From the dark tunnel came the roaring sound of the subway train.

Jostled by the crowd, Rachelle swam against the current, but the tide of humanity pushed her toward the yellow safety boundary painted on the platform floor. Frowning, she held on tight to her purse and tried to shimmy her way through the crowd.

The flat of a hand on her back startled her, and she jerked just as she was shoved hard, causing her to misstep and propelling her to the very edge of the platform. She lost her balance, her arms windmilling.

Terror ripped a desperate scream from her as she plummeted off the platform and onto the tracks.

Terri Reed
and

USA TODAY Bestselling Author
Valerie Hansen

Fatal Pursuit

Previously published as *Seeking the Truth* and *Trail of Danger*

LOVE INSPIRED
INSPIRATIONAL ROMANCE

Special thanks and acknowledgment are given to Terri Reed and Valerie Hansen for their contributions to the True Blue K-9 Unit miniseries.

LOVE INSPIRED®

INSPIRATIONAL ROMANCE

Recycling programs
for this product may
not exist in your area.

ISBN-13: 978-1-335-20964-1

Fatal Pursuit

Copyright © 2020 by Harlequin Books S.A.

Seeking the Truth
First published in 2019. This edition published in 2020.
Copyright © 2019 by Harlequin Books S.A.

Trail of Danger
First published in 2019. This edition published in 2020.
Copyright © 2019 by Harlequin Books S.A.

This edition published by arrangement with Harlequin Books S.A.

For questions and comments about the quality of this book, please contact us at CustomerService@Harlequin.com.

Love Inspired
22 Adelaide St. West, 40th Floor
Toronto, Ontario M5H 4E3, Canada
www.Harlequin.com

Printed in U.S.A.

CONTENTS

Terri Reed's romance and romantic suspense novels have appeared on the *Publishers Weekly* top twenty-five and Nielsen BookScan top one hundred lists, and have been featured in *USA TODAY*, *Christian Fiction* magazine and *RT Book Reviews*. Her books have been finalists for the Romance Writers of America RITA® Award and the National Readers' Choice Award, and finalists three times for the American Christian Fiction Writers Carol Award. Contact Terri at terrireed.com or PO Box 19555, Portland, OR 97224.

Books by Terri Reed

Love Inspired Suspense

Buried Mountain Secrets
Secret Mountain Hideout

True Blue K-9 Unit: Brooklyn

Explosive Situation

True Blue K-9 Unit

Seeking the Truth

Military K-9 Unit

Tracking Danger
Mission to Protect

Classified K-9 Unit

Guardian
Classified K-9 Unit Christmas
"Yuletide Stalking"

Visit the Author Profile page
at Harlequin.com for more titles.

SEEKING THE TRUTH

Terri Reed

For I know the thoughts that I think toward you,
saith the Lord, thoughts of peace, and not of evil,
to give you an expected end.
—*Jeremiah* 29:11

To the men and women of the NYPD
who protect and serve the vibrant city of New York.

To my fellow authors, Lynette, Dana, Laura,
Lenora, Val, Sharon, Shirlee and Maggie—
thank you for your support and patience with me.

To my editors, Emily Rodmell and Tina James—
I so appreciate all you do for me and the books.

And to my faithful friends Leah Vale and Jessie Smith
for reading every word and believing in me.

ONE

The smell of sweaty bodies, garbage from some unseen refuse container and the musty odor of grease from the subway rails lay heavy in the stale August air. Noise bounced off the ceramic tiled walls covered with a dinosaur motif, unique to the 81st Street and Museum of Natural History subway station on the Upper West Side of Manhattan.

The place was crowded due to the Central Park Walkathon. People of all ages and ethnicities mingled on the side platforms. Most wore the green shirts of the walkathon, but there were many other obvious tourists, what with it being late summer, along with local subway passengers.

Officer Carter Jameson kept vigilant for any sort of trouble as he and his K-9 partner, Frosty, an all-white German shepherd, moved from the uptown platform to the downtown platform and back again.

A family of three stepped into his path. The father held an adorable curly-haired toddler in his arms.

"We need to get to the South Street Seaport. Is this the right train?" the mother asked.

"Doggy!" the little girl squealed, her arms reaching

out for Frosty. She nearly tumbled out of her father's arms to reach the dog.

The father stepped back, securing his hold on the child. "The dog is working. We can't pet him."

Carter appreciated the father's words. "We are working, but we can take a short break if she'd like to pet him."

He looked down at Frosty and gave the hand gesture to sit, which Frosty immediately obeyed. "Play nice," Carter said, giving the dog the verbal signal that at this moment he was off duty.

Part of Carter's role as an NYC K-9 Command Unit officer assigned to the transit authority was public relations. To let the citizens know they were there to protect and to serve.

"You sure he won't bite?" the man asked, a wary expression on his face.

"Frosty is used to my six-year-old," Carter assured him. "She uses him as a horse."

"That's a cute name for a cute fellow." The mother held out her hand for Frosty to sniff. Frosty sniffed, then licked her hand, his tail thumping on the hard concrete platform.

"Doggy!" the girl cried again. The father kept her in his arms but squatted down for the child to rub Frosty's coat.

From the pocket of his uniform, Carter withdrew a sticker with the NYPD gold shield and squatted down next to Frosty. Holding out the sticker, he asked the girl, "Would you like to be deputized?"

She clapped her hands.

Peeling the back off the sticker, Carter placed the gold shield on her shoulder. "Now you are one of us."

"Thank you for taking the time with my daughter," the father said as he rose.

The words warmed Carter's heart. He worked hard to uphold not only the code of the NYPD to protect and serve, but also his faith. Not that he and Frosty wouldn't take the bad guys down in a heartbeat, but he'd do so with humility and as much kindness as possible.

Frosty's attention jerked to something behind Carter. The dog didn't alert, but his eyes were fixated on whatever had drawn his focus. Carter could feel a presence hovering.

He glanced over his shoulder. His gaze snagged on a pair of red pumps below well-shaped calves disappearing into a gray pencil skirt.

The reporter?

Two hours ago, his brother Noah, the interim chief of the NYC K-9 Command Unit, had called to warn Carter a reporter wanted to interview him regarding the upcoming national police dog field trials and certification competition, which would be held in two weeks. Carter and Frosty were favored to place high in the public demonstration competition.

A burn of anger simmered in Carter's gut. The way the press had hounded his family the past five months after the unsolved murder of his oldest brother, Jordan, bothered Carter. He had no patience for pushy journalists.

Turning back to the family, he said, "This is the uptown train. The downtown tracks are beneath us. You'll want to get off at Fulton Street. And then walk toward the water. It's easy to find."

"Thank you, Officer," the woman said.

The father held out his hand, which Carter took. "We appreciate your help."

The family turned and walked away.

Carter took a moment for a steadying breath. To Frosty, he murmured, "Work."

The dog's ear perked up, indicating he knew he was back on duty.

"Officer Carter Jameson?"

The honeyed voice, with just a hint of an accent, tripped down his spine.

Unnerved by the visceral reaction, he arranged his features into a neutral expression and turned around. "Yes. May I help you?"

The beautiful woman facing him was tall with long brown hair that floated about her cream-colored, silk-clad shoulders. Brown eyes framed by long lashes stared at him, and her full lips were spread into a tentative smile.

His gaze swept over her. She was dressed to impress, in her fancy blouse and gray pencil skirt. The red pumps were impractical. Though she had on a sturdy-looking cross-body type purse, not so impractical. The flowery notebook and pink pen in her manicured hand would have delighted his daughter, Ellie.

She tucked her pen behind her ear before holding out her hand while gesturing with the notebook to the newsstand that sat in the middle of the platform. "I'm Rachelle Clark with *NYC Weekly*."

He grasped her hand, noting the softness of her skin and the crazy frisson of sensation racing up his arm. "I can't say that I've ever read that particular one."

There were so many local NYC-centric newspapers and magazines keeping those living in the five boroughs up-to-date on the happenings, Carter couldn't possibly read them all.

She extracted her hand. "You don't want to know what's going on in your own community?"

Tucking in his chin, Carter said. "I didn't say that." He narrowed his gaze. "I believe my brother told you I was working."

She had the good grace to grimace. "True." Her smile reappeared. "However, he did tell me where to find you, so I took that to mean he wasn't opposed to me asking you some questions."

"Did he now?" Carter would have to chew Noah out for throwing him to the wolves, or wolf, in this case.

"How about this?" Rachelle said. "I can follow you around the rest of your shift. Just observe. I won't ask any questions." Her accent deepened into a definite Southern drawl. "I won't say anything. Just think of me as a little shadow."

Yeah, right. An attractive shadow. Like having her dogging his steps wouldn't break his concentration. He looked down at Frosty, who looked up at him with his tongue hanging out the side of his mouth.

"We'll take a break right now," he said. "You have five minutes."

"No, no, no. It would do my article so much good if I could see you in action. Even if it's just for a little bit. Then when you're off duty, I can interview you."

Carter rubbed at the tension in the back of his neck. "Like I said, five minutes."

Her gaze darted to his partner then back to him. "He's a handsome dog."

"He knows it," Carter told her.

She laughed slightly but didn't reach out to touch

Frosty. Carter wondered if she was afraid or being respectful.

He strode away toward a locked closet built into the staircase, fully aware of his "shadow" following. He tried to ignore the hint of lavender wafting off the woman as he brought out water for Frosty, who lapped it up thirstily. He grabbed his own thermos and drank deeply, his eyes on the reporter watching him.

She glanced around. "Was there a race today?"

"For a reporter, you're not very well-informed." He barely suppressed his amusement when surprise and a bit of annoyance flashed in her chocolate-colored eyes.

She recovered quickly and said through smiling lips, "I don't cover sports."

He couldn't contain the grin tugging at the corners of his mouth. "A walkathon for diabetes. Hardly a sport."

Her eyes narrowed slightly. "Are you expecting trouble?"

Only the kind tall brunettes posed. He shook his head, dislodging that thought. "No. We're just patrolling as a precaution."

"Right." She made a note in that flowery book of hers. "I suppose the walkathon could be a target like last month's Fourth of July celebration."

She was correct, but he didn't comment. No need to give her any more fodder on that score. Two of his fellow K-9 Unit members and their dogs were there when a bomb detonated in a park on the Lower East Side of Manhattan. Thankfully, no one was hurt.

"Did that bombing have anything to do with your eldest brother's murder?"

Carter glanced to her sharply. "Your five minutes is up."

"No, it's not," she countered. She tapped the gold watch on her slender wrist. "I have two more minutes. How close are you to solving your brother's murder case?"

"I thought you wanted to talk about the field trials?"

Her nostrils flared slightly but her smile didn't slip. "I do. Are you and Frosty competing?"

"Yes, we are."

"How many events will you participate in?"

"All of them."

Her dark eyebrows drew together. "Which are...?"

"Obedience and agility. Articles and boxes, which are timed. Apprehension with gun and without gun."

She wrote furiously in her notebook. "Could you elaborate on those?"

"Not now." He tapped her watch. "Time's up. You can attend the public demonstration."

A new flood of people rushed down the stairs toward the train platform. Carter carefully watched the throng and Frosty for any signs of an alert as the dog inhaled the air in short little bursts and sniffed at each person as they walked past him.

It was time to take his focus off the reporter.

Carter put their stash away and closed the closet. "Back to work." He let Frosty lead, his nose twitching in the air.

Awareness shimmied down Carter's spine with every step. He stopped abruptly and turned to face the woman on his heels. Her pumps skidded on the concrete floor, barely halting her in time to keep from bumping into him.

"What are you doing?" he demanded.

Her smile turned saccharine sweet. "There's no law against sharing the same space as you."

Barely refraining from snorting, he blew out a frustrated breath and stalked away.

Rachelle hurried after the handsome police officer and his dog. She'd seen him from a distance at Griffin's Diner, a neighborhood eatery near where she lived in Queens and close to the NYC K-9 Command Unit headquarters, but had never talked to him. Up close the man was downright gorgeous with his dark hair and blue eyes. And fit. She couldn't imagine wearing all the gear attached to his body on a daily basis, let alone in the dank and stuffy subway.

She was glad to see he was thoughtful of his partner to make sure the dog stayed hydrated. She made a note in her journal. She'd always liked dogs from a distance. Her parents had never allowed pets. Which made writing about the K-9 duo that much more fascinating.

It had taken some fancy talking to get her boss to allow her to write an article about the police dog competition because she'd already been assigned to cover an upcoming celebrity ball, which thankfully had some redeeming value as a fund-raiser for autism awareness.

Her hope with the article about the police dog field trials was to gain some insider information on the K-9 Unit and the unsolved murder of NYC K-9 Command Unit Chief Jordan Jameson.

Five months ago when Chief Jameson had failed to appear for a K-9 graduation, the department had known something was wrong. Their chief wouldn't disappear without a word. Then a few days later, Jordan had been found dead in what was made to look like a suicide, but evidence had proven Jordan's untimely death was in fact murder. Someone had killed the man in cold blood and remained at large.

A mystery she wanted to solve in order to be taken seriously as a journalist. If she could shed light on why Chief Jameson was killed, or better yet, solve the case by doing her own investigation…

Her work would be noticed and hopefully picked up by more prestigious media outlets.

She hustled to keep close to Carter and Frosty so she could hear and see what he and the dog were doing as they weaved and bobbed through the swarm waiting for the train. Bodies pressed in around her, the smells of the subway assaulted her senses. Odors she'd yet to get used to, having only been in the city for a year. Her skin itched with the need for fresh air and blue sky. Sweat dampened her blouse, no doubt ruining the fabric. Someone pushed against her, sending her stumbling sideways.

"Hey!" she cried out.

Carter whipped around, his blue eyes meeting hers. She regained her balance, gave him a reassuring nod and headed toward him, dodging a couple of teenagers who were jostling each other.

From the dark tunnel came the roaring sound of the train. People surged forward in anticipation of boarding, each hoping to make it through the doors, in case the train was already full.

Jostled by the crowd, Rachelle swam against the current, but the tide of humanity pushed her toward the yellow safety boundary painted on the platform floor. Frowning, she held on tight to her purse and tried to shimmy her way through the crowd.

The flat of a hand on her back startled her and she jerked just as she was shoved hard, causing her to misstep and propelling her to the very edge of the platform. She lost her balance, her arms windmilling.

Terror ripped a desperate scream from her as she plummeted off the platform and onto the tracks.

A woman's scream punctuated the air, loud gasps from the surrounding crowd following. Horror stole Carter's breath as Rachelle disappeared over the edge of the platform onto the subway tracks.

His heart jumped into his throat, galvanizing him into action. He pushed through the terrified crowd as he called into Dispatch asking for backup and for the incoming train to be notified there was a civilian on the tracks. He prayed the message would be relayed to the conductor in time to stop the train short.

Pedestrians yelled and urged Rachelle to get up. She appeared dazed as she pushed to her knees. Smears of grease and dirt marred her skirt and blouse. Shoving back her loose hair, she lifted her frightened gaze as if looking for help.

Frosty's frantic barking echoed off the tile and cement. Agitated, the dog paced the edge of the platform. Carter held tight to his lead, afraid the dog would jump onto the tracks to help save Rachelle.

The train wasn't far down the track. He could hear the strident squeal of the rails echoing down the tunnel. There wasn't time for her to climb back onto the platform.

He didn't think there was even time for her to run to the other end of the platform where there was a four-step ladder.

Only one option provided a hope of survival.

He knelt down and cupped his mouth to shout, "Lie down between the rails."

For a heartbeat, she blinked up at him as if trying to discern his words.

A gust of wind tore down the tunnel, whipping her hair in front of her face and plastering her skirt to her legs. The approaching train would arrive any second. "Hurry! Lie down. Cover your head!"

In a flurry of movement, Rachelle scrambled to do as directed. She lay prone between the inside tracks, her face tucked into the crook of her elbow.

Even if the train didn't hit her, there was no guarantee the equipment hanging down from the undercarriage wouldn't cause injury.

Nausea roiled through his gut as he pushed to his feet and lifted a prayer for this woman's safety. "Please, God."

Rachelle squeezed her eyes tight. Her heart hammered in her chest. She covered her head with her purse, thankful it hadn't flown off her body in the fall, and fought to lie as still and flat as possible.

If she survived this…

No! She would survive this—she'd be headline news. And could write about the fast-thinking officer who helped her stay alive.

The loud squeal of the rails shuddered through her. Her body tensed.

"Please, Lord. Please, Lord." She repeated the refrain over and over.

The sight of the incoming train filled Carter with terror. He waved his arms over his head, hoping to grab the train engineer's attention. Others joined in.

The sound of people crying mixed with the screech of the brakes as the train decelerated and came to a jerking halt within inches of Rachelle's feet.

A cheer broke out.

Sweat soaked Carter's back beneath his uniform and flak vest. "Thank you, Jesus."

To Frosty, he commanded, "Stay."

He dropped the dog's lead and then jumped down onto the tracks, careful to avoid the third rail, which supplied live electrical power for the subway to run efficiently. It was exposed and extremely dangerous. He hurried to gather Rachelle into his arms and lifted her off the ground. Her arms encircled his neck and she buried her face in his shoulder. Her body trembled. Shock, no doubt.

"You're okay," he assured her.

He carried her to the end of the platform. Several people rushed to help her up the stairs.

"My notebook and pen!"

Carter rolled his eyes at her priorities but quickly grabbed her items before climbing up the ladder behind her.

Rachelle's pretty brown eyes were wide, the pupils dilated. She wobbled on her pumps and gripped his arm. "Thank you. That was really close."

Tell me about it. "You're going to be okay."

He slid an arm around her waist and led her to the bench against the wall. He squatted down beside her, setting her notebook and pen on the bench.

Frosty put his chin on her knee. She stroked the dog behind the ears with one hand and placed her other hand protectively over her notebook.

"What happened?" Carter asked.

Her lips trembled. "Someone pushed me."

Shock reverberated through him. The platform was now a crime scene. He radioed in this new development.

"That's right. I saw the whole thing." An older gentleman stepped forward. "Guy wore a gray T-shirt, baseball hat and sunglasses. He had brown hair, medium height."

Carter rose and searched the pressing crowd. "Can you point him out?"

"As soon as he pushed her, the guy ran up the stairs," the older man told him. "I heard him say, 'You're getting too close.'"

"I heard him say that, too." A young woman wearing a walkathon T-shirt stepped forward. "I saw him put his hand on her back and push."

Carter's gaze snapped back to Rachelle. "Why would someone want to hurt you?"

She tucked in her chin. "You think I was targeted?" Something flashed in her eyes, some thought that made her frown, but then she shook her head. "No. It was crowded. He probably got claustrophobic. It had to have been a random act."

Carter wasn't sure what to think. He didn't have time to question her further as other police officers and paramedics flooded the platform. He greeted the officers, explained the situation and let them interview the witnesses. Carter would write up his statement when he returned to his home station in Queens.

The medical personnel fussed over Rachelle. She waved them away. "I'm fine. Nothing is broken. Nothing's twisted. I'll have some bruises, but you can't help with that."

Carter touched her shoulder. He'd already noted the

scrapes on her hands and the smudges on her knees. She'd dropped four feet onto hard concrete. "Let them do their jobs."

She huffed out a sigh and tucked her notebook and pen into her purse. "I've taken worse falls. My parents have a grand oak that rises a hundred feet in the air. I've fallen out of it more times than I can count. This was barely a tumble."

Her words were saying one thing, but her body was shaking beneath his hand. "Humor me."

Her lips pressed together, and she nodded. The EMTs checked her vitals, assessed her limbs for injury. They declared her okay but told her to rest and put ice on her knees.

When the paramedics retreated, she rose from the bench, straightened her dirt-smudged skirt and squared her shoulders. Looking him in the eye, she said, "What I would like to do is interview those witnesses, then get on with our interview."

She had gumption, he'd give her that. He admired that she wasn't rushing out of the subway system scared as a rabbit. Most people would be anxious to escape the area after experiencing something as traumatic as being pushed into the path of a subway train.

Who had pushed her? And why?

Random? Or a targeted attempt on her life?

TWO

"We're heading back to our unit's headquarters in Queens," Carter said to Rachelle as he reined her in from questioning the witnesses.

He was determined to discover the truth about why someone would want to harm her, which meant he needed to keep her close and grill her about the incident. "Come along with us."

"Wonderful. I live not far from there. Do you think I could get a tour of the station?"

"I'm sure that can be arranged." Carter looked down at Frosty, who stared at him with trusting eyes. "All right, partner, let's head out."

The dog's ears perked up, his tail thumped once and then he stood. The crowd had thankfully thinned. Yet, Carter couldn't shake the stress of seeing Rachelle tumbling off the platform onto the tracks.

"Let's go aboveground where we can hail a taxi."

"You don't have a vehicle?"

"I do, but parking in the city is nearly impossible for any length of time."

"Would you normally travel back to Queens via a cab?" she asked, her intelligent eyes studying him.

"No. Part of our job with the transit bureau is to ride the subway," he told her. "But we can take a cab today."

She shook her head. "Not on my account. I'd rather you do as you normally would. It would be better for my story."

Grudgingly, he respected her dedication. He shrugged. "Suit yourself."

They walked to the platform for the downtown train and stood behind the yellow painted barrier.

He doubted Rachelle realized he'd slowed his pace to keep her within reach so he could grab her and protect her at the first sign of danger. Coming from a family with a long line of police officers, protecting others was built into his DNA.

His cell phone rang. The caller ID announced his brother Noah. Again. Two calls in one shift? Carter quelled the spike in his pulse. Noah had offered to watch Carter's daughter, Ellie, on his day off because their parents were unavailable.

Keeping an alert eye on those around them, he pressed the button. "Hey, just about to leave the city. Your reporter friend has asked for a tour of the station." Carter glanced at Rachelle, watching her scribble in her flowered notebook.

Noah chuckled. "Not my friend, pal. But I'm glad you're not complaining."

"That will happen later. It's been exciting so far." *Traumatic* would be a better descriptor but Carter would save the story for when he saw Noah.

"Well, you can start complaining now. I've been called into headquarters. My day off is over, and my babysitting time is up."

Hope flared. "News on Jordy's killer?"

Rachelle's gaze snapped to his. Carter saw the curious gleam in her eyes. *Reporter, remember!* He couldn't let his guard down around her. He'd learned the hard way the media only wanted the sensational and twisted the truth to meet their own narrative.

Noah sighed. "No. Nothing to do with the case."

Disappointment curdled the hope.

"You'll need to come directly home," Noah continued. "Mom and Pop aren't back from Fire Island yet."

"Is Zach around?" Even though his youngest brother had married and moved out, he came around the family home often. His brothers took turns babysitting Carter's six-year-old when their mom and dad were not available.

"On patrol this evening. And Katie's not feeling well."

Katie, Jordan's widow, was five months pregnant. Carter's heart ached knowing his oldest sibling would never get to hold his child, watch his child take his or her first steps, or hear the sweet voice of his own kid calling him Daddy.

Carter cleared his throat before he could speak. "Why don't you bring the munchkin to the station house. I'll grab her there."

"Will do." Noah hung up.

Rachelle raised an eyebrow. "Everything okay?"

"Yes." He was saved from having to explain further by the arrival of the train. "Here we go."

They boarded a middle car. As usual, he and Frosty were greeted with a mix of nervous glances and stiffened spines or open interest. Carter gestured for Rachelle to take a seat near the car's end door. He and Frosty stood guard.

Until he was satisfied that the attempt on Rachelle's

life had truly been a random act of violence, he planned to unearth all he could about the pretty reporter and what she might be working on that would put her life in danger.

Rachelle kept her gaze on Carter as the subway train zoomed down the track. The rhythmic noise of the rails brought back the memory of the train bearing down on her. A shudder ripped through her, setting off a maelstrom of pain from the many bumps and bruises the fall caused. She forced the horrific images of what had happened earlier away. However, the fear lingered. She'd probably have nightmares tonight.

Or dreams of strong arms, making her feel safe and secure, lifting her from the train tracks while the thunderous applause from the crowd and the bark of the world's cutest dog rang in her ears.

She pushed the thought aside, too. It was fine she found Carter good-looking and she was grateful for his rescue, but she wasn't looking for anything more from him than a source that would provide her a front-page story to bring justice to the world.

Or, at least, justice for his brother.

And earn her notice from prestigious news outlets.

Consciously redirecting her mind to the phone call Carter had received, curiosity burned through her veins like a wildfire. She wanted to know more about Chief Jordan Jameson's murder. But the look of disappointment on Carter's face had let her know the call hadn't been about the investigation. "Who's 'the munchkin'?"

Carter folded his arms over his chest. "My daughter."

Ah. A call from the wife. Why would he be asking

his spouse about Jordan's murder? "Is your wife in law enforcement, also?"

His jaw hardened. He kept his gaze forward this time. Not even looking at her. His Adam's apple bobbed. For a long moment he stayed silent, his expression unreadable and she feared she'd just overstepped with her question.

"I'm a widower." His voice came at her low and sharp.

Her heart clenched. Had his wife died in the line of duty? An innocent bystander? Or an illness? Or some other horrible death? It was too much to bear thinking about. She went back to her earlier question. Munchkin was his daughter. "How old is she? Your daughter," she clarified.

"Six."

"That must be hard. Raising a child on your own. How old was she when her mother passed?"

He shifted his stance, tucking his hands behind his back and widening his feet. "These are not questions I choose to answer in this venue."

Properly chastised, she folded her hands over her notebook in her lap. Yes, this wasn't the place to ask about his personal life. Too many ears, too many eyes and too many unknowns. "Of course. Forgive me."

He remained silent, but his chin dipped slightly.

Rachelle would take the slight movement as forgiveness from a guy like Officer Carter Jameson any day of the week.

She glanced warily around the subway car. Several people were clearly nervous to have an officer and K-9 on board. It was a diverse group of individuals. Some were clearly families heading home from a day in the city. Others obviously were tourists, with cameras around their necks or holding subway maps in their hands. The rest of the passengers most likely were workers getting off from their city jobs, possibly heading home to one of the other boroughs where it wasn't so expensive to live.

She found herself looking for a man in a gray T-shirt and baseball hat with brown hair, of medium height. None fit that description in the car. Could the incident on the subway platform have been related to her investigation into Jordan Jameson's murder? She suppressed a shiver of dread.

A casual glance at Carter found him watching her with his inscrutable gaze. Unperturbed, she met his gaze fully and assessed him as he assessed her. This was a man who was used to intimidating others. With nothing more than a stony stare, a formidable stance and a big dog.

She'd learned a lot in the last year since moving to New York City. Who to stay away from, who might cause trouble and that at any moment some celebrity, thinking they were incognito, could appear right next to her on a subway car, a street corner or in a restaurant. Carter wouldn't be looking for celebrities. He'd be looking for the ones who were doing bad things.

Like the guy who'd pushed her off the platform. She knew to keep her eyes open and sharp. The fact that she'd failed to notice the danger really irked her. She should never have allowed herself to get close enough to the edge to be pushed off. Normally, she stayed back until the train came to a stop. The only explanation had to be she'd been too focused on Carter.

When the subway train pulled into the next station,

Carter and Frosty moved to stand near the opening doors. The dog sat at Carter's heels, his nose twitching at everyone who came in and out of the car.

"How did you come up with the name Frosty?" she asked him.

Carter glanced over his shoulder at her and arched an eyebrow.

Raising her hands in acknowledgment that she'd received the message—*not here, not now*—she opened her notebook and added more questions to her growing list. She kept her mouth closed for the remainder of the ride but couldn't help the impatient bounce of her foot as the subway car rolled along.

She was glad when they finally switched trains to head out of Manhattan to the borough of Queens.

As they exited the subway car, Rachelle was sure she heard several sighs of relief. She didn't understand why the dog and officer made people so anxious. Carter and Frosty were there to serve and protect. Yes, the police in general seemed to have a bad rap in the media over the last few years. And she wasn't naive—she knew there could be bad apples on any tree. But the NYC K-9 Command Unit had, until recently, a really good reputation.

However, people were losing confidence that the K-9 Unit could solve their own chief's murder, let alone any other crime. After five months with no answers, she had to admit she was frustrated, too. Which in part was what had prompted her to begin her own investigation.

Along with the fact she wanted to advance her own career.

But she'd rather think about the more altruistic reason she was diving headlong into Jordan Jameson's life. His murderer needed to be caught and justice served.

She and everyone else in New York would sleep better knowing a killer was off the streets.

A shiver traipsed down her spine, reminding her of the terrifying event she suffered in the subway. She rubbed at the dirt streaked across her skirt. The skin underneath protested. In fact, her whole body ached from the impact of the fall now that the shock had eased.

She really didn't want to contemplate why someone had pushed her off the subway platform. Better to chalk it up to a onetime thing than to live in fear. She refused to believe the incident had anything to do with her inquiries into Jordan's life.

With Frosty on Carter's left and Rachelle on his right, they walked away from the subway station and onto the sidewalk. This was her neighborhood. The residual fear and stress keeping her muscles bunched tight throughout her body began to melt away like butter on her grandma's biscuits. They neared the mini market where a slim man in his sixties swept the front walkway.

"Good afternoon, Mr. Lee," she called with a wave.

Mr. Lee looked up and smiled at her. "Ah, Miss Rachelle." His gaze narrowed at Carter and Frosty. "Are you okay?"

"Perfect," she replied. "You?"

"Well, thank you." He hurried inside the store.

They headed down the street with the late afternoon traffic buzzing by. She could feel Carter's curious gaze. She glanced at him sideways. "My apartment is only a few blocks from here. I stop in occasionally for fruit or milk." Her own curiosity prompted her to ask, "Do you two always receive that sort of reaction? I noticed on the subway that many people were nervous with you two aboard."

He shrugged. "It happens. Some people get antsy around authority figures. We're trained to discern the difference between a nervous Nellie and a real crook." He peered at her. "How did you end up in New York?"

"Who doesn't want to live in New York?" She wasn't about to tell him she had applied and accepted the job at *NYC Weekly* as a way to escape her family. "My hope is to write something that will be picked up by a major news source and lead to a job with them. And this New York job seems the best possible place for that to happen."

"Why journalism?"

She shrugged. "When it was time for college, my maternal grandmother suggested journalism." She affected a prim voice. "'Turn your rebelliousness to usefulness,' was her advice. I took it."

"She sounds like a wise woman."

Sadness slipped over her. "She was. She passed on while I was in college."

"I'm sure she would have been proud of you," he commented.

At the corner, they waited for the light to turn green before crossing.

"Thank you for saying so." She didn't add that her father had said the opposite when she'd made the decision to leave Georgia.

The walk signal appeared, and she stepped out onto the street.

The squeal of tires on the hot pavement filled the air. A car careened around the corner, aiming straight at her. Her lungs froze. Her body refused to move. Carter's hand wrapped around her biceps and yanked her back onto the sidewalk mere seconds before the brown sedan whizzed past, barely missing her.

She put a hand over her beating heart. "Crazy driver."

Carter regarded her with an intensity that set the fine hairs on her nape to high alert. He used the radio on his shoulder to report the incident and the fact the car's license plate had been removed.

"Come on." He ushered her quickly across the street to a three-story brick building with square windows and an American flag waving over the entrance. Carter stopped to open the glass doors of the public entrance.

"Would there be time for a tour?" She didn't like the way her voice quaked. The fright from nearly being run over still zoomed through her veins. Having her life flash before her eyes twice in one day made her nerves raw.

Carter's mouth lifted at one corner. "Yes, I'm sure that can be arranged."

Excited by the prospect of seeing the inner sanctuary of the K-9 Unit, she followed him inside. Carter and Frosty patiently waited while she went through security and then received a visitor's badge from the front desk officer sitting behind a large U-shaped desk.

Having never been inside a New York Police Department precinct, she found it fascinating. The lobby had a warmth to it she hadn't expected. Pictures of dogs and their handlers gave the beige walls life. The phones rang incessantly, keeping the receptionist busy.

Joining Carter and Frosty near a set of stairs, she observed, "Much different than the small police station back home."

Carter led her up a flight of stairs. "Really? Where

is back home and why do you know what the inside of the police station looks like?"

"Vidalia, Georgia. As to why…" A flush heated her cheeks. "I was a bit of a rebellious scamp as a child. I was caught picking flowers in Mrs. Finch's garden. My father thought he'd scare some sense into me by dragging me down to the sheriff's station and demanding that Sheriff Potter put me in jail. I think he wanted to frighten me straight as it were."

Pausing, Carter stared at her. "Seriously? The sheriff didn't…"

"No. He told me to apologize to Mrs. Finch and he never wanted to see me inside the station house again. He never did."

"Hmm."

She wasn't sure she wanted to know what he was *hmm*ing about.

They entered a large space dotted with cubicles for the officers and their dogs. At the far end were enclosed offices. Carter led her to his desk, where he locked his weapon in the bottom drawer. Frosty lay down on a large round fluffy bed underneath the desk corner.

"Can you tell me now how Frosty got his name?"

Carter hitched a hip on the edge of his desk. "He's named after William Frost. He was an officer with the NYPD back in the '80s. He was murdered in a gang-related shooting."

A pang of sorrow touched her. "That's so sad. Do all the dogs get their names from fallen officers?"

"They do, in some variation. I chose Frost rather than William because he was all white like a blast of winter frost."

"What breed is he?"

"German shepherd."

"Really? I've never seen one like him before."

"The white version of the breed comes out of Canada."

"That's funny. The Great White North." She wrote that down. "You said Frost, but you call him Frosty."

"Ellie, my daughter, liked Frosty better. And it stuck."

"What a pretty name. Ellie. Your daughter sounds charming."

"She is." He looked past her, and his features visibly changed, taking on a soft tender look that had her heart thumping against her rib cage.

She turned to see a blond-haired, blue-eyed pixie streaking toward them.

The little girl jumped into her father's arms. "Daddy!" she squealed.

She gave Carter big, noisy kisses on both cheeks.

Carter's deep rumble of a laugh hit Rachelle like an acorn from her parents' oak tree, digging into her psyche and making her want to hear more.

Holding his beautiful little girl on his hip, Carter smiled at Rachelle. "This is Ellie." The child regarded her with open curiosity. "My pride and joy."

There was no doubt about that. "Hi, Ellie, it's nice to meet you."

"Honey," Carter addressed his daughter, "this is Ms. Clark. She's a reporter."

The way he emphasized the word *reporter* had Rachelle stiffening her spine. Wariness entered the little girl's shining eyes. "She's one of those."

Rachelle tried not to take offense. Clearly the Jamesons didn't hold reporters in high regard.

"All right, you two," a deep masculine voice from behind Rachelle admonished. "No need to scare our guest."

Rachelle spun around to find herself face-to-face with Chief Noah Jameson. She'd seen his picture in the *New York Times*, as well as her own paper on numerous occasions over the past several months.

Dark circles were evident beneath his green eyes. She could only imagine the stress of losing one brother and taking over a high-profile position amid controversy.

Rachelle scribbled down her observations, her pink pen flying over the pages of her flowered journal.

"I like your book," Ellie said. "Can I see it?"

Rachelle clutched the notebook to her chest and gave a nervous laugh. "These are my work notes. I'm doing an article on your father. And Frosty."

Carter set Ellie's feet on the floor. "Okay, munchkin, I need a moment with Uncle Noah."

He glanced at Rachelle. "I need to tell Noah about today. All of it."

Rachelle swallowed back the sudden jump of residual fear. "We'll be fine here."

She looked at Ellie and was a bit disconcerted by the way the girl was assessing her, much as her father had done.

As the two men walked away Ellie asked, "What happened to your skirt? It's dirty."

Smoothing a hand over the mark, she replied, "I fell." She didn't add she'd been nearly run down in the street. And almost flattened by a train.

Ellie slipped her hand into Rachelle's. "Is my daddy helping you?"

Carter certainly had his hands full with this little perceptive child. "Yes. Yes, he is."

And she couldn't begin to express her gratitude to him for not only saving her life but also for being a path to furthering her career.

"Are you married?"

Taken aback by the little girl's question, Rachelle glanced up to see Carter had paused midstep as if he'd heard his daughter's query. His lips twisted in a rueful grimace before he turned and walked into Noah's office, closing the door behind him.

Smothering a grin, Rachelle shook her head at the little girl. "No, I'm not." And she had no plans to be for the foreseeable future.

Ellie's eyes lit up. "That's good."

Deciding it was best not to pursue that comment, Rachelle asked, "School must be starting soon, right?"

The little girl released Rachelle's hand and hopped onto her father's desk chair. With the heel of her hand on the desk, she sent the chair spinning. "Yep. In a couple weeks. I'm not looking forward to it."

"Why not?"

Ellie stopped spinning and stared at her. "It's school."

As if that should explain everything. Rachelle laughed. "Well, there is that. But aren't you excited to see all your friends and have recess and art? Art was always my favorite subject. I could get messy and not get in trouble." Though with budget cuts she wasn't sure art was taught anymore in public schools.

Ellie resumed her spinning. "Oh yes. I'm excited to see Kelly and Greta. I'll be in Mrs. Lenny's class. We'll get to do a garden project. My daddy said I could bring butterflies."

"He did, did he? That's fabulous. You have a good daddy."

"Yep." Ellie stopped the chair to peer at her. "He'd be a good catch, as my grandma says."

Uh-oh. Was she trying to play matchmaker?

THREE

Not going to happen. What to say that wouldn't offend or be rude? Rachelle settled for, "Interesting."

Ignoring Ellie's assessing gaze, Rachelle busied herself visually memorizing everything on Carter's desk. Everything in its place. Pens and pencils corralled in an NYPD mug. Reports stacked with clean edges on one side of the desktop while a dormant computer screen and keyboard took up the other half. No dust bunnies, either.

A family photo of the Jamesons sitting next to the computer caught her attention. Recently taken, by the looks of it. Carter and Ellie, much as the little girl appeared now, were crouched down in the front row, while Carter's three brothers, including the murdered Jordan, stood behind them. Snuggled up to Jordan was a pretty blonde woman. No doubt Jordan's widow, Katie.

Next to the Jameson family photo sat a gilded framed wedding photo of a young-looking Carter standing with his radiant bride. Ellie got her blond hair and delicate features from her mother.

A pang tugged at Rachelle's heart. No wonder Carter wanted Ellie to have butterflies in her life. They represented renewal and hope. "You can't have a garden without butterflies."

Ellie pushed off the desk and sent the chair whirling in a circle. "I have some carrot seeds that Aunt Katie got for me."

"That was nice of her."

"She said I should contribute to the vegetables, too."

A big word for a little girl. No doubt she was repeating what she'd heard. "Katie's a smart woman. Do you see her often?"

Ellie stopped spinning again. The corners of her sweet little mouth pinched inward. "She lives with us. She's very sad because Uncle Jordy went to Heaven."

Heart aching for this family's loss, Rachelle said, gently, "That's totally understandable. I'm sure you're sad, too."

The girl's eyes misted. She nodded. "I miss Uncle Jordy. He gave the best tickles. My daddy is sad, too. He misses Uncle Jordy and…because my mommy went to Heaven." Ellie's gaze was on the wedding photo.

Rachelle blinked to repel the sudden moisture gathering in her own eyes. "Do you remember her?"

Ellie shook her head. "No. Mommy died right after I was born."

Flooded with sympathy for this young little girl and her father, Rachelle didn't quite know what else to say. What could she say? The little girl had experienced more heartbreak than most people in her short time on earth. "So, does Frosty live with you guys?"

Ellie sent the chair spinning once more. "He sure does. Also Scotty—he's Uncle Noah's dog—and Eddie, Uncle Zach's dog. But Uncle Zach and Eddie moved out." Her little brow furrowed. "Snapper lived downstairs with Aunt Katie and Uncle Jordan, but we don't know where he is right now."

Rachelle remembered the name from the news reports. Snapper was Chief Jordan Jameson's missing dog.

"Now Mutt and Jeff live with us, too." Ellie giggled. "Those aren't their real names. That's just what Dad calls them."

"Your uncles?"

"No, silly." Ellie waved a hand in a swatting motion. "The puppies. They are both girls, but Daddy still calls them by boy names. They are with us to be—" She paused and appeared to concentrate as she said, "Socialized." She grinned. "But they're gonna be police dogs just like Frosty and Scotty. Frosty's not too fond of them. They get on his nerves. He growls, but they don't care. They just run right on top of him. Scotty's better with them. He just walks away when they bug him."

"Sounds entertaining." She would like to see the dogs and puppies together. Rachelle glanced at one dog in question. Frosty looked so peaceful lying there with his snout on top of his crossed paws. He opened one eye as if he sensed her attention.

Awareness cascaded over her flesh and she turned to find Carter approaching. The man exuded vitality even from five feet away. She mentally shook off the odd sensation.

"Ellie, sweetie," Carter said. "Can you hang with Frosty for a moment while I show Rachelle something?"

"Yes, Daddy." Ellie crawled off the chair and flopped down on the round bed on the floor, practically lying on top of the dog. Frosty's ears twitched, his tail thumped, but otherwise he made no move.

Amazed at how calm and loving the dog was with Ellie, Rachelle asked, "Are you sure he's a police dog?"

"He can be fierce when he needs to be," Carter told her.

She wasn't sure she believed his assurance. "If you say so."

"He has a really good track record of taking down criminals. He's a multipurpose trained dog. Part of our job with the transit bureau is public relations."

"Like with the little girl and her father today." Rachelle had been surprised to see the child petting the working dog when she'd approached Carter.

"Exactly." He cupped her elbow. "Come with me."

She sucked in a breath at the unexpected contact but forced herself to focus on the excitement of being given a glimpse of the rest of the precinct. Anticipating a tour of the facility, she was surprised by their first stop. He led her into a room filled with video monitors. A curvy female officer with long, curly blond hair tied back with a rubber band sat reviewing the screens. The woman turned to regard them with hazel eyes behind huge framed glasses. "Hey, Carter. What's going on?" Her gaze raked over Rachelle.

Uncomfortable beneath the other woman's curiosity, Rachelle fought the urge to fiddle with her purse strap or fix her hair. Best never to let anyone see a weakness. She lifted her chin, met her gaze and smiled.

"Hi, Danielle," Carter said. "This is Rachelle Clark. Rachelle, Danielle Abbott, our computer tech."

"Nice to meet you," Rachelle said, then winced inwardly at how her accent had thickened. It did that sometimes when she was nervous.

"Likewise." Danielle's curiosity sparkled in her hazel eyes.

"I need a favor," Carter said.

"Sure." Danielle's gaze snapped back to Carter. "Anything."

"Can you access the MTA database and bring up the video surveillance from the 81st and Museum of Natural History subway platform?"

"Of course. We have access to all the five boroughs' databases."

As Danielle's fingers flew on the keyboard, Carter told her the time frame he needed to review.

Rachelle's heart rate ticked up as she realized he wanted to see the push that had caused her fall. Steeling herself against reliving the nightmare, she hovered over Carter's shoulder.

"Here you go," Danielle said.

"Fast-forward a bit," Carter instructed.

It was strange to watch people in the video coming and going at a fast clip. There was the family she'd found Carter talking to when she arrived. Then she was on-screen talking to him. She couldn't help but critique herself. She hadn't realized she'd fidgeted with her notebook and pen the whole time she'd been talking to him. A nervous habit. One she intended to break.

"There!" Carter pointed to the screen.

Coming down the stairs was a man wearing jeans, a gray T-shirt, baseball cap and sunglasses. He stepped onto the platform and wandered from one end to the other, slowly making his way closer and closer to Rachelle with each pass.

Everyone surged forward in anticipation of the train's arrival.

The mystery man paused right behind Rachelle. From the angle of the video it was too hard to see his hand on her back, but then she was stumbling, her feet trying to find purchase on the slick floor. The man watched her go over the edge of the platform, and then he turned and fled back up the stairs just as the witnesses had said. The video screen froze.

A shudder of terror worked its way over Rachelle's limbs. She wrapped her arms around her middle. Definitely nightmares tonight.

Danielle turned to face her with wide eyes. "That was you."

Rachelle nodded, feeling a bit sick to her stomach.

"There's no good shot of his face. He obviously knew where the cameras were located." Frustration reverberated in Carter's voice.

Finding her own voice, Rachelle stated, "That still doesn't mean it was a deliberate act. He probably didn't realize how hard he pushed me, then got scared when I fell. He doesn't look familiar to me."

Carter frowned. "How would you even know if he was familiar to you? He was never directly in front of you, so you never got a good look at him."

She couldn't argue with his logic. She shrugged, hoping the fear stealing over her wasn't apparent. If this was a targeted incident…

"Danielle, I need to see what cameras we have on the street between here and the subway."

Without a word, the tech analyst swung back around to her monitors and typed on her keyboard. A few seconds later, traffic cameras from the area appeared.

"Go back about half an hour," Carter said.

The video was a blur in Rewind but then came into

sharp focus as Rachelle and Carter stepped into view to wait for the light to change at the corner. As the video rolled forward it caught Carter rescuing her from the careening sedan.

"I thought so," Carter muttered.

"What?" Rachelle asked, unsure what he'd seen.

To Danielle he asked, "Can you pull video from the street right outside of the subway station about ten minutes prior to when the sedan showed up there?"

When the video was running, Carter pointed to the sedan parked at the curb. It pulled away and slowly rolled down the street.

"The sedan was waiting. Whoever it is knows where you live and expected you to take the train home." His grim gaze met hers. "It deliberately tried to hit you."

"And the plates were pulled," Danielle mused, sending Carter a look even a noncop could decipher.

Rachelle swallowed back the bile rising in her throat. Her mind went numb. Someone was trying to kill her?

"Thank you, Danielle," Carter said as he put his hand on the small of Rachelle's back and led her out of the video monitoring room.

In the hallway, he stopped her. "Now we know. You're being targeted. Why?"

Hoping to buy time to make sense of things, she bristled. "Why are you making this out to be my fault?"

"I'm not saying it's your fault." He frowned. "I'm just wondering what kind of stories you've been working on that would generate somebody's animosity."

Someone like the person who killed Jordan Jameson?

She leaned against the wall as her knees weakened. "My assignments are fluff pieces," she told him, which was the truth. "In fact, I'll be covering the upcoming celebrity charity ball at The Met next week. I had to talk my editor into giving me a shot at writing an article about the K-9 trials. He wanted to give it to one of the boys."

"Boys?"

"The male staffers," she clarified, "though they usually act like teenage boys."

"Would one of them have a reason to want to harm you?"

She let out a grim laugh. "No. The guys are harmless. Macho, arrogant, egotistical, but harmless."

He peered at her closely. "What aren't you telling me?"

How did he know?

It could only be one thing that had put her in the crosshairs of a killer, but if she told Carter about her investigation into his brother's death then any hope of advancing her career by solving Jordan Jameson's murder would be gone.

But if she died, then what did her career matter?

Carter watched the play of emotions on Rachelle's pretty face. He wanted her to trust him but wasn't sure how to make that happen. They'd only just met. Trust had to be earned. But he'd saved her life twice. Such heroics had to go a long way toward building confidence in his ability to protect her. "Whatever it is, spit it out. I can help you."

The noise she made was half moan, half scoff. "I think I know what the guy who pushed me meant by 'You're getting too close.'"

"Go on. Tell me."

She licked her lips. His eyes tracked the motion.

"I am working on an investigative piece."

He jerked his gaze from her mouth to her eyes. "Into what?"

Inhaling as if to brace herself, she breathed out and said, "Your brother's death."

"Excuse me?" He reeled back a step, his mind grasping to comprehend her words. "You're… I thought you said you're only assigned fluff pieces."

"I am. This is something I'm doing on my own."

His fingers curled. "You're investigating Jordan's murder. Unbelievable." He hadn't been prepared for that. But she was a reporter, after all. He should know better than to think she would be different than the vultures who'd circled for weeks after Jordan's death. "You're interfering in a police investigation. Do you know how much trouble you're in?"

Her chocolate-brown eyes implored him to understand. "I'm seeking the truth. And there's no way I'm impeding the NYPD's investigation. But obviously I've struck a nerve somewhere."

Anger put an edge to his voice. "Yes. Digging into things you have no business digging into can do that."

She held up her hands. "Hey, all I've done is look up public records, searched social media, made a few dozen phone calls asking people for information. Information they might not be as willing to tell the police. Like the rumors of nepotism and favoritism."

He tucked in his chin. "What are you talking about?"

The look she affected was one of *are you kidding*. "It's a bit strange, don't you think, the way Jordan rose through the rank and file so quickly? Your grandfather with the NYPD, correct? Your father, too."

rawing up to his full height of six feet, he stared at

her. "Really? Lady, you don't know what you're talking about. Jordan excelled at his job. He rose to the top by hard work and grit. Just like Noah has."

"Okay, I'm only repeating what I've heard." Her gaze bored into his. "And then there's Jordan and Katie's whirlwind romance. They went from dating to marriage to baby super fast."

Stunned by her audacity, he could barely form words. "You have no right to invade our lives without permission. Katie and Jordan live…led—" the grief he kept under a tight leash bubbled to the surface, breaking his voice "—squeaky-clean lives. You're not going to find anything going down those roads."

"You may be right. But you're too close to the situation." Compassion softened her features, making her eyes warm. "You have to consider something in one or both of their pasts could have resulted in Chief Jameson's murder."

He hated that she was right. On both accounts. "I want that information."

With a resigned sigh, she nodded. "You can have it. I will gather everything and bring it to you tomorrow."

Taking her hand, he tugged her forward down the hall. "I need to inform Noah."

"Did you know that several criminals that Jordan arrested have been let out of prison in the past year?"

"Of course," he threw over his shoulder.

She dug her heels into the carpet, slowing their progress. "Most left the area or are trying to make something of their lives. But there was one guy who stands out."

Carter stopped. "Who?"

"Miles Landau. He was released the day before Jordan died."

"The drug dealer. We looked at him." She really had no confidence in the department. He knew the public was restless with the lack of development in the case, he just hadn't had it brought home to him in such an in-your-face way. "His operation was shut down when he went to prison."

She raised her eyebrows. "So you know about his property on the waterfront."

Carter's gaze narrowed. "What property?"

"I uncovered a deed to a warehouse near the marina in Flushing with the business name of MiLand, Inc. Mi as in Miles and Land as in Landau. I pulled the public record on the company. MiLand, Inc. was formed two days after Miles was released from prison. And the lease on the warehouse signed a week later."

His heart rate doubled. This was new information. "You have the address?"

Lifting her chin, she nodded. "Yes, I do. And the first name of a woman, Ophelia, whom he might be seeing or staying with, though I can't seem to find her last name."

As much as he didn't want to admit it, her snooping might be helpful. And very dangerous. "Why are you doing this?"

"Doing what?"

"Looking into Jordan's murder?"

She made a face. "Reporter, remember?"

There was more to it than just her job. "But you're not being paid to write about Jordan's murder, so why? What do you hope to gain?"

"I want what everyone wants. The truth."

"You expect me to believe that's your only motive?"

He shook his head. "You want to exploit my brother's to further your career, am I right?"

"Not exploit. Never. I'm not that person." Her tone was one of pleading. "I'm doing my job. And yes, I hope if I write a great article with some meat to it, it will propel my career forward. What's wrong with that?"

"Everything, because it comes at the expense of my family."

The tenderness on her face made his stomach clench. "Your family has already paid an awful price for whatever motivated someone to kill Jordan. Don't you want the truth? It really is freeing."

Her words rang with sincerity. "What do you mean by that?"

Her expression closed, like a door slamming shut in his face. She may not realize how transparent she was, but he glimpsed the pain in her eyes before she hid it. She shrugged. "Nothing."

"Oh, something." He wasn't going to let her make a statement like that, then back away. "What truth set you free?"

"This isn't about me." She started walking down the hall. "I'd like to leave now."

He let it go. He didn't want to get invested in this woman in any way. He matched her steps. "After we tell Noah."

Noah listened, his face grim. Finally, he said, "I'll put people on Miles Landau. Though I'm skeptical he's our suspect. We looked at Miles. He doesn't have a record of violence. He's strictly low-level. However, Miss Clark, I would like to see your notes and research."

"As I told him—" she tipped her chin in Carter's direction "—I can bring it all tomorrow. It will take me some time to gather everything. I'm not the most organized individual."

Noah inclined his head. "Tomorrow, 10:00 a.m., then. I'll tell the front desk I'm expecting you. For now, I'll have Carter escort you home."

"I can't right now." Carter shook his head. "I have Ellie. Send Faith."

Noah nodded and picked up his phone to call for Officer Faith Johnson and her dog, Ricci.

"I'll leave you to it." Carter left the room without so much as a glance at Rachelle. If he never saw the reporter again, it would be too soon.

"Thank you, Officer Johnson," Rachelle stopped at the locked entrance to her apartment building.

"Of course," the petite female K-9 officer said with a smile. "I can walk you up." Her dog, a handsome German shepherd, sat patiently at her side.

Rachelle rattled the doorknob. "It's a secure building. No one can get in without a key. I'll be fine." She was exhausted. Two attempts had been made on her life. If Carter hadn't been there…

Now all she wanted was to get into her apartment before her roommates came home. A hot bath, a change of clothes and a tall glass of sweet tea were in order.

Officer Johnson looked around as if assessing the threat level. "Okay. We're just a phone call away."

Rachelle smiled because the irony was the NYC K-9 Command Unit was so close she could probably scream and be heard by the extraordinary dogs. "I appreciate you taking time for me."

"Chief said to be back here in the a.m. to escort you to his office. I'll see you then." Officer Johnson nodded, her dark, chin-length bob moving jauntily beneath her NYPD cap.

Rachelle unlocked the door and hurried inside, making sure the door closed completely behind her and the lock was secure. Through the small square window at eye level in the door, she watched the officer and dog walk away.

Breathing out a tired sigh, she headed to the elevator only to find a handwritten note saying, Out of Order.

Great. Just what she needed. She veered away, resigned to taking the stairs to the fourth floor. She trudged up each step at a slower pace than she normally would. Her legs were tired and sore and bruised. So was her ego. All her hopes for a career boost with her investigative report into Jordan Jameson's murder had slipped out of her control.

When she told Carter about the article on his brother's murder, his expression had made her lungs constrict and even now she was struggling to catch her breath. He'd been hurt, shocked and angry. He couldn't even look at her when they were in Noah's office.

She was glad she hadn't given in to the temptation to tell him her own family drama but thankfully, she'd managed to keep it inside. He wouldn't think her issues were anything compared to the losses he'd suffered. And he was right. Her heart ached for the Jamesons.

Two flights up, she turned the corner in the stairwell and found the way blocked by a man wearing a gray T-shirt. Shock constricted the muscles in her throat. Rough hands grabbed her and spun her around so fast she didn't have time to look at his face. A muscled arm slid around her neck and squeezed while her attacker's other hand pressed a smelly cloth over her nose and mouth.

She breathed in, preparing to scream, and gagged.

Her eyes watered. Her surroundings grew dim while her oxygen supply depleted, leaving her head woozy.

Her mind screamed, *Dear Lord, help me.*

FOUR

Capitalizing on the adrenaline flowing through her veins, Rachelle used what little remained of her strength to claw at the hand over her mouth and the arm squeezing her neck. She jerked her head side to side in an effort to find the crook of his elbow to relieve the pressure crushing her throat. She wildly kicked backward with the heel of her shoe and was rewarded with a grunt from her attacker.

From a floor above them a door banged open and the sound of feet on the concrete stairs echoed off the walls. Hope bubbled. *Please!*

Her attacker swore, then gruffly muttered, "Call off your investigation!"

She was abruptly thrust aside, hitting the wall with a thud while the assailant rushed down the stairwell.

Gasping for breath, Rachelle slowly slid down the wall to sit on the stairway landing and put her head between her knees.

A moment later, her upstairs neighbor, Yvette Grant, a nurse at Flushing Hospital Medical Center, appeared around the corner in her green scrubs. Rachelle had never been so happy to see anyone in—well, forever. "Yvette." The word came out a croak.

Another resounding bang reverberated off the walls as the man left the building.

"Rachelle!" Yvette knelt beside her, checking her pulse. "Are you okay?"

Rachelle shook her head. "No." She cleared her throat and pushed through the pain to add, "I need to call the police."

Yvette's dark eyes rounded. "Were you assaulted?"

"Yes." Rachelle attempted to stand.

Yvette put a restraining hand on her. "Stay where you are." She quickly dug her cell phone out of her purse and dialed 911.

"Can I talk to them?" Rachelle asked, holding out her hand.

Yvette relinquished the phone.

"Nine-one-one, what's your emergency?" a female voice answered in a calm and steady tone.

"Hello. I, uh, was attacked in my apartment building," Rachelle answered. She'd never called for help before and wasn't sure what to do or say.

"Can you give me the address?"

Rachelle recited the street number. "I'm in the stairwell."

"Are you hurt?"

Touching her tender throat, Rachelle grimaced. "Yes. Ish."

"Are you safe?"

"Yes." The question helped Rachelle collect her thoughts. She squared her shoulders. "Yes, I'm safe." *Thank You, God.* "My neighbor is here with me."

"Will the officers be able to gain access to the building?"

"No. The front door is locked." Yvette motioned she'd go downstairs. "My neighbor will let the police in."

"I'll make a note of it," the dispatcher said. "Can you tell me what happened?"

As Yvette hurried down to the lobby, Rachelle explained about the attack and that she believed it was the same man who'd pushed her off the subway platform earlier that day. "Can you inform Chief Jameson of the NYC K-9 Command Unit?"

She wondered if Carter would be told. She hoped he'd want to see that she was okay, but she knew he was angry with her and probably wouldn't care.

And that left her feeling hollow inside.

"Sweetie, go wash up and we'll have a snack," Carter told Ellie as they entered the apartment they shared with Noah on the top floor of the three-family house. Jordy's widow, Katie, had the second floor, and their parents had the ground level. Zach used to occupy one of the bedrooms in Carter's place, but after his marriage to Violet Griffin, he moved out with his bride. So now the room was a catch-all for stuff they weren't sure what to do with.

Frosty went to the water bowl in the kitchen and lapped greedily at the cool liquid. Carter didn't blame him. The heat and humidity was brutal in August.

"Okay, Daddy. Be right back." Ellie ran down the hall to the bathroom, slamming the door in her wake.

Carter winced but decided to refrain from getting after her about closing the door more gently. It was a constant battle.

Remnants of Ellie and Noah's tea party littered the

small living area and kitchen space. Apparently, Noah hadn't taken time to clean up before leaving for the precinct. Resigned to taking care of it, Carter washed the tea set and placed the tiny cups, saucers and teapot on the dish drainer to dry. Cookie crumbs were scattered across the top of the miniature purple dining table in the center of the living room and on the rug. With a shake of his head, he vacuumed up the mess. When he turned off the vacuum, he heard the chime of his cell phone.

Carter glanced at the caller ID. It showed Noah's private line at the precinct.

Ellie ran into the living room. "Can I watch my show?"

Distracted, he nodded and answered the phone. "Noah?"

"Hey, just thought I'd let you know Miss Clark was attacked in her apartment building."

The news sliced through Carter. Guilt flooded the wound. "What happened? I thought Faith was escorting her home."

"She did. All seemed fine, so Faith left."

As he would have. The NYPD didn't have the resources nor the manpower to provide around-the-clock security for any one person. Almost afraid to, he asked, "Is Rachelle okay?"

"Yes. Shaken. A neighbor scared the guy off."

Relief soothed the inner chaos a bit. "Is she at the precinct?"

"No. Officers are with her at her apartment."

Pacing, Carter stated, "Whatever hornet's nest she stirred up by probing into Jordan's life brought this on." The grim knowledge made his chest tighten.

"Agreed."

"She's not safe staying in her apartment."

"Again, agreed. She needs around-the-clock protection until we can eliminate the threat to her life."

He wondered if her family could afford a private security team. "We also need her research notes. If these attacks are connected to her investigating Jordy's death…"

"Yes. Carter, I want you to handle this. Find a way to keep her safe and get the information."

Though he wasn't looking forward to seeing Rachelle again, he knew it was crucial that he press through his own issues with her being a reporter and step up to not only protect her, but also discover why she was being targeted. And he prayed in the process they would uncover the truth of his oldest brother's death.

"Text me her address, will you? Maybe Katie can stay with Ellie."

"Aren't Mom and Dad back yet?"

"I don't know. I'll check." Alexander and Ivy Jameson lived on the bottom floor of the house they'd purchased to raise their kids in. For years the two upper-floor apartments had been rentals, until the four brothers were ready to have their own space.

As the oldest, Jordan, and eventually Katie, had taken the second floor, while Carter and his late wife, Helen, had taken the top floor. But then Helen passed, leaving him to raise Ellie alone. Noah and Zach had moved up from their parents' apartment on the first floor to live with Carter and Ellie.

"Sending you Miss Clark's information now."

A short ding announced the arrival of the text. "Got it. Heading over there ASAP." He was glad he hadn't changed out of his uniform yet.

Carter clicked off the phone with his brother. "Ellie girl," he said, tucking his phone back into the pocket on his vest. "Let's go downstairs and see if Grandma and Grandpa are home."

Without hesitation, Ellie jumped off the couch and raced to the door. "Frosty," she said. "Let's go see Grandma and Grandpa."

Frosty was slower to move off his bed, but he happily trotted over to her side and squeezed past her out the door.

Carter followed the two down the staircase to his parents' apartment. Using his key to unlock the front door, he heard movement in the kitchen. Ellie raced through the rooms with a squeal of delight. Carter entered the kitchen, where his parents were unloading groceries. Frosty went in for a quick pet before settling on a large dog bed in the corner of the dining room reserved for when one of the K-9s came to visit.

Ivy Jameson smiled and held out her arms for her grandchild. "Hello, love bug!"

Ellie jumped into her grandma's arms. Carter's heart swelled. His parents had been so great. After his wife passed he had been at a loss, unsure what to do, or how he was going to raise a child on his own. His whole family had stepped up and helped. Especially his parents.

Carter greeted his mother with a kiss on the cheek and his dad with a hug.

"Would you to be willing to watch Ellie for a little bit? I've been called back in to work."

Three sets of eyes stared at him. His father nodded his understanding. The worry in his mother's eyes churned Carter's gut.

Ellie tilted her head. "Are you going to see Rachelle?"

Carter dropped his chin and stared at his little girl. How on earth had she known? "Yes, honey. I have to talk to her again."

Ellie nodded. "You need to help her some more, Daddy."

Love for his child swelled in his chest. She was so compassionate. "I will, sweetie."

"You could bring her home for dinner," Ellie said.

His mother arched an eyebrow. "Rachelle?"

Before Carter could reply, Ellie said, "She's a reporter and she fell down. Daddy's helping her. She's really pretty and I liked her—so did Frosty."

Inwardly groaning, Carter shook his head. "I'm not bringing her home."

His mom ruffled Ellie's hair. "Why don't you go into the den and set up a board game for us."

"Yippee!" Ellie ran off, leaving Carter to face his parents' questioning gazes.

"You're helping a reporter?" His dad's tone brimmed with incredulity. "They're piranhas. Why would you want to help anyone in the media?"

Knowing how frustrated his family had been by the press over the past five months, Carter understood his father's sentiment. "Dad, she's in trouble. She's mixed up in something very dangerous. She's already had three attempts on her life today."

His mother frowned. "That doesn't sound good, though it doesn't surprise me. Reporters go snooping around whether they are wanted or not."

His mother's words were so spot-on that for a moment Carter didn't have a reply.

"Can't someone else help this woman?" his dad asked.

Carter remembered the look of compassion and empathy on Rachelle's face when they'd talked about Jordan. He shook off the image. "She's in trouble and it's my job to protect her."

His mother turned away to handle the groceries. "Let somebody else be her hero. The media have raked our family over the coals enough. We don't need any more contact with reporters. And there are certainly enough police officers who could deal with her."

"I was given a direct order from Noah," Carter said. "You can take it up with him. In the meantime, yes or no to watching Ellie?"

His mother paused. "Of course we will."

His father came over to him and put his hand on his shoulder. "Use caution. Don't get caught up emotionally. Stay focused on the job."

He was emotionally involved because whatever Rachelle had stirred up had something to do with Jordan's death. But he couldn't say that to his parents.

"I'd tell you not to worry, but I know that won't stop you," he said. "So, I'll just say Frosty and I will be careful."

At the sound of his name, Frosty scrambled to his feet.

With a morose sigh he couldn't contain, Carter grasped his dad and gave him a hug. "Love you, Dad."

"We love you, son."

His mother hurried over for her own hug. "We can't lose you, too."

With a kiss to his mother's cheek, Carter stepped back. "I'll let you know when I'm headed home."

He paused at the front door to call to Ellie. "Sweetie, I'm going."

In a whirl of arms and legs, Ellie ran out of the den,

where his parents had a plethora of board games and other toys for Ellie and the next soon-to-be grandchild. She launched herself into his arms. "Okay, Daddy. You be careful and take care of Rachelle."

Holding her tight, he breathed in the soft scent of her shampoo. His heart expanded in his chest. "I will." He kissed her on the top of the head and set her down. With a salute, he and Frosty exited the house.

With the dog at his heels, he jogged to the department-issued K-9 vehicle that he used to cart Frosty around. He had to park up a couple of houses because curbside parking was scarce in the neighborhood. The short driveway had room for two cars. Katie's car was already in the driveway. The other space they reserved for Noah. His parents didn't drive anymore since they preferred public transportation and walking.

He entered Rachelle's address into his GPS, hit the siren and headed out.

When he arrived at Rachelle's apartment, he was greeted by Officer Faith Johnson and her dog, Ricci.

"I feel so bad," she said. "The building was secure. There was nobody else around. I should've walked her inside. I knew it, but I had to get back to my other duties."

"You did nothing wrong. I'd have done the same thing." Though his motive for leaving wouldn't have been for the job. He'd pawned off the duty to Faith to begin with because he didn't want to have anything more to do with the reporter. Guilt wormed a hole through his conscience. "She's safe now," he continued. "That's what matters." And he would make sure she stayed that way despite his own feelings.

Faith nodded, "True. Thank you."

He and Frosty entered the building and found Rachelle sitting on the bench in the lobby talking with two plainclothes detectives. A dark-haired woman in green scrubs held her hand.

Rachelle's gaze snapped to his and the look on her face nearly upended him. *Relief? Joy?* She should be angry at him for leaving her in the lurch.

She rose and came toward him, the dirt on her gray pencil skirt and cream-colored silk blouse stark reminders of how close she'd come to being killed in the subway. The new red abrasion at her throat tied his stomach up in knots.

Stopping two feet away, she said, "I— You're here."

Frosty nudged her hand with his nose.

"Noah called me," he told her as he watched the way her fingers slid through the dog's fur in the spot behind his right ear that he loved to have scrubbed. At first glance the movement seemed casual, but she was clearly soothing herself as much as the dog. He cleared his throat before he spoke to make sure his question would come out as gently as possible. "Can you tell me what happened?"

As he listened to her story, concern grew and spread through his chest. "Are you sure it was the guy from the subway?"

She shrugged. "He had on a gray shirt. I didn't get a look at his face."

The other woman walked up, sliding her arm around Rachelle's waist. "Can she go to her apartment now?"

"And you are…?"

"This is my upstairs neighbor, Yvette Grant," Rachelle answered him. "If she hadn't come along when she had I'd be dead." A visible shiver racked her body. Frosty leaned into her, as if offering his support.

"Let me confer with the detectives." Carter stepped aside with the two detectives and they filled each other in on the day's activities.

Detectives Sanchez and Walsh introduced themselves. Then Sanchez said, "The guy gained access to the building by posing as a floral delivery man. The forensic tech didn't find prints on the vase of carnations left in the stairwell."

"We're going to canvass the area and see if we can find where he obtained the flowers," Walsh added.

Carter handed them his card. "Keep me updated. I'll be handling Miss Clark."

The detectives nodded and left the building. Carter went to Rachelle. "Let's go get your things. You can't stay here."

"She can stay with me," Yvette offered.

Shaking his head, Carter said, "She needs to be away from this building. The assailant knows where she lives." He turned his gaze to Rachelle. She stared at him with what appeared to be shock and confusion. He explained, "We need to get you out of the city. Do you have family somewhere we can call?"

Seeming to absorb his words, she tucked in her chin. "No, I'm not calling my family."

His heart twisted in his chest. He wondered what the story was there. Obviously, they weren't close. He couldn't imagine life without his family.

"I'm not leaving New York." There was a stubborn glint in her eyes that didn't bode well. "I don't mind going to a hotel."

He sighed. "Let's discuss this in your apartment."

With a frown, she headed for the elevator.

"This was just a trick to make me take the stairs." She yanked the Out of Order sign off the door and pushed the button. A second later, the doors slid open. She stepped inside, tapped her foot and crossed her arms over her chest. "Are you coming?"

Exchanging a glance with Frosty, Carter muttered, "This is going to be fun."

FIVE

When the doors opened on the fourth floor, Carter and Frosty put a hand up to prevent Rachelle from stepping out first. He made sure the hallway was empty, then held his hand on the elevator door to keep it from closing. "We're good."

Rachelle quickly turned and hugged Yvette. "Thank you so much. You are a blessing."

"Be careful, okay?" Concern laced Yvette's voice.

"I will." Rachelle clung to her for moment, then stepped back.

Yvette shot Carter a quick glance before saying to Rachelle, "Let me know if there's anything I can do for you."

Rachelle nodded and stepped out of the elevator car. The door shut behind them. Without a word, Rachelle led Carter and Frosty to the last apartment at the end of the hall. He had to admit he admired her strength under pressure. The woman had a spine of steel.

She dug into her purse for her keys. With shaky hands, she attempted to unlock the door.

"Here, let me." As Carter took the keys, his fingers brushed over hers. She was cold, no doubt still reeling from the most recent attack. He slid the key in the lock and opened the door.

She hurried to block the way. "It's small," she warned. "We're not tidy. I have two roommates. They share the bedroom. My domain is the living room." She bit her bottom lip, her cheeks pinkening.

Carter shrugged. "I'm not going to judge you. I live with a messy six-year-old. I just need your notes and you need to pack a bag."

Looking unconvinced, she moved aside so he could enter first. Frosty sniffed the air, then lay down, indicating there was no discernible threat.

Carter barely refrained from whistling. Okay, this was messy, beyond what three men and a six-year-old could do, back when Zach still lived with him, his daughter and Noah.

In a flurry of apparent nervousness, Rachelle grabbed the clothes on hangers dangling from the ceiling fan and hung them in the entryway closet. Then she righted the sofa bed, which had been out and unmade.

The dining room table had stacks of notebooks and loose papers, pens and highlighters, covering every square inch. Up against the wall was a freestanding whiteboard written on with notes and arrows and circles. There was a small kitchenette and a short hall with two closed doors, presumably the bath-and bedroom.

The place was hardly big enough for one person let alone three.

Moving to stand beside the dining room table, she gestured to the disorganized chaos. "Everything I have on Jordan's case is here." She gestured to the whiteboard. "And here."

He joined her by the table, taking in the looping

cursive covering the pages. "You do all your notes by hand?"

"I have some things on the computer, but I think better with pen and paper. I do all my first drafts by hand, then type them in."

He couldn't imagine taking that time or having the patience to work that way. He hated doing his reports. He typed by hunt-and-peck. If he had to do them by hand, then type them in, he'd... Well, it would make for a very bad day.

"I don't know how we'll get the board out of here with just you and me," Rachelle said. "You might just want to take pictures of it."

"Good idea." He liked that she problem-solved. Taking out his cell phone, he went about the task of photographing the whiteboard.

"I'll see if I can find some boxes to throw everything into and then I can organize it later."

"That's fine. But you also need to pack your clothes."

She hesitated. "If it's not safe for me here, then it's not safe for Grace or Roxanne."

He appreciated her concern for her roommates. "You're right. They are going to need to leave, as well. Can you text or call them to let them know? They should find other accommodations for the time being."

Shoulders slumped, she nodded. "I can't believe we're having to do this."

"If you or your family can spring for a security team, then you could stay. I'm willing to wait until they arrive."

Straightening, she shook her head. "I'm not calling my family. I'll text the girls. I'm sure we can all find somewhere else to crash for a few days." She looked at him steadily. "It won't be more than a few days, will it?"

"I can't honestly say. I don't think you'll be safe coming back here to the apartment or the building. But maybe in a day or so, they can. But they can't know where you've gone."

She shuddered and dug out her cell phone from her purse. After she sent several texts, she went into the living room, where a set of dresser drawers was pushed up against the bookcase.

"Why don't you want to call your family?" For him, family was everything. He didn't know what he would do without them.

She opened some doors and stared at her clothes. "I left Georgia to be out from under their control. I'm not going to invite it back into my life."

He wasn't sure what to say. He ached for her because she obviously didn't feel supported by her family.

Turning away from the dresser, she moved to the sofa bed and knelt down on the floor to drag out a suitcase from beneath. She pulled out a couple of flat boxes, as well. He rushed over to help her.

Standing, she held out a roll of tape. "Do you mind taking care of these?"

"Not at all." He took the tape from her hand, and the boxes.

While she packed, he put together the boxes and filled them with everything on the table.

"I've taken several pictures of the whiteboard," he told her. "You need to erase it."

Leaving her suitcase by the front door, she grabbed her own phone and snapped off several images before taking a black felt eraser and wiping the board clean.

"There." She set the eraser down and picked up her cell phone. "Now to find a hotel."

As Carter watched her searching the internet, Ellie's words reverberated through his head. *You better help her some more, Daddy.*

His daughter was right. He couldn't in good conscience send her off alone. And though he didn't want to do this, he knew there was only one option. "Forget the hotel. You're coming home with me."

Rachelle froze. Stunned, she lifted her gaze to meet Carter's. Surely she'd misunderstood him. He wanted to take her home? To his home? That couldn't be right. "What did you say?"

He sighed and ran a hand through his dark hair, leaving behind grooves from his strong, capable fingers. She had the craziest urge to touch his hair, to smooth down the ruffled strands. She tightened her hold on the phone.

"Listen, whatever you've stumbled on could be the break we need in solving my brother's murder. I can't leave you alone again. My family home has plenty of rooms. It's a temporary solution until we can find a secure safe house."

Her mouth dropped open. She snapped her lips together as a protest gathered on her tongue. But then her mind latched on to the fact she'd be staying with the Jamesons. Inside the family home, where she could gather more insight into Jordan's life and death.

Carter's gaze narrowed. "Don't even think about continuing with your investigation or your story."

She drew back. Had she been that transparent? "How can I stop when I've gathered more intel than the police? If you let me work with you…we could accomplish much more as a team."

He barked out a laugh. "Really? A team." Then he seemed to give it some thought. "Okay. We'll team up to go through your notes once we get back to my house."

That wasn't exactly what she meant but she'd take it for now. "Deal."

They left the apartment with Carter balancing two full cardboard boxes filled with her notes in his arms. Frosty trailed along at his side while she dragged her suitcase behind her. She appreciated that Carter had her wait to exit the elevator until after he and his partner were satisfied there were no visible threats. Her throat still burned where the man had pressed his arm against her neck and squeezed. An involuntary shudder racked her.

As if sensing the tremor racing through her, both Frosty and Carter stopped and looked at her.

"You okay?" he asked, concern darkening his blue eyes.

She swallowed past the soreness. "Yeah. Of course," she hedged, unwilling to show any weakness. She lifted a quick prayer asking for the strength to see her through this ordeal.

Carter set the boxes on the sidewalk beside his blue-and-white K-9 Unit vehicle. Using the fob on his key chain, he popped open the back hatch.

"Load up," he said.

Frosty jumped into the back compartment without hesitation.

Impressed, Rachelle said, "Wow, he really is well trained."

"We work eight to ten hours a week at the training

center and then more intense specific training with others in the K-9 transit unit once a month."

"I'd really love to see the training center and witness some training. Will you be doing any drills for the upcoming K-9 trials?"

He nodded as he picked up the boxes. He gestured with his chin toward the rear passenger door. "Can you get the door?"

She opened the side back passenger door and he set the boxes on the seat, then hefted her suitcase inside, as well. He turned to look at her. "I still owe you a tour of the station house. That would include the training center. Frosty and I need to run through our obstacle courses before next Saturday."

"May I watch?" She couldn't wait to see the two in action.

He shut the back door and opened the front passenger door and leaned on the frame. "Yes. In fact, it would probably be a really good idea for you to walk the course so you can get an idea of what it's like out there."

She slid into the passenger seat, catching a whiff of his aftershave. She'd noticed the spicy, masculine scent earlier in the day. She liked the way he smelled. "That sounds fun."

"It will be." He winked and then shut the door, leaving her to wonder what he meant.

As he started the SUV, she fingered a pink scrunchie stuck in the cup holder. Ellie's, no doubt. She had to admit she was looking forward to seeing the little girl again. She was charming, just like her dad. Rachelle didn't have much experience around children. She'd never babysat like some of her friends had done during high school. Her after-school job had been office work in her father's law firm. Not that he'd paid her, saying she needed to earn her keep. She shook off the memory and paid attention to where they were going.

Carter drove them out of Forest Hills and into Rego Park. They passed the popular four-floor shopping center with its multilevel parking garage, then wound their way through the neighborhoods of tall apartment buildings that gave way to detached homes.

He brought the vehicle to a halt in front of a three-story house with a nice front yard and beautiful full tree providing some shade.

She stared at the three-story, multifamily building. "Are the upper floors apartments?"

"Yes. Ellie, Noah and I share the top floor. Jordan and—" His voice faltered. "Katie lives on the second floor."

He climbed out before she could offer sympathy. She couldn't imagine how hard it had to be for the family to have Jordan gone and his murder unsolved.

Carter let Frosty out, then he came around to her side as she stepped out of the vehicle. He retrieved her suitcase and placed it on the paved walkway. Then he grabbed the boxes and led the way up the porch stairs to the front door.

Nerves suddenly fluttered in her stomach. "Are you sure about this?"

There was just the briefest hesitation before he said, "It'll be fine."

She wondered if he was hoping to reassure her or himself. "Did you let your family know I was coming?"

He set the boxes down and faced her. "No. My parents aren't terribly fond of reporters. The press has been less than kind to our family since Jordan's death."

She grimaced. Remembering some of the headlines. Especially in the beginning when the death at first had appeared to be a suicide. She wanted to tell him it was nothing personal. The reporters and the newspapers had a job to do. But she understood there were some who acted carelessly. She tried not to be biased one way or another in her reporting. But then again, there wasn't much to be biased about in giving an account of a new doughnut shop opening up or what a celebrity was wearing at one of the many gala events that she was assigned.

"Maybe I shouldn't be here."

"Too late. Besides, this is the best option." He opened the door and ushered her inside.

As she stepped into the house, she wondered why he was adamant that he and his family provide her shelter and security. Why not pawn her off to someone else like he'd done earlier? Guilt, she decided. He felt guilty for not having been there when she was attacked in her apartment building. "You don't have to do this."

He cocked his head. "Do what?"

"Take me in like this. It wasn't your fault I was attacked."

His mouth twisted in a rueful way that had her pulse skipping. "You caught me. I do feel guilt for not seeing you home. But bringing you here is also selfish. I want the information in these boxes."

"Ah." She wasn't sure if that made her feel better or worse. She looked away and took in the house.

The living room was cozy with well-worn leather furniture, a large-scale TV on a wood stand, shelves filled with books and magazines on the coffee table. A colorful afghan lay folded across the back of the couch. To her left was a dining room with a large dining table and enough chairs to accommodate the whole Jameson clan.

Carter set the boxes on the dining table. "You can leave your suitcase over there." He pointed to the mouth of the hallway. "Your room will be down that way. I'll show you to it after I introduce you to my parents. They're out back."

He walked through the doorway into the kitchen. With trepidation making her nerves jumpy, she followed him. Carter opened the back door and they stepped out onto a patio overlooking a grassy yard. There was a dog run and a couple of kennels. Frosty trotted straight out to the grass where two puppies, one black and one yellow with a black smudge on one ear, were chasing each other. For a moment, Rachelle watched the rambunctious pair, enraptured by the cuteness.

"Daddy!" Ellie exclaimed, scrambling out of her chair and drawing Rachelle's gaze.

An older couple and a pretty blonde also sat at the patio table, their curious gazes raking over Rachelle. Subconsciously, she smoothed her hand over her skirt wishing she'd taken the time to change into some clean clothes.

Ellie wrapped her arms around her father's waist and held him tight, and then she turned her bright blue eyes onto Rachelle. "Are you doing better now? Are you hungry?"

Disarmed, as she was earlier by the cute kid, Rachelle nodded. She was safe and famished. "Yes and yes."

Ellie released her father and slipped her hand into Rachelle's, tugging her toward the table. "Come on."

Sending Carter a questioning glance, to which he

shrugged, Rachelle allowed herself to be pulled toward the table.

The elder Jameson, wearing cargo shorts and a T-shirt with the logo of the Mets emblazoned across the front, stood, his gaze locking with Carter's. He was tall, handsome and formidable. She decided the Jameson men took after their father. "Are you going to introduce your friend?"

Moving to stand beside Rachelle, Carter said, "Mom, Dad, Katie, this is Rachelle Clark." He gestured with his hand. "My sister-in-law, Katie, and my parents, Alex and Ivy."

"Hello," Rachelle said with her best smile.

She could tell from the disgruntled look on his mother's face that her presence definitely wasn't a pleasant surprise. Her blue eyes, so like her son Carter's, were wary. Her dark hair was swept up in a topknot and she wore a skort and polo top, looking comfortable and sporty at the same time. An outfit Rachelle's mother would have curled a lip at.

"Rachelle needs a safe place to stay tonight," Carter said.

"She can stay with us!" Ellie piped up.

"Actually, honey," Carter said. "I'm hoping Grandpa and Grandma can put her up in their spare bedroom."

Rachelle's gaze snapped to him. He was putting his parents on the spot. Totally uncomfortable, she said, "That's okay. I can find a hotel."

"But I want her to stay with us," Ellie protested. "She could have Uncle Zach's old room."

Carter shook his head. "No, honey, that's not going to happen." He looked to his parents. "Mom, Dad?" There was steel in his tone that made Rachelle shiver.

She didn't want to cause a rift between Carter and his family.

Carter's mother gave her a tight smile. "Of course. I'll make up the bed after dinner." She gestured toward an empty seat. "Please, join us."

Feeling as welcome as a swamp breeze, she debated turning tail and sprinting for the door. The heat of Carter's hand at the small of her back jolted through her. His gaze locked with hers. The message clear in his blue eyes said she wasn't going anywhere.

And for some reason she suddenly didn't want to leave. Which was as scary as facing down her attacker in the stairwell.

SIX

After excusing herself to take a few moments to clean up and change out of her soiled clothing into jean capris and a blue, cap sleeve shirt, Rachelle hesitated at the back door before joining the Jameson family on the patio. *What am I doing here?*

Maybe she should go home to Georgia. At least there, she knew what to expect—her parents' disapproval and assertion that she shouldn't have left in the first place. Here, she wasn't sure the Jamesons would accept her, despite the invitation to join them.

But she wasn't a quitter. And running home wasn't something she could stomach. So she squared her shoulders, lifted her chin and stepped out onto the patio.

Carter rose from his seat and held out the chair between him and Ellie. She wasn't sure what to think of that but smiled her thanks and caught Katie Jameson's curious gaze.

Rachelle's own curiosity surged. She wanted to ask Jordan's widow some questions about her husband and about their whirlwind romance, but this definitely wasn't the time or place.

"What can I get you? Hot dog or hamburger?"

Redirecting her focus, Rachelle said to Alex Jameson, "I'll take a hamburger, thank you."

Carter resumed his seat next to her, so close his knee bumped against hers. The little jolt of awareness that raced up her leg made her bounce a bit in her seat.

He looked at her, his eyebrow hitched ever so slightly, then turned to his father. "The same. With cheddar." Looking back to her he asked, "Cheese?"

Not about to tell the family she was lactose intolerant, she shook her head and simply said, "No, thank you."

For several awkward moments, there was silence so thick she could have cut it with a butter knife. Then Ellie started chattering about ponies. And the two puppies raced around beneath their feet, making everyone laugh. Rachelle began to relax, enjoying the novelty of a loud and boisterous family dinner. Her hamburger was tasty and satisfying. Much better than the salad she'd planned on having tonight.

"Miss Clark, where do you come from?" Ivy asked. "There's just a little bit of an accent in your voice."

Ugh. The stress of the day had her slipping and rendering her diction practice useless. She tried to modulate her voice as she answered, "I'm from Georgia."

"Ah. We haven't ventured much to the southern states. New York must be a whole different way of life to you," Ivy commented.

She inadvertently caught Carter's gaze. She didn't know how but she was certain he was thinking of her sprawled flat on the sharp gravel between the tracks of a subway train, waiting in terror for what might be a horrible death. She blinked away the awful image and gave him, then his mother, a toothy smile. "Yes, but I'm getting used to it. I like the fast-paced lifestyle. Much different from the small town where I grew up."

"Your family must miss you," Ivy said.

Rachelle figured they hardly noticed her absence. They barely paid attention when she was around except to find fault with her. For the way she dressed, the way she wore her hair or talked. She never was able to live up to their expectations.

"She doesn't have contact with her family," Carter interjected.

Slanting him a glance, Rachelle inhaled sharply. She didn't appreciate him answering for her.

Carter lifted an eyebrow.

"We aren't speaking at the moment," she said. She didn't tell him that she'd uncovered a secret that had not only explained many things for her but also caused a rip through the fabric of their family.

Thankfully, the subject matter changed to the Jamesons' recent visit to Fire Island and the upcoming K-9 trials. Rachelle soaked it all in, deciding she would have to take a trip to see the lighthouse at the tip of Long Island. And the more she heard about the K-9 trials the more excited she was to write about the event.

Ellie tapped her on the shoulder and leaned over. In a loud whisper, she said, "Will you come to the K-9 trials and sit with me? It's so much fun to watch Daddy and Frosty. They do some funny things."

"That's my plan, Ellie." Touched by the child's requests, she added, "I'd love to sit with you. If it's okay with your dad."

Ellie grinned. "It's okay, right, Daddy?"

"Yes, sweetie," Carter answered, his gaze meeting Rachelle's.

She couldn't decipher what had him looking so intense.

"Daddy, may I be excused now?" Ellie asked. "I ate well." There were just a few little remnants of her hot dog and potato salad on her plate.

"You did good," Carter agreed. "You may be excused."

Ellie raced down the porch stairs to play in the grass with the two little Labrador puppies, while Frosty watched from beneath the shade of an awning.

Katie stood, picking up her plate and her father-in-law's, then started into the house.

Needing something to do, Rachelle followed suit, gathering the empty plates. "I'll help you."

She hesitated before taking Ivy's plate.

The older woman gave her an assessing glance before lifting the plate to stack it on top of the others in Rachelle's hands. "That's very sweet of you, dear."

"The least I can do," Rachelle replied with a smile. "I need to earn my keep."

Ivy smiled back, her features softening. "That is not necessary."

Unsure how to respond, Rachelle followed Katie into the kitchen, where Katie set the plates in the sink. For a moment, she leaned against the counter rubbing her back.

Stacking her own pile of dishes in the sink, Rachelle eyed Katie with concern. "Are you okay?"

"Yes. I just battle with bouts of fatigue. It's been a very emotional five months."

Empathy spread through Rachelle's chest. "I can imagine. I'm so sorry that you're going through this."

Katie turned on the water faucet and rinsed the

dishes before putting them into the dishwasher. "Not much I can do but pray Jordan's killer is caught."

"Here, let me do that." Rachelle shooed Katie aside. She took over rinsing the plates and silverware and putting them into the dishwasher. "I'm sure something will break in the case soon." She glanced out the window over the sink, making sure that Carter was still with his parents. She turned off the faucet and turned to Katie. "I'm actually working on a story about your husband's death. That's why I'm here."

Katie frowned. "What do you mean?"

"Carter will probably get mad at me for telling you this, but the attempt on my life today must have something to do with my investigation into Chief Jameson's murder."

Katie put a hand on the counter as if the news had weakened her knees. "I don't know what to say."

Noticing that Katie's face had lost its color, Rachelle dragged a chair in from the dining room. "You should sit."

Katie sank onto the wooden chair. "I feel like I've let Jordan down. I promised myself I wouldn't rest until they found out who killed him. But to be honest, these days, resting is about all I can do. I'm glad you're investigating. But I don't like the fact that your life is in danger."

Rachelle felt better about her investigation knowing that Katie appreciated her efforts. "Thank you for saying that. Carter's not terribly happy with me, but at least he's willing to team up."

Katie tilted her head, a speculative gleam in her eyes. "Team up, huh? That's interesting. He must really like you."

"I don't think 'like' is the right word. He finds me an

irritant. He's only working with me for my notes. If he could read them without my help, I wouldn't be here."

"What do you mean?"

"A lot of my notes are written in my own form of shorthand. I'm the only one who can transcribe them."

Katie nodded approvingly. "Clever girl. And I'm not sure you're correct in thinking Carter finds you irritating," she said with a smile. "He went all he-man with his parents over you. I've never seen him do that before."

Hoping to change the subject, Rachelle asked, "Do you know if you're having a boy or girl?"

Katie put her hand on her tummy. "A girl." Tears gathered in Katie's eyes. "Jordan so wanted to be a father."

Aching for her, Rachelle said, "It's really good that you have so much support from the Jameson family."

Katie nodded and wiped her eyes. "Yes, they've been really great. My own parents are long gone. Everybody has been so kind to me. A couple of ex-boyfriends and several coworkers have all offered to help in some way or another. Even my college roommate, who I'd lost touch with when she moved to Europe, made contact and said I could go live with her if I needed."

"Would you go?"

Katie shook her head. "No. This is my family now." She rubbed her belly. "Our family."

"You're a teacher, correct?" Rachelle vaguely remembered something about Katie's job in one of the articles she'd read after Jordan's death.

"Yes, fifth grade at Rego Park Elementary School. Though I'd resigned for this coming school year as Jordan wanted me to be a stay-at-home mom." She sighed.

"Maybe I'll go back to teaching once the baby is old enough. Ivy has offered to provide day care."

"I'm sure Mrs. Jameson is looking forward to taking care of another grandchild."

"Oh yes. I don't know what I would do without Alex and Ivy. Of course, Carter and Ellie and Noah will be here to help out. Zach and his new wife, Violet, have offered to pitch in, as well. Like I said, family."

"I have to confess I envy your close-knit family."

"I married into it," Katie said. "My parents died years ago." She tilted her head. "Why are you not on speaking terms with your family?"

The ache and hurt from learning she was adopted reared up to clog her throat. She wasn't ready to talk about learning the reason she was never accepted by the man and woman she'd called her mother and father. "It's complicated."

"Do you have siblings?" Katie asked.

"I'm an only child. I was a surprise that came along later in my parents' life." An unwanted guest that stayed too long. "They had chosen not to have children. But apparently, God had other plans."

"There's no arguing with God and His plans," Katie said. "I'm sure He has great things in store for you."

Liking Katie and appreciating her kind words, Rachelle smiled. "Thank you for that."

"So, are you married? Dating anyone?"

"No, to both questions. I'm focusing on my career right now."

"There's no reason you can't be married and have a career," Katie pointed out.

"Maybe someday," Rachelle said. "But not anytime soon."

"What do you think of Carter?"

Oh no. She was trying to play matchmaker. Not happening. "Please don't go there." Remembering the wedding photo on his desk, she added, "I get the sense that he's still mourning his late wife."

"Perhaps. I never met Helen. But from what everybody has told me of her she was a wonderful person. It would take a special person to replace her." Katie tilted her head, her gaze speculative. "I have a feeling you could be that person."

The back door opened, and Carter stepped inside. His gaze bounced between Rachelle and Katie and back again. "What's going on?"

Cheeks flaming, Rachelle quickly went back to the dishes. "Nothing."

Rachelle reminded herself not to get attached to him or his beautiful little daughter. Because there was no way she could be special enough to fill the empty hole left by his wonderful wife.

The next day Carter packed the boxes back into his SUV and he and Rachelle and Frosty headed to the NYC K-9 Command Unit headquarters.

Rachelle had been quiet the rest of last evening and again this morning as they prepared to leave. He'd asked her to wear comfortable clothing for their trip to the training center. He tried not to notice how cute she looked in her loose-fitting pants and T-shirt with the words Hello Sunshine written across the front.

She had been a ray of sunshine last night. The way Ellie and Katie responded to her made his heart glad that he'd brought her home, despite his mother's less than warm welcome. Mom could be a tough cookie, but he knew she'd warm up to Rachelle in time. Not that he needed her to for his sake. Far from it.

When he'd walked into the kitchen to find Rachelle and Katie talking, it was the first time in a long time that Katie hadn't looked to be on the verge of tears.

Of course Ellie adored Rachelle. Too much, in fact. All Ellie could talk about as he was putting her to bed was Rachelle. *Isn't she pretty, Daddy? Isn't she so nice, Daddy?*

And when Ellie asked if Rachelle would come and sit with her at the K-9 trials, he had to fight the need to warn both of them not to get attached. He just hoped he could end the threat to Rachelle sooner rather than later so they could all go back to their normal, separate lives.

He pulled into the parking lot behind the brick building housing the NYC K-9 Command Unit.

After releasing Frosty from the vehicle and attaching his lead, Carter hefted the two cardboard boxes into his arms.

She reached for the top one. "I can carry that. You don't have to do it all yourself."

For the briefest moment he thought of protesting. But then decided she was right. And it would free him up just a bit in case he needed to drop the box if something were to happen between here and the precinct. He nodded. "Thanks. I appreciate it."

Her smile reached her eyes this time. He liked the way her brown eyes lit up and crinkled at the corners when she was genuinely smiling.

Frosty nudged his leg, drawing his attention. The dog no doubt wanted to know why they weren't on the move. Because he was enjoying staring into Rachelle's eyes. He mentally gave himself a shake and started walking.

Carter stopped at the training center to drop Frosty off with the lead trainer.

He could tell Rachelle wanted to linger. "We'll come back here later."

She nodded and followed him to Noah's office. He'd come home late last night and left again before Carter had gotten up to get Ellie ready for an outing with his parents.

"I take it those are your case notes," Noah said, eyeing the boxes they held as they entered the room.

"Yes, sir. As promised," Rachelle responded.

Carter liked that she wasn't a shrinking flower. She was bold and strong. She had to be if she was digging into his brother's death. Acid churned in his gut. Something in one of these boxes would lead them to the truth.

"Take the conference room," Noah instructed. "Shut the blinds. I don't want anybody interfering." He leveled Carter with a direct look. "This is for your eyes only. Not even Dad or Zach."

Surprise washed through Carter. His brother's confidence in him was pleasing. He gave Noah a sharp nod and led the way to the conference room. For the next several hours, he and Rachelle went about the task of laying all the notes out. Some of her writing was indecipherable to him.

"My shorthand," she said. "I learned from my father's law clerk."

"Your father's a lawyer." Lawyers were right up there with reporters as far as he was concerned. Good when you needed them, but the rest of the time he wanted nothing to do with them.

"Can you un-shorthand them so I can read them?"

"Of course I can. It will take some time. Might be easier if I just read the notes to you."

"Good idea. Let's try that." He grabbed his pad to take notes of his own.

She took a seat and picked up a ledger. "Recent releases from the jail system." She read the list of names in her slightly accented voice that filled the room. She had a nice voice and he had to concentrate to stay focused on listening to the words and not just the warm, honeyed tone.

Partway down the list was Miles Landau. But there were other names he hadn't heard before. He lifted a hand. "Hold up. All of those inmates had some connection to Jordan?"

"Yes. Going back through public records." She put emphasis on the word *public*. "Jordan was involved in each of these cases in some way. In some he was the first responder to the scene. Those are from back when he was a rookie. Other cases as the arresting officer, while in many he was the officer in charge of the investigation."

Carter tumbled that information through his head. Could Jordan's death have something to do with a case from the past?

"Okay." He decided to pursue this line of thought. "You've pulled case files on each of these ex-cons?"

"I have. Many of their files are very thick and some not so much. Several were a slam dunk, while others the state had to really dig deep to convict. I've also dug into various social media outlets to see what I could find about where they are now and what they are doing."

She was a go-getter; he'd give her that. "Let's start at the top and dig our way through all of the files."

"You don't want to start with Miles? He was released the day before your brother's death. And I have the most information on him. Photos from before he was incarcerated and after."

"We have no way of knowing if he's the culprit. It could be any one of these guys."

"My instincts tell me Miles is up to something," she insisted. She handed him a photo of the man standing on the deck of what looked like a fancy boat, a bottle of alcohol in one hand and a pretty woman next to him.

Carter wasn't sure he trusted her instincts. He stared at the photo. Was this man responsible for Jordan's death? "Noah put a man on finding and trailing Landau. If he makes any strange moves, we'll know."

For a moment, he thought she'd continue to argue but instead she took the picture back and replaced it in the file.

"All right, then." She read the top name again. "This guy was a pusher who beat his girlfriend. The state's case against him put him away on drug charges as well as attempted murder. Your brother was the first officer on the scene."

"Tell me everything you could find out about him."

The ring of a cell phone echoed off the conference room walls.

"That's me," Rachelle said. "Sorry. I thought I turned the ringer off." She hurried to where she'd hung her purse across the back of a chair and answered the phone. "Hello."

At that exact moment, Noah opened the conference room door, his expression grim. "We have a situation."

Carter went to his brother, while keeping his eyes on Rachelle. Her face had gone white at whatever was said on the other side of the cell phone conversation. He heard her exclaim, "Oh no! I'll be right there."

Carter's gaze whipped to his brother as dread cramped his chest. "What's going on?"

The hard set of Noah's mouth sent unease sliding through Carter.

"There was a break-in at the *NYC Weekly* offices." Noah tipped his chin toward Rachelle. "Her desk space specifically was targeted."

Carter's gut clenched. "Whoever was after her wanted these notes."

"My thought exactly," Noah said.

Rachelle rushed to the door with her purse slung over her shoulder. "I have to go. It's the office."

"I know," Carter said. "Come with me to get Frosty and we'll head over there."

"I can't wait!" She slipped past him and Noah and hurried toward the front staircase.

"Go get your partner," Noah instructed him. "I'll keep her from leaving without you."

Carter peeled away and headed down the back stairwell to the training center while Noah went after Rachelle.

Frosty was sleeping in a kennel but as soon as Carter stepped into the large space reserved for the dogs to have some downtime, Frosty rose and stretched. Carter let him out of the kennel. "Time to work, boy."

Without a word, the lead trainer, Olivia King, handed him a lead.

"Thanks." He leashed up and hustled out of the kennel room.

"Be safe," Olivia called after him.

"From your lips to God's ears," he muttered beneath his breath.

When Carter and Frosty reached the lobby, Noah was talking to Rachelle, hopefully keeping her from acting impulsively. She tapped her foot as he approached.

Noah waved him on. "Go."

With a nod, Carter led Rachelle and Frosty through the exit. Because her office building was only a few blocks away, they didn't need to drive. The sidewalk was crowded as they joined the flow of pedestrians. They reached the intersection just as the Walk sign flashed.

Up ahead, the sidewalk was blocked by a hand truck stacked with aluminum kegs. He slowed, hoping to give the workers time to get the hand truck out of the way.

"We have to go around them," Rachelle insisted and stepped off the curb, skirting past the parked cars.

Clenching his jaw, he and Frosty followed but were waylaid by pedestrians taking the same route in the opposite direction.

At the next corner, a white panel van pulled up in front of Rachelle, blocking her path. The side door opened and two men with ski masks covering their faces jumped out. She skidded to a halt and attempted to backpedal, but the men grabbed her by the arms to drag her into the van.

SEVEN

Carter's heart jumped into his throat at the sight of the two men grabbing Rachelle. He surged forward, through the crowd. "Police. Move!" He dropped Frosty's leash as he ran. "Attack!"

Carter trusted the dog's training to know the difference between the aggressor and the victim in this situation. Plus, Frosty knew and loved Rachelle.

Frosty raced to launch himself at the closest kidnapper. The dog's powerful jaw snapped closed and his teeth sank into the man's forearm through his black long-sleeved windbreaker. The guy screamed with pain behind his black ski mask, releasing his hold on Rachelle as he tried to shake off Frosty.

With her free hand, she landed a well-placed punch to the second man's face. Blood spurted through the nose hole of his mask after she made contact. He dropped her arm to grab his face. She pivoted and ran toward Carter.

The two men, one still struggling with Frosty, jumped back into the panel van as the driver hit the gas. Frosty ran alongside, still clamped onto the man's arm as he screamed, punching and kicking in a useless effort to force Frosty to let go.

Fearing for his partner's safety as the van picked up speed, practically dragging Frosty, Carter yelled, "Out!"

Immediately, Frosty released his hold on the man and veered in an arc back to Carter's side as the van's panel door closed and the vehicle sped away. Carter had no way to follow, but he noted the plates were missing, like the sedan. These guys were making it hard.

Wrapping his arms around Rachelle, Carter took deep breaths, willing his heart to slow down. Within his embrace, her body shook. Frosty leaned against Rachelle's legs as if offering his support.

"You're safe. I've got you." He couldn't believe his voice sounded so calm, because inside he was quaking. Witnessing another assault on Rachelle nearly stripped him to the very core. He couldn't let anything happen to this woman.

Ellie would never forgive him.

He would never forgive himself.

She lifted her frightened gaze to his and curled her fingers around his flak vest. "How did they know I'd be here?"

"I can only guess the break-in was also a way to flush you out," he told her.

Keeping an arm wrapped securely around her, he radioed in the incident, telling Dispatch to put the van's description out to all units and to call the area hospitals alerting them to watch for a man with a dog bite on his left arm and another man with a broken nose.

Picking up the leash with his free hand, Carter hustled them toward her office building. Caution tape barred the entrance. He nodded at the officer standing guard, who lifted the tape for them, allowing them access. Once inside the building, Rachelle led him to her cubicle. The drawers of her desk were upended, and her computer hard drive gone.

Carter's stomach sank. He leaned in close to her ear. "Please tell me you didn't back up all your work onto your office computer."

She shook her head. "No. I told you, I've been working on this at home. Never here."

For that he was grateful.

"Rachelle," a deep voice called.

She pushed past Carter and Frosty and hurried to where a man with salt-and-pepper hair stood in an open doorway. The placard next to the door read Editor in Chief.

"Are you okay?" the man said. "I just heard two men tried to kidnap you."

"I'm fine, Quinn, thank you. Is everyone here okay?"

"Yes. The break-in happened overnight."

"I don't know what to say. I'm so, so sorry this happened."

"This isn't your fault," he said.

"Yes, actually it is," she replied. "I've been working on a side project looking into Chief Jordan Jameson's murder."

Carter was proud of her for taking ownership.

Quinn's bushy eyebrows rose. "You don't say." He shook his head. "I told you to let it go. But since you didn't, you can fill me in on what you have."

Carter stepped forward. "Sir, this is a police matter. And confidential. I will be taking Miss Clark with me."

The man sized Carter up. "Is she in trouble?"

Before Carter could respond, Rachelle said, "This is Officer Carter Jameson. Jordan Jameson's brother."

Carter wouldn't have thought it possible but the older man's eyebrows rose even higher, nearly disappearing into his hairline.

"Indeed."

Rachelle turned to Carter. "This is my boss, Quinn Seidel."

Carter stuck out his hand. "Mr. Seidel."

"Officer. My condolences on your brother."

Extracting his hand, Carter turned to Rachelle. "We need to get going."

She nodded but turned back to her boss. "I'm still going to cover the K-9 trials and the celebrity ball. Please, don't take these assignments away from me."

Carter stared at her. Really? That's what she was worried about? Her assignments? Figured. Her ambition went before anything else. He would be wise to remember that.

"I don't know," Quinn said. "I—"

"Carter is helping me with the K-9 article," Rachelle quickly interjected. She gave Carter a pleading look. "Right?"

Jaw tightening, Carter nodded. He still needed her help to decipher her notes. "Yes."

She swung back to Quinn. "See? And he's going to escort me to the ball."

Carter choked on a laugh. "What?"

Her brown gaze implored him to agree. "As my bodyguard." She mouthed the word *please*.

His mouth dried. Every instinct inside of him screamed for him to decline her request but he thought

of Ellie and how disappointed she would be if he refused to help Rachelle.

"Is that correct, Officer Jameson? You'll be in attendance at the ball?" Quinn asked. His piercing blue
eyes assessed Carter. "It would be good to have a police presence there considering all the mayhem going
on these days."

Rachelle gave him an impish smile that did funny
things to his insides.

"Yes. Fine. I'll be escorting Rachelle to the ball."

Putting her hands in a prayer position, Rachelle
mouthed, *thank you*. She turned back to her boss. "I'd
like to work remotely for a while if that's okay."

Quinn narrowed his gaze for a moment, then relented. "That's probably for the best."

Carter wasn't sure whom it would be best for.

With another officer in tow, Carter ushered Rachelle and Frosty into the veterinarian clinic, where the
vet, Dr. Ynez Dubios, gave him a thorough once-over
and determined he'd suffered no injuries while protecting Rachelle.

Grateful for his partner's clean bill of health, Carter
felt the tightness in his chest ease as they walked the
short distance to the station. When they reached the
lobby, he paused. "You should talk to the psychologist
the department uses," he said to Rachelle. "Dr. Benchley is really good at helping victims process their feelings."

"You're very thoughtful to think of it," she said, her
gaze tender. "I wouldn't mind talking to someone."

Glad he'd had the idea, he ushered her to the desk
sergeant and got the phone number for Dr. Brenda
Benchley.

She tucked the number in her purse. "I'll give her a call later to set up an appointment."

His stomach rumbled with hunger, reminding him they'd missed lunch. "Let's grab food from the commissary and then head to the training center, where Frosty can get some water. We can eat down there, too, and you can make the call."

She gave him a wan smile. "I'm not sure I can eat right now."

"You need to at least try," he told her. "Keep up your strength."

Securing the strap of her purse higher over her shoulder, she said, "I could go for another of your father's hamburgers. He does barbecue right."

Carter laughed, glad for the lighter topic. "He's a master at it."

"Has he taught you how to grill?"

"All of us had to learn. Not only how to barbecue but to mow the lawn and fix what needed repair. 'No slackers in my house,' Dad would say."

"I'll bet he made it fun, though," she said with a wistful tone. "You all bonded over projects."

He gave her a sideways glance as they took the stairs down to the basement level. Frosty's nails clicked on the cement steps. "Yes, we did bond. He was really good about making sure we each got one-on-one time with him throughout the years."

"That's really special."

Love for his father infused his voice. "Yes. He's been a good dad. A good role model both personally and professionally. He and my grandfather were both NYPD."

"The family business."

"There were also times when Dad made the four of

us kids cooperate and work together." Remembering those times brought an ache to his chest. Now there were only the three of them left. "*Teamwork*, was another of his big phrases. Of course, Mom used teamwork to mean housework."

"You were blessed to have such involved parents."

In the commissary, they grabbed salads and bottles of water and took their bounty to the training center, where he dropped Frosty off with Olivia for some water.

"We'll be back shortly," Carter told Frosty.

"Do you always talk to him like a human?" Rachelle asked as she followed Carter to the break room.

He shrugged as he settled into a chair. "Dogs understand way more than we can know. I read a study once that claimed dogs processed words with the left side of their brains just like humans and they use the right side of their brains to understand tone and pitch."

"That's fascinating," she said, taking a seat next to him. "I had no idea. I never had a pet growing up."

Carter couldn't imagine not having an animal to care for. Dogs had been such an integral part of his life.

"Tell me about your family," he said as he unwrapped his salad. He hoped to keep her talking while the rush of adrenaline from earlier ebbed away. "Why are you not speaking?"

She made a face. "It's a long story."

"We have time."

"Dad was a prominent lawyer in town until he retired last year. Mom…" She hesitated, pushing her lettuce around with her fork. "She likes to be involved." There was an edge to her voice. "She volunteers for any committee she can. She likes to keep busy."

"Your dad retired young," he commented.

"They were older when I—" She seemed lost in thought.

"Was born?" he prompted.

She let out a humorous laugh. "Yes. My parents are actually my aunt and uncle."

"Okay."

She set down her fork. "I didn't know I was adopted until college. I was doing a paper on my family genealogy and discovered my birth was a scandal. Lily Clark, my father's youngest sister, was unmarried when she had me."

He covered her hand with his. "You must have been shocked and hurt."

"Yes." Her lips twisted. "Once I knew, so many things made sense. Like why I could never measure up to my mother's standards."

"What happened to your birth mother?"

A sad light entered her gaze. "She perished in a car accident while I was still an infant. My dad took me in, but my mother hadn't wanted children."

He squeezed her hand. "I'm sorry."

She smiled. "It is what it is."

He realized her smile was her default mode when she wanted to keep an emotional distance. His heart ached for her.

"I had a string of nannies, none of which stayed long, because, well, I didn't make life easy for them."

"You liked to climb giant trees and fall out," he said, remembering her story about the oak tree.

"Little girls were not supposed to do things like that. But I did everything I was not supposed to do. Nothing criminal, but certainly nothing deemed proper by my parents. Even my choice of college went against their wishes. I attended the state school instead of a prestigious private one."

"I'm surprised they didn't push you to get married and have children," he said, not liking the picture she was painting of her parents.

She glanced at him sharply. "Oh, they tried. They even picked out someone for me. Wallace Thompson." She set her fork down, leaving her salad untouched. "I dated him, trying to be the good daughter, hoping for Mom's and Dad's approval." She blew out a breath. "But I realized Wallace just wanted a partnership in my dad's law firm. He didn't really care about me, and I certainly didn't love him. So I broke it off and moved to New York. I decided to focus solely on my career."

"Good for you. Though I find your choice of career lamentable."

She cocked an eyebrow. "As do I yours."

He drew back. "What?"

Her gaze was direct. "You have a daughter. Why would you stay in a career that puts you in harm's way? Look what happened to your brother. Now Katie's left to raise their child alone. What if something happened to you? Ellie would lose her father, too."

Her words sliced through him like a double-edged sword. "That's not fair. Life and death happen. We can't control any of it."

He'd learned the harsh lesson the hard way as he'd watched his wife die in childbirth. And now Jordan was gone, too.

Sorrow burned at the back of his eyes.

He battled back the anger at God for allowing Helen to die that occasionally tried to surface. The grief counselor Carter had seen in the first few years after her death had helped him to see that blaming God instead of turning to Him for comfort only heightened the pain. Believing that God grieved with him was the only way he made it through the dark days.

Rachelle reached across the table and covered his hand. "You've lost so much. I'm so sorry."

He stared at their joined hands. Her hand so much smaller and feminine compared to his large, rough paw. Warmth spread up his arm from the contact. He couldn't remember the last time he'd let anyone close who wasn't family. He couldn't let himself become involved with this woman.

She flexed her fingers; the pressure against his wrist made his pulse jump.

"We're going to find the answers. We'll solve your brother's murder. Together. Like a team."

He swallowed as he fell into her brown-eyed gaze. For five months with no leads, he'd almost given up that they would bring Jordan's killer to justice. He hated that there were crimes that people got away with, that were never solved. He'd prayed that Jordan's death would not be one of them. And this woman's assurance that, together, they could do what a whole department couldn't, bolstered his flagging hopes and made him want to believe in her, in them, as a team.

But he couldn't let himself become emotionally attached to this woman. Or any woman. He had no intention of opening himself up again to the kind of loss he'd experienced when Helen died.

He cleared his throat and pulled his hand out from beneath hers. "Temporarily a team. Only until we have answers and find the person who wants you dead."

The sparkle left her eyes. "Right. Of course."

Carter noticed Rachelle had barely taken more than a few bites of her salad as they cleaned up the remnants of their lunch. He figured his reminder of the danger she was in had stolen her appetite. He dismissed the idea that she was upset that he'd made it clear they were only a temporary team. She had to know this was a onetime thing. And for the sole purpose of keeping her safe and finding his brother's killer.

They returned to the conference room but neither of them could concentrate. Rachelle kept reading the same words over and over and it wasn't until the fourth time he heard the repeated sentence that he realized they weren't progressing. Finally, he held up his hand. "Rachelle, take a break."

"I'm sorry," she said, looking dejected. "I'm struggling."

She needed a distraction. They both did, because he was having the same problem. He kept reliving the moment the van pulled up and the two men grabbed her. If not for Frosty...

He rose and held out his hand. "Come with me."

There was a brief hesitation before she slipped her hand into his. It felt natural and right to have their hands clasped together. He was reluctant to let go when he locked up the conference room and pocketed the key. Tucking his thumbs into his utility belt to keep from reaching for her again, he escorted Rachelle to the kennel room, where they picked up Frosty. As soon as the kennel door opened, the dog went to Rachelle, his tail wagging as he leaned against her legs.

"He seems to really like you," Carter said, a bit flummoxed by the dog's show of affection.

She rubbed Frosty in the perfect spot behind his ears. His eyes practically rolled in his head with bliss.

Shaking his head, Carter said, "This way. I want to show you something."

He led the way to the center of the training floor covered in Astroturf. There were several obstacles set up. Not as many as they'd run through during the upcoming K-9 trial but enough to keep them sharp.

"I've watched a little agility on TV," Rachelle said as she took in the training equipment. "These don't look like normal agility obstacles."

"They're not." He gestured toward the eight-foot-long wooden tunnel. "The crawl obstacle is for when we have tight spaces only the dogs can get through, like under a porch or in a culvert." He pointed to three large crates with windows cut out at the top on all four sides. "Those three boxes in the middle of the room are for scent work. Meaning, during competition, somebody will hide in a crate and then Frosty will have to find which crate the person is in."

She dug out her pink flower notebook from her purse. And started scribbling in it as he talked. Frosty lay down at her feet.

Eyeing his partner, Carter continued, "This helps us when we're doing searches and we have a suspect who thinks he's going to hide in a garbage can or in the vents of a building. Humans give off more than just body odor. Their scent is released every time they breathe and every time their skin cells drop off their body."

"This is great stuff," she said. "I can't wait to write this article. Oh, pictures. Would you mind if I take some?"

"You'd be better off waiting until the actual trials.

Those will be much more interesting and dramatic. These are only a fraction of what we'll be doing in competition."

"Right. Good point." She gestured to the other side of the floor's center. "What about that wall with the window? Does someone hide on the other side of that?"

"No. Frosty has to go through the window."

She stared at Frosty. "He can jump that high?"

"I give him a boost. Part of being a K-9 handler is making sure that we can lift our dogs while at the same time having the fifty or so pounds of equipment strapped to our body."

She whistled. "That's crazy." She wrote it down.

"It's necessary. We're going to run the course so you can see how it works. And then you are."

She barked out a laugh. "You're not serious."

He rubbed his hands together. "Yes, I am."

"There's no way I can lift that dog high enough to go through the window."

"Don't worry. I'll make sure you can do it."

She gave him a doubtful look. "I'm glad you're so confident."

"I am. You might want to stand over by the door. Once we get going you don't want to be in the way."

She nodded and hustled to plaster her back against the wall. Her pen poised over her notebook.

He patted his side and Frosty lined up next to him. In tandem, they walked to the far end of the training center.

"Sit." Frosty obeyed. Carter stepped away then said, "Find."

Frosty ran around the room, with his nose bouncing from the floor to the air. He went to the boxes and sat down in front of the far right one. Carter went over and opened a latch that allowed a door to open. Inside he found a small blue bucket filled with liver treats that Olivia kept inside. "Good boy." He gave the dog a treat.

"What did he find?" Rachelle called out.

He held up the bucket. "The dog knows where his snacks are."

She smiled and wrote in her notebook. He put the treats back.

As he patted his side, Frosty fell into step with him. They lined up for the crawl and the jump to the window. "Go!" They both ran as fast as they could, and then Frosty squeezed through the open end of the crawl space. Carter met his partner at the other end. They ran for the window.

Frosty jumped into the air, his front paws reaching for the windowsill. Carter caught him by the haunches and lifted Frosty the rest of the way. The dog leaped through the opening, landing easily and circling back to Carter's side.

Rachelle clapped. "That was amazing."

"Now your turn."

She shook her head. "Not a chance."

"You can do it. Put your purse down and come here." He cocked an eyebrow. "Or are you too chicken?"

Her mouth popped open in obvious indignation. She snapped her lips together and laid her purse on the floor. "All right, hotshot. Show me how this works."

Gratified to see her taking his challenge, he said, "Call Frosty to your side by patting your outer thigh. And call his name."

She did as instructed. Frosty's gaze bounced between Rachelle and Carter. He nodded, giving the dog permission, and Frosty trotted over to her side and sat beside her.

Her face lit up with delight and Carter's breath stalled in his chest. Shaking his head, he stepped to the side. "When you're ready, say *go*. Then you're going to run as fast as you can to the crawl. While he's taking the tunnel, you keep running toward the window. He'll meet you there."

Her eyebrows dipped together. "And you expect me to lift him?"

"You help push him up and through. I'll be right alongside you."

She grinned. "Just like a team."

"Like a team."

She took a deep breath and said, "Go." She ran. Frosty darted forward with Rachelle racing behind. Carter couldn't keep from grinning as he ran alongside her. Frosty took the crawl. When he emerged, Carter gave him a hand signal to slow down since Rachelle hadn't reached the window yet.

Once she was there, Carter motioned for Frosty to take the window. As he leaped, Rachelle reached out to place her hands on his haunches. Carter moved in to help, his hands covering hers. Together, they boosted Frosty through the opening.

Rachelle clapped her hands, a big smile on her face. "That was fun. And you do that with all your gear on? I am so impressed."

Pleased by her praise, he said, "I'm glad you enjoyed it. Your story will sound authentic now."

"You're right. I appreciate you doing this for me." The warmth in her gaze sent his heart pounding. The air around them seemed electrified. Frosty nudged him in the back of the knee. He took a step toward her as alarm bells went off in his head.

"Uh, we should get back to work." He spun away and strode toward the door, his heart pounding in his chest like he was sixteen again.

EIGHT

"I'm telling you we should be looking closer at Miles Landau and finding this Ophelia woman. She might know something," Rachelle stated, referring to the name that she'd uncovered in a social media post by Miles before his incarceration six years ago. Why wouldn't Carter listen to her?

They sat across from each other at the conference table. He'd brought Frosty with them and the dog lay across her feet, keeping her toes warm in the air-conditioned room. Her eyes felt gritty from looking through her notes and her throat was sore from reading most of her handwritten pages aloud to Carter.

"Noah has Miles under surveillance." His voice held a sharpness to it.

Ever since they had returned to the conference room after running the obstacles with Frosty, Carter had been distant with clipped answers and hardly looking at her.

Which seemed so odd considering she'd thought they were connecting in the training center. He'd been so kind to provide her a distraction from the horror of nearly being abducted.

But what did she know? He was a confusing man.

All protective and caring then standoffish and brooding. She decided the stress of the case and the attempts on her life were making them both tense and edgy.

He sighed, long and loud, as if he'd just lost an argument he'd been having with himself, then he spoke as if he was explaining something to a very slow-witted person. "I ran the name Ophelia through the national database," he continued. "Nothing noteworthy popped. Danielle, our computer tech, has been cross-referencing the name with Miles but hasn't come up with anything. The name probably refers to the new rooftop bar that opened in the city and not a woman at all."

Fearing he could be right, she stared at her notes with frustration pounding at her temples. Her stomach rumbled loudly. Embarrassment heated her cheeks. Frosty lifted his head and placed his chin on her knee. She rubbed him behind the ears.

Carter frowned. "You need to eat." He stood and stretched. "Let's go. We can continue this tomorrow."

"I'd rather keep working," she said. Her life was on the line. They needed to figure out who and why someone was trying to kill her. "Can we order in?"

His parents had called to say they were taking Ellie to dinner and a movie, which meant she and Carter were on their own. The prospect of an intimate meal shared with Carter was both thrilling and unnerving.

"How about we go to Griffin's?"

The diner was an established neighborhood haunt and one of her favorite places located not far from the NYC K-9 Command Unit and her small apartment. The thought of seeing a friendly face or two appealed. She relented. "Sure."

He picked up the lead from the chair where he'd

placed it when they'd entered the room and made a clucking sound with his mouth. Frosty rose and went to his side to be leashed up.

They left the building and Rachelle's breath caught in her throat when Carter snagged her elbow, pulling her close. He smelled good, masculine and musky, and his protectiveness made her feel special. Which was ridiculous. She wasn't special. He was doing his job, nothing more.

They stepped through the diner's door and the aromas of savory dishes had her tummy cramping and her mouth watering.

"Well, look who's here! Our own Georgia peach!" Lou Griffin's loud voice boomed as he came out from behind the counter.

Glad to be out of the August humidity, Rachelle broke away from Carter and Frosty with a grin as she headed over to give the older gentleman a hug. "Hey, Lou."

Extracting herself from Lou's bear hug, she looked past the new appliances, gleaming counters and filled tables of the main diner to the area in the back they called the Dog House. An area designated for NYPD K-9 officers to eat while providing a place of rest for their canine partners.

The walls were covered with pictures to honor fallen officers. Rachelle's attention caught immediately on the newest photo that had been added to the display— Jordan Jameson.

She really wanted to invade that sacred space, to question the other officers and get their take on Jordan's murder, but she knew her questions wouldn't be welcome. More to the point, *she* wouldn't be welcome.

At least not on her own. But if Carter invited her—though there was no way he would allow her to ask anyone about his brother.

Carter shook Lou's hand and commented, "If I didn't know, I'd never guess you had a fire here."

More specifically, a bomb. Rachelle shuddered to think what could have happened if K-9 officers Gavin Sutherland and Brianne Hayes hadn't been eating in the diner that night and if their dogs hadn't alerted, allowing the two officers to evacuate everyone from the building.

Because she knew the owners and had been there the night of the explosion, she had made a case to her boss that she should write an article about the bombing and the arrest of both the bomber and the real estate developer who was behind the destruction in an attempt to force Griffin's out for gentrification of the neighborhood. But her boss had assigned the story to a more "seasoned" male counterpart. She knew she shouldn't let the twist of frustration deep in her chest change her, but she woke with it every morning and she hadn't been able to let the story go.

Barbara Griffin walked out of the back tying an apron around her waist. "The remodelers did a really good job, didn't they?" She opened her arms.

Rachelle moved in for a hug. The Griffins had appointed themselves as the welcome committee for this transplanted Georgia girl.

Barbara released Rachelle, then gave Carter a hug. "It's been a long time since we've seen you here."

"I know," he said, his gaze straying to the Dog House wall.

Patting his arm with obvious sympathy, she said,

"Violet's working on a grand reopening celebration. I hope you both will attend."

Violet was their adult daughter who helped run the diner when she wasn't working at the customer service desk at LaGuardia Airport. She had recently married Carter's brother, K-9 Officer Zach Jameson, in a small wedding that was attended only by family and close friends. Rachelle had to admit to a spurt of envy for Violet and Katie. To be welcomed into the Jameson family, to feel their love and support, would be a dream come true.

Good thing she'd learned that dreams and reality rarely coincided.

"Of course I will attend the grand opening," Rachelle assured Barbara, touched by the invitation. The perfect opportunity for her to do a follow-up story that her boss couldn't refuse. "I'll even do a write-up about it for the paper."

"We will not be pushed out by gentrification," Lou heatedly vowed. "You can print that."

Barbara put a hand on his arm. "Don't get yourself worked up again, dear."

He covered her hand. The obvious love they shared made Rachelle ache in a strange way. She'd never seen her own parents display genuine affection for one another. Nor had she experienced it herself.

"I know, I know," Lou said. "Think of sailing calm waters on a balmy day. *Relax.*" He drew the last word out.

Barbara went up on tiptoe to give her husband a peck on the cheek. "Exactly."

Carter looked at Rachelle. "Do you want to eat here or get dinner to go?"

Knowing this might be her only opportunity to sit in the Dog House, she said, trying not to sound too eager, "Here."

"Sounds good. Let's go get a table."

"I'll meet you back there. I need to wash my hands," she told him.

Carter and Frosty walked into the back section.

When they were out of earshot, Barbara sidled up to Rachelle. "Oh, what's going on here? You and the handsome officer? Do tell."

A heated flush rose up Rachelle's neck. "No, we're not... Our—" She hesitated to call what they had a relationship. "We're working on something together. Professionally."

Lou went behind the counter. "The way he was watching you, I'd say he has more than a professional interest in you."

With her heart fluttering at the suggestion that Carter felt anything more than duty toward her, she shook her head. "It's really not like that. We've only just met."

"Carter deserves some happiness," Barbara observed. "It was tragic the way his wife died. It's past time for him to find love again."

Not sure how to respond to her statement, Rachelle excused herself and hurried to the restroom. She put some cool water on her face, but nothing could calm the secret yearning to be more to Carter than a burden from taking root inside of her.

She'd never considered herself one to willingly take on heartache but that was exactly what would happen if she allowed herself to hope there was a chance at a future with the handsome Jameson brother.

Slapping a hand to her forehead, she told herself, *Get*

a grip. Stay focused. Staying alive and furthering her career were the priorities. Not romance. And certainly not with a man who had made it clear she was a temporary fixture in his life.

Girding her emotions behind a well-constructed wall, she entered the Dog House portion of the restaurant and scanned the busy room. There were many tables with officers of various ranks. Carter had taken a seat at a table near the back with three officers. Frosty was in the porch area with several other dogs.

Carter waved her over. As she approached, she was aware of the curious glances of everyone in the room. She was a stranger entering a strange land. Nervous flutters had her tummy jumping as she slid into a seat beside Carter.

A female officer with auburn hair and big brown eyes smiled at her. "Carter was just telling us about you. I'm sorry to hear you've had a rough time of it lately. But you're in good hands with Carter." She held out her hand. "I'm Brianne Hayes."

"Nice to meet you." Rachelle shook the woman's hand. "Thank you. Carter's been great. Very protective."

A speculative gleam entered her gaze. "I would hope so." She gestured to the man next to her. "This is Gavin Sutherland."

He reached across Brianne to shake Rachelle's hand. "Welcome." As he settled his arm around Brianne in a way that made it clear they were couple, he said, "Carter mentioned you're a reporter."

Rachelle braced herself for the disdain she was sure would come. "I am. For *NYC Weekly*."

"I've seen you in the diner." The third officer, a big

man with brown hair and hard features, eyed her warily with his dark brown gaze. "No comment."

Tucking in her chin, Rachelle said, "Okay."

"Knock it off, Tony," Carter said with a smile. "She's off duty." He turned his blue eyes on her. "Right?"

"Right. Except..." She smiled at him. "I am writing an article about you and the police dog field trials so..." She looked around the table. "I'd love to include anything you all could tell me about the competition."

Tony sat back and pointed a finger at Carter. "He and Frosty will win."

"I'll be happy to place," Carter said. "There's some stiff competition this year. I've been hearing good things about the team from Boston PD."

"Is anyone else from the command unit competing?" Rachelle asked.

"Are Luke and Bruno running the course this year?" Brianne asked.

Carter looked thoughtful. "I believe so."

Barbara came over to take their orders. Rachelle ordered the daily special of Atlantic salmon over rice and mixed vegetables. Carter went for the meat loaf plate.

The conversation turned to politics, which created a lively debate on several issues facing the NYPD.

"You're not from New York," Brianne observed. "I detect a Southern accent."

"You're correct," Rachelle admitted. "Georgia."

"Tell us about home," Gavin said. "I've been to Florida."

Rachelle laughed. "Not exactly the same sort of Southern." She told them of growing up in the onion capital of the US. "In the spring we have a world famous Onion festival."

"What does one do at an onion festival?" Carter asked.

"It's a big deal. The festival is shown on the Food Network and all sorts of culinary events take place showcasing the sweet onion. There's a carnival and concerts with some big name country artists, a Little Miss Onion pageant for the up-to-twelve-year-olds. A Teen Onion and Miss Onion pageant. A parade—"

"And which year did you win?" Carter's teasing tone sent a ripple of laughter through his friends.

A blush crept up her neck. "What makes you think I entered?"

His eyebrows dipped together. "You didn't?"

"I did," she said, and hated how her voice sounded defensive. "I won when I was ten."

"Ah." He gave her a smug smile. "I knew it."

"And again when I was fourteen."

Tony let out a soft whistle. "Whew. We're in the presence of royalty."

Carter grinned. "Two wins. Good for you."

She sighed. Embarrassment curled her toes within her shoes. "Actually, I won again when I was seventeen."

"Nice," Brianne said. "Way to go."

Her face flamed. She was sure they thought she was as vain as they came. She didn't mention that her mother had pressured her to enter each time. And hoping to gain her approval, Rachelle had complied only to be disappointed when her mother still found fault with her even after being crowned.

Hoping to steer the conversation away from the pageant, she said, "The other claim to fame we have is the Vidalia onion was an answer on *Jeopardy*."

Barbara arrived with their orders, stalling any more conversation about her hometown. Instead, as they ate, the officers talked shop and she was content to listen, absorbing the nuances of their speech and the shorthand language they used.

Lou came over to clear their plates. "Dessert?"

"Apple pie for me," she told him. "No ice cream."

"Me, too." Brianne said. "With an extra scoop of ice cream."

"I'll have the same," Gavin said.

"Not me," Tony said. "I need to head out." He rose and nodded to Rachelle. "Nice to meet you." He took his dinner ticket to the cashier station to pay Barbara.

"Can I have a bite of your pie?" Carter asked Rachelle. "I don't want a whole piece of my own."

Surprised and pleased, she nodded. "Of course."

When Lou brought the slices of pie, he handed Carter an extra fork.

Sharing the warm gooey pie with Carter, Rachelle told herself not to read too much into the gesture. It was only pie they were sharing, not their hearts.

After their desserts, Rachelle said goodbye to her new friends and then fell into step with Carter and Frosty and headed for the exit. She'd enjoyed meeting the officers and learning more about them as individuals and as a team. "My dinner was delicious."

"Agreed. Barbara's meat loaf is almost as good as my mom's," Carter said, placing his hand at the small of her back as they stepped outside. While still light out, twilight was approaching and the heat and humidity from earlier in the day had eased considerably.

"You know, it's funny that you and I hadn't met before the other day," he said. "You seem to be very close to the Griffins."

"They've been very good to me. I'd seen you in the Dog House with your brothers and the other officers," she told him. "But as a civilian, I never dared venture into that part of the diner."

"Ah. I guess I wasn't paying very good attention." He guided her around the K-9 Unit building to the back, where he'd parked his vehicle.

She wasn't sure how to take his words. Was he saying he was remiss in not noticing her? The thought was thrilling.

Once they were safely inside the vehicle, she let out a breath that eased the constriction in her chest. She hadn't realized how the tension of the day had tightened her nerves and irritated her already-sore muscles. Even being in the coveted inner sanctuary of the Dog House, surrounded by a dozen other officers, hadn't set her mind at ease.

"I've been thinking," she said as he started the engine.

"Uh-oh. That could be trouble."

"What?"

The corners of his mouth tipped upward. He was teasing her.

Warmth spread through her. "What if the name Ophelia isn't a woman or a restaurant, but a boat?"

His eyebrows rose. "A boat?"

"Yeah. Lou mentioned sailing calm waters and it occurs to me that many boats have a female name. One of the photos I found on his social media was of him on a boat, remember?"

"You could be onto something there." The approval

in his tone tickled her. "Tomorrow we'll search for any registered boats with the name Ophelia."

"Or we could take a quick detour to the World's Fair Marina in Flushing Bay. See if we can spot a vessel with that name."

"Trouble with a capital *T*," he stated. "No."

"We wouldn't even have to get out of the vehicle," she told him. "Just drive through the marina. Nothing dangerous about having a look."

"Every moment with you is dangerous," he muttered beneath his breath.

Obviously he didn't like having to protect her. "I'm sorry I've been such a bother." She crossed her arms and looked out the side window. "I would think you'd want to do everything possible to find your brother's killer."

"You're not a bother," he said. "And I do."

She turned to face him again. "Then let's check out the marina."

He drummed his fingers on the steering wheel. "What makes you think Miles owns the boat?"

"The picture, remember? I could totally be off base but it would be worth the time and effort to see. We have nothing to lose if I'm wrong."

"Why the World's Fair Marina?"

"It's the closest marina to the warehouse owned by Miles in Flushing," she replied.

She watched his internal debate play across his handsome face.

"Ellie's with your parents," she offered. "We don't have to rush home."

Her automatic urge to refer to his family's property as home made her ache with a yearning she wasn't willing to consider.

"I guess it wouldn't do any harm," he said, albeit grudgingly.

"Thank you." She settled back with satisfaction. They were doing something proactive. As a team. And she'd be grateful for however long it lasted.

Carter pulled the vehicle to the curb near the gate leading to the docks of the World's Fair Marina just as the sun set, casting long shadows across the water of Flushing Bay. Lampposts shone a warm glow over the various-sized boats tied to cleats on the dock. All appeared quiet. Except at the far left side of the marina, a light was out. Unease slithered up his spine and settled at the base of his neck.

"We'll have to come back," he said. "The gate has a keyless entry."

Popping the passenger door open, she said, "Let's get a little closer." She hopped out and shut the door.

"Hey!" *Unbelievable.* Irritation mingled with dread as Carter scrambled from the vehicle. He quickly released Frosty, leashed him up and hustled after Rachelle. "You promised you'd stay in the car."

"I made no such promise," she drawled, giving him an affronted look. "I said we wouldn't have to get out. But I didn't promise I would stay in the car."

He pinched the bridge of his nose where a headache was brewing. "Semantics."

"No, not semantics." She put a hand over her heart. "I never break my promises."

She sounded so sincere he had trouble hanging on to his annoyance. "Whatever. We need to leave."

"We have to get in there." She turned away to inspect the gate.

"I'm not climbing over the fence and neither are you."

She sighed and started walking along the fence line. "I wish I had binoculars. I can't see the names." She halted. "Wait there's one called *Riptide*. Do you know that I've never actually been out on a boat?"

Carter shook his head. "You are an interesting woman."

"I imagine you say that to all the girls." She gave him a cheeky smile.

"No. I don't."

She titled her head and studied him for a moment before quickly looking away. "There's a streetlight out at the other end of the dock."

He'd been hoping she wouldn't notice. But he had a feeling she noticed everything. "Not much we can do about it tonight. Let's go."

"Wait." She shrugged off his hand. "There are people out there."

He squinted and, sure enough, he saw movement. Acid churned in his stomach. Nothing good could be happening in the dark in such an isolated place. He needed to get her out of there.

"Don't you want to check it out?"

"I don't have a warrant or probable cause. A burned-out light is not enough."

A low growl emanated from Frosty's throat and then a series of alerting barks. Carter spun around and noticed two men coming toward them. One had a bandage over his nose and the other a bandage around his forearm.

The men who'd tried to abduct Rachelle.

Had they followed them to the marina?

Alarm pulsed through Carter.

One of the men held a gun.

NINE

"Halt!" Carter yelled. "Police."

The man with the gun aimed at them.

Fearing for Rachelle's safety, Carter snagged an arm around her waist and pulled her down behind a metal garbage container just as shots rang out and bullets pinged off the metal. He reeled in Frosty's lead, tucking the dog close.

Pulse pounding in his ears, he unholstered his weapon and peered around the edge of the garbage container as he radioed for backup.

The two men ran to the gate and entered the code into the keyless lock. The gate opened, and they ran through and along the docks toward the darkened corner. The guy with the gun continued to fire off random shots at them.

"Carter, you have to go after them," Rachelle said.

"I'm not leaving you."

An engine roared to life. Carter jumped to his feet in time to see a lighted boat speeding away from the dock. Carter took out his cell phone and snapped off pictures. He doubted the photos would be any help, but he had to do something.

He called the situation in on the radio attached to his shoulder as they hurried back to his vehicle. And he asked for the harbor patrol to search for the boat. Though he knew by the time the patrol got out on the water, the escaped vessel could be miles away in a multitude of directions.

Hustling Rachelle to his vehicle parked at the curb, Carter glimpsed a white van parked in a far corner of the lot. The same van used by the men who'd tried to kidnap Rachelle earlier.

As they waited inside the vehicle, Carter said, "You know, I'm going to catch flak for bringing you here."

"Surely your brother can't get mad at you for following a clue."

"Oh yes, he can."

And he was proved correct a short time later when Noah climbed out of his K-9 Unit vehicle with his dog, Scotty, a majestic rottweiler trained for emergency service work. Along with Noah was Gavin Sutherland and his dog, Tommy, a springer spaniel who excelled at bomb detection. After instructing Gavin and Tommy to check out the van, Noah and Scotty headed to where Carter, Rachelle and Frosty waited by the curb.

The disgruntled expression on his brother's face didn't bode well. "What are you two doing down here?"

"Following a hunch," Carter said.

"It's my fault," Rachelle said. "I talked Carter into coming down here to search for a boat named *Ophelia*."

Carter stared at her. Why would she try to protect him from Noah? A strange sort of pleasure infused him and made him stand taller.

Noah arched an eyebrow. "I doubt, Miss Clark, that you could talk my brother into anything he didn't want to do. I know I have not been able to over the years." Noah shifted his attention to Carter. "So tell me, brother, how did you come across this lead?"

"It wasn't my clue," Carter told him. "It was Rachelle's. She figured it out." Carter smiled encouragingly at Rachelle. "Go ahead, tell him."

She blinked, clearly surprised and pleased. For some reason pleasing her filled his chest with warmth and tenderness.

"I was scouring Miles's social media sites. And I found a reference to the name Ophelia. I thought maybe an old girlfriend or employee. But we had no luck tracking down a woman by that name. But then I thought maybe the name belonged to a boat. I came across a photo of Miles on one, so it stood to reason…"

"As it turns out," Carter said, "she was right."

He showed his brother the photo of the retreating vessel. Though the image was blurry, they could make out the name painted in blue letters across the back— *Ophelia.*

"All clear," Officer Gavin Sutherland called. "Tommy didn't alert."

Tommy was an excellent bomb detection dog and Carter trusted the canine's nose. Carter let out a relieved breath. He hadn't expected there to be an explosive in the van, but one never knew. It was best to be prepared.

Noah donned latex gloves and opened the side panel door. Carter tugged Rachelle behind him just in case there were any surprises waiting inside.

The van was empty. There were splashes of blood inside the cargo hold and on the door frame. From where

Frosty had bitten one thug and Rachelle had broken the nose of the other.

Frosty strained at the end of his lead.

Noah nodded. "Let's see what he can find."

Carter dropped the lead and Frosty jumped into the back of the van. He sniffed around and then let out a bark.

"He's found something," Carter said, leaning inside, careful not to touch anything. "I can see brass under the passenger seat."

"All right, everyone step back," Noah instructed. "I'll have our forensic team scour the van for evidence."

Once Carter had Frosty back in control, Rachelle asked, "Brass?"

"Unspent bullet," he clarified.

"You two head home. We've got this," Noah said.

Carter heard Rachelle's little humph of frustration. He felt the same way.

"We'd like to stay," Carter said. "These men tried to kidnap her today and shot at us. I want to know what they're up to and how this relates to—" He stopped himself from saying Jordan's name. His gaze flicked to Gavin and back to his brother.

Noah gave a slow nod. "Understood. Fine. Stay back."

Carter ushered Rachelle and Frosty away from the van and stopped a few feet away.

Rachelle slipped her hand into Carter's. "Thank you."

The place where their palms pressed together created a firestorm engulfing his arm and heading for his chest. "For what?"

"Everything."

He wasn't sure he deserved thanks. He'd only been doing his duty.

As they waited for the forensic team, he was achingly aware of Rachelle, her fingers flexed around his and her lavender scent teasing his senses. He saw the curious and speculative glances of his brother and Gavin but chose to ignore them.

When the forensic team was done, Noah walked over. His gaze flicked to where Carter still held Rachelle's hand. For a split second Carter thought of retracting his hand from Rachelle's but then dismissed the idea.

He liked holding her hand; he liked the connection.

He met Noah's steely gaze, daring him to say something. No doubt he'd get an earful from his brother later about keeping a firm line between work and personal feelings. Carter had never had trouble keeping an emotional barrier between him and, well, everyone else. But this woman was slowly, methodically, undermining his walls.

But guilt was piling on fast. Reminding him he couldn't let himself feel anything. He owed it to Helen not to give his heart away again. Carter loosened his hold on Rachelle, but she tightened hers, keeping his hand trapped within her grasp.

Noah's mouth quirked at the corner. He shook his head and then cleared his throat. "The forensic team found a high-caliber bullet underneath the front seat. No fingerprints."

"What about the blood?" Carter asked.

"We'll type it," Ilana Hawkins, one of the forensic techs, said as she paused next to Noah. "Not sure it will lead anywhere but if our suspects have DNA in any database, then we'll be able to ID them."

"Thank you, Ilana. Good work," Noah said.

She smiled and walked to where the other two techs waited by their mobile forensic unit vehicle.

"Now what?" Rachelle asked. "Do you raid Miles's warehouse?"

"I can make a case with the commissioner to get a warrant," Noah said. "I've got people sitting on the warehouse. There's been no activity in the past twenty-four hours."

"He must have other property," Rachelle said. "We need to get back to the station and get back to work."

"Not tonight," Carter told her. "We're done for now. Tomorrow we can keep searching."

"But—"

He squeezed her hand. "No. I want to see my daughter."

Rachelle's eyes grew wide. "Oh, of course. Forgive me. Yes, let's go home."

"We'll see you there." Noah's chuckle rankled.

Carter tugged his hand free of Rachelle's and narrowed his gaze on Noah. "Not a word."

If Noah blabbed to their parents that Carter and Rachelle had stood holding hands like a couple, Carter would never hear the end of it.

Noah held up his hands in mock surrender. "I have no idea what you're talking about."

Shaking his head, Carter led the way to his vehicle. When they arrived back at the house Carter was able to park at the curb in front. He used his house key to open his parents' front door. "Hello."

The sound of pounding feet echoed through the house. Ellie tore out of the living room, followed closely by his mother and father. And two little yipping puppies.

"You came back!" Ellie cried and launched yourself into Rachelle's arms and hugging her tight.

Carter's jaw dropped. *Seriously?*

Over Ellie's head, Carter met Rachelle's surprised gaze. His insides twisted. He wanted to be the center of his daughter's world. If that made him selfish, then so be it. "Hey, what about me?"

Ellie wiggled out of Rachelle's arms and threw herself against Carter. "Daddy!"

He picked her up and held on tight, relishing the feel of his precious child.

The puppies nipped at Rachelle's pants. Laughing, she got down on the floor to shower the two miscreants with snuggles and praise. Frosty even edged his way in to lick her face. Her laughter was infectious. Carter's heart squeezed tight.

Giggling, Ellie shimmied out of his arms to join the lovefest on the floor. She pushed her way onto Rachelle's lap and joined in the fun with the puppies and Frosty, who now lay down with his paws on Rachelle's knee. The sight, so achingly sweet and tender, was almost more than Carter could bear.

And he found himself jealous of his daughter, the puppies and Frosty as Rachelle lavished her affection and attention so easily on them. He wanted it for himself. Which made no sense at all.

He tore his gaze away and found his parents watching the scene with bemused smiles. Carter had to put a stop to this now. Everyone was getting too close, too attached, too emotional.

He clapped his hands to gain everyone's attention. A trick he'd learned from Ellie's preschool teacher. "All right. It's time for a bath and bedtime stories."

Ellie leaned back into Rachelle's arms. "Can Rachelle read my bedtime stories to me tonight?"

Carter's stomach sank. Way too attached. "Honey, it's been a really long day, and I would really like to spend some time with you."

"Your father's right. It's been a very long day." She stifled a yawn. "I can read to you another time."

Grateful for her assist, Carter bent to pick Ellie up into his arms and then held out a hand to help Rachelle to her feet.

For a moment she clung to him. And he had the strangest sensation that if he could allow it, they could be a family.

Jolted by the thought, he quickly disengaged and stepped away from Rachelle. "We'll see you in the morning." He set Ellie on her feet. "Give Grandma and Grandpa kisses and thank them for your special day."

She ran to her grandparents and gave them noisy kisses. "Thank you, Grandma and Grandpa."

Ellie then raced back to Rachelle and wrapped her arms around her legs. "You'll still be here tomorrow, right?"

Rachelle rubbed Ellie's back. "I believe I will be. Now off with you. Sweet dreams."

Carter grabbed a puppy under each arm. "Ellie, get the door, please. Come on, Frosty. 'Night, Mom, Dad."

Ellie opened the front door so Carter and Frosty could pass through. As she shut the door, Carter heard Ellie say, "Sweet dreams to you, too, Rachelle."

The next morning Rachelle awoke to the smell of bacon and coffee. Hungry and eager to start the day, she quickly dressed in navy capris and a flowered top that had flounces at the elbows and the neckline. The top was feminine and made her feel pretty. And she had to admit to herself that she wanted to look pretty and hoped that Carter noticed.

"Really?" she asked her reflection in the bathroom mirror as she plaited her hair into a single braid down her back because the heat index was to reach triple digits. "What do you hope will happen? Carter will declare his undying love for you? Ha!" Shaking her finger at herself, she said, "Don't get all gooey about Carter. You are not looking for romance."

They were only together to solve a crime and keep her alive. With a shudder, she really hoped and prayed that today would not be a repeat of yesterday. Nearly being kidnapped and shot at had never been on her bucket list. In fact, none of this had been on her bucket list.

When she'd decided to write an investigative piece on Jordan Jameson's murder she never dreamed she would become a target herself or that she would end up ensconced deep within the Jameson clan.

Or find herself longing for Carter Jameson.

Frustrated with herself, she stuffed those feelings deep inside. There was no room in her life for emotions that had no place to grow. Carter wasn't interested in her romantically and once her life was back to normal, she'd probably never see Carter or his adorable daughter again. The thought saddened her more than she wanted to admit.

When she stepped into the kitchen, Carter and Ellie were at the counter eating bacon, pancakes, fresh berries and drinking orange juice. Through the window in the back door, Rachelle could see Alex Jameson in the backyard with the puppies. Frosty lay on the porch observing. She assumed Scotty had gone with Noah to the NYC K-9 Command Unit headquarters.

"Good morning," Rachelle said.

Carter smiled. "Ellie wanted to see you. So we came down for breakfast."

Touched, Rachelle hugged the child. Ellie gave her a sweet kiss on the cheek.

Ivy Jameson handed her a cup of coffee. "Milk?"

"No, thank you. You wouldn't by chance have an alternative creamer?"

"Let me check the cupboard. I usually keep a variety of things here for when we host Bible study." She pulled out a powdered nondairy creamer. "Will this work?"

Rachelle would've preferred an almond beverage, but she took the nondairy creamer. "Thank you so much." She applied a liberal amount to her coffee and stirred with the spoon Ivy handed her.

"Sit here." Ellie patted the bar stool beside her. "I'm going with my friend Greta and her mom to Prospector Park."

"Prospect Park," Carter corrected.

Taking a seat, Rachelle said, "I've never been there. Is it an outdoor playground?"

"It's one of the biggest parks in the five boroughs," Carter told her. "With lots of shade trees."

"I'm sure you will have lots of fun, Ellie." Rachelle skipped the pancakes but took a spoonful of berries and several pieces of bacon, which she doused with syrup.

"Do you not like pancakes?" Ellie asked.

Rachelle shook her head. "Not really. But I love bacon."

Carter's soft chuckle heated her cheeks. "A little bacon with your syrup?"

She grimaced. "I wasn't allowed much in the way of sweets as a kid so now I go a little overboard."

He cocked his head and looked like he wanted to ask questions. Hoping to keep him from delving into her childhood, she stuffed her mouth. Thankfully, he let her comment go.

After breakfast, Rachelle helped Ivy with the dishes while Carter and Ellie went to their apartment so Ellie could get ready for her outing with her friend.

"Thank you, my dear," Ivy said. "Carter told us what happened to you yesterday." Concern laced her words. "Despite my initial reaction to your occupation, I hope you know you're welcome to stay here with us as long as you need. Between Alex and Carter and Noah and the dogs, we will keep you safe."

Touched to the point of tears, Rachelle blinked rapidly and busied herself drying the dish in her hand. "I really appreciate your offer."

And she did, more than Mrs. Jameson could ever know. She felt wanted here, like she belonged. She knew she was getting herself in too deep, emotionally. She really needed to take a step back. But that time would come eventually. And it would hurt, but until then she would enjoy the sense of family, of belonging.

"Are you ready to go?" Carter stepped into the kitchen a few minutes later.

Drying her hands off on the dish towel, Rachelle nodded. "Yes." She was eager to get digging more into Miles Landau's life. "Thank you, Ivy, for breakfast."

"My pleasure," the older woman said. She turned to Carter. "Keep her safe."

A flash of surprise in Carter's eyes turned to determination. "Of course."

When they arrived at the station, there was a buzz of activity going on. Carter led her to the conference room. "I'll be right back. I'm going to see what's happening."

He shut the door behind her. Wondering if there was news regarding Jordan's case, Rachelle immediately went to work looking for something that would lead them to Miles.

An hour later Carter returned just as she was getting up to go look for him to share what she'd found.

"Everything okay?"

"Yes. The August heat brings out the crazy in everybody." He ran his hand through his thick dark hair. Her gaze tracked his movement and her fingers curled against the itch to feel his hair, to brush back the stray lock that fell over his forehead. "There was some gang activity and a robbery. Nothing unusual."

Forcing herself to focus, she said, "I think I found something that might be useful."

He crossed the room to her side with purposeful strides. "Show me."

"I was reading through all the comments on Miles's Facebook page. He has quite the list of friends and followers. Anyway, this is from a couple of days after his release from prison."

She showed him the post. It was a picture of Miles mugging for the camera outside the prison. His shaved head gleamed like a recently polished bowling ball. His thin frame was muscled and his dark eyes had a feral light. The caption accompanying the photo read, *Watch out, here I come.*

"Ominous but not a direct threat to anyone in particular," Carter said.

"This is what I wanted to show you." She scrolled down through the two hundred-plus comments and landed on one that read, *Looking forward to you coming home.*

"Who is that from?"

"Cecilia Landau," she said. "I checked out her social media pages and I believe she's Miles's mother. He might be hiding out at her place."

"That is a good catch."

Approval resonated in his tone and pleasure infused her.

"I'll let Noah know and he should send officers over." He headed for the door.

"Wait."

Carter stopped and arched an eyebrow.

"You and I should go over. She might talk to me."

He shook his head. "No way. I'm not putting you back out in the field. After what happened last night…"

"But you and Frosty would be with me," she argued. "Though I would suggest putting on civilian clothes." She gestured to his uniform. "Less intimidating that way."

"Noah will never go for it."

She hurried to his side. "We won't know unless we ask him."

"Suit yourself." He gestured for her to precede him out of the conference room.

Carter rapped on Noah's door, then opened it so she could pass through first. She really liked the way Carter was so polite and thoughtful.

Despite the nervous flutter in her tummy, she told

Noah what she'd found and what she'd like to do. Even before she finished he was shaking his head.

Frustration ate a hole through her patience. "Listen, both of you. I appreciate that you're trying to protect me but if we don't find Miles this will never end. Mrs. Landau is not going to willingly talk to the police—I can guarantee you that. But she might talk to me. If I come at her saying I'm doing a report on recently released inmates and want to include her son, she might be more inclined to talk to me. Everyone wants their fifteen minutes of fame."

"It's too big a risk," Carter said. "If Miles is the one after you he would have told his mother about the nosy reporter."

"Maybe not," she countered. "She may be in the dark about his current activity."

Noah rubbed his chin. "We could bring Mrs. Landau in for questioning."

"Then she's guaranteed not to talk," Rachelle stated.

"I won't authorize a visit, it would be too risky, but a phone call couldn't do any harm," Noah said.

Forcing herself to be content with a call, Rachelle hurried back to the conference room to look up the number.

She would have to employ all of her charm to get Mrs. Landau to talk to her.

Rachelle was up to the task.

TEN

At the end of the day, Rachelle was discouraged. Mrs. Landau had hung up on her at the first mention of her son, Miles.

And though Rachelle and Carter had gone through every last scrap of her notes and research, they'd come up with nothing solid. No new leads on Jordan's killer.

She prayed the police caught Miles soon. Then they'd know one way or another if he was the murderer they sought.

When they arrived home to the three-story house in Rego Park, Ellie hadn't returned from her outing to the park. Carter went upstairs to his apartment to change out of his uniform.

Needing some downtime as well, Rachelle went to the spare bedroom in his parents' portion of the large multifamily home that had become hers for the past few nights. It was a nice, comfortable room, with a double-size mattress and decorated in sea-foam green and cream.

She wondered if at one time this had been one of the boys' bedroom. Maybe Carter's?

With a sigh, she decided she really needed to keep

her mind off the too-handsome officer. Nothing would come of letting herself pine for him when he had repeatedly made it clear he wasn't interested.

Lying on the bed, she closed her eyes to rest. The bang of a door opening, then Ellie's sweet voice drew her out of the bedroom like a butterfly to a flower.

Rachelle hung back in the shadow of the hallway as she watched the Jamesons greet each other. Carter, now wearing jogging shorts and a T-shirt, swept his daughter into his arms and kissed her face. She giggled as he made raspberry sounds against her neck.

Rachelle's heart ached with love and longing for this family. But they would never be hers. Saddened and dismayed at the same time by the thought, she began to retreat, deciding it was time to distance herself. But Ellie spied her before she had taken two steps.

"Rachelle." Ellie broke away from her father and ran to Rachelle, giving her a warm hug.

"Well, hello there," Rachelle said, aware of Carter's gaze on her and his daughter. "Did you have a good time at the park?"

"I did." Ellie slipped her hand into Rachelle's and drew her into the living room. "We had a picnic and Greta and I met some nice girls to play with. I even saw Snapper."

"What?!" Carter and his parents, who had joined them, all stared at the child.

Rachelle tucked in her chin. "Isn't Snapper...?"

"Uncle Jordan's partner," Ellie said. "I hugged him and told him he should come home with me." Sadness crossed her face. "But he ran away and no one else saw him. Greta's mom was upset when I told her about Snapper. She said I shouldn't touch dogs without permission from their owner. But Snapper is family."

"Ellie, are you sure it was Snapper?" Alex asked, his voice breaking slightly.

"It could have been a different German shepherd, Ellie," Carter said gently. "And Greta's mom is correct. You know better than to approach a dog without permission, and even then, only if I'm with you."

Ellie shook her head adamantly. "It was Snapper. He had on his black collar."

Carter exchanged a look of disbelief with his dad.

Snapper disappeared the day Jordan had died. If the dog were still alive... Rachelle knew this was momentous. "We should go to the park," she said to Carter.

"There's no *we*," he said. "You're not going anywhere." He looked at his father. "I'll call Noah on the way."

Alex nodded, already moving to the hall closet, where he grabbed two flashlights.

Carter squatted down in front of Ellie. "Sweetie, can you describe where in the park you were when you saw Snapper?"

She scrunched up her little nose. "We were in the funny trees. We pumped water into a trunk and played in the sand."

"Sounds like they were in Zucker Natural Exploration Area," Ivy said. "It's just off Nellie's Lawn in the northeast part of the park."

"Got it." He gave Ellie a hug.

"Are you going to bring Snapper home?" Ellie asked.

"I'm going to try." He stood and met Rachelle's gaze. "You'll stay put?"

Though he had reason to ask, the question rankled.

"Yes. I'll keep Ellie occupied while we wait for you to come back."

He gave a sharp nod before leaving with Frosty and his father.

"Who would like to help me fix dinner?" Ivy asked, breaking the silence.

Rachelle immediately said, "I will." Anything to keep her mind off being left behind while Carter and his father went in search of Snapper.

"Me, too," Ellie cried.

"Great." Ivy headed to the kitchen. "I'll send Katie a text and ask if she'd like to come down. She wasn't feeling well earlier. She has been so tired. The pregnancy is really taking its toll."

Rachelle would imagine the death of her husband was more the culprit. Her heart hurt for this family and all they had suffered. She wished she could solve the crime. She didn't want to find the truth for herself anymore. She wanted it for Carter and his family.

"Do you think she really saw Snapper?" his father asked as Carter drove them to Prospect Park, located in the neighboring borough of Brooklyn.

Steeling himself against the hope in his father's voice, Carter said, "I don't know, Dad. We can pray so."

Taking out his phone, he called Noah and told him what was happening. "Dad and I are on our way there now."

"I'll join you," Noah said, and clicked off.

Carter didn't think Ellie would make up a story about something so important, though she was an imaginative child. If Snapper were out there, he would have come home, wouldn't he? There had been so many sightings over the past five months and every time it was either the wrong dog or just a fool's errand. But if Ellie really had seen Snapper, then they had to try to find him.

By the time Carter pulled to a stop along Flatbush Avenue, two other vehicles from the NYC K-9 Command Unit pulled up behind him. Noah and his dog, Scotty, got out of his SUV. Tony Knight and his dog, Rusty, a male chocolate Lab specializing in search and rescue, climbed out of the next vehicle.

Carter shook hands with Tony. The man had been Jordan's best friend growing up. "Glad to see you."

"I was in with Noah when you phoned," Tony said. "I will do anything to help bring Snapper home."

"I put the call out," Noah said. "There will be others arriving to help in the search. The park is over 500 acres. Snapper could be anywhere or not even in the park by now, but we have to try."

Alex grabbed Snapper's bed from the back seat where he'd placed it before leaving the house and held it out for the dogs to sniff. "I snagged this so the dogs could get Snapper's scent."

"Good thinking, Dad," Noah said.

After Scotty, Frosty and Rusty had taken a whiff, Carter said, "Dad, Frosty and I will take the Zucker Natural Exploration Area."

Noah nodded. "Tony and Rusty, head toward the zoo."

As Carter, Frosty and his dad set off, more police vehicles arrived. Carter was glad to have Noah coordinating their search effort.

With the beam of their flashlights bobbing through the dense woods, Carter and his dad called Snapper's name. Frosty picked up a scent. Encouraged, Carter let the dog lead him and his dad through the park toward the west side. Frosty left the wooded, grassy area and stopped at the one-way road that bordered the park. He whined, indicating he'd lost the scent.

Had Snapper been picked up in a car?

A few moments later, several other dog and handler teams emerged from the woods. Apparently all the dogs had picked up Snapper's scent but the trail went cold at the road.

Disappointed and discouraged, Carter feared they might never find Snapper.

Late Friday afternoon, Carter finished up some last-minute paperwork, stalling, really, because tonight was the celebrity ball Rachelle was covering for the newspaper. He wasn't looking forward to attending. He wasn't much for swanky shindigs. Give him a baseball stadium or dog park, he felt comfortable. The Metropolitan Museum of Art, not so much.

"Hey, shouldn't you be headed home?" Noah stopped by Carter's desk.

"Soon."

While Carter had resumed his duties, Rachelle had remained safely in his parents' house with Ellie and his mom and dad. Dad would protect them all.

Carter hated admitting to himself how much he looked forward to going home at the end of every shift, not only because his daughter would be waiting, but also Rachelle.

He liked the way Rachelle's brown eyes lit up when she saw him, though she'd quickly try to hide her reaction. Just as he hid his own joy at seeing her. He wanted to believe it was only the close proximity heat-ing up emotions between them. Not something deeper. He couldn't do deeper.

He really needed something to break on Rachelle's case. The more time she spent with his family, the harder it would be for them all when she left.

"Still no news on Snapper?" Carter asked, hoping to deflect his brother.

Unfortunately, Snapper hadn't been found at Prospect Park or anywhere in the vicinity despite every law enforcement officer keeping an eye out for the dog. Though Carter had worked his normal shift patrolling the subway system, he'd taken a walk through the park on his own several times hoping to find Snapper. Ellie had seemed so certain.

Noah shook his head. "All we can do is pray Snapper will find his way home if he's still alive."

Carter clenched his fist at the thought. "Yes. I'm not… I don't—" Carter stalled out, searching for words to voice the anguish lodged in his chest.

Noah put his hand on Carter's shoulder. "I know. Me, too." For a moment they were silent. Grief snarled in Carter's chest and he lifted up a prayer to ask that Snapper really was alive and would come home. It would do them all so much good.

Squeezing his shoulder before releasing him, Noah said, "Very impressive article she wrote for the *NYC Weekly* newspaper about Snapper and the search for him. She has a real gift with words."

Pride for Rachelle swelled in Carter's chest. "She did a great job. She's a skilled writer." He'd been a bit leery when she told him about the article but when he'd read it before she turned the piece in, he'd wanted to hug her for her kind and compassionate way of asking the public for help while still maintaining the family's privacy.

Noah grinned. "And I'm sure she'll do just as excellent a job reporting on tonight's event. Ellie has been talking nonstop for the last two days about this ball you and Rachelle are going to. I think it's great you're willing to escort her."

Carter snorted. "I can't very well let her go on her own and she's bound and determined to go."

"True. It's not like she's under house arrest. She could leave on her own if she chose to. She has to continue to do her job, after all."

The thought of Rachelle out from under his protection, vulnerable and alone, made Carter's insides twist.

"I heard Mom say the girls were going shopping today," Noah said.

"What?" Carter's spine stiffened. "She left the house?"

"Calm down, calm down." Noah put up a hand like a traffic officer. "They have a uniformed escort."

Carter wasn't placated.

"Plus, Dad's with them," Noah added. "You know he's not going to let anyone near the ladies."

Taking a breath to calm his racing pulse, Carter let some tension ease from his body. When it came to protection, their father was the best. And Carter trusted him. If Dad felt there was a threat he'd take action. Carter just wished they had a dog with them.

As if reading his thoughts, Noah said, "Plus, I had Dad take Scotty with them. It's good for my partner to get out and stretch his legs during the day, instead of being cooped up in the office while I'm pushing paper as the interim chief."

Carter wanted to hug his brother. Except they weren't the hugging sort. "Thanks, man. I appreciate it."

"Of course. You would do the same for me."

"You know it. And I've no doubt the commissioner will make you the permanent chief. There's no one better suited after—" Carter swallowed back the sharp stab of grief. "Jordy would be proud of you. As am I."

A flash of surprise, then acceptance and brotherly love shone in Noah's eyes. "Thank you." Noah cleared his throat. "You better get on home. You have a penguin suit to squeeze yourself into."

Chuckling at the reminder, Carter said, "I do. You think they'd let me bring Frosty if I put a bow tie around his neck?"

Noah laughed. "You're both on guard duty. I think you should."

Rachelle sat on a stool in the middle of the Jameson guest bathroom wearing a belted robe as Katie and Ellie fussed with her hair. She winced slightly when Ellie tugged a little too hard. But she bit her lip, refraining from saying anything.

Today had been one of her most treasured experiences. She and the Jameson women had spent hours looking for the perfect dress and shoes for her to wear tonight to the celebrity ball. Though they'd had Alex and another patrolman, along with a beautiful rottweiler dog named Scotty, as their escorts, Rachelle, Ellie, Katie and Ivy had giggled their way through several shops until they'd found success and Rachelle had purchased a new gown.

Rachelle had planned to wear her one good dress, a long, black tank style she wore with pearls. Nothing fancy, just serviceable. But Katie and Ellie had taken one look at it and declared the dress wouldn't do. So now there was a stunning red dress with lace overlaying silk hanging on the back of Rachelle's bedroom door and a pair of new sparkly sandals waiting to be worn. She'd put it on a credit card, deciding the expense was worth the price.

All the attention and pampering was overwhelming. She could be the heroine of her own Cinderella story.

Ivy walked into the bathroom and clapped her hands. "Oh my, you look lovely."

"They won't let me look," Rachelle complained with a smile.

"Almost there," Katie said around a mouthful of bobby pins.

"Just a few more flowers," Ellie said.

Rachelle had the sinking feeling she might look like a wood nymph when they were done. Ellie had insisted on putting baby roses in her hair.

Katie had done Rachelle's makeup, and again she hadn't let her take a peek.

"Okay," Katie said as she stepped back, holding her hand out for Ellie. The little girl skidded around Rachelle's knees with a big smile on her face. "It's time for you to take a look."

Rachelle stood up gingerly so as not to dislodge whatever they'd done with her hair. As she gazed in the mirror, she swallowed past the lump in her throat. Her makeup was dramatic, yet not heavy. And Katie and Ellie had done some sort of a fancy twist around the crown of her head and gathered her hair into a long ponytail going over her shoulder. Little red, baby roses were embedded in her hair along the twist with a few woven into the ponytail. The effect was stunning.

Tears burned the back of her eyes. She blinked rapidly so she didn't ruin her mascara. She turned to the others. "Thank you. I don't know what to say." She looked in the mirror again. "I barely recognize myself."

Katie and Ellie and Ivy beamed at her.

"Carter's upstairs getting ready," Ivy said.

"Let's get you dressed," Katie said.

They hustled Rachelle to her bedroom. As Rachelle slipped into the red dress, she felt compelled to say, "I've never had anything like this before."

"It's a striking dress," Katie said while zipping up the back.

"It is, but that's not what I mean." Rachelle faced her new friends. "This girl time. I can't express how special today has been." Her throat grew tight. "I was an only child. My mother wasn't the touchy-feely type."

Katie put a hand on her shoulder. "You're one of us now. No matter what happens going forward, you will always be our friend."

Choking back tears, Rachelle smiled. "Thank you. I really am so grateful to all of you for everything you've done for me over the past week."

Ellie clapped her hands. "I can't wait for Daddy to see you."

A knot of anxiety formed in Rachelle's tummy. Would Carter think she was pretty?

They heard Carter's deep voice talking with his father in the living room.

"I guess I should go." Rachelle smoothed a hand over the front of the gown.

"Wait," Katie said. She picked up a jewelry box she'd

placed on the dresser. "This will complete the look." The box held a sparkly strand of crystals and a matching bracelet. "These aren't real. They were a gift and I never wear them, but they would look lovely on you."

"Thank you." Touched by the other woman's thoughtfulness, she turned so Katie could close the clasp on the necklace.

The Jameson women walked ahead of Rachelle, giving her a moment to collect herself. She picked up the little sparkly black bag Ivy had lent her, which now held her flowered notebook and pink pen, her ID and some cash. She took a deep breath and walked into the living room.

"Here comes the princess," Ellie announced with much fanfare.

Rachelle caught sight of Carter and her heart stuttered and then pounded. She'd thought him handsome in his uniform and his casual clothing but in the tux, *wow*. His dark hair had been styled back off his forehead and his jaw was clean-shaven. Sitting beside him, Frosty wore a black K-9 police vest and a black bow tie rested beneath his chin.

They made quite a picture.

Carter's blue eyes collided with hers. They were icy and unreadable. A flutter of uncertainty made her want to look away. Instead, she lifted her chin and smiled.

Carter bent down to give his daughter a kiss. "You can stay with Aunt Katie tonight. We'll be home late."

"Okay, Daddy." With her little hands, she turned his face back toward Rachelle. "Doesn't she look pretty?"

"Yes. Very pretty." His voice was devoid of any inflection.

Rachelle swallowed the hurt of his nonreaction. She

didn't need his approval or appreciation. This night wasn't about them. This night was about her career. She had a job to do. He was just her bodyguard. And she would repeat the phrase to herself over and over again all night long.

ELEVEN

Carter's heartbeat was so fast in his chest he was surprised Rachelle didn't hear it as he escorted her up the red carpet at The Metropolitan Museum of Art. Cameras flashed. People *oohed* and *ahhed* over the guests arriving. He really didn't like all this pomp and circumstance. But it was part of the deal. And Rachelle deserved to be fawned over. She was gorgeous. The red dress fit her to perfection and made her warm brown eyes shine. The crown of roses on her head made him think of one of Ellie's fairy tales. Rachelle was indeed a princess.

Inside the famed art museum, they followed the crowd to The Charles Engelhard Court in the American Wing. Twinkle lights dangled from the ceiling of the glass-enclosed courtyard and danced off the stained-glass windows. At the far end of the courtyard, in front of a facade of the Bank Branch of the United States, a band had been set up, complete with a dance floor.

Amid the large marble and gold-plated American sculptures, linen-clad tables with gold-rimmed china and sparkling crystal stemware created an intimate feel for the myriad guests squeezing into the space.

Carter usually didn't suffer claustrophobia, but he was beginning to understand the feeling as he and Frosty trailed in Rachelle's wake. She appeared comfortable among New York and Hollywood's elite. She stopped to talk to women in stunning and sometimes awful gowns, jotting down names of designers and accessories that made his head spin. More than one man paused to admire Rachelle as she moved through the throng. Carter had never considered himself the jealous type but as the night wore on, he found himself wanting to push a few overly eager men off their feet for getting too chummy with Rachelle.

After the dinner of chicken smothered in sauce alongside rice and vegetables, the band struck up their first set and people moved to the dance floor. Tired of the small talk with those at their table, Carter settled Frosty near a statue away from the crowd, snagged Rachelle's hand and drew her to the dance floor.

They moved to the music, a classical piece that permeated the air and for a moment made Carter feel as though they were the only two people on the dance floor.

Holding her close, he said against her ear, "How soon can we get out of here?"

She leaned back to look at him, her eyes sparking with amusement. "It took longer than I expected."

"What?"

"I figured you'd become bored much sooner."

"Not bored." *Just tired of sharing you with everyone.* The thought made him stumble.

He twirled her in a circle and then steered her away from the dance floor toward a side exit leading to an outside balcony. He let out a soft whistle; a moment later Frosty joined them, trotting along at Rachelle's side.

"I need some fresh air," Carter explained as they left the revelry of the celebrity ball behind them.

She stepped out of his arms to lean against the handrail. He wanted to pull her back into his embrace.

"It's a beautiful night," she commented, gazing up at the stars.

"You're beautiful." In the moonlight he could see the surprise in her eyes.

A slow smile, different than any other he'd seen on her face, appeared. "I didn't think you noticed."

"Oh, I noticed. So did every man here."

She shrugged. "I'm here to do a job. I don't matter to any of these people beyond getting their name in the paper."

"You matter to me. More than I care to admit." Before he could stop himself, he fingered the long strands of her hair draped over her shoulder. Silky, smooth and so pretty.

"Carter?"

His name on her lips was like an elixir, taming the riot of emotions bouncing through him. "This thing between us can't go anywhere." The words were directed more at himself than her.

She stepped closer. "Why?"

"I'm not prepared to replace—" His chest hurt with grief. "I care for you, Rachelle. But I'm not free to—I can't offer you my heart." He hated to be so blunt, but he had to make sure she understood. He needed to keep his heart safe. He couldn't imagine going through the kind of pain he'd experienced when Helen died. Better not to love again than risk heartache.

She breathed in and slowly exhaled. "I understand. But we have this moment in time. It may be all we'll ever have."

The deep, honey tone of her Southern voice spread through him, overrunning his walls and making him believe her words. Giving in to the yearning for closeness, he cupped her face and lowered his lips to hers to kiss her the way he'd wanted since the moment he'd held her in his arms after her near miss with the subway train.

Rachelle couldn't breathe. But who needed air with Carter kissing her, curling her toes inside her little strappy sandals. Only this moment on the museum's ballroom balcony mattered. She clutched at the lapels of his tux to keep from melting into a puddle at his feet. A sense of rightness, of belonging, of being noticed, filled her every cell.

When they broke apart, they were both breathing rapidly as he touched his forehead to hers.

"Wow." His voice was husky and deep as if he, too, was having trouble catching his breath.

"Hmm, yes," she murmured, wanting so badly to repeat the experience but too shy to initiate another kiss.

He took a breath and lifted his head. "I didn't mean—"

A flood of embarrassment and irritation chased away her shyness. She stepped back and put a finger to his lips. "Don't you dare say you didn't mean to kiss me. Because I hope you did mean to, if only this once."

One corner of his mouth lifted in a salty grin. "Oh, I meant to kiss you. I've been wanting to for a long time."

For a long moment, he held her gaze and she was lost in the swirling blue depths. Then his grin faded, and his eyes seemed to cool. He disengaged from her. "This can't happen again. I can't allow anything to develop between us. I can't do that to Ellie, and I can't betray the memory of my wife."

Stricken to the core, she clapped her hands together in front of her. Suddenly the mild evening air was cold against her bare arms. "Of course."

He was still in love with his late wife. She could never compete with his memory of her. She lifted her shoulder in hopes to downplay the hurt spreading through her. "I understand."

She turned and hurried back inside the museum. She wandered aimlessly through the crowd, a smile plastered on her face. She needed to find the restroom or some little dark alcove where she could melt down in private. Or as private as it could get with over a hundred people milling about. Her lower lip trembled. She clenched her teeth together. She would not cry in public.

She headed for the far exit, where the restrooms were off to the right and the caterer's station off to the left. She passed the threshold into the hallway outside of the exhibit hall when a strong arm wrapped around her shoulders and something sharp poked in to her left side.

"Just keep walking," a deep voice said in her ear. "Or I'll gut you here. The boss doesn't want a scene. He wants you out of the way."

Her breath caught in her throat. She slanted a glance sideways. The tall man wore a waiter's jacket. His face was bruised around his nose and eyes. She swallowed as realization hit full force. This was one of the men who had tried to kidnap her the other day. The one whose nose she'd broken.

He steered her toward the catering doors. Horror

filled her veins. If she let him take her through those shiny, swinging doors she was going to die.

Better to die here where there was a chance he would be caught. She had to do something. Cupping her left fist with her right hand, she took a deep breath and used as much force as she could muster to jab her elbow into his rib cage while at the same time she stomped down on his foot with her spiked heel.

He let out a foul curse, his hold on her lessening enough that she twisted away, running back toward the party. He grabbed the back of her dress and yanked her off her feet. She went down with a jolt onto the hard floor. Pain reverberated through her, stealing her breath.

A woman screamed.

Then she heard Carter's voice. "Attack!"

The scrabble of nails echoed on the marble floor and then the whirlwind of white fur flashed by as Frosty sprang at her attacker. Despite the agony pulsing through her body, she spun to face the assailant with her feet up and ready to defend herself. But she didn't need to. Frosty was standing on top of the man's chest, snarling and snapping his jaw.

"Hey! Get him off me!" The terrified man withered beneath Frosty.

Carter raced forward to kick the knife away. "Don't move or he'll bite."

The man froze.

Security guards and policemen rushed forward to take the man into custody. Carter called Frosty off so the man could be put in handcuffs and taken away.

Carter squatted down beside her and cupped her cheek. "Are you okay? Can you stand?"

"I'm just sore. Nothing broken." She hoped. She allowed him to help her to her feet. She tested her legs, her back and arms to reassure herself there were no broken bones.

Despite his earlier assertion that nothing could happen between them, she clung to him. He was her safeguard. Her anchor in this strange and violent storm.

And she knew there was no way she could fight her feelings for Carter. She could only hope she could hide them.

After giving their statements to the officers on scene, they were cleared to leave.

Carter handed her the little black purse she'd been carrying. He must have grabbed it from the table on his way to find her.

Going home sounded like an ideal plan. She had enough information to write her article about the fundraiser and all the celebrities in attendance, and of course the part about being attacked by a rogue waiter would add drama, especially when she highlighted how a certain handsome officer and majestic white dog came to her rescue. She was still shaking from the scare. She sent up praise to God above for sending the pair to her aid when she needed them the most.

"He said the boss didn't want a scene. He wants me out of the way," she said. "Do you think Miles is his boss?"

"I'll find out when I question him," Carter replied as he guided her through the gathered crowd and toward the museum exit.

Carter called for a car to pick them up. They didn't have to wait long. They slid into the back and Rachelle leaned against the headrest, taking a few calming breaths.

Frosty lay curled on the floorboard. Carter had his face turned away from her as they traveled through the city.

She wanted Carter to hold her, but she wouldn't ask. If he didn't want to explore their growing attachment, then so be it. She had to learn to live within the parameters he'd set. She was used to craving love and affection and having it denied. There must be something wrong with her, that no one wanted to love her.

All the more reason to focus on her career.

The town car headed onto the Ed Koch Queensboro Bridge, taking the outer lane. From the side-view window Rachelle could see the borough of Queens laid out in yellow dots reflecting the night sky. Below the bridge lay the wide expanse of the East River.

The silence between them became too much for her to bear.

"Did you know the East River isn't really a river?" she asked Carter.

"No?"

She heard a hint of amusement in his tone but ignored it. "No. Despite its name it isn't truly a river but a saltwater tidal strait connecting Upper New York Bay with Long Island Sound."

"That is correct."

Definitely amused. "Did you know that water of the strait flows in different directions depending on the time of day?"

"I think I remember learning something about that in school," he said drily.

She rolled her eyes at him even though it was too dark inside the car for him to notice. "I know you grew up here, but this is all new to me. The closest river near where I grew up, the Oconee River, provides drinking water for thousands of people in the state."

"You don't want to drink the East River water."

"I see people fishing in it."

"You don't want to do that, either. There are much better waterways to find good fish." He shifted to face her. "Do you fish?"

She shook her head. "My father took me fishing when I was young, much to my mother's dismay."

"Did you catch anything?"

"A cold," she confessed. "I wasn't patient enough to stand in the water with a pole, waiting for some wide-mouthed bass to bite."

"That sounds about right."

"What does that mean?"

"In the time I've known you I can say you aren't the type of person to sit idle for long."

True. She did like to keep busy. Either physically or mentally. "I don't see you relax much."

"Between the job, Frosty and Ellie, there's no time for relaxation."

"When was the last time you took a vacation?"

He rubbed his chin. "I took some time off when Ellie was born."

Her stomach clenched. Time to mourn his deceased wife. That didn't sound like a vacation. The man needed some downtime. For himself and for Ellie. "Have you considered taking Ellie to Disney World? I was about her age when my grandmother took me."

Though she couldn't make out his expression, she could feel his gaze on her in the shadowed interior of the car. "You still remember the trip?"

"Like it was yesterday." She reached across the seat

to find his hand. "Take your daughter on a memorable trip. Let her dress up like a princess."

He gave her hand a squeeze. "I might do as you suggest."

The sound of a roaring engine filled the car's interior as harsh light shone in through the back window. Frosty lifted his head and growled.

From the front seat the driver said, "What's this guy doing?"

Rachelle sat up straight and glanced through the rear window and was momentarily blinded by multiple headlights on the large vehicle tailgating their car.

"He's awfully close," she said.

"Step on it," Carter told the driver. The car sped forward but so did the big truck behind them.

Carter grabbed his cell phone from the breast pocket of his tux jacket. He said, "Carter Jameson, 10-13Z, Queensboro Bridge." He explained their predicament.

"What was that code?"

"Civilian clothed officer in trouble," he said. "Put your seat belt on."

She scrambled to click the belt into place.

Carter patted the seat between them. Frosty jumped up. "Help me put the center seat belt on Frosty."

"What's happening?" She stretched the seat belt over Frosty, as he craned his neck behind him, barking into her ear.

The truck roared up right behind them.

"Brace yourself," Carter instructed. "I have a bad feeling about this." Fear infused his tone, betraying the gravity of the situation.

Her body tensed, and she dug her fingers into the seat to brace herself.

With a rev of its big engine, the truck struck the back of their vehicle. The vibration of the hit jolted through Rachelle. Her head bounced off the back seat. Their car fishtailed. Their driver lost control of the wheel, sending the car spinning.

The big truck lurched forward. Rachelle ducked and covered her head as the large silver grill rammed into her side of the vehicle. The sickening sound of metal crunching as the car buckled inward filled the interior. The car slammed into the concrete barrier, keeping them from going over the side of the bridge.

Terrified, Rachelle prayed, "Lord, please, get us out of this."

The trajectory of the town car jerked to a halt. For a moment, Rachelle opened her eyes, then quickly shielded them from the glaring light still shining through the passenger side window.

Carter grabbed at her buckle. "We need to get out."

Before he could unbuckle her, the engine on the big truck rumbled. Fearing her legs would be crushed, Rachelle drew her legs up onto the seat an instant before the side door crumbled inward, bending with a loud shriek. Glass flew through the air and she barely felt the pricks as tiny shards hit her skin.

The big truck pushed their car like it was nothing more than a child's toy.

"Save yourself," Carter yelled to the car driver.

The driver managed to extract himself and stumbled away from the car to safety.

Carter opened the sunroof. "Unhook yourself," he instructed Rachelle. "And Frosty. Hurry!"

He climbed out through the window and reached back inside to help Frosty out onto the roof of the car.

Heart pounding in her ears, she grasped Carter's outstretched hand. He pulled her through just as the truck squished the metal frame of the car.

"This way!" Carter took her hand and drew her onto the top of the concrete barrier. Frosty jumped off what was left of their car onto the road and barked, the frantic sound heartrending.

Beneath her feet, the barrier shook as the car broke through a chunk of cement and the back end dangled over the river.

Surefooted, Carter ran across the barrier to safety. Rachelle's strappy sandals slipped. For a moment, her arms cartwheeled, before she bent her knees and crouched, clinging to the barrier with both hands.

"Move forward," Carter yelled. "You can do it!"

She crawled as best she could until she cleared the front end of the car. Carter reached for her and drew her to his chest as gunfire erupted from the cab of the big truck. Taking her by the hand, he ran with her in a hunched, serpentine fashion toward the line of cars that had stopped.

"Down! Everyone get down," Carter yelled at the people who'd climbed out of their cars.

The pinging of bullets hitting cars and spitting asphalt shuddered through Rachelle. She couldn't believe this. Why were they so determined to kill her?

TWELVE

The sound of sirens punctuated the air. Carter dragged Rachelle down behind the tail end of a large newspaper delivery van. Frosty sat beside them. She buried her face in the dog's fur. The irony wasn't lost on her, and she would have laughed if she weren't so frightened. Here she was, desperately trying to solve Chief Jordan Jameson's murder, following clues that led her to Miles Landau, and she might die hiding behind a newspaper's van.

They heard the squeal of tires on pavement and the roar of the big truck's engine. Carter glanced around the side of the van. "They're leaving."

She gripped his shoulder and peered around him to see the big heavy hauling truck tearing down the roadway away from them, its horn blaring as cars that had stopped on the other side of the accident either scrambled to get out of the way or were pushed out of the way by the heavy grill.

"You're okay," Carter told her.

She nodded, grateful once again for his quick thinking.

For the next hour, there was organized chaos as uniformed officers and other K-9 Unit officers, along with their dogs, converged on the scene. Medics saw to the injured.

Rachelle had sustained a few cuts from broken glass on her shoulders, hands and face. The paramedics also confirmed she hadn't sustained any injuries from her earlier attack. Carter's hand was bandaged for a cut and a shard of glass had to be removed from one of Frosty's paws.

Once the paramedics released her, Rachelle followed Carter to a K-9 Unit vehicle. Her heart beat too fast and her hands shook as she accepted a bottle of water from a tall, brown-haired, brown-eyed officer. Beside him sat a handsome bloodhound, whose deep chocolate eyes studied her with a tilt of his droopy-jowled head.

"Thank you," she said to the officer.

"My pleasure. Name's Reed Branson," Reed told her, his voice low and empathic. "You two have had an exciting evening."

"That's an understatement," Carter muttered as he tilted a bottle of water to his lips and drank deeply.

"Hop in," Reed said, gesturing to his vehicle. "I've been instructed by the chief to get you both home safely."

"I need to go to the station to interrogate the suspect arrested earlier," Carter told him.

Reed shrugged. "Take it up with your brother." He opened the door. "Until I hear otherwise, get in."

"I should get my own rig, anyway," Carter stated. He held out his hand for Rachelle.

She allowed him to help her into the back seat while Reed put his dog and Frosty into the dog compartment. Carter sat up front on the drive to the house in Rego Park.

When they arrived at the Jamesons', Carter handed

her off to his parents, then he and Frosty left in his official vehicle. She burned to go with him, to hear him interrogate the suspect and learn if this man worked for the person responsible for Chief Jordan Jameson's murder.

She would have to wait and see if Carter would divulge any information to her. For now, she just wanted to ease the aches and pain with a hot shower and a good night's sleep. If such a thing was even possible.

The next three days went by in a blur for Carter. Between dealing with the aftermath of the attempts on Rachelle's life and doing his certification competitions, he was both wired and exhausted.

And unfortunately, no closer to taking down Miles Landau. The thug from The Metropolitan Museum of Art who had attacked Rachelle had lawyered up and wasn't talking. They had him dead to rights on attempted kidnapping and attempted murder. Still, his lawyer maintained that Attilo Hunt was acting alone and had nothing more to say. And unfortunately, the police department couldn't connect Attilo to Miles Landau.

And the haul truck hadn't been found, despite every cop in all five boroughs searching high and low for some sign of the destructive vehicle.

By the morning of the police dog field trials public demonstrations, Carter was wishing he wasn't competing. He was afraid he wouldn't be able to concentrate.

Ellie appeared in the doorway to Carter's bedroom. She'd dressed herself in the unicorn-covered dress Rachelle had apparently purchased for her on their shopping excursion before the fund-raiser ball. The whimsical motif soothed Carter's ragged emotions a little.

"Can I go downstairs for breakfast?"

Needing a few more minutes alone to gather his thoughts, he said, "Sure. I'll be down shortly."

Over the past week he'd tried unsuccessfully to ignore the tension between him and Rachelle that ebbed and flowed in a disturbing way he had never experienced.

When he was away from her, he wondered what she was doing, if she was safe. And every once in a while he'd catch a phantom whiff of lavender and think she was nearby. And then, when he returned home at night, she'd be there with his parents, Katie and Ellie. They'd have dinner ready and would gather like a family. And he'd want to pull Rachelle into his arms and kiss her again.

He didn't know how much more of her being within the bosom of his family he could take without losing his sanity.

But today, he couldn't think about her and his unexpected and unwanted feelings for her. Today he had to focus on the course. Today was about him and Frosty representing the NYC K-9 Command Unit against over forty other teams from all over the nation.

He grabbed his duffel bag filled with all of Frosty's paraphernalia and water bottles for them both, plus a few granola bars, and headed down to his parents' apartment, determined to keep Rachelle out of his head and his heart.

Rachelle sat at the patio table across from Katie. She opened her flowered notebook and found a blank page. Katie had offered to talk to her about her marriage to Jordan. An unexpected boon. Rachelle picked up her pen, held it poised over the page. "How did you two meet?"

"He taught the self-defense class I took when I first moved to Queens." Katie rubbed her tummy with a sad smile. "I thought he was so handsome, but I didn't talk to him. But then he and Snapper came to Rego Park Elementary School to do a demonstration. And oddly enough he recognized me."

"Why oddly?"

Katie shrugged. "I just never imagined that a man like him would take notice of someone like me."

Rachelle reached across the table to place her hand over Katie's. "I understand the sentiment. But from everything I've learned about Jordan Jameson he was a rare man and I'm sure he was smitten with you from the moment he saw you."

Katie nodded, her gaze unfocused on the yard, where Frosty lay on the grass watching the two puppies tugging on the same toy. "We didn't have a long engagement. In retrospect, I wish we had taken more time to—"

The back screen door banged open and Carter walked out. His gaze zeroed in on Rachelle like a heat-seeking missile. "What are you doing?"

Taken aback by his less than friendly demeanor, she sat up straighter and said, "Good morning to you, too."

He glanced at the little flowered notebook in front of her and the pink pen her hand. "You're interviewing Katie," he accused. "You're still writing an article about Jordan, aren't you?"

She closed her notebook and very slowly set the pen on top. "Yes, I am."

"You promised me you would stop this."

She narrowed her gaze and leaned her elbows on the table. "Carter, I never promised you anything. I told you I would hand over my notes and research. I never said I'd stop writing this article." Uncovering the truth was too important, especially now that she knew and cared for the Jameson family. And adding the personal touches to the story of Jordan's life and love would make him more real to the reader. She wanted people to care about Jordan as a man as well as the chief of the NYC K-9 Command Unit.

"Carter, it's okay," Katie said. "I offered—"

He held up a hand, stopping her. "No, it's not okay, Katie. She's using our family to further her own career."

"Daddy!" Ellie ran out of the house. "Grandma and I finished our puzzle. Isn't it time to go?"

"Yes. It is." Carter's voice sounded a bit strangled.

Ellie skirted around Carter and climbed up on Rachelle's lap. "You're coming with us, right?"

Loving the feel of the little girl in her arms, Rachelle held Carter's gaze. She wouldn't go where she wasn't wanted, but she wasn't going to make it easy for him. Not when she longed to be a part of the Jameson clan for as long as possible. "If it's still okay with your father."

For a long moment, he didn't respond. Rachelle wavered in her determination to stand her ground. She should bow out because he apparently didn't want her to go.

"If Rachelle wants to attend, she's free to," he finally said. He directed his focus on Ellie. "Can I have a blessing kiss?"

Ellie slipped off Rachelle's lap and hurried to her father. She took his face in her little hands and kissed his forehead, his nose, each cheek and his chin. "May you be blessed with a good run today. Whether you win or lose, Daddy, I will love you no matter what."

The tender show of love between daughter and father had Rachelle's eyes tearing up.

Carter placed a kiss on Ellie's golden head, then he whistled for Frosty. The dog trotted toward the porch stairs with the puppies scampering close behind. Frosty followed Carter into the house, the screen door closing behind them. A moment later, Ivy stepped out with treats for the puppies, which she gave to Ellie. The little girl and the puppies raced around the yard.

"Carter's not used to sharing Ellie with somebody outside the family," Ivy said without preamble. "Ellie's become quite attached to you."

"And I her," Rachelle said. "I'm sure Carter wants to protect her. At some point I will be leaving." The thought brought a pang of loss she wasn't looking forward to.

Ivy sat next to Katie. "That could be true."

Could be true? What did she mean by that?

Rachelle wanted to probe Ivy's words but before she could ask, Ivy continued, "You should have seen Carter in the early days. He needed our help, but boy, he wanted to do it all himself. But he's like that." Ivy sat next to Katie. "The doer has a hard time delegating. Unlike Noah, who is a master delegator. He would delegate doing the dishes when he was a kid." Ivy chuckled. "I would come into the kitchen and the three boys would be washing and drying and loading the dishwasher. And there would be Noah, supervising."

Rachelle itched to write these details down but refrained as Carter's words about using his family echoed in her head. "Who's older? Noah or Carter?"

"Noah, by a couple of years." Ivy shook her head. "Those two were always vying for attention."

"I'd guess Jordan was the one loading the dishwasher," Katie said. "He liked things done a certain way."

"Yes," Ivy said. "Jordy would come in and rearrange the dishwasher behind me sometimes." Her smile faded. "I really miss him."

Katie reached over to awkwardly hug Ivy. "We all miss him."

Rachelle dropped her gaze, feeling out of place.

Ellie ran up the porch stairs. "Are we gonna go?"

Ivy wiped at her eyes. "Yes, we are. Grandpa made some sandwiches so we don't have to buy anything at the concession stand."

"Oh," Ellie grumbled. "I wanted to get some cotton candy."

"That's between you and your daddy." Ivy headed back inside. "You know how he feels about sugar."

Rachelle took Ellie's hand. "They have cotton candy? I haven't had cotton candy since I was your age." She winked at the child. "I may just have to buy myself some."

Ellie grinned at her. "You'll share, right?"

"Of course."

Katie rose from the patio chair and looked at Rachelle. "You're playing with fire."

Rachelle shrugged. "What's a little more disapproval in my life?"

The stadium seats were filled. The crowd buzzed as Rachelle filed through the entrance of the sports complex housing the police dog field trials. The large grass field was dotted with various pieces of equipment like those in the NYC K-9 Command Unit's training center.

Rachelle hadn't been sure what to expect and was bemused by the excitement in the air and the multitude of people who'd come out to watch the K-9 dogs and their handlers demonstrate their abilities.

Her look must've given her away, because Alex said, "Folks from all over the region come out for these trials. It's a big deal."

"So I'm gathering." She followed the Jamesons to their seats, which were in a really good place where they could see the whole field. Zach and his wife, Violet, along with Mr. and Mrs. Griffin were already seated. A sense of belonging seeped through her and it tore her up inside to know there would be a day when she'd have to leave them.

She sat between Ellie and Alex. "How often do they hold these trials?"

"The regional ones are twice yearly," Alex explained.

"I'm very blessed that I was here for this one." Rachelle traced Carter's name on the glossy program. There was another team from the NYC K-9 Command Unit listed: Officer Luke Hathaway and his German shepherd, Bruno.

Katie said, "We'll be blessed if we don't walk out of here with our backsides numb."

Rachelle had to laugh. The seats weren't the best, but they weren't the worst she'd ever sat on.

"Hi, everyone." A pretty woman with long brown hair and big blue eyes scooted into their row and sat on the other side of Katie.

Katie hugged the woman. "Sophie, I wasn't sure you'd make it."

"I wouldn't miss Luke and Bruno for anything," Sophie said. She leaned forward. "Hi, Ellie."

Ellie jumped up and shimmied past Rachelle to give the newcomer a hug.

"Sophie, this is Rachelle Clark," Katie said. "Rachelle, this is Sophie Walters, Noah's assistant and soon to be Luke Hathaway's bride."

"We talked on the phone when you called to ask about interviewing Noah," Sophie said, extending her hand that bore a beautiful engagement ring.

"Yes, we did. Thank you for your help that day. I was happy Noah offered up his brother," Rachelle said as she shook Sophie's hand. If Noah hadn't suggested she talk to Carter, she wouldn't be here right now. Literally. Carter had saved her life that day and many times since.

As the announcer welcomed the attendees and introduced the participants, Rachelle settled in her seat with Ellie on her lap. A roar went up from the crowd as each duo was presented. Rachelle yelled and clapped along with the Jamesons when Carter and Frosty trotted onto the field. They also cheered for Luke Hathaway and Bruno.

The demonstration got underway. Rachelle followed along with the program as the teams competed on the different obstacles. Her heart raced every time it was Carter and Frosty's turn to compete. The pair was so in sync. She was sure they'd win.

"Okay," Alex said, in a lull between events. "If anybody wants anything from the concession stand you better go do it now. In about ten minutes there's an official break."

Katie pulled herself to her feet. "I need to find the restroom."

Ellie tugged on Rachelle's sleeve. "Cotton candy?" she whispered.

With a grin, Rachelle stood. "We'll go with you."

They shimmied their way out of the stands to the main concession area. Katie waddled away in search of a restroom, while Rachelle and Ellie joined the line at the concession stand.

As they moved forward, Rachelle could feel a presence behind her. Not liking the invasion of her personal bubble, Rachelle glanced over her shoulder and locked gazes with a young woman with black hair beneath a baseball cap. Rachelle moved forward and the woman did, as well. Chalking it up to the New York way, she ignored how much the woman was crowding her space.

There were only three more people ahead of them when the woman latched on to Rachelle's shoulder. She leaned in close. "If you don't want anything to happen to this pretty little girl and her father," the woman whispered in a raspy tone into Rachelle's ear, "you better stop snooping into things that are none of your business."

Rachelle whipped around, shrugging off the woman's hand. The woman darted out of the line and blended into the crowd. Heart racing with the ominous words ringing inside her head, Rachelle fought back hot tears of frustration. It was one thing to put her life, and even Carter's, in danger. But to put Ellie in jeopardy was unacceptable.

Rachelle could not allow anything to happen to Carter's sweet little girl.

It was time for Rachelle to leave the safety of the Jameson home, as soon as possible.

THIRTEEN

Carter had just tucked Ellie into bed and kissed her good-night when he heard a knock on the front door to the apartment. Since Noah was still working, Carter quietly shut Ellie's bedroom door and hurried to open the apartment door to find his mother standing there. Unexpected disappointment shoved him hard in the chest. He wasn't sure why he had been hoping Rachelle would be at the door. They'd hardly spoken two words to each other all evening.

"You better get downstairs," his mother said by way of greeting. "Rachelle's packing and planning to leave."

The news was like a punch to the gut. "What do you mean she's leaving?"

"I don't know. Something must've happened at the field trials because she's been..." His mom paused, seeming to search for the right word.

"Subdued?"

"Yes. Exactly."

He'd noticed after the competition that she'd been very un-Rachelle-like. She'd been quiet and reserved when they all went to Griffin's Diner for a celebratory meal. Though he and Frosty placed second and Luke and Bruno placed third behind the team from Boston PD, Carter had been jazzed to represent the NYC K-9 Command Unit and was grateful for placing so high.

"Go," his mother urged. "I'll stay with Ellie."

He hurried downstairs, belatedly realizing he had no shoes. Didn't matter. He needed to find out what was going on with Rachelle. He entered his parents' apartment, and his father, standing sentinel, pointed down the hallway. With a nod, Carter strode to Rachelle's closed bedroom door and knocked.

"Come in," she said.

He pushed the door open and saw the suitcase she was packing on the bed was already nearly full.

She glanced up at him. A little *V* appeared between her eyebrows. "What are you doing here?" Her eyes widened with fear. "Is Ellie okay?"

The quiver in her voice sent an alarm through his system. "Of course she's okay. Why wouldn't she be?"

She let out a noisy breath and turned back to her task of packing. "Good."

He put his hand over hers, stilling her movements. "Rachelle, tell me what's going on."

She kept her head bent, her eyes downcast. Light from the overheard fixture created shadows over her cheeks. "Why does something have to be going on?"

"You're packing your bags. Why are you going?"

"You can't make me stay here."

He drew her hands to his chest, forcing her to face him even though she refused to meet his gaze. "You're right, I can't make you stay," he said carefully. "But I don't understand why you want to leave now. Is it because I was upset with you earlier?"

A pained expression flittered across her face. "No. That has nothing to do with this."

"Then what has happened? Tell me."

She tugged her hands away and moved several steps back. "Nothing. Nothing happened."

"Right. You haven't been acting yourself ever since the field trials. My mom even noticed."

Rachelle bit her lip. She seemed to be wrestling with a decision she was struggling to make.

"Talk to me," he pressed. "Trust me."

Finally, she said, "It's not safe here. I need to leave."

Her words made zero sense to Carter. "Of course it's safe here. You're safer here than anywhere else."

She shook her head. "You don't understand. They know."

His breath stalled in his lungs. A chill of dread worked down his spine. "They who?"

"Whoever's targeting me. Miles, if he's the killer. And if he's not, then *whoever is* Jordan's killer. Maybe more than one person is responsible. I don't know, but somebody knows I'm here and—" She clamped her lips together.

"And what?" He stalked forward, stopping within an inch of her. He gripped her shoulders. "Tell me what happened."

She swallowed, looking trapped and afraid. He eased his hold on her to cup her cheek. "Rachelle, whatever it is, whatever happened to you, whoever threatened you, you can tell me. I will keep you safe."

Turning her head into his palm, she closed her eyes. When she opened them, they were filled with determination and she stepped out of his grasp. "It's not me I'm afraid for. It's Ellie."

His heart dropped. "What do you mean?"

"Today when Ellie and I went to the concession stand, a woman told me that I better back off or they would hurt you and Ellie." She shook her head. "I can't let anything happen to your little girl."

A deep fury ignited in his chest. Not directed at Rachelle, but at these unnamed, faceless people who were threatening her and now his daughter. "You don't have to worry. You're both safe here. I will get armed guards to cover the front of the house and the back."

Darting around him, she resumed packing. "I'm leaving. You can't stop me. If I'm gone then she's out of danger."

"But you won't be out of danger." The thought of something happening to her tore him up inside. He couldn't let her leave.

"It doesn't matter," she insisted. "What matters is Ellie."

He frowned at her logic. "You do matter."

She waved away his protest. "Ellie is all that matters. Her safety. Your parents' safety. Your safety." Her voice broke on her last words. "I've brought nothing but trouble into your life."

Now she was being silly. "Rachelle, listen to reason."

She held up a hand. "Carter, I am not under arrest. You can't force me to stay here."

From outside the house a horn blared.

"That's my ride." She zipped up the suitcase and pulled it off the bed. She grabbed her purse and slung it over her shoulder. "Please, just let me go."

"Where are you going?" His heart beat so fast he thought it might jump out of his chest. He wanted to demand she stay put but she was right, he couldn't stop her. She was an adult with the right to exercise the free will God gave everyone. But he wished he could compel her somehow to stay within the protection of his family, within his protection.

She dragged her suitcase across the carpeted floor toward the door. He rushed forward. "Here, let me take that."

He considered holding her suitcase hostage. Instead, he helped her out to the curb, where a black town car sat waiting.

The driver jumped out and came around to take the suitcase and stashed it in the trunk.

Carter wanted make sure the guy was legit. "Let me see your license and registration."

The driver paused with confusion on his face. "Excuse me?"

He heard Rachelle give a little sigh. He didn't care. She was going to be safe no matter what it took.

"Carter." She put a hand on his arm and allowed the driver to slip back into his seat.

He faced Rachelle. A desperate sensation curled through him. She let go of him to put her hand on the rear passenger door handle.

He stopped the door from closing. "Rachelle, this is crazy. Tell me you aren't going back to your apartment."

She gave him a droll look. "Of course not."

"Are you going home to Georgia?"

Letting out a beleaguered sigh, she shook her head. "No. I'll be at The Elms. It has a twenty-four-hour concierge, state-of-the-art security and I have a room high up."

"I should go with you," he said.

"You have no shoes on."

"Give me five minutes to put some on."

She tugged on the door. "Carter, just please let go."

He didn't want to let go. Deep inside he never wanted to let her go. And the realization nearly took him to his knees.

"Call me when you get there," he insisted. "And check in frequently."

"I will. Thank you for all you've done. Keep Ellie safe."

"Of course." His stomach clenched. He wanted to reach out and cup her cheek, to smooth away the worry from her brow. His kept his hands at his sides. "Be careful."

"Of course." She gave him the smile she used on him when she was convincing him she knew what she was doing, or her boss when trying to get the assignment she wanted. Carter realized the truth behind her smile: false bravado. Was she trying to convince the world, or herself?

Yet here she was, making the brave choices anyway.

And he had no option but to let her. He couldn't compel her to stay. He had no say in her life. Short of begging…

"Please reconsider. We can put you in a safe house somewhere else. I can't protect you if you run away."

"I'm not running away. Don't you understand?" Her voice rose. "I couldn't live with myself if something happened to your family because of me. If you can arrange a safe house then I'll go there but until then—" Her lips firmed and steel entered her eyes. She tugged on the door again.

He released the handle and she shut the door. The car rolled away, disappearing around the corner.

Would he see her again?

And his heart ached with the knowledge that he was well on his way to unwittingly falling for Rachelle.

Guilt swamped Carter and he lifted his eyes heavenward. "Lord, I don't understand. How can I allow her into my heart?"

He never understood how it could still beat inside his chest since the day Helen died. He'd been living for Ellie and Ellie alone. Now there was somebody else he wanted in his life. But he couldn't do it. He couldn't dishonor the woman who had given birth to his daughter.

He turned to head back into the house and found his father standing on the porch. "You let her go."

The accusation was like a slap. "I had no choice. I couldn't hold her hostage."

"Do you know where she's going?" Alex asked.

"Yes. The Elms."

"On the Upper East Side? I know the place. It's in a good neighborhood."

"But she's alone and unprotected. I have to arrange for a safe house." He swiped a hand through his hair in frustration. "I'll call the hotel security and make sure they are aware she's in danger."

"Both are good ideas," his dad said. "But more importantly, did you tell her how you feel?"

"How I feel?" Carter moved past his father toward the staircase. "I don't know what you mean."

Alex grabbed him by the arm, stopping him in his tracks. "Don't try to deny it. I know you too well. You love that young lady. But you're just too bullheaded to face the truth."

"I am not in love with Rachelle. I can't do that to Ellie. I can't betray Helen." He needed to build up the walls around his heart once again. To protect himself from pain.

Alex put his hand on Carter's shoulder and turned him so they were face-to-face. The porch light shone on his dad's face, revealing the compassion in his expression. "Son, Helen would want you to be happy. She would want Ellie to be happy. Rachelle makes you both happy."

Carter shook his head in a futile attempt to protest what his heart already knew. Ellie loved Rachelle, and he could if he allowed himself to. "But there's no future for me with Rachelle. There just can't be. I'm not ready to let her or anyone else in, Dad. What if something happens to her?" His voice cracked, and he jerked out of his father's grasp. He ran for the staircase leading to his apartment as if he could outrun the truth of his fears.

"Love is worth the risk," he heard his father say. "Excuses will only leave you lonely."

The next day Carter's stomach hurt, and acrid worry chomped through him as he sat at his desk. Rachelle had called when she'd reached the hotel and had given him her room number as promised. He expected her to check in this morning but so far hadn't heard from her, which caused his blood pressure to rise with every passing second.

Last night, he'd talked to the hotel security and they seemed competent. Still, he didn't like the idea of her alone and vulnerable even for a short time.

He'd spent the past hour arranging for a safe house, which was taking longer than he'd expected, much to his frustration. Jumping through red tape was like eating shards of glass. Nothing was within his control and he hated that he couldn't speed up the process.

From his office doorway, Noah called out, "Miles Landau has been spotted. Everyone is gathered in the conference room."

Carter's heart rate tripled. Finally, if they could get Landau, Rachelle would be out of danger.

Carter rushed to the conference room and squeezed in between Tony and Reed.

"We've had Miles Landau under surveillance," Noah said to the group. "Today he was seen entering the warehouse in Flushing. I just now received word that a detective from the Brooklyn precinct leaned on one of his confidential informants and discovered a way into Landau's crew. The CI's cousin or something. He says Miles has been ranting and raving about a reporter."

Carter's heart froze for a moment, then pounded in big painful beats. The property he'd purchased after he'd served his sentence from the first time Jordan had sent him to prison. Clearly he'd resumed his illegal activities, but he has mostly been obsessing over some reporter...

"He has to be talking about Rachelle." She obviously hadn't given up on doing her own investigating into Miles while at the Elms. "We have to pick him up before he finds her."

"We will," Noah told him. "Unfortunately, he sent thugs out to take care of the problem."

Carter slammed his hand on the conference room table. "How do they know how to find her?"

"I have no idea," Noah told him. "We'll bring the whole weight of the NYPD down on his head. But first we have to get to Rachelle before he and his minions do. I've sent local officers to her location."

Carter was already heading out the door. "I'm heading there now."

Rachelle sat at the desk in front of the window of her twenty-fourth-floor hotel room. She was safe so high up, and the view of the city in the distance was spectacular. There was a watchful doorman and video security cameras everywhere.

Though she missed the Jamesons something fierce, she'd made the right decision. Now there was no chance Ellie could be hurt because of Rachelle.

This time in isolation had given Rachelle an opportunity to finish and turn in the two articles she'd been working on. Her boss had been very pleased with the story she'd done on the celebrity ball fund-raiser for autism. And for her article about the police dog field trials, she couldn't help but highlight Carter and Frosty a bit more than she did any of the other dog and officer teams. They were local heroes and she wanted to make sure everyone knew it.

With both of the stories in the can, she turned her mind back to Miles Landau. She looked at the information on her laptop computer screen. She had found more information on Miles's company. MiLand, Inc. held stock in a trucking company. One that supplied heavy hauling trucks like the one that had tried to crush them on the Queensboro bridge.

Tapping her fingers on the desktop, Rachelle wondered aloud, "What are you up to, Miles Landau? What do a warehouse in Flushing, a boat and a trucking company have to do with Chief Jordan Jameson's murder?"

The hotel's desk phone rang and she froze. No one would call her through the hotel's system. She checked her cell phone on the charger. Three missed calls from Carter. She'd left the ringer off.

She snatched up the receiver and said, "Hello?"

"Why aren't you answering your cell phone?" Carter's terse words were accompanied by the sound of a siren.

"Sorry. The battery died this morning. And I forgot to turn the ringer back on. I turn it off at night when I go to bed." Dread gripped her in a tight vise. "Did something happen? Ellie?"

"Ellie's fine. However, Miles Landau knows where you are. We have to get you to safety. I'm on my way to you now. Almost there. But local officers will be arriving shortly."

Her stomach dropped with trepidation. She stood and paced. "How did he find me?"

"I don't know. What have you been doing that would draw his attention?"

A pang of dismay made her wince. "I've been searching through more public records." She removed the thumb drive she'd used to back up her work from the laptop and shut the device down. "He owns stock in a trucking company that serves the whole Eastern Seaboard."

"You know how dangerous he is. Why do you insist on pursuing your own investigation?"

She could feel the reprimand through the phone line. "You can't tell a zebra to change its stripes," she told him. "I'm a reporter and I am going to find out why Miles Landau wants me dead and how he's connected to your brother's murder."

She thought about the phone call she'd made earlier.

Better to come clean and face his wrath over the phone rather than in person. "So I—uh—called the trucking company Miles has stock in posing as a potential client. I asked the woman who answered about their fees, potential routes and drivers." She looked around the room for a place to hide the thumb drive.

"Is that all?" The exasperation in his tone reached through the line and tweaked her conscience.

Pulse thumping in her veins, she grimaced as she attempted to drag the desk chair beneath the air vent in the ceiling. The phone wouldn't reach. She paused to say, "I asked if I could speak to Miles Landau."

He groaned. "They could have called the number back and found out where you were staying."

"I realize that now," she said. "Hold on." She put the receiver on the desk so she could put the chair under the air vent, then stepped up and slid the small, silver memory stick through the slats. She jumped off the chair and picked up the receiver.

"Rachelle!"

Carter's frantic yelling pierced her ear. "Here. Sorry, sorry. I was hiding the backup of my computer."

"There's a street fair blocking off the road," he told her. In the background she heard music and voices. "We're on foot. Just minutes away. Haven't the local officers arrived?"

"They haven't," she said, the edges of panic closing in on her. "I'll put my shoes on and meet you downstairs."

"No! Stay put. Wait for me."

The sound of the hotel room doorknob rattling raised the fine hairs on her arms. Panic squeezed her chest. She could barely breathe. "Carter, someone's at the door."

FOURTEEN

"**D**on't take any chances—hide!"

Taking Carter's order to hide seriously, Rachelle dropped the receiver and ran toward the bathroom in hopes to lock herself inside long enough for Carter to reach her. She'd taken two steps when a loud thwack reverberated through the room and the door splintered, the locks popping open. Two men entered with guns drawn.

For a split second, she froze in shock. Then self-preservation kicked in and she darted for the bathroom.

Thug One vaulted forward and caught her with big, rough hands. "Oh no, you don't."

Thug Two grabbed her laptop from the desk. "Let's go."

Hoping to buy enough time for Carter to reach her, she resisted, kicking and screaming.

"You're a little wildcat." Thug One shoved her forward. She dropped to her hands and knees. If he wanted to take her, he was going to have to carry her. Instead, he raised his gun, aiming for her head.

"No!" Thug Two shouted. "The boss wants to take care of her himself."

Thug One growled and reached out to yank her to

her feet. He towered over her as he cursed at her and dragged her toward the door.

In an effort to continue to stall them, she said, "I need my shoes."

A feral grin spread over Thug One's face. "You don't need shoes where you're going."

If he'd meant to ratchet up her fear, he'd succeeded.

With his gun pressed into her rib cage, Thug One forced her out of the room and down the hall to the elevator. Her bare toes sank deeply into the surprisingly plush hall carpet she hadn't even noticed before now. She prayed the doors would open and Carter and Frosty would be there. Her heart plummeted when the car arrived empty. Thug One shoved her inside.

"Why?" she asked as the elevator descended.

Neither man answered.

"Miles Landau is your boss, right?" she pressed.

"Shut up," Thug Two said.

"Did he or you kill Chief Jordan Jameson?"

The two men exchanged a confused look before Thug Two repeated, "Shut up."

They reached the lobby and stepped out. Rachelle's gaze sought Robert, the concierge, but he wasn't at his post. Dread seized her and tightened her chest. "What did you do to Robert?" And where was the security team? The police officers?

Without getting an answer, Rachelle was shoved out the sliding doors of the hotel. Frantic, she searched the crowd. Half a block away she spied Carter and Frosty pushing their way through the crowded street as they raced toward her.

The squeal of tires jerked her attention to a black sedan as it halted at the corner.

Thug One jammed the gun hard into her ribs. "This way."

Panicking, she twisted around, her gaze locking with Carter's. "Carter!"

"Halt! Police!" came his cry.

He released Frosty, and the dog raced forward. Thug One raised his gun. Fearing for Frosty, Rachelle rammed her elbow into his side. He let out a grunt, then wrapped his arm around her body, using her as a shield as he hauled her backward toward the sedan that had pulled up, driven by a third man. Thug Two opened the back door and tossed her computer inside. "Move it! Let's go."

Frosty barked and lunged. Thug One jerked Rachelle around like a rag doll, keeping her in front of him. They reached the sedan and the thug climbed in, dragging her with him. Frosty instead latched on to the arm of the other bad guy, snarling viciously and tugging him away from the car as the engine revved and the sedan shot forward, taking her away from Carter, Frosty and any hope of rescue.

Chest heaving with panic and adrenaline, Carter aimed his drawn weapon at the man trying to shake Frosty off his arm.

"Out!" Carter commanded Frosty. The dog released his hold on the assailant and backed up, his tail high and his teeth bared.

"Don't move," he yelled at the man.

Carter watched helplessly as the sedan carrying Rachelle away roared down the street with its horn blaring, forcing pedestrians and other cars to get out of the way. The vehicle careened around the corner and disappeared.

With one hand still holding his gun, Carter used his radio to call in the license plate of the sedan that had just kidnapped Rachelle. The dog whined.

"I know, buddy." They'd failed to protect Rachelle, and he could only imagine the horror of what would happen to her now.

Carter quickly handcuffed Rachelle's attacker. "Where are they taking her?"

The man smirked. "Lawyer."

"Tell me." Carter shook the man.

Frosty growled a warning.

Gaze darting between Carter and Frosty, the man replied, "I said lawyer."

Several police cruisers screeched to a halt in front of The Elms. Carter had no choice but to pass the guy off to another member of the NYPD, who read him his rights before putting him in the back of a cruiser just as Noah arrived along with several other members of the NYC K-9 Command Unit.

Carter told Noah about the sedan that had taken Rachelle away.

"We have to find her," he told his brother.

Noah clamped a hand on his shoulder. "We will, Carter. I'll put out a BOLO."

"The warehouse," Carter said. "He'll take her there."

"We've got the place locked up tight," Noah told him. "Miles wasn't there. Apparently he no longer deals drugs but weapons. We rounded up his men and they all lawyered up."

Just like the other two criminals working for Miles.

"Where are the local officers who were supposed to be here?" Noah asked.

Dread squeezed Carter's chest. "I didn't see them or the hotel security."

Noah's jaw firmed. "We'll search the building for them. And pray they are alive."

Frustration beat a steady pulse through Carter's veins. "Rachelle said something about a trucking company that Miles's company owns stock in."

"That's something," Noah said. "Did she give you the name and location?"

"No. But it would be on her computer in her hotel room."

He whirled and raced into the hotel with Frosty at his heels.

At the elevator, Carter jammed his finger on the call button as he heard Noah saying to the others, "Find the doorman, the security guards and the local officers who were sent to this location. Check the hotel's video and get it to Danielle so we can identify Miss Clark's kidnappers."

The elevator arrived, the door sliding open. Carter and Frosty entered. Before the doors could close, Reed and his dog, Jessie, stepped inside.

"I can't let you go through this alone, man," Reed said.

Appreciating his friend's support, Carter nodded, not sure he could speak without his voice revealing the fear tearing him up inside. What if he didn't reach Rachelle in time? What if he lost her, too?

He couldn't take another death of someone he… He couldn't finish the thought.

On the twenty-fourth floor he stepped out of the elevator and ran down the hall to Rachelle's room. The door hung off its hinges. His heart lurched. He remembered the horrifying sound of the door busting open and Rachelle's screams. He shuddered as nausea roiled through him.

Letting his emotions get the better of him wouldn't help Rachelle. Determined to keep focused on doing the job, he entered the room with Frosty. The dog sniffed the carpet. Behind him, Reed and Jessie entered.

Rachelle's laptop wasn't on the desk by the window. He opened the closet and the drawers of the dresser. "Her computer isn't here." He snapped his fingers. "The thumb drive. She hid one somewhere in here."

The desk chair had been pulled to the center of the room. Her cell phone was on the charger, plugged in to the outlet on the desk. The hotel phone lay on the floor.

While Reed searched under the bed and between the mattress and box spring, Carter circled the chair. Why was this here? He tilted his head back and eyed the vent in the ceiling. Would she have hidden the device there?

He stepped onto the chair and probed at the vent. She could have shoved the USB between the slats. He dug into his duty belt for his multitool. He used the screwdriver portion of the versatile tool to undo the screws holding the vent plate in place. When he removed the plate, a small, silver memory stick fell to the floor. Frosty sniffed at it and whined, no doubt picking up Rachelle's scent from the device.

Picking up the thumb drive, Carter said, "We have to get this to Danielle."

Rachelle wasn't surprised when the sedan pulled into the gravel driveway of Smith's Trucking Company in

Flushing. The same company that Miles Landau owned stock in. She sent up a prayer that Carter would make Thug Two tell them where to find her. She only wished she'd told Carter where she'd hidden her thumb drive in case Thug Two refused to talk.

Sitting in the back seat next to Thug One, who kept his gun pressed into her side, she looked for possible escape routes as a metal gate closed behind the car. They had passed through an industrial area until they reached the compound, which had a high chain-link fence covered over with sheets of corrugated metal preventing anyone from seeing inside. A dozen large hauling trucks were parked in two rows of six. A building near the front looked like the company office.

If Rachelle managed to get away from her captors she could hide in the trucks or go to the office for help. But would she find help there? Most likely Thug One would only catch her or shoot her as she ran or tried to climb the fence. And she doubted there was anyone on the other side to hear her screams. They were pretty isolated at this far end of the borough.

"It's not too late." She sat forward to address the driver, who'd yet to say a word. "You could let me go. The police know about this place. They'll be here any minute and y'all will go to jail."

Thug One yanked her back as the car rolled to a halt. His wide-set eyes held anger in their depths. "When we're done with you, there won't be anything left for the police to find. Now shut up."

A shiver of terror coursed over her skin at his ominous words. She was hauled unceremoniously out of the sedan. Rocks dug into her bare feet as she was pushed toward a metal building at the back of the property.

Biting back yelps of pain, she lurched through the door behind the thug who'd driven them here. The smooth, concrete floor eased the pain in her feet as Thug One continued to poke at her with his gun. She wished Frosty had taken another bite out of the man.

The door clanked closed behind them. Musty and humid, the heat of the day would have been suffocating if not for the large fan whirling overhead, the noise bouncing off the walls. Sunlight filtered through the grimy windows, illuminating the large space. Large crates, stacked two and three high, lined the opposite wall. In the center of the building sat a man at a metal desk. She recognized Miles Landau from the pictures in his police file.

Sweat beaded his bald head. He steepled his hands and stared at her, his dark eyes unnerving. "So you're the pain in my neck. I wanted to see you for myself. You're just a slip of a thing yet so hard to get rid of. Do you have any idea of the trouble you've caused me?"

Thug One shoved her forward. She stumbled a few steps. "Trouble?"

"Yes. My buyers have become nervous from all your snooping." He gestured to the crates. "Now I'm stuck with product I can't move. All because you've been poking around into my life."

"You're back to selling drugs," she said.

Miles barked out a laugh. "I've moved up in the world." He waved a hand toward the crates. "Show her."

"Boss, I think that's not a good idea," Thug One said.

Miles glared at him. "I don't pay you to think."

The driver of the sedan moved to one of the crates and slid the lid off to reveal multiple weapons inside.

"You've become an illegal arms dealer." That wasn't

what had led her to investigate him. "Did you kill Chief Jordan Jameson?"

He narrowed his gaze. "I heard about his death. I can't say I'm too sad as he's the reason I went to prison, but—" he shrugged "—I also would thank him since that's where I made the contacts to start my new business."

Unsure that she believed his protest, she clarified, "Are you saying you didn't kill him?"

"Not me," Miles said. "Is that why you've been snooping into my life? You thought I offed Jameson?"

"You were released only a few days before his death," she said. "You vowed revenge at your trial."

"True. And unfortunate timing, but I didn't kill him." He rose. "However, I won't be able to say the same of you."

Another wave of fear crashed through her. "The police know about this place."

"She's been claiming that all the way here." The driver finally spoke.

"We should just do away with her now," Thug One insisted. "I'll gladly do the deed on behalf of Attilo."

Rachelle thought about the man who now sat in jail after failing to take her at the fund-raising event.

"We can't take the chance that she told the police about this place, too," Miles said. "We have to move. We've already lost the warehouse and the inventory there." He shook his head. "All my hard work destroyed." His lip curled. "I was going to take my time killing you, but now we're in a hurry. Ken, take her out back and don't leave anything for the vultures to take away."

"Gladly." Thug One, Ken, bared his teeth at her like a rabid dog.

She shrank back. "Please, Miles. Don't make things worse for yourself. Killing me isn't going to solve anything."

"Maybe not," Miles said. "But it will send a message to anyone else who tries to mess with me and my operation." He made a rolling gesture with his finger. "Get moving."

Danielle had no trouble accessing the thumb drive's information. Carter grabbed the address of the trucking company and hustled out of headquarters with Reed and Jessie to very end of Flushing where Smith's Trucking was located. They pulled to a stop outside the ten-foot-high chain-link fence lined with sheet metal. Stacking behind them were Noah with Luke Hathaway and Tony Knight along with Carter's youngest brother, Zach.

They gathered at Noah's vehicle. "We'll need bolt cutters," he said, eyeing the fence. "That metal looks thin. Easy to bend."

"Sure hope it's not electric," Luke said.

Carter grabbed a handful of dirt and threw it at the fence. No sparks ignited. "Nope."

"I've got a set in my rig." Tony peeled away.

"Me, too," said Reed.

"Good. I do, too," Noah said. "Zach, you go with Tony and take the west side of the compound. Luke and I will take the east." Noah looked at Carter. "You and Reed head to the back."

"What if they come out the front?" Zach asked.

Noah pointed to the NYPD cruisers pulling up. "Those guys will be waiting to take whoever comes out into custody. They have a stake in arresting Miles, too. The officers that had been dispatched to Rachelle's hotel, along with the hotel security, were found unconscious and tied up in the janitor's closet. One of the officers has a concussion."

Carter was relieved to hear the men were alive.

After retrieving their dogs, the K-9 Unit dispersed.

Carter lifted a prayer they weren't too late to save Rachelle as he and Frosty took off with Reed and Jessie close behind. He kept an eye out for video surveillance equipment but didn't see any.

They reached the back of the compound. Reed cut through the chain-link fence and bent back the sheet of metal and they found themselves facing the backside of a metal outbuilding. They squeezed through, keeping the dogs close.

A low growl emanated from Frosty. Carter gave him the hand signal for silence.

Carter peered around the building, his heart stuttering to a stop at the sight of Rachelle being manhandled by a large, beefy guy—the same guy who'd abducted her from the hotel. He was attempting to drag her toward the fence, but she wasn't making it easy.

Relief that she was still alive and fighting lifted Carter's spirits.

Drawing his weapon, Carter whispered to Reed, "Cover me."

Reed nodded and withdrew his weapon.

Keeping a tight hold on Frosty, Carter stepped out from around the back of the building. "Let her go."

The assailant stilled with one arm wrapped around Rachelle's waist. With his other hand, he reached behind him and produced a gun, which he shoved into her rib cage. "Don't come any closer," he yelled. "I'm taking her with me." He pulled her toward the closest haul truck.

"There's nowhere for you to go," Carter told him. Frosty strained at his lead. "You have nowhere to run."

The door of the metal building banged open and a man came out holding an AK-47 semiautomatic rifle.

"Halt," Reed called as he aimed his weapon at the newcomer.

Without warning, the man holding Rachelle aimed and fired at Carter. The retort of the gun echoed through Carter's head as white-hot pain tore through his leg.

"No!"

Rachelle's cry sliced through Carter's heart. He buckled, going down hard to the ground, losing his hold on Frosty. "Go," he said.

The dog rushed forward.

From all around there were shouts as the K-9 team and officers of the NYPD flooded the compound, quickly subduing the man and leading Miles Landau out of the metal building.

And yet Rachelle's captor refused to give up. He held the gun to her head and backed away. Frosty followed, barking and lunging, but the man was too adept at using Rachelle as a shield.

"Drop your weapon," Noah shouted.

"No way. I'm a dead man if I do," the guy shouted. "She's my ticket out of here."

Carter fought through the agony burning his leg. Using what remained of his energy, Carter lifted his weapon. He met Rachelle's terrified gaze. He prayed she'd understand as he yelled, "Drop!"

Trained to follow the command, Frosty dropped to

his belly. A fraction of a second later, Rachelle went limp in the man's arms, creating an opening.

Fearing for Rachelle and knowing in his heart of hearts that he couldn't fail her now, Carter made a difficult choice and fired, striking the man square in the chest. The man crumpled to the ground and Rachelle was free.

Drained, Carter flopped onto his back and stared at the blue sky overhead.

Then Rachelle and Frosty were at his side. Her lavender scent filled his head. Her soft hands soothed his fevered brow. She gathered him in her arms. Frosty whined and licked Carter's cheek. He wanted to reassure them both he was all right. It would take more than a bullet to the leg to do him in. Yet, he couldn't form words. His tongue felt thick. His brain fogged like a window in winter. A chill passed over him. Fire licked at the wound in his leg.

From a distance, he heard Rachelle's sweetly accented voice calling to him. "Stay with me. Please, Carter. Don't you dare leave me."

I won't. The thought flittered through him. *Lie or truth?*

He didn't know. He couldn't hold on to the light. Darkness pulled, the allure of oblivion, where there'd be no more pain. No more heartache.

But Ellie! Rachelle!

They needed him. He fought to stay in the light, to stay with her, but the last of his strength ebbed into the gravel beneath him.

Darkness settled in, scrubbing the edges off the pain as he lost sight of Rachelle's tearstained face.

FIFTEEN

"Help him!" Rachelle held Carter half on her lap. His head lolled to the side, his eyes closed. There was so much blood on the ground, seeping into the earth from the bullet wound just above his knee. She pressed her hands against his leg, but crimson liquid oozed through her fingers. Her heart stalled out. They were going to lose him.

An ambulance siren split the air.

Hurry, hurry, she silently urged. *Please, dear God, don't let him die.*

Noah rushed to her side. He placed his hands over hers on his brother's leg. "The medics are here."

Two paramedics knelt down beside Carter, nudging her aside. She watched helplessly as they checked his vitals, dressed his wound, stuck an IV in his arm. With Noah's help, the medics moved Carter onto a gurney. She scrambled to her feet and stayed at his side as the men carried him to the back of the ambulance.

"I'm going with you," she told them, and climbed inside the back as Carter was loaded inside. Frosty jumped in with her.

The medic frowned. "Ma'am, that dog can't—"

"It's okay," Noah told the guy. "Let them both go with you." He met her gaze. "When you get to the hospital, call my parents."

She took a shuddering breath as the weight of responsibility and trust being placed on her settled around her like a heavy blanket. "I will. I promise."

He nodded. "I'll be there as soon as I can."

The door of the ambulance shut and the van rolled out of the trucking company parking lot. Through the small windows in the back doors, she saw a handcuffed Miles and his minions being led to a cruiser.

Frosty leaned against her and put his paw on the gurney as if the dog needed to touch his master. She understood.

Carter lay so still. His face was ashen, his lips tinged blue from lack of blood. Her heart lurched.

She gathered Carter's hand in hers. His palm was clammy. She smoothed a hand over his brow as she silently prayed for his survival. Frosty set his snout on her knee as if he sensed her prayers.

When they reached the hospital, medical personnel whisked Carter away, leaving her and Frosty to quickly follow. Her hand tightened around Frosty's lead as the adrenaline of the day seeped away and tears streamed down her face. Furiously she wiped at them. She had to call the Jamesons. She needed to find a phone.

"Miss?" A nurse—Sue, her name tag read—drew Rachelle's attention. "You're bleeding."

"What?" She looked down at her clothes. Carter's blood stained the fabric. Her breath stalled. "It's not mine."

"Your feet."

Glancing at the floor, she noted a trail of blood leading to her bare feet. In the chaos, she'd forgotten about her feet. "Oh." She dismissed her own need for care with a shake of her head. "I need to make a phone call."

"Let me tend to your feet, then you can make your call." Nurse Sue took her to an exam room. "Are you with the police?" She gave Frosty a wary glance.

"Uh, not me. He is, though," Rachelle said as Frosty stared at them. She reached out and he nuzzled her hand. His vest had splotches of blood embedded in the gold lettering. "His handler was just brought in. I have to call his family."

"You don't want to get an infection in your foot. Let's get this done. I'm not going to lie—this might hurt." Nurse Sue treated her feet for a couple of minor cuts, picking out bits of gravel before bandaging the wounds. Emotionally overwrought, Rachelle hardly felt the nurse's ministrations.

Nurse Sue helped Rachelle into a pair of socks and disposable slippers.

Slipping off the exam table, her feet hit the floor with a sting but she ignored the discomfort. "Is there a phone I can use?"

"This way."

Rachelle shuffled after the woman to the nurses' station. Frosty's nails clicked against the hard floor alongside of Rachelle. He sat with his back to the desk as if keeping watch.

Rachelle picked up the receiver and paused as she realized she didn't know the Jamesons' home number by heart. It was stored in her phone back at the hotel. Despairing she'd fail at the promised task, she frantically dialed the number for information only to be thwarted because the Jamesons' number was unlisted. Frustrated, she called the NYC K-9 Command Unit and asked for Sophie Walters.

"This is Sophie." The woman's voice wavered slightly as if she were upset.

"Sophie, it's Rachelle Clark," Rachelle said. "I need Alex and Ivy Jameson's home phone number. Carter was—" Her voice broke. She swallowed back the sob threatening to undo her. "I need to tell them where he is."

"We've heard the news." Sophie sniffled. "I can call them."

"No. I promised Noah I would, but I don't have their number. Please, I need to—" A fresh wave of tears coursed down her face, dripping onto the nurses' station counter.

"I understand." Sophie gave her the number.

"Thank you." Rachelle hung up and quickly dialed the Jameson home.

"Hello," Alex answered.

Hearing his voice made her knees buckle. She clung to the counter and mustered every bit of control she possessed to speak coherently. "Alex, Carter's been shot. He's at New York-Presbyterian Queens in Flushing."

There was a moment of silence, then Alex said, "We'll be right there." The line went dead.

Rachelle hung up the phone, feeling raw and desolate. *Now what?* She pushed away from the counter, with Frosty at her side. They wandered down the linoleum hallway until she paused at the door to the hospital's chapel. She entered and sank onto a bench.

Folding her arms over the back of the bench in front of her, she lowered her head and sobbed. Frosty lay beside her, his head resting on her feet.

She wasn't sure how long she remained there, quietly pleading with God to save Carter. Frosty whined and rose to his feet. Rachelle lifted her head and found Ivy sliding onto the seat beside her.

The knot in her chest twisted. Dread clawed up her throat. "Carter?"

"He's in surgery," Ivy said. "He's going to need a knee replacement, but he'll live."

Rachelle sagged with relief even as more tears fell from her eyes. "I'm so sorry," she whispered.

Ivy's eyes were red-rimmed as she gathered Rachelle in her arms. "This was not your fault."

"But if I hadn't kept investigating—" Her throat constricted with guilt.

"Then you wouldn't be you," Ivy said. "None of us can predict the future. All we can do is trust every moment we have to God."

She leaned away. "I should be the one comforting you." Another wave of guilt crashed over Rachelle. "You were right not to want me in your lives."

Ivy shook her head. "No. I will admit I was wary at first, but we've come to love you, Rachelle. Especially Carter."

Rachelle's breath hitched as pain seared her heart. "No. Not Carter. He told me there was no room in his life for me."

"Don't give up on him yet," Ivy said. "He may need time to adjust to his feelings, but once he realizes the truth…" She smiled. "I can't wait to see what happens."

Rachelle didn't want to burst Ivy's bubble, but Rachelle had no illusions. There was no future for her with Carter.

A beeping sound, annoying and grating, drew Carter through a groggy haze toward consciousness. The scent of lavender filled his lungs.

He knew that scent.

Rachelle.

Heart leaping with the need to see her, his eyelids fluttered open. Light stung his retinas. After several blinks, his focus adjusted on a water-stained ceiling, sterile beige walls and that incessant beeping to his left. He turned his head to see a monitor gauging his heart rate and blood pressure. An IV bag hung from a stand. His gaze followed the tubing down to his hand, where it disappeared beneath white gauze. He was in the hospital.

The scrape of chair legs on the linoleum floor pierced his ear and echoed inside of his head. He winced.

"Easy now."

He knew that voice.

Rachelle. She really was here.

A cool hand pressed against his forehead, soothing and gentle. He sighed and closed his eyes, his mind wanting to sink back into murkiness. He fought against descending into the bliss of oblivion. He needed to see her dear, lovely face.

"Stay down," she said.

Who was she talking to?

Forcing his eyes to reopen, he turned his head to find her standing beside him, her dark eyes filled with worry even as a smile played on her lips. She wore a pink, feminine top and khaki capris. Her dark hair was clipped back at her nape, the long ends draped over her shoulder. Dark circles under her eyes made his stomach clench. Then Frosty's head appeared over the top of the hospital bed, his dark eyes on Carter's face. Joy at seeing them both spread through him, filling all the empty places.

Where was Ellie? He needed his daughter to complete...

"You're awake," Rachelle said. "We were beginning to think you were going to sleep like Rip van Winkle."

Memory of when he'd last seen Rachelle jackknifed his pulse. A man holding her hostage. The searing pain in his leg. The split second to make a decision that would save Rachelle's life. Her tears.

He jerked, trying to sit up but his head was so foggy and his leg felt heavy, weighted down. "Are you safe?" he questioned. He looked toward the closed door. "Why isn't there a guard? You should be under protection."

If anything happen to her...

She stroked his cheek. "Shhh. Everything is fine. I'm fine." She started to turn away. "I need to tell them you're awake."

He lifted a hand to stop her. "What happened?"

She stepped out of his reach. "Let me get the doctor."

As Rachelle hurried from the room, Frosty put his front paws on the bed next to his head and licked Carter's face.

"I missed you, too, buddy," Carter murmured. He lifted his head and looked at his legs. They were covered with a blanket, but the left knee was propped higher.

The door to the room opened and a man in a white lab coat, a stethoscope around his neck, walked in. He was in his midforties, medium height with jet-black hair and kind hazel eyes.

Behind him, Rachelle slipped back into the room and leaned against the wall, out of the doctor's way.

"Off," Carter instructed Frosty. The dog retreated. "Down." Frosty settled on the floor, his gaze on Carter.

"Well, it's good to see you're alert, Officer Jameson. I'm Dr. Garcia. I've performed your surgery."

"Nice to meet you, I guess," Carter said. "I was shot in the leg."

Dr. Garcia nodded. "Yes. We extracted the bullet from your knee. You lost a lot of blood and you're going to be weak for a little while, but your prognosis is good."

"My knee?" That didn't sound good.

"We reconstructed your left knee. It'll be a while before you'll have full function of your leg. You'll need physical therapy once you're healed enough."

Anxiety twisted in Carter's chest. "Will I be able to walk again?"

"Yes," the doctor said. "However, you may not have full function of your left leg to the same capacity you did prior to your wound."

Carter wasn't sure what to make of the doctor's words. He was just glad that he hadn't lost his leg. But what would that mean for his career with the NYC K-9 Command Unit?

Dr. Garcia made notes on his chart. He noticed Rachelle and smiled. "I'll leave you in good hands."

Rachelle dragged a chair close to the bed. She took his hand in hers. "Your family is waiting to see you. But I just wanted a moment to tell you thank-you. You saved my life." She let out a small, rueful laugh. "Again."

"Miles?"

"Arrested and in custody," she told him. "His men turned on him. They confessed to being a part of Miles's newly formed crew. Apparently, Miles had decided while in prison to take up a new profession as an arms dealer."

"Did he confess to killing my brother?" He held his breath, hoping they'd solved Jordan's murder.

Rachelle shook her head. "No, he denies any connection to Jordan's death. And so far there's been no evidence to put him at the scene of your brother's murder."

Disappointment punched him in the gut. So they were back at square one. But at least Rachelle was safe now.

He thanked God for that huge favor.

"Carter, I—"

A commotion at the door cut Rachelle off as his family pushed through the door.

"Daddy!"

His daughter's sweet voice made his heart leap with joy. Rachelle stepped aside, allowing Ellie to rush the bed. Noah followed and picked Ellie up so that she could lean over to kiss Carter on the forehead. His parents, Zach and Violet and Katie circled the bed.

"Hi, sweet pea. I love you," he told Ellie.

Her bright blue eyes sparkled with tears. "I love you, Daddy. We were all so scared."

He looked at every face in the room. His family. He was a very blessed man. Tears of gratitude gathered in his eyes.

Rachelle slipped behind Noah and Ellie, pausing to say something to Katie and then she walked out the door. Frosty stood and stared after her.

Carter wanted to call her back but Ellie was talking and his head began to pound as pain flowed up his leg. He did his best to listen as each person took a turn to speak to him. He appreciated the love and support even as he gritted his teeth as the ache in his knee intensified.

"Okay, everyone," Ivy said. "We need to let Carter rest."

She urged the others out of the room. His father remained at his side and gathered his hand in his.

His mom came back and sat in the chair Rachelle had vacated. "You're quite the hero."

"Just doing my job," Carter said, his voice cracking.

"Not the way Noah tells it," Alex said. "And you know he's not one to give a ton of praise."

Yes, his stoic brother who didn't like to let his emotions show. If Noah called his actions heroic...

"How long will I be in here?"

"Doc said at least another week," his dad replied.

Carter frowned. "How long have I been here?"

"Three days," his mom said. "And Rachelle has hardly left your side."

"That young lady loves you," his father stated.

Overwhelmed by the thought and the agony rippling through him, Carter turned his head. "I'm tired. My knee is on fire."

His mother patted his hand. "I'll tell the nurse."

But Carter doubted the nurse would bring him anything that could deaden his feelings for Rachelle.

With deep, welling satisfaction, Rachelle sat in her apartment holding a copy of the *NYC Weekly* newspaper and stared at the front page. Her article detailed her ordeal with Miles Landau and the heroic efforts of the NYC K-9 Command Unit, and specifically Officer Carter Jameson and his partner, Frosty, in taking down the arms dealer and keeping this reporter alive.

Her article on the front page! She wanted to dance around the room in joyous abandon. She wanted to shout from the rooftop. She wanted to tell Carter.

Instead she sank farther into the cushions of the couch and grabbed another cookie.

With a sigh borne of heartache, she set the newspaper aside and picked up her computer. She wanted to buy a thank-you present for the Jamesons for all they had done for her. And a gift for Carter and Frosty.

Better to buy something for the dogs. It would be less complicated, have less meaning. No, not less meaning. She owed her life to Frosty, as well as Carter.

She admired and respected the great dogs and men and women of the NYC K-9 Command Unit.

But most especially Carter.

She blew out a frustrated breath. No matter what she did or how much she'd tried over the past three days, she couldn't eradicate Carter from her thoughts. Or the feelings that had flooded her when all the Jamesons had joined her and Carter in his hospital room. There'd been an outpouring of love and support among them and between them.

Leaving her feeling like an outsider.

The familiar sensation had nearly drawn her to her knees right there. Instead, she'd made a quick exit.

She just had to face the knowledge that she'd always be an outsider, no matter where she went or whom she was with.

Maybe some retail therapy would help. The computer was open on a page for dog paraphernalia.

First a little something for Frosty, Scotty and the puppies and the Jamesons, then a little something for herself.

As she scrolled through the various items the cutest thing caught her eye. She smiled.

That's the ticket!

And she placed an order.

SIXTEEN

"Five days," Carter fumed at the doctor reading his chart. "I've been here five days. I want to go home."

And at least twice every day he had picked up the phone to call Rachelle and then talked himself out of dialing her number. He didn't know what to say. He'd never been good at small talk. But it wasn't really the small talk that was the problem. He had a problem telling her of his feelings and broaching the subject of their relationship. He wasn't good at talking about the big stuff.

Dr. Garcia smiled. "You are making great strides. Your blood pressure has normalized, and your blood volume has come up significantly. Alonzo tells me your PT is going well."

Carter snorted. "You mean the torturer torturing me is going well."

Dr. Garcia chuckled. "Yes, physical therapy can be painful."

Carter arched an eyebrow. "That's putting it mildly."

But he was motivated to be able to walk again. He had Frosty to think about. He needed to get back out in the field eventually. Though every time he thought about returning to his beat, Rachelle's words echoed in his head. *Why would you stay in a career that puts you in harm's way? What if something happened to you?*

A bout of panic stole over him. Carter held it in check. The last thing he needed was to go see the department psychologist. Or maybe it was the best thing he could do. Yes, he decided, he would seek help from the department's psych doc.

He didn't want to be a statistic with post-traumatic stress disorder, flinching every time he thought about work.

There was a knock on the door to his hospital room.

Dr. Garcia replaced his chart. "I will come back and check on you later."

He left and in strode Reed Branson and his partner, Jessie. The big female bloodhound trotted at Reed's side.

"Hey, buddy," Reed said. "How are you doing?"

Carter pinched the bridge of his nose. "I've been better. Tell me something interesting. Fill me in on what's going on at the command unit."

Reed pulled up a chair. "Mostly business as usual. There have been reports of a German shepherd matching Snapper's description seen with a bunch of teens at Coney Island. We're going to check it out." He stroked one of Jessie's ears.

Carter's heart jumped with hope. "Ellie still maintains she saw him in Prospect Park."

"Everyone is keeping an eye out for him," Reed said. "We'll do our part. Jessie's tracking skills are top-notch."

"If we could find Snapper that would be a huge blessing." Carter hated to think they'd never see the dog again. "I wish I wasn't stuck here. Frosty and I would go with you."

"I'd like nothing better," Reed said. "Soooo," he drew out the word. "Rachelle."

Carter glanced at his buddy sharply. A stab of fear hit him in the chest. "What about her?"

"Haven't you heard the good news?"

"What good news?"

"She has a job interview with the *New York Times.*"

Surprise and pleasure erupted inside Carter's chest, melting the fear away. "That's great." He wondered why his parents and his brothers hadn't mentioned it. Probably because every time they brought Rachelle up, he shut them down. He sighed. "I'm so proud of her."

"Did you read her article about you?"

Carter glanced at the stack of *NYC Weekly* newspapers on the bed tray. He still couldn't believe she mentioned him, calling him a hero and touting his and Frosty's finesse. His heart swelled with affection when he read and reread the articles she'd written. And every time, he tamped the tender emotion back into the box of things he'd rather not deal with.

"She's got a thing for you, you know." Reed waggled his eyebrows.

"Yeah, that's what everybody keeps saying. But I don't believe it." More like he didn't want to believe it. Because if she cared for him, she'd only end up hurt in the end, because he couldn't…

"Dude, she would hardly leave your side. After you were shot, she was the one who ran to you and put her hand over the wound. She rode in the ambulance with you and Frosty. And she stayed here until you woke up."

"I understand she needed to make sure I was okay,

because I saved her life. And then she left." Without saying goodbye or anything. He'd been surprised by the hurt that had burrowed in deep after her abrupt departure.

"Did you ask her to stay?"

"She didn't give me a chance."

Reed tucked in his chin. "There's this thing called a phone. You could call her and ask her to come back."

Carter shook his head. "I would only interrupt her life. Complicate it. I don't want to mess up what she has going for herself."

Reed shook his head. "I never thought you'd be one to hide from the truth."

Carter stared. "What do you mean, hide from the truth? I'm not hiding from anything."

Reed rubbed his chin. "Maybe not, but maybe you are hiding from your own truth."

His friend's words dug deep inside of Carter, breaking loose something he'd tried so hard to ignore, to deny. Something he'd been hiding. He did love Rachelle.

But the truth was he couldn't do anything about it. He just couldn't. He wasn't brave enough, no matter what Rachelle had written about him.

Two days later, Carter was finally home. At least to his parents' apartment. He wouldn't be able to take the stairs to his, Ellie's and Noah's apartment quite yet. His dad had built a wheelchair ramp so that they could wheel him through the front door of their place.

A chorus of "Welcome home" erupted and echoed throughout the house and inside his heart. There was a Welcome Home banner stretched across the wood beam separating the dining room from the living room. There was a cake on the table.

He searched for Rachelle but she wasn't there. Disappointment lay heavy on his heart even as he smiled and opened his arms for Ellie to climb up onto his lap.

"Hey, munchkin."

"Welcome home, Daddy. We love you."

His heart swelled with love for his daughter and those gathered around.

There was a scratch at the back door.

His mother hurried over and opened the door. Frosty, Scotty and Eddie rushed in, followed by the growing bundles of fur that were the puppies. Honestly, they had doubled in size since he'd last seen them. Frosty ran to the side of the wheelchair and propped his paws up on the arm of the wheelchair. Carter leaned over and nuzzled the dog. Frosty licked his face. Everyone laughed.

Carter drew back and looked at Frosty. "What is he wearing?"

Frosty had a black T-shirt with white lettering that read, "I'm the big dog, don't mess with me." Scotty had on a T-shirt that read, "I'm the other big dog, don't mess with me."

Ellie slipped off his lap and picked up one of the puppies. "Rachelle sent them."

Ivy picked up the other. "Aren't they adorable?" Ivy asked.

Each pup had on a navy T-shirt that had gold lettering that read, "K-9 In-Training."

He looked at the puppies then back at Frosty. He laughed. "That is so thoughtful and funny and so Rachelle."

His heart ached with missing her.

"Somebody get this man some cake," his father said.

Later, after the party, Carter sat with Noah and Zach in the living room while Ellie helped his mom clean up in the kitchen and his dad was out back with the dogs.

"We invited Rachelle," Noah stated.

"Let me guess," Carter said. "She declined." His stomach clenched. He couldn't blame her.

Noah's jaw tightened. "She did. Citing she had to work. But really I think she was being stubborn."

"Stubborn?"

"Yes, just like you're being," Noah chastised.

"I don't know what you're talking about."

Zach punched Carter on the shoulder. "That woman loves you—we all know it."

Noah sat on the coffee table in front of Carter and placed his elbows on his knees, steepling his fingers, looking like he was settling in for a lecture. "Brother, you know we love you. And so you have to understand this comes with love."

Uh-oh. Noah was using the *L* word—this was pretty serious.

Zach nodded. "You're our brother. We want to see you happy."

"Like you're happy?" Carter suggested.

Zach grinned. "Exactly. I am blissfully happy. Violet is the best thing in my life."

Carter looked at Noah. "Don't tell me you believe in love."

"Not for myself, but I can recognize it when I see it. You love Rachelle and she loves you. And you're both being stubborn and idiotic." He ran a hand through his hair. "All I'm saying is, you have a chance at something wonderful with a wonderful woman. Don't blow it."

Carter's heart thumped against his rib cage. "Her career is taking off. She's interviewing with the *New York Times*. I would only hold her back."

Zach scoffed. "It's not like she moved away. She can have her dream job and be with you and Ellie."

"But what if her career takes her somewhere else?" He knew he was grasping for an excuse not to accept their words.

Zach made a choking noise. "What's bigger than the *New York Times*?"

Noah narrowed his gaze on Carter. "You're afraid." He nodded his head, satisfied with his assessment. "Yeah, that's it. Carter is afraid of love."

Carter gripped the handrails of the wheelchair.

"No. I loved Helen. I love Ellie."

Zach put his hand over Carter's. "Brother, what's holding you back?"

Carter slipped his hand out from under Zach's and grabbed the wheels and pushed but the wheels wouldn't budge. He wanted to get away from them, get away from this line of questioning. But the brakes were on the wheelchair. Giving up on rolling away, he tried to push himself to his good foot but his brothers pushed him back down into the chair.

"You're not going anywhere until you face this," Noah said in his most commanding tone.

Trapped, Carter spit out, "Fine. I'm afraid." The confession burst from him. "I'm afraid of losing her. I'm afraid of loving and going through the kind of pain I had when Helen died."

Zach nodded. "I understand. I really do. When Violet was being threatened, I knew my life would end if something happened to her."

"But you saved her. You protected her," Carter said.

"Just like you did for Rachelle," Noah pointed out. "Just as you would in the future."

"But what if something happens that I can't control?" Carter's voice broke. He hadn't been able to protect or save his wife. Her death had been out of his control.

Zach and Noah looked at each other. Then back at Carter.

"You know what Mom says," Noah stated.

"Only God's in control," Zach finished.

Carter had heard his mother and others say this his whole life. But accepting the words took faith and he wasn't sure he had enough faith for a second time.

He felt a hand on his shoulder and looked up at his mother. Beside her, Ellie clutched her hand. "Son, we love you. We all love you and we know Helen would want you to be happy."

His dad had said the same thing. But was it true?

Ellie climbed up into his lap and took his face between her little hands and stared into his eyes. "Daddy, do you love Rachelle?"

He could never lie to his child. Emotion swelled in his throat. He swallowed convulsively before he could speak. "Yes, honey, I do." The admission allowed peace to flow through him. No more hiding from the truth.

A beaming grin broke out on his daughter's face and she let out a loud whoop before she slipped her arms around his neck and hugged him.

"I do, too," Ellie whispered into his ear. He could feel her wet tears on his neck.

The back door opened and his father walked in, along with five curious dogs.

Frosty sat next to him and whined; clearly the dog

sensed that Carter was upset. Carter patted Frosty re-
assuringly.

"What's going on in here?" Alex demanded.

Noah stood up and clapped his dad on the back. "I'll
let them explain. I need to get back to the command center." He whistled for Scotty, who followed at his heels
as Noah strode out the door.

Zach rose, and his dog, Eddie, a floppy-eared bea-
gle, hurried to his side. "Violet's upstairs with Katie.
I'm going to go see the ladies." As he and Eddie passed
by Carter, Zach squeezed his shoulder "Proud of you,
man."

While Ivy filled in Alex, the puppies barked and
raced around the room, a cute distraction.

"Daddy?"

Carter looked into his daughter's serious gaze. "Yes,
sweet pea?"

"Don't you think we ought to go tell Rachelle?"

He chuckled. Leave it to his daughter to point out
the obvious. "Yes, I think we should."

Ivy clapped her hands. "We'll drive you."

"Now?" Carter questioned with a laugh.

"No time like the present," Alex interjected, grabbing the back of the wheelchair and unlocking the
wheels.

"Can the dogs come, too?" Ellie asked as she climbed
off her father's lap.

"Sure, why not?" Carter said. "Let's make this a
family affair."

They loaded him up into the wheelchair-accessible
van that his father had rented.

"Do you mind if we stop at a store on the way?"
Carter asked.

Ivy beamed at him. "Flowers! Good thinking, son."

That hadn't occurred to him. But flowers would be good, too.

But he had something else in mind, as well.

Rachelle completed the finishing touches on the article about the zoos in the five boroughs, then hit Submit, and off the document went to her editor at *NYC Weekly*.

She hoped and prayed at some point she'd be able to write a story about how the NYC K-9 Command Unit finally closed the case on Jordan Jameson's death and captured the villain who'd taken their chief, friend and family member's life.

Maybe even for the *New York Times* if they called her back for a second interview. She thought the first one went well. She'd had other news sources calling, showing interest, but she quickly realized they only wanted insider information on the K-9 Unit and the Jameson family specifically. She shut down those inquires fast and hard.

A knock at the door startled her. She wasn't expecting anyone. She opened the door to find Carter sitting in a wheelchair, a brown paper bag in his lap and a bouquet of flowers in his hand. Ellie stood on one side of him, her sweet little face beaming, and Frosty on the other side of Carter while Ivy and Alex stood behind him, each holding a puppy.

The dogs were wearing the T-shirts she'd sent them. Her heart raced. Happiness to see the Jamesons had her pulse tripping over itself. "This is an unexpected surprise."

Frosty trotted in and sniffed around.

"May we come in?" Carter asked.

Where were her manners? "Of course, please."

She stood back. Alex handed off his pup to Ivy, then pushed Carter into the middle of the living room. Ellie rushed forward to wrap her arms around Rachelle.

Heart thumping, Rachelle bent and picked her up in a tight hug. Fighting back tears, she set Ellie down as Alex gave Rachelle a quick hug before taking Ellie by the hand and backing out of the apartment to stand next to his wife in the doorway.

"We'll be out here in the hall," Ivy said, and she grabbed the door handle and shut the door.

Surprised and a bit wary, Rachelle turned to Carter. "I don't understand? Why are they not coming in?"

For a long moment, Carter just stared at her. There was a look in his eyes that made her both nervous and thrilled at the same time.

He thrust out the bouquet of gerbera daisies. "These are for you. I didn't know what kind of flower you like. But these were the brightest and prettiest. Ellie thought that you would like them."

She took the flowers and hugged them to her chest. "I love them. Gerbera daisies are actually one of my favorite flowers. And you're right, so vivid. All the pinks and oranges and yellows. They can brighten any gloomy day."

Carter frowned. "Are you having a gloomy day?"

She didn't want to tell him she'd been having many gloomy days lately. Ever since he'd been shot.

"It's my fault," he said.

"What? What are you talking about?"

"Your gloomy days," he said as if he'd somehow read her thoughts. "I'm sorry, Rachelle. I have to confess something to you."

The wariness turned to dread. "Should I be sitting down?"

He gave her a wry smile. "No, this isn't anything earth-shattering. I'm sure it's something you already suspect."

Wanting to stall whatever he had to tell her, she moved into the kitchen to grab a vase. Her hands shook as she filled the vase with water and put the flowers in and carried the vase to the dining room table. Finally, she bolstered her courage and turned around. "Okay. Tell me."

Carter licked his lips. He looked at the bag he was holding. He held the bag out to her. "Oh, this is for you, too."

Curious what he'd bring her in a brown paper bag, she took the bag and peeked inside. Surprised pleasure spread through her as she lifted out the almond-based ice cream.

"How did you know?"

"You didn't think I noticed that you don't drink or eat dairy. But, Rachelle, I notice everything about you." His voice turned husky with emotion. "I see you for who you are. A kind, compassionate and loving woman."

Tears gathered in her eyes as she stared at him. "This is the sweetest thing anyone has ever done for me."

His eyebrows rose. "Aw, Rachelle. That breaks my heart to hear that giving you ice cream is the nicest thing anybody's ever done. If you let me, I will do so much more for you, for us."

She blinked as tears fell down her cheek. "Carter, what are you saying?"

"I'm saying I've been afraid. Too afraid to allow my heart to open up to anyone except my family. I realize that isolating myself wasn't being fair to Ellie or to the memory of Helen."

Rachelle sucked in a breath. "You still love your wife."

"Yes," he said. "I always will. But I know Helen would want me to make room in my heart for more love. She would want me to be happy." He held out his hand. "You make me happy, Rachelle."

She couldn't believe what she was hearing. Words she'd longed to hear her whole life.

Carter let his hand rest back on the wheelchair arm. "I would understand if you don't feel the same. But I just need you to know that I love you."

Her feet felt rooted to the spot. All the love she felt for him welled up until her throat closed and she felt like she would pass out from the lack of oxygen. A gentle nudge at her knees drew her attention away from Carter. Frosty pushed her gently toward his partner. It was all the encouragement she needed.

She closed the distance between her and Carter and went down on her knees next to his wheelchair. Setting the ice cream aside, she looked at him with all the love and joy she possessed. "I love you, too, Carter."

He breathed out a breath and smiled as he framed her face with his hands and leaned in to kiss her. His lips molded exquisitely against hers.

For a long moment, she lost herself in the sensations rocketing over her and through her, heart beating with joy and love.

Frosty let out a single bark.

The tiniest squeak of the front door alerted her before there was an eruption of clapping and whooping as Ellie, Ivy, Alex and the puppies charged inside the apartment.

Reluctantly, Rachelle drew away from Carter with a bemused smile.

He stared at his family. "Were you listening at the door?"

Alex pointed to Ivy. She shrugged, totally unrepentant.

"Does this mean you're going to get married?" Ellie asked as she squeezed in between Rachelle and Carter, wrapping an arm around each of them.

Rachelle met Carter's gaze, her breath caught in her lungs as she waited for his response.

"If she'll have me," he said.

"Yes. Yes, a thousand times over," she answered.

Ivy clapped her hands again. "Another wedding. I'm so excited."

"We're going to have to wait, though," Carter said. "I want to be able to stand at the altar. Without crutches."

Remembering something Katie had said about wishing she and Jordan had had more time to get to know each other, Rachelle nodded. "I don't mind waiting. It'll give us an opportunity to get to know each other better without all the drama and danger."

Carter frowned. "It won't be that long. I'll double my PT regimen and do whatever I can. Maybe in a month or two?"

"That's perfect," Ivy said, pulling Rachelle to her feet for a hug. "We'll have to go dress shopping right away."

Overwhelmed with joy, Rachelle felt like she was going to burst.

Carter captured her hand. "You won't just be marrying me," he said, his gaze intent and serious. "You will be joining our family, which includes the NYC K-9 Command Unit."

She touched his cheek. "I couldn't ask for more."

Carter turned his head and kissed the palm of her hand.

* * * * *

Valerie Hansen was thirty when she awoke to the presence of the Lord in her life and turned to Jesus. She now lives in a renovated farmhouse on the breathtakingly beautiful Ozark Plateau of Arkansas and is privileged to share her personal faith by telling the stories of her heart for Love Inspired. Life doesn't get much better than that!

Books by Valerie Hansen

Love Inspired Suspense

True Blue K-9 Unit: Brooklyn

Tracking a Kidnapper

True Blue K-9 Unit

Trail of Danger

Emergency Responders

Fatal Threat
Marked for Revenge

Military K-9 Unit

Bound by Duty
Military K-9 Unit Christmas
"Christmas Escape"

Classified K-9 Unit

Special Agent

Visit the Author Profile page
at Harlequin.com for more titles.

TRAIL OF DANGER

Valerie Hansen

Train up a child in the way he should go:
and when he is old, he will not depart from it.
—*Proverbs* 22:6

Special thanks to my fellow authors
Lynette Eason, Dana Mentink, Laura Scott,
Lenora Worth, Terri Reed, Sharon Dunn,
Shirlee McCoy and Maggie K. Black, as well as to our
editor, Emily Rodmell. This was a wonderful group
of women chosen to portray the courage
and dedication of NYC officers and K-9s.

It was a true honor.

ONE

Abigail Jones stared at the blackening eastern sky and shivered. She was more afraid of the strangers lingering in the shadows along the Coney Island boardwalk than she was of the summer storm brewing over the Atlantic. Thankfully, the air wasn't uncomfortably cool. It would be several months before she'd have to start worrying about the street kids in her outreach program during frigid New York weather.

Early September humidity made the salty oceanic atmosphere feel sticky while the wind whipped loose tendrils of Abigail's long red hair against her freckled cheeks. If sixteen-year-old Kiera Underhill hadn't insisted where and when their secret rendezvous must take place, Abigail would have stopped to speak with some of the other teens she was passing. Instead, she made a beeline for the spot where their favorite little hot dog wagon spent its days.

Besides the groups of partying youth, she skirted dog walkers, couples strolling hand in hand and an old woman leaning on a cane. There was no sign of Kiera. That was troubling. So was the sight of a tall man and enormous dog ambling toward her. As they passed beneath an overhead vapor light, she recognized his police uniform and breathed a sigh of relief. Most K-9 patrols in her nearby neighborhood used German shepherds, so seeing the long floppy ears and droopy jowls of a bloodhound brought a smile despite her uneasiness.

Pausing, Abigail rested her back against the fence surrounding a currently closed amusement park, faced into the wind and waited for the K-9 cop to go by. His unexpected presence could be what was delaying Kiera. Street kids were wary. Once he and his dog were far enough away, the teenager would probably show herself.

"Come on, Kiera. I came alone, just like you wanted," Abigail muttered.

Actually calling out to the girl would be futile. Between the whistling wind and small groups of rowdy youth, there was no way she'd be heard. "Too bad I left my bullhorn at home," she joked, intending to relieve her own tension.

Kiera had sounded panicky when she'd phoned. That was concerning. *Ah, but she's a teenage girl*, Abigail reminded herself. *They can be real drama queens.*

"Here. Over here," drifted on the wind. Abigail strained to listen. Heard it again. "Over here."

The summons seemed to be coming from inside the Luna Park perimeter fence. That was not good since the amusement facility was currently closed. Nevertheless, she cupped her hands around her eyes and peered through the chain-link fence, trying to make out a human figure among the deep shadows. It was several seconds before she realized the gate was ajar. *Uh-oh. Bad sign.* "Kiera? Is that you?"

A disembodied voice answered faintly. "Help me! Hurry."

Abigail's heart was in her throat. If the teenager was inside the park, she was trespassing. Looking around nervously, Abigail gave the gate a slight push and it swung open on squeaky metal hinges. An icy shiver shot up her spine despite the muggy night. Something was definitely wrong. "Kiera?" Her mouth was cottony, her insides quivering. "It's Abby. I'm at the gate. You shouldn't be in there. Come on out."

As an outreach coordinator for troubled teens, Abigail was basically charged with taking care of those who came into her office. However, her past had been rough enough to compel her to respond to the girl's summons and venture out tonight. That was one of the reasons she was so successful. She was able to personally identify with the street kids she was trying to aid.

And this one sure sounded as if she was in trouble. "Kiera. Come out."

"Help me."

There it was again. A plea that Abigail could not ignore. She'd have to trespass herself in order to set the girl straight about respecting the law.

Checking to make sure the officer and his dog were far enough away to keep from spooking the girl, Abigail sidled through the gate. Although she could have enlisted his aid, she didn't want to give Kiera the mistaken notion that she had broken her promise and called the police.

Lingering odors of popcorn and other food would have been a lot more pleasant fresh. "Kiera? C'mon, honey. We shouldn't be in here. Let's go back to the boardwalk."

Pausing, Abigail listened. Thunder rumbled. Wind whistled. Paper trash that the cleaning crews had missed tumbled along the ground and began to pile up against the fences and bases of the silent rides.

Abigail couldn't help feeling edgy. She, who took pains to never break the law, was currently doing so. Yes, she had a good reason, but that didn't mean it was legal. She looked heavenward briefly and prayed, "Please, Father, show me what to do now?"

A noise to the far left startled her. She froze, straining to listen and peering into the shadows. Lightning flashed. In that instant she did see a person. Two people, to be exact. And they were men. *Imposing men.* Neither of them looked a bit like the slim young girl she was seeking.

Then, the men stepped apart and a third figure appeared between them. This person did resemble Kiera and seemed to be struggling to break away. Of all the situations Abigail had faced in her troubled past, this was the kind she'd most feared. The scenario that had given her untold nightmares.

Despite being unarmed and alone, she knew she had to do something. *What?* How could she possibly rescue Kiera, or whoever the smaller person was, without weapons? Fear urged flight. Duty insisted she act. Good sense demanded both.

How long had it been since she'd seen the police officer and his dog? Maybe she could return to the gate and call him back to rescue the captive.

But first, she had to distract the kidnappers, slow them down. Ducking behind a post, she took full advantage of the deep shadows, cupped her hands around her mouth and yelled, "Let. Her. Go!" It worked so well she almost cheered. The men froze and stared in the direction of her voice.

As she pivoted to make a dash for the gate, lightning illuminated the area around her like the noon sun. Someone shouted, "There she is! Get her!"

Oh, no! Abigail's heart leaped. She stumbled and almost went to her knees trying to get a running start. Her pulse was pounding. Her body felt numb, as if it belonged to a stranger.

She gasped, nearly falling a second time. Shouts were getting louder, closer, more menacing.

Almost there!

A gloved hand reached past her and shoved the gate closed, blocking her exit. Someone had a death grip on the back of her lacy vest. She twisted and shed the garment. Her attacker flung it aside and grabbed her arm.

She ducked and wrenched. Pulled and flailed. It was no use.

Finally, she filled her lungs and screamed. High, loud and repeatedly. "Help!"

Officer Reed Branson's K-9 partner, Jessie, stopped plodding along with her nose to the boardwalk, lifted her broad head and looked back.

"What is it, girl?" Reed also listened. Whatever his K-9 was hearing was too faint for human ears. Nevertheless, he trusted his partner and reversed their direction. They could try to pick up Snapper's trail later, assuming the latest supposed sighting of the missing police dog was a valid lead. So far, none of the other tips had turned up the valuable and beloved German shepherd.

Jessie picked up speed, ears flopping, hips swaying beneath rolls of extra hide meant to protect her in battle. He strained to hear despite the rushing wind and the dog's panting. His demeanor as he passed small groups of teenagers this time was different enough to scatter them. Adults cast wary glances and shied away, too.

Jessie led him straight to a gate at Luna Park. The chain was unfastened, the padlock hanging open on the wire mesh. He reached for his mic and identified himself, then said, "Ten-thirteen at entrance C, Luna Park. Possible break-in."

Dispatch answered in his earpiece. "Copy. Ten-thirteen. Requested assistance dispatched. Advise on a ten-fifty-six."

Good question. Did he need an ambulance as well as police backup? He hoped not. Hot summer nights were notorious for mischief and simmering tempers, whereas cold weather kept many New Yorkers off the boardwalk, particularly when rain was threatening. This night was a mix of both. Unpredictable.

Reed tightened his hold on Jessie's leash, pushed open the gate and undid the snap on his holster, just in case. The seasoned K-9 was on high alert, stopping to check out a small item of clothing crumpled on the ground. Reed picked it up. It was pristine, not like something that had been discarded when the park was last open. Instinct told him it was time to put Jessie to work. He presented it to her.

She was sniffing, showing eagerness to track, when a muffled noise in the distance put her hackles up and she gave voice as only a bloodhound can. Her mix of a growl, bark and then deep howl carried throughout the park, bouncing off the uneven surfaces to echo back as if a dozen hunting dogs were pursuing fleeing game.

The hardest thing for Reed, as a handler, was convincing the born and bred tracker to be silent. He laid a hand against the side of her muzzle. "Hush, Jessie. Quiet."

Slurping and drooling, she danced at his feet, mouth only temporarily closing. That was enough. Reed heard it now. A woman's scream. He grabbed the mic again as he gave Jessie her head and broke into a run. "I'm ten-eighty-nine, foot pursuit, inside Luna Park. I can hear a woman screaming."

The high-pitched protest continued, then broke off, then started again. Reed lengthened Jessie's lead but kept a firm hold of her leash so she wouldn't race into danger alone. She wasn't trained as an attack or protection dog, meaning she was nearly as vulnerable as whoever was yelling for help.

Except dogs have big teeth, he countered. Judging by the tone and volume of the screams he'd heard, this victim was not only female but likely young.

Suddenly, the night went silent. Jessie slowed, tilted her head to the side and tested the air for odors. Reed strained to listen. Nothing.

He gathered up the extra length of leash and gripped the handful tightly, every sense keen, every muscle taut. His K-9 acted puzzled for a few seconds, then started to strain to the left. Their quarry, or victim, or whatever, was apparently on the move.

Reed presented the vest again, braced himself, commanded, "Seek!" and they were off like a shot.

Abigail kicked and clawed and threw herself from side to side, trying to break loose as the first man picked her up like a sack of potatoes and jogged through the park to where the other waited. Frantic, she searched the dimness for the smaller person she'd spotted earlier.

There was no sign of her or him. That was some relief. Now she could concentrate on her own escape without worrying about collateral damage to anyone else. "Let go! You're hurting me."

Her captor set her on her feet, kept hold of her wrist, and focused on his partner. "What happened to the other one?"

The second man snorted. "Almost got away. I was tyin' her to a post so I could go help you when she ran off. I caught her and locked her in the car trunk."

"As long as that took you, it's a good thing I didn't need any help." Shoving Abigail forward, he cursed.

The second man huffed wryly. "Hey, you ain't the boss."

"Neither are you."

"Never mind that. What made you think it was a good idea to bring that one back here where she could see my face?"

"Your ugly face, you mean. I had to do something with her, didn't I? She was watching us when we…"

"Shut your yap. You ain't got a brain in your pin-head."

"Oh, yeah?"

"Yeah."

Abigail felt a slight lessening of his grip. The more the two thugs concentrated on each other, the less attention they paid to her. It took enormous effort to relax her arm and give the impression she was no longer struggling to break free.

"So, what're we gonna do?"

"How should I know?"

"What about keepin' this one? A bird in the hand?"

"Too old. See?" The captor released her arm and

started to grab her shoulders, apparently intending to turn her around for his partner's inspection. Before he could get a fresh grip, Abigail continued her spin, kicked one of the men in the side of his knee and punched the other in the stomach.

Neither blow was serious but together they were enough. Abigail ducked, dodged and sprinted away. Adrenaline gave her speed and made her feel invincible. For a few seconds.

Then they were after her again. Shouting. Cursing at her and at each other. Abigail had barely enough breath to keep going. Her initial burst of speed was waning fast. Where could she hide? How close were they? She didn't dare look back.

The night became surreal. Surroundings blurred as if she were navigating a nightmare. An impressive antique carousel loomed ahead. Despite knowing the ride was closed, she imagined seeing its wooden horses prance and paw the air. Her brain whirling, her lungs fighting to fill, she made a critical decision.

After vaulting over a low decorative fence, Abigail gained the circular platform with a leap and made a lunge for the closest steed. Her arms closed around its carved nose and she used her momentum to swing past to the second row. The horses grew uniformly smaller as she worked her way toward the center control booth. It had a door she could close. Even if it wouldn't lock, maybe her pursuers would overlook her in there.

Abigail jumped down and landed with both palms against the mirrored center pillar. Circled looking for the camouflaged door. Found it. Threw herself inside and pulled it closed behind her, stumbling backward as she did so and landing against a bank of switches.

Suddenly, calliope music began, slowly rising in speed and volume until the air vibrated. Had she bumped something? Accidentally flipped a switch? Was her hiding place useless? Undoubtedly. And it was already too late to stop the music. The damage had been done.

Stunned, she clamped her hands over her ears, pressed her back against a side wall and began a slow-motion slide to the floor as sheer panic began to dull her senses and render her helpless.

The walls pressed in on her. Reality receded as her mind shut down, and she gladly accepted the enveloping darkness of unconsciousness.

TWO

Reed and Jessie had detoured past the Shoot-the-Chutes when the calliope music had begun to play, starting low and winding up to quickly gain intensity. During the day when the park was crowded and other attractions were operating, the distinctive tunes blended in. Tonight, the solo music was deafening. And eerie, particularly since the rest of the ride wasn't lit or moving.

Jessie would have tried to climb the sides of the water ride and plunged through the cascading stream if Reed had not guided her around. The screaming had stopped. As painful as it had been to hear someone in that much distress, this was far worse. Silence could mean the danger had eased, but he knew it was more likely that things had worsened. A screeching victim was a breathing victim. It was as simple as that.

Reed approached a low fence that kept riders from cutting the line. A hand signal sent Jessie leaping over and he followed. Man-sized shadows shifted on the opposite side of the wide, round platform. Reed looked to his dog, read her body language and drew his sidearm. "Police. Freeze."

The figures froze all right—for a heartbeat—then parted and dashed off in opposite directions. Not only could Reed not pursue them both, he still didn't know where the screaming victim was or how badly she may have been injured. Finding out came first.

"Seek!"

Jessie led him in a weaving pattern between horses while Reed radioed his position and circumstances. The K-9 went twice around the center pole of the carousel before stopping and putting her enormous paws up on one of the beveled mirrors.

"Sit. Stay," Reed commanded. The door release was cleverly hidden but he found it. "Police," he announced, his gun at the ready.

The hair on the back of his neck rose and perspiration trickled down his temples. He pulled open the narrow door and struck a marksman's pose with his gun and flashlight.

Instead of the panicking, wild-eyed victim he'd expected, he saw a small figure curled up on the cement floor. His light panned over her. She had long, reddish hair that made him think she was a teen until he took a closer look.

He'd seen that face. Tonight. She'd passed him on the boardwalk not more than a few minutes ago. She was no kid but she wasn't middle-aged either. Reed guessed her to be younger than he was by five or ten years, which would put her in her twenties. What in the world was she doing out here in the middle of the night in the first place?

Holstering his gun, he bent and lightly touched her arm. Her skin was clammy. "Ma'am? Are you hurt?"

There was no reaction. The woman didn't even act

startled when he held her wrist to take her pulse but he did notice that the fair skin looked irritated. "Can you tell me what happened?"

Still nothing. He could hardly hear himself speak over the rollicking pipe organ music. A quick scan of the control panel showed one switch out of place, so he flipped it to kill the noise. Propping the narrow door open for ventilation he stood with one booted foot outside and radioed in the details as he knew them. "That's right. She's really out of it. I don't see any serious signs of physical trauma but I can't get a response, so you'd better start medics. The victim may have internal injuries or be drugged. I'm pretty sure she was the one doing all the screaming."

He paused and listened to the dispatcher, then stated his case. "Jessie acts like this is the same person she was tracking before, and I have no reason to doubt my K-9. Put a rush on that ambulance? I don't want my victim to code while I wait, okay? I'm going to take a chance and move her out onto the carousel floor where she can get more air. Tell backup to hurry."

One more check of his surroundings and a long look at his dog assured Reed the area was clear. He bent and gently lifted the victim in his arms. She was lighter than he'd imagined. "Take it easy," he said, speaking as if to a frightened child. "I'm a police officer. You're safe now."

She stirred. Her lashes quivered.

Reed placed her carefully on one of the chariot bench seats. It was too short for her to lie down all the way so he propped up her feet and lowered her shoulders, bringing more circulation, more oxygen to her brain.

She blinked and stared directly at him. He had expected at least a tinge of leftover panic but there was none. The woman didn't even flinch as she studied him.

He gave her a minute to process her thoughts, then asked, "What happened to you? Why were you screaming?"

"Screaming? I don't think…" She coughed. "My throat hurts."

"I'm not surprised," Reed told her. "What's your name?"

The blue eyes widened and filled with tears. "It's— it's Abigail. I think."

Abigail's instincts told her to trust this man even before she realized he was wearing an NYPD uniform. He had kind brown eyes and his expression showed concern. What struck her as odd was her sense of overall peace and security in his presence.

Looking past him, she saw elaborately carved wooden carousel horses that reminded her of the ones on the restored antique ride at Luna Park. *Luna Park?* What she was doing there? And why was a police officer acting as if he thought she needed help?

"Abigail?" he asked softly. "That is your name, right?"

"Of course it is." Affirmation came easily.

"How about a last name?"

"Um… Jones?"

His lopsided smile made his eyes twinkle. It was clear he didn't believe her. Thoughts solidified in her muddled mind and affirmed her choice. "It really is Jones. I'm sure it is."

"Okay. How are you feeling? Are you hurt?"

Abigail worked her shoulders and rubbed her right

arm. "I think I pulled a muscle." Her eyes widened. "Did you see something happening to me?"

Reed shook his head. "Sorry. No. By the time I got here you had stopped screaming and were hiding. All I saw were shadows."

He paused, studying her so intensely that it made her ask, "Shadows? Of who? What?"

"Don't you remember?"

Her earlier peace was giving way to the uneasiness of the unknown. How much did she remember? And why did she feel a creeping fear when she tried to draw those memories out?

Head throbbing, she sniffled and pressed her fingertips to her temples. "I don't know anything." She concentrated on her rescuer. "Why can't I remember?"

"Trauma can do that sometimes. It'll all come back to you after a bit." His radio crackled and he replied. "Copy. Tell them to pull as close as they can to the carousel. She's conscious but disoriented."

Abigail grasped his forearm. "What's wrong with me?"

"The ambulance is on scene. Medics will look you over and take good care of you from here on."

He leaned away and started to stand but she held fast. "Don't leave me. Please? I don't even know who you are."

"Officer Reed Branson." He reached into his pocket and handed her a business card. "Hang on to this. It'll help you remember me later. I'm part of the NYC K-9 Command Unit, not a detective, so I won't be investigating your case, but you may have questions for me once you get your memory back."

"Canine?" She peered past him. "Where's your dog?"

A hand signal brought a panting, pleased-looking bloodhound to his side, where it sat obediently, staring up at him as if he were the most important person in the world. That tongue, those floppy ears, the drooling lips. Abigail almost gasped. "I remember him. I saw him somewhere."

"Out here. Tonight," Reed said. "We passed you on the boardwalk. And it's *she*. Jessie is a female."

"She found me?"

"Yes. She heard your calls for help before I did. That led us into the park, where we found this." He pulled a crumpled crocheted vest out of his pocket. "Is it yours?"

"Yes!" Abigail was thrilled to recognize it.

"Jessie used it to follow your scent. I'm a little surprised she was able to do it so well with this storm brewing. Wind can throw trackers off."

Abigail's headache was intensifying to the point where it was upsetting her stomach. She knew she wouldn't have ventured out at night, alone, without a valid reason, so what was she supposed to be doing?

She tried to stand. The carousel and objects beyond began to move. At least, she thought they did. Given her undeniable unsteadiness, she wasn't sure if the platform beneath was spinning or if her head was. Or both.

Instinct urged her to reach out to the police officer, to draw on his strength. Instead, she covered her eyes with her hands. "I'm sorry. I get terrible headaches when a storm is coming but I've never had one this bad before."

Someone—was it her rescuer?—cupped her shoulders and guided her to the edge of the circular platform where other gentle hands lifted her down and placed her on a gurney. She could smell the bleach on the sheets. A bright beam of light stabbed into her eyes.

Abigail tried to cover her face again but someone was restraining her. A wide strap crossed her upper torso and tightened. She began to struggle. Being held so still was frightening, although she couldn't pinpoint a reason for her rising panic.

"No! Let me go!"

A low masculine voice cut through her protests and brought calm. Large hands gently touched her shoulder. "Easy, Abigail. It's okay. They're just trying to help you."

"Don't let them strap me down! Please!"

"All right." She saw Reed casually wave the medics away. "I'll be right here. Nobody will have to restrain you as long as you lie still. Understand?"

"Uh-huh."

"Good. Now let them take your blood pressure and pulse, okay?"

A strong urge to resist any involuntary movement of her arms arose as soon as one of the medics began to work on her again. Thankfully, this tech was a woman who made short work of checking her vitals, listening to her ragged breathing with a stethoscope and reporting to a doctor via radio.

The numbers quoted didn't matter to Abigail. All she cared about was having the police officer close by. It didn't occur to her that he wouldn't be able to climb into the ambulance with her until he stepped back at its door.

She reached out. "Aren't you coming?"

"Can't." The attendants paused while he explained. "I have a responsibility to Jessie, not to mention my reason for being out here tonight. I was in the middle of a different search until you screamed."

No matter how logical his answer was, she couldn't

accept it. "Promise you'll follow me? You're the only one who has any idea what happened out here."

"You'll be fine once you're under a doctor's care." The way he patted the back of her hand as he spoke reminded her of a parent trying to soothe a child who was throwing a tantrum. That unfortunate comparison was hard to take, particularly since her head was still pounding and her vision blurred whenever she moved.

Abigail jerked her hand away, turned her head and closed her eyes. "Fine. Go. Save the rest of the world if that's what you want." Tremors wracked her body. Nobody had to tell her she wasn't herself. Her conscience was doing a good job of that without any outside help. Harsh words and snappy retorts were not her usual reactions to difficulties, nor was she sarcastic. People at work were always complimenting her on her even temperament.

Work? Yes, work! She was an outreach coordinator for AFS, A Fresh Start, and helped homeless and troubled teens. That she remembered well. She could picture the tiny office in Brighton Beach, her desk stacked with file folders, and even the potted violet plant atop the bookcase beneath the window.

"That's better," she whispered with a sigh, not expecting anyone to take notice.

The female medic smiled. "Good to hear." She held out a clear plastic mask fitted with a narrow tube. "Just let me give you a few breaths of oxygen and you'll feel even better."

The plastic contraption hovered over Abigail's face. There was a continuing urge to resist being treated, but now that she'd recalled more about her life, she'd settled down enough to control herself. "Okay."

Elastic straps held the mask in place. She took several deep breaths.

"That's it. Nice and slow." The medic was hovering over her, looking directly into her eyes. "Now, the law says I have to secure you before we can hit the road, so here come the straps again. I'm sorry to have to do it but I could lose my license if I didn't make sure you were safe."

Abigail inhaled more of the enriched air, then lifted the mask to speak. "I'll try to behave. I promise. I don't know what came over me before."

"Leftover trauma, if I had to guess," the woman replied pleasantly. "I almost wouldn't mind trading places with you if I could get Reed Branson to look at me the way he looked at you just now."

"That cop?"

"Oh, yeah." She chuckled as she tightened the safety strap. "What a hunk."

"I didn't notice."

"Really?" The medic fitted her with an automatic blood pressure cuff and checked the flow of oxygen to the mask, then smiled. "Maybe you need your vision checked, too."

Reed's first duty was to notify acting chief Noah Jameson that he had diverted from his tracking assignment in order to intervene in a crime. Then he checked in with fellow police officers while they were still on scene. Some had dispersed to search the shadowy amusement park while others guarded the carousel and busy crime scene techs. The Coney Island boardwalk was relatively safe most of the time but it did draw a rougher element late at night, particularly in warm weather. A hot summer or fall day brought out every troublemaker in the state of New York at night. Or so it seemed.

Adding to the foreboding atmosphere, wind-driven rain began pelting the rides and the ground as if bent on settling a score with humanity. Reed kept Jessie fairly dry under the canopy of the carousel while CSIs dusted the control booth mirrors for fingerprints and filled tiny plastic envelopes with dust and debris from the floor of the wooden turntable.

"Needle in a haystack?" Reed asked a familiar crime scene investigator.

"More like a needle in a stack of other needles. There's virtually no chance we'll scoop up usable clues. They've probably blown all the way to Flatbush by now."

Reed nodded. "Agreed. Sorry I didn't get a better look at the guys who tried to grab the victim."

"Any chance this is connected to the rash of disappearing teens?" the CSI asked, pausing to glance up at him.

"Remotely. This victim looked pretty young until I got up close. You'd think anybody who was after kids would be able to tell the difference, though." He scowled. "I'm sorry she had to go through this, but she probably stood a better chance than an inexperienced kid would have."

"Do you know her?"

"Not the way I know you and most of these others." Reed indicated a group of NYPD regular officers sweeping the area with flashlights and sloshing through puddles. "Going by what she told me after Jessie tracked her down, her name is Abigail Jones. That's so common I didn't believe her last name until the medics found ID on her."

"Jones? I wouldn't have bought that, either."

"Are you about done here?"

"Why? You got a hot date?"

Smiling slightly, Reed denied it. "Nope. Just wondered. Chief Jameson released me and I thought I'd check on the victim before my shift ends."

The man chuckled. "Your car is going to smell like wet dog, Branson."

"Probably. It often does."

Reed had a standard-issue yellow slicker and a modified cover for Jessie, too. In his Tahoe SUV. Three blocks away. He sighed, waved goodbye to the friendly tech and stepped off the carousel.

Big drops were still falling so close together it was impossible to stay dry. Jessie snapped at a few of them as if it were a game. "You're thirsty, aren't you girl? Hang in there. I'll pour you a drink as soon as we get back to the car."

Because he was paying close attention to his dog, Reed noticed a slight change in her behavior as they walked up the street. That was part of being a K-9 handler. He and the dog were supposed to read each other without fail. And right now Jessie was acting as if she sniffed something familiar. Since Abigail was long gone, Reed could only surmise she was getting a whiff of the thugs.

He delayed radioing his suspicion until he had walked a little farther, following his dog until she paused at a curb and turned in circles several times. When she looked up at him he could tell she was disappointed.

"Well, you tried, girl," Reed said. "And I forgot to reward you the last time, didn't I?" Handing the K-9 her favorite toy, a piece of frayed mooring rope, he ducked into a doorway to call dispatch. "This is Branson, K-9 Unit. Jessie just led me to an empty parking space. It's in front of a falafel stand on West Fifteenth almost to Surf Avenue. There's a tourist trap with souvenirs next to it. We may see something on surveillance cameras if we pull up tonight's recordings."

"Copy. I'm showing you on West Fifteenth Street a little north of Bowery."

"That's affirmative. I'm about to head for the hospital to check on the victim, then I'll be ten-sixty-one. It's been a long night."

"Copy that."

Visions of Abigail's pale blue eyes and ginger hair remained vivid, not that he was pleased to have noticed. His life was complete. He had the perfect job, a peaceful private life and the best tracking dog in the unit, maybe in the whole state. The K-9s and his fellow officers, which included his sister, Lani, as a rookie, were all the *family* he needed. Theirs was a dangerous profession. Just look at what had happened to his former boss, Chief Jordan Jameson, six months ago.

The entire NYC K-9 Command Unit was still mourning deeply, as were others. Losing Jameson had been hard to accept, especially for Zack, Carter and Noah Jameson, Jordy's brothers. The glue of respect and friendship that had held their unit together had been sorely tried after Jameson's murder and Noah's interim promotion into his vacated position.

The killer had been clever, even leaving a suicide note, but Jordy's team of officers hadn't bought it. Between the four branches of the K-9 Unit—Transit, Emergency Services, Bomb Squad and Narcotics—they had all the expertise they needed to pursue the truth. To help homicide solve the crime, one way or the other. No one in his unit was content to sit back and wait for results from other divisions.

Yet life went on. It was true that New York City never slept. Reed knew what his duty was and did it to the best of his ability. Now and then, however, a puzzle came along that fascinated him enough to seek answers on his own time, such as, what had happened to Abigail Jones tonight.

THREE

"I just want to go home," Abigail kept telling anyone who entered her hospital room. What was wrong with these people? Why were her wishes being ignored?

The graying patient in the other bed snorted as a harried nurse beat a hasty retreat. "Might as well save your breath, sweetie. You ain't gettin' out of here tonight."

Desperate for someone who would listen, Abigail fought tears of frustration as she said, "I don't understand why they won't discharge me. They did a brain scan and the doctor told me there was no damage."

"I believe he said, 'No visible damage.'"

"Same thing."

"Not hardly." The other woman coughed. "I heard him asking questions. You didn't have a lot of answers." Another cough. "You hidin' from an abusive man or avoidin' the cops?"

"Of course not!" *I'm not my mother.*

"Okay, okay, don't get your jammies in a twist. I was just askin'. What happened to you, anyway?"

Abigail chewed on her lower lip before admitting, "I don't know. I remember getting ready to leave the office. The next thing I knew it was dark and I was looking up at a stranger."

"Did he hurt you? If he did, you gotta report it, you know. We can't clean up these streets if we don't all do our part."

"I know," Abigail said sadly. "I work with homeless teens all the time."

"So what really happened to you? You can tell me. I won't breathe a word."

Frustration took over. Her voice rose, then cracked. "I don't know! I can't remember."

As she took a shaky breath there was a knock at the open door and a man in a dark blue uniform entered the room. No, not *a* man, *the* man. She might not recall anything else from her ordeal but she'd never forget Reed Branson. Or his dog.

He smiled, dark eyes twinkling. "Good to see you awake and recovering."

"Yeah. I'm pretty happy about that, too." Abigail mirrored his expression. "They tell me there's no brain damage but they won't let me go home."

Approaching her bed, he pulled up a chair and sat. "Do you know where you live?"

"Of course I do. I have an apartment in Brighton Beach."

He held up his hands, palms out. "Okay, okay. Just asking. What else have you managed to remember since I found you?"

"Not a lot." Abigail sobered. "I was just telling my new friend here that it's a blank."

"I heard part of that before I came in."

"You were eavesdropping?"

"Not exactly. You'd be surprised how often we overhear a lot more than people are willing to disclose officially. I'm not the enemy, Ms. Jones. We really are sworn to protect and serve."

Sighing, she nodded at him. "Well, at least you know I'm not holding back. I'd give almost anything to remember what made me walk over to Coney Island at night. I'm usually more cautious. Any big city like ours will rise up and bite you if you're not careful, I don't care whether you're a native or not." Studying his face, she noticed a small scar on his chin and wondered if he'd gotten that in the line of duty. Rather than spoil his looks it gave him a rugged edge.

"Will you be all right when you do go home? I mean, do you live in a secure building?"

"Why?" She inhaled sharply when she fully grasped his implication. "You don't think anybody will come after me there, do you?"

"Probably not. I wish I knew more about the guys who were manhandling you tonight, though."

"So do I." Mulling over her predicament, she added, "I can only hope I'll recognize them soon enough to protect myself if I see them again."

"Tell you what," Reed said. "I'll go look your place over on my own time if the department doesn't send another officer to do it. How's that sound?"

Abigail frowned at him. "Why are you being so nice to me? You don't even know me."

"I'm not real sure," he admitted with a grin. "Maybe because my being in the right place at exactly the right time to rescue you seems like such an odd coincidence. Plus, I had Jessie with me. She did all the tracking. I just followed her lead. That strikes me as providential, if you get my drift."

"Why did you say were you down on the boardwalk?"

"Jessie and I were sent to follow up a tip on a missing K-9 that means a lot to the department, to my unit. Snapper is a highly trained German shepherd who used to be the chief's partner."

The flash of grief she saw pass over Reed's face took Abigail by surprise. She could understand missing a dog as if you'd lost a friend, but the officer's emotions seemed stronger than that. She had to ask. "What happened?"

When Reed swallowed hard and said, "Chief Jordan Jameson was murdered by a person or persons unknown. Snapper was his K-9 and has been missing since," her stomach knotted. He wasn't merely looking for a lost dog, he was searching for a cop killer. That made all her troubles pale in comparison.

"I'm so sorry."

"Thanks. Me, too."

Before Abigail could decide what to say next, the handsome K-9 officer got to his feet. "You take care. I'll get your address off your file, then speak to your super and make sure your apartment is safe before you're discharged. I promise."

He wheeled and was gone before she had time to decide to stop him. Pride urged her to object to having her privacy violated but good sense intervened. There was nothing secret in her life, nothing that anyone could hold against her.

Except my childhood, she added. Those records had been expunged but she hadn't hidden her past when she'd applied for the job at A Fresh Start. If anybody could understand street kids, it was her. Success proved it.

The image of a pretty blonde teen popped into her mind. Kiera Underhill was one of her toughest cases, a girl with a chip on her shoulder the size of Lady Liberty's torch.

Abigail shivered despite the warm room. Thoughts of Kiera were unduly disturbing for some reason. A sense of foreboding had settled over her like winter fog, yet the harder she tried to access her locked mind, the more blank it became.

She scooted down in the bed and pulled a sheet over her head, blotting out the world the way she had as a little girl.

Irony brought unshed tears. If she was going to forget something traumatic and painful, why couldn't it be her childhood?

It had been several days since Reed had visited Abigail in the hospital. Why was he having so much trouble getting the pretty redhead out of his thoughts? They had no actual connection other than their accidental meeting at Luna Park, unless you counted the city's problem with homeless kids and Abigail's job assisting them. He'd had more than one difficult encounter with young teens along the boardwalk and in nearby neighborhoods like hers. Many were victims who put on a show of being capable and happy while hiding their true situation. They found safety in numbers, yes, but get one of them alone and you could often glimpse the fear lurking behind a facade of bravado and arrogance.

When he tried to phone Abigail at home and got no answer, he left messages, which she apparently ignored. Checking with her place of employment didn't help either. She'd been put on medical leave.

Consequently, he decided to visit in person, parked as close as he could, about three blocks west, and walked over with Jessie. Reed let her sniff along the narrow sidewalk because she wasn't on duty. Street-side trees that had once enhanced the old neighborhood crowded the four-and five-story brick apartment buildings as if in a battle for dominance. Eddies of sand and trash waited against the curbs for city trucks to sweep away.

After reaching Abigail's building, he found her name on the tenant list and pushed the worn brass intercom button. "Ms. Jones? It's Reed Branson." There was no answer, no buzz to unlock the front door. He tried again, speaking more slowly and identifying himself as a K-9 officer. The result was the same.

Not good. Even off-duty he needed to watch his professional image, so he hesitated before randomly pushing other buttons. A tenant leaving solved his problem. Reed grabbed the edge of the exterior door before it could close behind the other man, nodded pleasantly and slipped inside with Jessie.

Reed chose to take the stairs to the third floor rather than chance riding an elevator that was probably older than his grandfather. The halls were swept clean, which was a plus, but the ancient building exuded an aura of age and use. Cooking odors seeped into the hallways, reminding him of the street fairs he'd attended around the city.

His knock on Abigail's door was not demanding— until he got no response.

He called to her. "Ms. Jones? Abigail? It's Reed Branson. And Jessie. Are you all right?"

Still no answer. He knocked again. Louder. Called out to her. "Abigail?"

Frustration made him want to force his way in but what if she simply wasn't home? A quick trip back downstairs and he was knocking at the superintendent's door.

An apartment dweller across the hall stuck her graying head out of her own apartment and gave him a scathing look. "Hush. You're spoiling my show. I was about to find out if Reginald really murdered his half brother."

It took Reed the space of several heartbeats to realize she was referring to the plot of a daytime soap opera. "Sorry. But I can't get the tenant in 312 to come to the door and I'm worried. Do you know if she's gone out?"

"Not likely. She would have said. Does she know you?"

"Yes." Since he was in civilian clothes he flashed his badge wallet. "Officer Reed Branson. I was the one who helped her when she ran into trouble a couple of nights ago."

"Well, in that case, thank you." She stepped out. "I'm Olga Petrovski." A ring of keys jingled in her hand as she locked her door behind her. "That poor girl's a basket case and nobody seems to care. She's turning into a worse hermit than she was before. Doesn't even have a cat for company. Can you imagine?" The woman led the way up the stairs, surprising Reed with her ease of movement in broken-down shoes that looked as if they were about to fall off.

"You have keys? I thought Mr. Rosenbaum was the super."

"He is. But he's in Jersey visiting his daughter. When he's gone, I handle the building." She squinted at Jessie. "That dog better be house-trained."

Reed paced her. "She is. Jessie's a police officer, too, K-9 unit. We're just not in uniform today."

They reached Abigail's door. The woman knocked gently. "Abby, honey. It's Olga. You need to open up so we can check on you. Please?" Casting a worried look at Reed, she spoke aside. "Like I said, I look after her and she never goes out these days. She has to be in there. You didn't scare her, did you?"

He shrugged. "Not purposely. She seemed to be doing pretty well when I saw her in the hospital right after the incident but she's not returning my calls." Glancing at the woman's fisted hand he said, "I think you should use your key."

She did. The door swung open slowly. "We're coming in, dear. It's Olga and…"

"Officer Reed Branson," he called. "I brought K-9 Jessie, too. I'm sorry to disturb you."

Still there was no reply, no sign of the apartment's occupant. Heavy drapes were pulled, shutting out most of the available daylight. The odor of pizza or something equally spicy lingered, although he couldn't spot takeout containers. Abigail Jones's home was spotless yet unwelcoming. She had created her own dungeon and locked herself away in it.

Reed unclipped Jessie's leash and quietly ordered, "Seek."

Seeming to sense the need for finesse, Jessie didn't give voice to her quest. She merely snuffled along the carpet, clearly on the trail of something or someone. Reed came next, followed by the acting super.

The K-9 entered a bedroom and circled the bed, then barked once at a closet door. Reed moved in. "Abigail?

Ms. Jones? It's the police. Your friend Olga from downstairs is here, too. She let us in."

He eased open the door.

Abigail pulled her knees closer. Instinct warred with the part of her mind that knew there was no real danger. She wanted to stand up and act more normal, but some inner power refused to let her move.

A clicking pattern on the bare floor jarred her. She heard heavy breathing and her heart stopped for a moment before she realized the noise was a dog's panting. A broad wet nose poked through a crack in the door. *The bloodhound!*

Jessie panted against Abigail's cheek, then slurped her ear with a tongue wide enough to cover it. That was enough stimulus to snap her out of her fugue.

She focused first on the affectionate hound and rubbed her droopy, velvety ears, then forced herself to look up at Reed and Olga. "Hi."

"Hello," Reed said.

Olga followed with, "Are you all right, hon?"

The ridiculousness of her location triggered Abigail's wry wit despite feelings of unease and embarrassment. "Fine and dandy. I always sit on the floor of my closet. Doesn't everybody?" When Reed offered his hand, she took it and let him pull her to her feet. "In other words, no."

"I get that," he said. "How about coming out here with us? I'd like to have a talk."

Abigail managed to overcome lingering reluctance by keeping one hand atop the dog's broad head. "I'm sorry I caused worry. It's just... I don't know. For some reason I couldn't make myself come to the door when you buzzed and then knocked."

"How about my phone calls? I left messages. Did you get those?"

"I—I must have. I probably didn't recognize your number and I didn't listen to anybody who had a deep voice."

"I'll go make some coffee," Olga offered. "You two have a seat and visit."

Abby chose the sofa, relieved as the police officer took an easy chair. Even in jeans and a polo shirt instead of his uniform, he had the bearing of someone in command. Someone to trust and lean on in times of trouble. Beyond the fact that she found him handsome, there was an unexplainable attraction. That, she attributed to his heroic actions. Why wouldn't she admire somebody who had rescued her the way this K-9 cop had?

To her delight, Jessie jumped onto the couch and plopped her enormous head in Abigail's lap. It was a relief to rhythmically stroke the tan fur. "I think she likes me."

"No doubt. Are you feeling better now?"

"Yes. Thanks. I don't know what came over me."

Reed sobered. "Have you seen a doctor since you left the hospital? It's normal to be uptight after a traumatic event, but it's troubling to see you so fearful. I think you should seek professional help."

Her hand stilled. "You think I'm crazy?"

"No, no." Reed leaned forward, elbows resting on his thighs, hands clasped between his knees. "What I'm trying to say is that sometimes we need to talk it all out, to try to make sense of whatever has happened to us. Posttraumatic stress can hit anybody. Surely you've seen it in some of the homeless kids you work with."

She nodded.

"Then you know it's not a sign of weakness, Ms. Jones, it's a manifestation of your mind's self-defense mechanism. We all get scared sometimes. It's when we get stuck in that emotional state that it becomes a problem."

Abigail's fingers slipped under Jessie's collar and she wiggled them. Pure bliss filled the dog's soulful brown eyes and she actually sighed in contentment. Searching for a smidgen of similar peace, Abigail asked, "So why don't I remember my attackers?"

"Short-term amnesia, I assume. A health care professional can tell you more."

"No way. I can't afford to be judged mentally unstable. It might cost me my job. I won't abandon those kids. It's bad enough that I've stayed home as long as I have."

"Surely no one holds that against you."

Abigail huffed. "I do. I haven't been able to push myself to set foot out of this apartment all weekend."

"The trip home from the hospital went all right?"

"Yes, but I thought…"

He leaned closer. "What? You thought what?"

"You're going to think I really have lost my mind. I thought I heard the voice of one of my attackers on my way home in a taxi."

"The driver?"

"No, no. Passing on the sidewalk. A man yelled and he sounded so menacing I almost jumped out and ran."

"Where was this? What street?"

"I'm not sure. I covered my eyes."

"I can take you over the same basic route, if you want. Maybe he lives or works around there."

She was so astounded by his suggestion, she was temporarily speechless. Finding her voice, she finally said, "Do you think I *want* to find him? No way. If I never run into him again it will be too soon."

Even as she was speaking, Abigail somehow knew a repeat encounter was possible. It didn't matter how big the city was or how carefully she moved through it, she could meet her attacker again. And until her memory recovered, she was a sitting duck for any evil he had planned. If only she could remember more. Put faces and descriptions together and help the police.

But those memories were all gone, sunken into an abyss of her own making and leaving her a prisoner in a cell with invisible bars.

FOUR

Watching Abigail unwind while petting Jessie gave Reed an idea. If she continued to refuse to see a doctor about her mental hiccup, perhaps he could help her another way.

"Jessie sure took to you. You must be a dog lover, too."

He noted a flush of her cheeks. "I don't really know. I mean, I've fed strays before but I've never had a pet of my own."

"Not even when you were a kid?"

The warmth he'd sensed was swept away by a scowl and a shake of her head. "Sometimes I wonder if I was ever a child."

Concerned, he regarded her soberly. "You're serious."

"Very."

"Care to explain?"

"Not really."

Although Abigail rested her hand atop Jessie's head, Reed noticed that she had ceased stroking. The friendly bloodhound did her best to encourage further attention, finally rolling onto her back, all four paws in the air, tail thumping the sofa cushions.

Reed waited for Jessie's antics to relax Abigail again

before he mentioned his idea. "Since you're so naturally good with dogs, how about volunteering to foster one of our extra pups."

She scowled at him. "Do *what*?"

"We received an amazing working dog as a gift from the Czech Republic. Unfortunately, there must have been a miscommunication because Stella delivered a litter soon after she arrived."

"What does that have to do with me?" Abigail looked so astonished he decided to play up the underdog, literally.

"After her pups were weaned and tested for various abilities, most of them qualified for our training program and are being fostered." Reed paused for effect. "One little female is right on the cusp of flunking out and we'd like to find her a new foster home to see if lots more one-on-one attention helps. I'm not asking you to commit to giving her a permanent home but it will help her develop to her full potential if she's well socialized and loved while she's young."

Abigail was shaking her head. "I have enough problems without adding a puppy."

"You wouldn't have to keep her. Just get her off to a good start."

"Me? I can hardly handle my own life these days and you want to add an impressionable youngster to it?"

Shrugging, Reed blew out a breath that was so evident it even caught Jessie's attention. "I just figured, since you were so good at rescuing needy kids, you might be willing to do the same for an innocent animal."

Judging by the way Abigail was looking at him, Reed could tell she wasn't totally buying his analogy. "It's true. All of it," he insisted. He pulled out his phone and paged through the photo files, smiling and holding it out for her to view once he located the shot he wanted. "This is Midnight. Look at those sad eyes. How can you refuse to help her?"

The instant Abigail saw the picture, her whole body reacted and she pouted. "Oh, poor thing. She looks so lonely all by herself."

Reed let her take his phone so she could study Midnight in detail. She may have told him no but her body language said otherwise. All he had to do was be patient.

"What a sweet face. And those floppy ears. Will they stand up like a German shepherd's when she's older?"

"No. We did genetic testing on the litter. They're purebred Labs like their mama. The only difference is, Stella's coat is yellow. That's going to be another problem in placing Midnight if she doesn't make it through our program. Black dogs are statistically the last to be chosen at the pound."

"You're not sending this poor baby to the dog pound!"

"Well, I hope not, but…"

It was all Reed could do to keep from grinning. When her eyes met his he could tell she realized he'd been leading her on.

Abigail began to smile and slowly shook her head. "You're good. I could use somebody with a smooth technique like yours at work. You could charm those wild kids into shape in no time."

His grin escaped with a quiet chuckle. "Does this mean you'll take the pup?"

"No." She handed his phone back to him. "But I will

agree to meet her, no guarantees. You could fill a book with all the things I *don't* know about raising a dog."

"That's okay. I'll teach you." He stood before she could change her mind and called out to Olga. "I'll take a rain check on the coffee, ma'am."

"You're leaving?" the older woman asked, peeking around the corner from the kitchen.

"Not for long. I'll be back ASAP. I promise."

Already thinking ahead, Reed signaled to Jessie, clipped her leash to her collar and headed for the door with a brief wave goodbye. His intention was to leave before Abigail thought it through and had time to change her mind. Once she met Midnight he was pretty sure she'd fall in love.

With the dog, he added to himself when a stray thought intruded to remind him how attractive the young woman was.

Reed shook off any whispers of impropriety. He had not come there looking for romance. He'd sought out Abigail because of a sense of duty. When he'd rescued her he'd stepped into her life enough to care, which was not necessarily a wise reaction. Nevertheless, he was determined to do what he could to help. This was a win-win situation. A needy pup would help Abigail heal as well as benefit the less than stellar young dog.

He jogged down the stairs with Jessie at his side. Midnight might still blossom in the right foster home even though she'd done poorly so far. As long as he stuck around long enough to get Abigail and the pup off to a good start there was a chance of redemption. He could already see her taking Midnight to work with her when she was ready to go back. A loving puppy would help reach the street kids, too, and perhaps show aptitude as a future service dog. They needed the nonjudg-mental acceptance K-9s provided.

Together, Reed and Jessie broke out into the sun-shine and headed for his SUV. There was a spring in the dog's gait and she almost looked as if she was smiling.

Reed empathized. He was pretty happy, too. If the narrow sidewalk hadn't been so crowded he might have jogged back to his vehicle instead of settling for a brisk walking pace.

Suddenly, Jessie gave a tug on the leash that jarred Reed out of his reverie. He paused. Looked behind him. Heard the bloodhound growl and saw the hackles on her back bristle.

"What is it, girl?"

Jessie never took her eyes off the people who had just passed. Reed scanned the group. There were too many for him to pick out which one had excited his K-9.

Given the probability that someone nearby was car-rying drugs, he wasn't too surprised. Even though Jessie wasn't trained to sniff out illegal substances, she had smelled them often enough on subjects she had tracked.

But that didn't mean he was on board with the un-easy feelings Jessie's behavior was bringing out. The sooner he picked up Midnight and returned to Abigail Jones's apartment, the better. For everybody.

As far as Abigail was concerned, Olga's presence was a plus. She would never have asked her friend to keep her company, but since she was already there, she hoped she'd stay.

The older woman emerged from the kitchen carry-ing two steaming mugs. "That one has a lot of nerve."

"He promised he'd be back."

"I hope he's happy. He made me miss my soap."

"We can watch it here," Abigail offered, blowing on the hot coffee before chancing a sip. "My cable box lets me run programs back to the beginning. You won't miss a thing." She reached for the remote. "What channel?"

"You want I should stay? I don't want to bother you."

"Yes, please. It's no bother. I—I don't like being alone all the time."

"So get yourself a fella," Olga said, taking the remote from her and quickly locating the correct TV channel. "Girl like you shouldn't have any trouble attracting a decent man." She smiled. "What about the one that just left?"

A shiver raced up Abigail's spine and prickled the nape of her neck. "I've seen enough bad relationships to stay away from all of them." She blushed. "I'm not letting any guy move in on me the way…"

"The way what?" Olga asked.

Abigail lowered her gaze. "The way my mother used to. That was almost as bad as her insisting I call every one of them Daddy." Embarrassed beyond words, she wished she hadn't spoken so bluntly. So truthfully. Yet now that she'd started to bare her soul she yearned to go on.

"What about your real papa?"

"I don't even remember what he looked like. My mother got mad at him once when I was little and destroyed every picture. I have nothing to remember him by."

"Did you ask her? Maybe she kept some for herself."

Shaking her head, Abigail took another sip before continuing. "I haven't seen Mama since I was sixteen. I have no idea where she even lives."

Olga began patting her free hand. "All right. I'll stay." She lifted her own mug as if in a toast to the soap opera. "Now we watch my show. I know some people say I'm foolish to want to see what happens, but you can learn a lot about life this way."

"I wish my life was as easy to understand," Abigail said softly. "I thought I was on the right track, helping homeless teens and doing good for society. Now I wonder."

"Nobody ever said doing the right thing was easy. That doesn't mean it isn't still right." Olga paused until the drama switched to a commercial, then said, "You keep the dog your friend is going to bring you, Mr. Rosenbaum will probably raise your rent."

Abigail hadn't thought of that but it fit with the way her days had been going lately. If it wasn't one thing, it was another. She had just about decided to tell Reed to take Midnight back where she came from when Olga added, "Of course, there's nothing like a big dog barking to scare off thugs." She chuckled. "Might not be such a bad idea after all."

Three flights of stairs and a frightened, gangly puppy were a bad combination, Reed mused, breathing hard as he carried wiggly, floppy, excited Midnight up to Abigail's. Before he had time to put his furry burden down, Jessie barked. The door was jerked open.

He set the pup on its big feet and smiled as he straightened. The look of astonishment on Abigail's face added to his amusement.

Eyes wide, she snapped her jaw closed and pointed. "That's a *puppy*?"

"Uh-huh. She's about five months old. They grow pretty fast at first."

"Yeah." Remaining in the doorway, Abigail held her hands apart to demonstrate something about the size of a domestic cat. "I was expecting, you know, a puppy. Little? Fluffy? Cuddly on my lap?"

"Midnight will cuddle you. Give her a chance."

Although she did step back, Reed could tell she was anything but sold on his idea even before she said, "All right. Come on in. But this is not going to work."

Jessie was first through the door and already on the couch by the time Reed was able to coax Midnight inside. Instead of compliantly trotting along on the end of the leash as she had at the training center and coming up the sidewalk from his SUV, she threw herself down, splayed out on her belly, and was sliding across the wood floor, inch by inch, while he tugged and cajoled. Astonishing! If she'd been trained to resist he'd have understood, but this was a puppy who was supposed to be leash-trained.

Abigail began to laugh. "Well, that's good if I need my floor dusted. What other tricks does she do?"

"She's pretty good at eating," Reed joked, knowing he was blushing. "I promise you, she was behaving perfectly when I picked her up at the kennel and put the harness on her. This is very unusual. Working dogs need to be confident and unafraid."

"Maybe she senses my moodiness," Abigail offered. "Don't judge her by one incident. I'm sure she'll be fine once you take her back to where you got her."

"Mind if I catch my breath first? She wasn't crazy about climbing stairs, either."

Laughing, Abigail said, "What? A big, strong guy

like you can't carry a puppy up three flights without getting winded? Does your chief know how out-of-shape you are?"

Reed started to argue, then realized she was teasing. "She was hard to hang on to," he said. "I almost dropped her a couple of times until I figured out she liked her front legs draped over my shoulder."

Abigail laughed again. "Can I get you a cup of coffee now, or would you rather have a sports drink?"

"Plain water's fine, thanks."

Eyeing Jessie and realizing the bloodhound wanted to follow Abigail, Reed unsnapped the pup's leash and gave Jessie a release command.

Off they went in Abigail's footsteps, one after the other, as if they were both tracking. Curiosity moved him to continue watching. He circled an easy chair and walked softly across the hardwood floor toward the kitchen.

What he observed was a Rockwell picture of Americana. Abigail was standing with her back to the refrigerator door, a bottle of cold water in each hand. The dogs were sitting politely at her feet, tails sweeping arcs on the floor, and acting as if their favorite human was about to serve the tastiest treats they'd ever eaten.

He waited to see what would happen. He wasn't disappointed. She began to speak to the dogs as though they were hers.

"What do you girls want, huh? A drink of water? I can probably manage that, but I'd better ask the officer first."

Jessie stayed in place. Midnight, excited by the kind tone of voice, wiggled and circled at Abigail's feet. Then she glanced over at her canine buddy and managed to resume a seated position without quivering too badly. The pup was smart, all right. She'd learned to beg after one impromptu lesson.

Waiting to see what happened next, Reed was startled by the loud ringing of a cell phone. He watched Abigail pale as she set the water bottles aside, reached for her phone and looked at the number. It must have been familiar because she quickly answered.

"Hello?"

Whatever the caller said caused her to lean against the counter. Was she shaking? Perhaps it was bad news and she needed moral support. Convinced he was right, Reed joined her and the dogs.

"I—I can't. I'm not ready," Abigail said, listening to the caller's reply before she added, "Are you sure?"

Apparently the answer was affirmative because her tight grip on the phone began to whiten her knuckles. He gently cupped her elbow and mouthed, "What's wrong?"

Distracted, she lowered the phone. Her eyes were wide and moist, her lower lip quivering slightly. "It's one of my kids. A girl I've been working with for several months. She insists she has to talk to me in person."

"Where?" Reed asked.

"She's at the AFS office where I work. That stands for A Fresh Start. It's only about six blocks away, right here in Brighton Beach. I usually walk, it's just that…"

"I understand. How about if we go with you?"

"You'd do that? Really?"

"Of course."

Abigail lifted the phone to her ear again and agreed to the rendezvous. "All right. I'll manage. Tell her to meet me there in thirty minutes."

Her blue eyes were still wide and misty when she ended the call and looked at Reed. "I hope that's enough time."

"It will be if we drive instead of dragging this pup on a leash. I'd like to see her relate to teens."

"Some of them are very troubled," Abigail told him.

"All the better for temperament testing."

"Right."

He saw Abigail standing very still and eyeing a purse that sat at the end of the kitchen counter. Clearly, she was far from over the trauma of nearly being abducted.

"Tell you what," Reed said, keeping his voice light and pleasant, "I'll go get my car and come pick you up. How does that sound?"

The smile she gave him showed great relief. "Sounds good. That way we won't have to drag Midnight and get her all dirty from the sidewalks."

He matched her smile with a wider grin. "I'll leave them both with you so Jessie can help influence the pup." After snapping short leashes on his K-9's collar and Midnight's harness, Reed handed the opposite ends to her. "You're in charge."

"Hey! Wait. I don't know what to do."

"It's easy. You just stand where you are or sit back down on the couch. They'll follow you."

"Like this puppy followed you up the stairs, you mean?"

Reed chuckled. His ploy had worked. Abigail was concentrating on handling the dogs instead of dwelling on her pending trip outside. Anything he could do to relieve her angst was a plus. It was likely that her healing would depend upon taking baby steps, such as initially venturing out with him as her companion and the dogs for distraction. She was certainly acting less afraid than she had when she'd first taken the phone call.

He gave Jessie the hand signal to stay, turned, and was almost to her door before Abigail called, "Hurry back."

That sounded so much better than the state in which he'd found her when he'd first visited, he was thrilled. The sooner she got over her fright and regained her memory of the incident at the carousel, the sooner the NYPD would be able to locate and arrest her assailants. At least, he hoped so. No matter how much he enjoyed the young woman's company, he was going to have to back off soon. His official duties didn't allow for much of a social life, not to mention the inadvisability of spending free time with the victim of a crime.

Jogging along the narrow sidewalk and dodging pedestrians, Reed realized he felt the absence of his K-9 partner. Jessie was so much a part of him, on and off duty, it was as if a critical element was missing. He could count times like this when he'd left her behind on the fingers of one hand.

The faster he moved the stronger his sense of foreboding grew. He had to get back to Abigail—and to Jessie—as fast as possible.

FIVE

Edging sideways toward the sofa, Abigail was surprised to find both dogs keeping her company the way Reed had promised. Once she was convinced they weren't going to go berserk, she began to relax a little and sat down. One of the dogs stepped on her toes. She didn't have to guess which one.

"I'm sorry, Midnight," she crooned like a mother to her baby, "this just isn't going to work out between you and me. You see that, don't you? Hmm? It's not that you're being difficult right now, it's just that I've never had a dog, let alone a puppy. I'd probably confuse you so badly you'd never become a police dog."

The pup's brown eyes sparkled, her ebony coat glistening. She wagged her whole rear end and panted at Abigail's feet, leaving a small damp spot on the right knee of her jeans. "See what I mean? Why can't you be still and easy to handle like Jessie is? Huh? Look how good she's being."

It took only a moment for Abigail to realize she'd goofed again by calling a name. Jessie, who had been calmly waiting at her feet, leaped onto the sofa next to her and took up the place she had chosen on her initial visit. That left Midnight alone on the floor, and it was clear she didn't intend to stay there when her canine companion was cuddling up to a friendly human.

Big, soft front paws landed in Abigail's lap as the puppy made an unsuccessful leap to join the party. Abby instinctively leaned forward and reached out to keep her from falling. She managed to hug the younger dog's shoulders, felt the texture of the glistening fur and received a wet slurp under her chin for her efforts.

"Eww! Stop," she ordered, chuckling in spite of herself. Rather than push Midnight back down she hoisted her onto the sofa on the side opposite Jessic. To say the pup was overjoyed was an understatement. It immediately crawled closer, succeeding in getting only its front half into her lap.

There was something very special about the unbridled attention and obvious acceptance of both dogs. When she'd been petting Jessie earlier, Abigail had thought she'd felt mild contentment. Having Midnight draped across her lap, gazing up at her and leaning that blocky head against her chest, was unbelievably comforting. Encircling the puppy in a gentle hug she stroked the velvety floppy ears and heard the youngster actually sigh. Who knew dogs could be so expressive?

Beside her, a growl rumbled in Jessie's throat. Was she jealous? Oh, dear. Now what?

"It's okay, Jessie," Abigail said quickly. "I love you, too."

That didn't placate the bloodhound. The quiet growl was followed by stronger rumbling, then a bark. Midnight's head whipped around. Both dogs were staring at the closed apartment door.

Abigail scooted forward to perch on the edge of the

sofa, her body as still and tense as that of her canine companions. Something metallic was making a scratching sound. The doorknob was moving!

Before Abigail could decide what to do, Jessie began to give voice in a way that left no doubt she was extremely upset. Whoever was on the other side of that door was definitely not officer Reed Branson. And his K-9 partner knew it.

Finding a parking place directly in front of Abigail's apartment building was impossible, so Reed flipped on the blue-and-white Chevy Tahoe's flashing lights and left it idling as close to already parked cars as possible.

He stepped out. Listened. Heard a dog barking. Traffic noise nearly drowned out Jessie's angry warning but the closer Reed got to the outer apartment door, the more sure he was. He slammed his palm into the bank of buttons on the intercom and was able to enter almost immediately because several residents responded.

Howling and guttural barking echoed down the stairwell, giving Reed's feet wings. He'd reached the second floor landing and was turning to start up to the third when a figure going the opposite direction bumped his shoulder so hard the blow nearly knocked him down!

Adrenaline enabled him to take the final section of stairway two and three steps at a time. He skidded to a stop at Abigail's door. Jessie was still barking. Puppy yips were background noise.

The hallway around him was empty. Reed knocked. "Abigail. Ms. Jones! It's me."

Not only did the dogs fall silent, it was quiet enough for him to hear her footsteps approaching. "It's really you?"

"Yes." He held his badge in front of the peephole. "See?"

Abigail opened the door and instead of ushering him in, threw both arms around his neck and fell into his embrace.

At their feet, Jessie was panting and wagging her tail. Midnight was so excited she ran in circles around the couple and wrapped their legs together with the trailing leash.

Reed braced himself against the doorjamb for balance. "Whoa. What happened? What's wrong?"

"I—I don't know."

"Okay. One thing at a time." He checked to make sure there was no immediate threat, then bent to unravel the snare of the short leash. "There. Let's go back inside."

Abigail didn't comply as quickly as he liked so he slid an arm around her waist and half carried her through the open doorway. Jessie entered ahead of them with the pup bringing up the rear, much to Reed's relief.

He closed the door, then escorted her to the sofa, sat down with her and clasped her hands. "All right. Tell me everything."

Although her blue eyes were wide and she still looked frightened, she said, "I think the dogs heard a prowler in the hallway. I—I heard a funny noise and thought I saw the doorknob turning but nobody came in."

"Not surprising considering the racket Jessie was making. She's not trained for personal protection but she knew she was supposed to look after you—and the puppy."

"Midnight barked, too. It would have been kind of cute if I hadn't been so scared."

"Well, there's no way we can prove someone was trying to break in," Reed said, choosing to keep his stairwell encounter to himself so Abigail wouldn't be as stressed. Reporting his suspicions to the 60th Precinct would suffice for now, since he had such a poor description of the possible suspect.

"Do you need a few more minutes or are you ready to leave?"

The emotions flashing across her pale, lightly freckled face came and went so fast Reed could hardly sort them out. Duty warred with fear. Where determination began and fright ended was less clear.

Abigail stared at him. "I promised I'd meet Kiera at the office. I have to go. How much time is left?"

"About ten minutes," he said cautiously. "Are you sure you're up to doing this?"

"No," she said with a tremor in her voice, "but I'm going to do it anyway."

He got to his feet and held out a hand to her. "Okay then. Let's get this show on the road."

"Dog," she said with a loud sigh.

"I beg your pardon?"

"This *dog* show. What in the world are we going to do with the puppy?"

The moment Reed's glance located Midnight he groaned. "Oops. I knew I should have walked her longer before I brought her in. I'll take care of your kitchen floor, then we'll take both dogs to my car and be on our way."

"Want to tell me again how much fun I'm going to have raising a half-grown pup?"

Speechless, he just rolled his eyes and hurried to take care of the housekeeping problem. Behind him he heard Abigail giggling. For a short time she had set aside her looming fear and was enjoying the moment. That relief was without price.

"You're double-parked!" Abigail was peering out through the glass fronting the foyer of her building.

"We do what we have to," Reed countered. "There was no place close by and I figured you'd appreciate a shorter walk."

"I do." She would have slipped her hand through the bend of his elbow if he hadn't needed both arms to carry the floppy pup.

"Okay, I'll go first with the dogs. Stick close behind me and you'll be fine."

"I'd rather carry Midnight and let you watch my back," she said, trying to mask her growing unease.

"She's pretty heavy."

"I'm stronger than I look." Abigail extended her arms.

"All right. We want to make the trip to the car ASAP. Be careful going down the steps."

"Oof!"

"Told you she was a chunk."

"It's fine. I've got her." What she also had was the perfect opportunity to receive more doggie kisses, like it or not. "Eww. Why does she keep trying to lick me?"

"It's a pup's instinctive reaction to its mama. She's transferring her affection for Stella, her mom, to you."

"She thinks I'm her mother?"

"In a manner of speaking." Reed led the way to the SUV and opened the passenger side door, and Abigail climbed in, pup and all. One end of Midnight was on the center console, the other hanging off the right side of Abigail's lap.

"Give her to me and I'll put her in the back with Jessie."

"Can't she ride like this, with me?" She scooped up the rear of the gangly pup and gathered her long legs, tucking them under like the hem of a blanket.

"Not if we follow the law," he countered. "Being a cop is no excuse for rule breaking."

"I suppose not." Reluctance to let him take Midnight made her pull the pup into a bear hug, which resulted in more wiggling and expressions of joy from her furry burden.

Horns honked behind the idling SUV. Reed chuckled. "Okay. I'll put Jessie in the back, then come around and hook Midnight's harness to a seat belt. You fasten yours."

Abigail looked at her lapful, then at the clasp for the belt. "Sure. Easy-peasy. I'll do that with my extra two hands."

She heard Reed laughing as he let his bloodhound into the rear compartment, then slid behind the wheel and reached for the young Lab. Although Abigail tried to help by positioning Midnight for him, the entire operation was anything but smooth. By the time her harness was fastened everyone was breathing hard.

"Sorry," Abigail said. "The next time I'll let you put her in back with Jessie."

"I was just about to say the same thing." Reed shut off the flashers and signaled to pull into traffic. "Which way to your workplace?"

"Basically downtown Brighton Beach. Do you know where the open-air fruit and vegetable market is?"

Reed nodded.

"We're a couple doors past that. AFS leased a vacant storefront rather than pay exorbitant rent in an office building. Besides, we figured the kids we help would be more likely to wander into a place that looks less official. Know what I mean?"

"Absolutely. You need to use every trick in the book to bring them in."

"We're not tricking them," Abigail countered. "It's all about gaining their trust and providing aid without making them feel as if they have no choice."

"The way their parents treated them?"

She nodded slowly, pensively. "In some cases. Other kids come from situations that were so bad they feel they're better off wandering the streets with their friends. What they fail to see is how dangerous that lifestyle can be." A shiver zinged up her spine, reminding her to be cautious to the point of fear.

Sensing Reed's glance, she met it with her own eyes. "What?"

"I just saw you shiver. Are you okay?"

"I'm fine." *Just remembering being a lost kid myself,* she added silently. Traffic had slowed as they'd entered the old shopping section of Brighton Beach and she was relieved to have a reason to change the subject. She pointed. "There. See it? The sign in the window isn't very big, but that's the storefront."

"Got it. Want me to circle until I find a parking place or let you off?"

"Oh." That was a tricky question if she'd ever heard one. If she climbed out right there she could enter the A Fresh Start office quickly, but Reed and the dogs wouldn't be with her. If she insisted he park and escort her in, she might be late for her meeting with Kiera.

Abigail made a face at him. "I don't suppose you could do both, could you?"

"Sure. Hang on."

After angling into a narrow alley between buildings, he used his emergency lights again, circled the vehicle, got Jessie and met Abigail at the passenger door with a satisfied smile. "We'll walk you in, then I'll go park and come back for you."

Relieved, she asked, "What about my puppy? It's too hot to leave the poor little thing in the car."

One of his dark eyebrows arched and his grin widened. "What did you say?"

"Midnight." Abigail was frowning at him. "She can't stay in a hot car while we go inside." Climbing out to stand beside him and Jessie, she heard Midnight whining. "See what I mean? She doesn't want to be left behind."

"And if she got bored she'd probably rip the upholstery off any seat she could get her teeth into," Reed said. "I won't abandon her. I promise. This will only take a second and I'll lock her in with the AC running. Now let's get you inside for your meeting."

Abigail had already noticed how much more wary he was acting now that they were on foot. Good thing she hadn't been up to walking over from her apartment.

With Reed between her and Jessie, she hurried across the crumbling, cracked concrete sidewalk and ducked into her place of business. There were a few tattered posters taped to the walls, three old metal desks, a sofa with faded brown-and-gray upholstery and a couple of odd chairs. The well-used living room furniture was grouped in a back corner by a refrigerator to encourage more casual gatherings.

Abigail didn't see Kiera, but her boss, Wanda, greeted her with a smile. "I'm so glad you were feeling up to this. Kiera insisted she won't talk to anybody else."

"I understand. Where is she?"

"She didn't want to wait. I expect her back any minute." Wanda patted her on the shoulder. "Who's your friend?"

"This is…" She hesitated to give his job title where they might be overheard by prejudiced kids, so she merely said, "Reed." Smiling, she pointed. "And this is Jessie."

"We don't usually allow dogs in here," the slightly older woman said pleasantly, smoothing her bob and tucking longer strands of dark hair behind her ear on one side. "But in your case I may make an exception."

Flabbergasted, Abigail realized that her boss was flirting with the off-duty cop! She stifled a wry smile. *Well, well, well.* What a surprise.

"See you ladies again as soon as I go park," Reed said.

"I can comp your parking at the lot around the next corner if you want."

"No need. I'm just dropping off Ms. Jones for her meeting." He nodded politely and started to back away.

As he turned, his gaze caught Abigail's and she was sure she saw mirth twinkling in the rich depths. When he winked for her eyes only, she was positive.

Watching him saunter away with his K-9 partner was enough to dampen Abigail's joy. Yes, he would be back soon. And, no, she shouldn't be fearful doing the job she truly believed God had given her, yet she was. There were still too many unknowns lurking in the depths of her subconscious for her to fully relax in any situation, particularly one away from her apartment.

Before she had time to think herself into a snit, she spotted a familiar pierced and tattooed teenage girl with pink-fluorescent-streaked hair loitering outside the display window. Kiera had shown up.

Whatever was on the teen's mind was more important than Abigail's personal problems, she reminded herself. She'd faced her fears and braved the outdoors to get there. She wasn't going to blow a chance to offer the girl counseling.

If her memory didn't recover soon, maybe she'd take Reed's advice and see a professional herself. Remaining clueless indefinitely was unacceptable. And dangerous.

She clutched a file folder to her chest like a shield as the door opened and Kiera Underhill ducked through. The back of her long hair was gathered with an elastic band. She wore silver-and-pink chandelier earrings and a stud in her right eyebrow.

There had been a time when Abigail, herself, had delighted in marching to a different drummer, and she admired Kiera's spunk. What worried her was the teen's antagonistic attitude toward authority.

"Been there, done that," Abigail murmured, thinking back on the risks inherent in her own mistakes. If not for the grace of God and a few good influences at just the right times in her life, she wondered if she'd have survived to pass on the hard lessons she'd learned.

SIX

Abigail watched Kiera's approach and assessed her as nervous and perhaps deceitful. Well, that wasn't too surprising, given the girl's background. After being abused or abandoned or both, as in Kiera's case, it took time to heal.

No, *healing* was the wrong word, Abigail decided. It was more an adjustment of attitude and an acceptance of the mistakes of others, particularly one's parents. Some adults simply could not relate to the immature thought processes of a teen. Others had so many problems of their own they didn't even try to understand—or make the slightest effort at reconciliation with runaways. Those families produced the kids who were hardest to reach. They'd accept food and clothing and whatever else was offered but they never truly trusted. It wasn't in them.

Instead of the greeting Abigail had expected, Kiera sneered. "At least you showed up."

"I beg your pardon?" She faced the teen's ire while Wanda made herself scarce, leaving the two of them essentially alone.

"Whatever," Kiera muttered. She bypassed Abigail and headed for the refrigerator. "Got any cold beer?"

"You know better than that."

"Yeah. I guess I'll have to settle for soda."

"Fine. Help yourself."

The teen not only did so, she threw herself backward into the center of the sofa and propped both feet on the scarred coffee table before she popped the top of the frosty can.

Displaying a good counselor's calm demeanor and posture, Abigail took the nearest chair, file folder on her lap, and leaned forward. "You wanted to talk to me?"

"Maybe."

Self-control had helped get her this job in the first place and she needed it now. She waited quietly, knowing that the more she probed, the more she urged the girl to open up, the less likely it was to happen.

"So," Kiera began, focusing on the soda can instead of her companion, "how are you?"

"I'm all right. Why?"

"Just wondered."

There was so much unsaid, Abigail felt unsteady, as if she were floundering in the waves that were ebbing, returning and breaking on the nearby shore. Her mind had suddenly made an unexpected jump and provided a startlingly clear image of a beach with storm clouds threatening. Just like the night she'd been attacked! She shivered, hoping the teen hadn't noticed.

Maybe Kiera hadn't, but Wanda had. She approached behind Abigail, laid a steadying hand on her shoulder and explained, "Ms. Jones was involved in a frightening attack down by the Coney Island boardwalk. She isn't feeling well but she came in today because you insisted you needed to speak with her. Please get to the point so she can go back home and rest."

The slim, tanned girl swung her feet to the floor and sat up straighter. "You were hurt? H-how? Did they…?"

"I just have a few bruises," Abigail assured her. "My main problem is my memory. I don't even know why I was over by Luna Park so late at night, let alone what happened to me, other than what I've been told."

"You—you don't?"

Abigail was getting the idea that Kiera knew more than she was telling. Speaking softly, she said, "No. Do you?"

"Naw. Not me." Kiera threw her body back against the sofa pillows again.

"Okay. So why did you want to speak with me today?"

"I don't. Not really." She lunged to her feet, splashing a few drops of the soda on her tank top. "Um, I gotta go."

Abigail saw Wanda start to intervene and held up a hand to signal her to stop. Obviously Kiera did know something about the incident in Coney Island. Her expressions and changes of mood gave her away, although she undoubtedly believed she was fooling the adults. That was all right. The time would come when she'd speak up. It almost always did when the runaway was kind-hearted behind a facade of bravado. Kiera wasn't a bad kid, she was just young and scared and trying to fight her way through to a better life with no idea how to go about it.

Kiera was on her way to the door, wasting no time, when Abigail called after her, "I expect to be back at work next week. Stop by anytime."

A raised soda can was the girl's only answer. She didn't even look back.

"What do you think is going on?" Wanda asked when they were alone.

"Maybe nothing, maybe plenty," Abigail said. "I got the idea she was fishing to find out what I knew. As soon as I admitted I couldn't remember what happened, she clammed up."

"I noticed. I'm surprised you let her get away with it."

"Right now, there's no way I can prove or disprove whatever she tells me," Abigail said with a sigh. "I sure wish I could remember at least a little about that night."

"You will," her boss said. "It just takes time. Do you really think you'll be ready to resume your duties by next week? That seems awfully soon."

"Pretty sure. Everybody keeps telling me it's not unusual for a brain to blot out trauma. I wish mine were not quite so efficient."

"Oh, I don't know," Wanda drawled. "If you stay the way you are, you'll probably have a lot more visits from your favorite cop."

Abigail's cheeks warmed and she knew her fair, freckled skin had begun to look sunburned even though it was not. "I never asked him to take an interest in my case. He says he's doing it because he was the one who found and rescued me and he feels some kind of divine assignment or something."

"Whatever works." Wanda was chuckling. "If you decide you're not interested, let me know." She nodded toward the front of the store. "Looks like he's still on volunteer guard duty."

The sight of Reed's back and broad shoulders through the glass made Abigail's pulse speed and stole breathable air from the surrounding atmosphere. How long had he been standing there? Had he seen Kiera leave?

If so, why hadn't he come inside? Was he waiting until she gave him the okay?

Well, it was *very* okay for him to rejoin her, she decided easily. Being with Reed and the dogs gave her a morale boost as well as keeping her from jumping at shadows.

Abigail froze. *Shadows!* She remembered seeing shadowy figures. Trying to bring the hint of memory into focus, she closed her eyes and concentrated on the blurry picture. It was… It was gone.

Her shoulders sagged with disappointment. So close, yet still too far away, too buried in the labyrinth of her mind. Was seeing Kiera again the trigger? She supposed just getting out of her apartment and back into the office might have helped, too. So did Reed's presence, although she had yet to figure out why, other than equating it with him showing up at Luna Park after the attack.

It had been real. She was sure of that much. Bruises on her arms and wrists showed the patterns of large hands. Male hands. So one or more men must have grabbed her. Reed said his dog had alerted to screaming and her throat had hurt, so she figured the screamer had been her. And he'd found her hiding in the carousel control booth, another sign she'd been threatened.

Those facts were the bare bones of her ordeal. In order to flesh it out and provide clues to the attackers, she was going to have to get past her nerves and unlock her mind. That was easier said than done. Until she remembered more details she didn't even know what questions to ask.

Thinking about this latest encounter with Kiera, however, she had a pretty good idea where to begin.

* * *

Reed glanced over his shoulder into the AFS office after he noticed a teenage girl leaving. Reflections of passing traffic and other pedestrians made it hard for him to see through the glass. He was about to approach the door when Abigail opened it and beckoned. Her serious expression turned to a smile when she noticed he'd brought both dogs this time.

As soon as Midnight spotted her, the tug-of-war was on. Reed had the pup's leash looped around his wrist, and her lunge toward Abigail pulled him sideways. A quick step and slight stagger set his balance right again. Some valiant defender he was, he mused. He must look like a flailing fool.

"Come on in. And bring your furry friends," Abigail said, chuckling, "before they flatten you."

"She caught me off guard, that's all. I can see she needs a lot more leash training."

"Will you show me how to do that?"

Reed pushed the door shut behind him and stepped farther into the office. "Seriously? Do you think you're ready to hit the streets with her?"

Good humor fled. "Well, no, but you can take her outside for me and I can walk her up and down the hallway for practice. That will help, won't it?"

"Sure, as long as you don't let her lead you. We're not sure of her strongest traits but she is headstrong."

"And so cute it's impossible to be mad at her. I'm not supposed to spank her, am I?"

"No. Absolutely not. That could make her afraid of all human contact and she needs to use her brain to tell the good guys from the bad guys."

"Police dogs really do that?"

"All dogs do to some extent," Reed said. "The secret is teaching them proper responses." He nodded to Wanda before turning his concentration back to Abigail. "So, what did the girl want to tell you that was so urgent?"

She shrugged. "Beats me. Kids like Kiera are masters at avoidance, but her body language gave me the idea that she may have seen what happened to me down by the boardwalk."

The short hairs at the back of Reed's neck prickled. "What makes you think that?"

"Her attitude, mostly. And the way she changed the subject when I asked her if she knew anything about it." Abigail sighed audibly. "I am sure she was worried I'd been hurt because she asked me. That's a positive sign. She does have a tender heart, she's just learned to hide those feelings, and it's going to take more than one meeting to convince her she should share information. Maybe she heard rumors from some of the other kids. I don't know."

"Okay." Reed shortened the puppy's leash to keep her close to his side and inclined his head toward the door. "Let's get you home and settled in again, then I'll go by headquarters and check up on her via computer. Do you know if she has a juvenile record?"

"I don't think so. I haven't known her for very long. There's a tremendous turnover in kids who hang out at the beach in the summer. Most have homes to go to and unless they show a need or happen to drop in here with friends, it's hard to tell much about them."

"How do you know they aren't scamming you?"

That question brought a sweet, pensive expression to Abigail's face. "We don't. We do check, of course, but getting their real names is tough enough, let alone the true story of their past. It takes time to develop rapport and some are only here for a short time. Foot traffic dies down in the winter."

"I imagine so. Do you take them in if the weather turns bad?"

"We don't, but we have connections with some of the area churches and other charities that do. I'd never let my kids suffer on the streets."

That statement, her owning of the lost children, struck Reed as the crux of her personality. She was a nurturer. Oh, she might not know it or might deny it if asked, but that was what she was. Everybody's mother. The other notion that stuck in his mind was wondering how such a young, seemingly fragile woman had developed the inner strength to carry off the daunting task of tending to a myriad of ungrateful strangers, week after week, year after year.

When—if—he got to know her better, he might even ask.

Abigail managed to leave A Fresh Start without too much angst because of Reed and the dogs. At first she felt hesitant, but as they walked toward the lot where he had left his car, she began to actually enjoy the brisk day. Temperatures had moderated since the storm the night of her attack and the weather was about as perfect as fall along the Atlantic could get. Some seagulls whirled overhead while others, and smaller birds, squabbled over bits of food in the street and along the curb.

"That reminds me," Reed said, "are you hungry? I'll buy."

His offer startled her. Under other circumstances she

might have been flattered, but eating out would mean a delay in getting back to her apartment and was therefore unacceptable.

"Sorry. No," she said too quickly.

"I'm the one who should apologize for asking," he told her. "You seemed so calm I thought you might be up to it."

"I am better. Who wouldn't be on such a beautiful day? But I still feel as if I'm being watched."

"Why didn't you say so?"

Abigail huffed a chuckle. "And convince you I'm paranoid? I don't think so." She concentrated on watching the dogs rather than meet his gaze. Thinking about the weather and the birds and the dogs had distracted her some, but it hadn't taken much to pull her back into survival mode. There was no way she was even close to being normal.

The crush of pedestrians around them, the noise of traffic, the calls of vendors and incessant chatter along the busy street were drowning Abigail in sensory stimuli. Everything pressed in on her as if she were being swamped by a tsunami of sound or lost in a forest of trees so close together there was no clear avenue of escape.

"My car is right around the next corner," Reed said. "Do you think you can take charge of Midnight for a bit until I get Jessie loaded?"

A nod was all she could muster. He handed her the leather leash and she slipped her hand through the end loop. Reed's concern was evident. If there had been a way to explain how rapidly a sense of looming disaster had overcome her, she would have done so. Gladly. All it had taken was a simple question and she was headed straight over a figurative cliff again. There had to be a way to stop these panic attacks. There had to be. Because if she failed to get control of her own emotions she wasn't going to be fit to help anyone else.

It was one thing to study human behavior in school and quite another to apply that knowledge to her personal life, let alone those of others. Head knowledge didn't erase irrational fear any more than wishful thinking did.

So, what options did she have? Abigail asked herself. Wanda would cite total reliance on faith and prayer, she knew, and if that had ever worked well for her in the past, she might consider it. Night after night she'd prayed that her father would return and that her mother would stop partying and bringing home strange men, yet nothing had changed. Inevitably, she had run away and become a street kid just like the ones she was now trying to aid.

Abigail froze as her thoughts came full circle. The unanswered prayer had forced her to leave, sent her into the streets and eventually to school, where she became qualified to do what she was currently doing for others. If God had given her the results she'd prayed for, who knew where she'd have ended up or what she'd be doing for a living?

Looking back, she suddenly realized she was acting like a foxhole Christian, only praying when she was out of other options or too scared to think straight. No wonder she assumed God wasn't listening. The only time she called on Him was during an imminent disaster.

Like the assault, she added, stunned by the recollection.

A sharp intake of breath drew Reed's attention. He wheeled. "What is it? Did you see somebody?"

"No." Although she was a bit breathless, she nevertheless explained. "I just remembered something I did the other night before you found me."

"Running? Hiding? Getting grabbed?" he asked, finishing loading his K-9 and stepping closer to Abigail.

She shook her head. "No. Praying."

Instead of congratulating her on bringing back a lost fact, Reed began to smile. Seeing that was disconcerting enough for her to ask, "What's so funny?"

"Not funny. Gratifying," he drawled. "It feels good to be the answer to someone's prayers."

"How do you know you are?"

The self-satisfied smile grew into a grin. "Because you probably asked for help and I was sent. Go ahead. Deny it."

She sighed and shook her head. "I don't remember what I prayed for. I just thought it was a good sign that I recalled doing it."

"It's always good," he countered, loading the puppy into the secure second seat space, then opening the front passenger door for her.

As she slid in and reached for her seat belt, she was frowning. "Which one? Praying or remembering an inconsequential detail like that?"

"Talking to God is never inconsequential," Reed admonished gently. "Answers always come in one form or another. All we have to do is accept them when they come and recognize how blessed we are."

She waited until he slid behind the wheel before she said, "It's never worked that way for me."

"Sure it has." Reed started the SUV and merged into traffic. "You just haven't been looking with your heart."

Mentally working on a logical argument, Abigail saw something flash in her peripheral vision. She tensed. Opened her mouth to warn Reed of the anomaly.

It was too late. A white box truck sped out of no-where and smashed into the side of the SUV with a rending of metal and shattering of glass.

Abigail gasped, intending to scream, but the air was knocked out of her by the impact. Her seat belt grabbed her chest and kept her from being thrown across the front seats.

They were sliding sideways into oncoming traffic. She threw her arms across her face and braced for a second impact as the airbags exploded.

SEVEN

It had taken Reed a split second to realize there was no way to take evasive action. Even if he had seen the danger long before they were hit, he couldn't have maneuvered out of the way. A box truck had left the alley accelerating, tires squealing, and had smashed into the Chevy Tahoe before he'd had time to even brace himself.

Glass had shattered from the impact. They slid across the street into oncoming traffic and barely missed connecting with a city bus before jumping the curb and coming to rest against a power pole. Thankfully, their speed had slowed enough by then to keep that damage to a minimum.

Reed shouted. Abigail screamed. Around them, cars bumped each other like a line of toppling dominoes.

He'd felt the seat belt bruising his ribs as he'd mashed down the brake with all his strength. It was hard to let up once the vehicle came to rest but he knew he had to.

"Are you all right?" he shouted to Abigail.

"I—I think so. I saw the truck coming but I didn't have time to warn you."

"It wouldn't have mattered." As the airbags collapsed

he was able to reach the ignition and shut off the engine, then key his radio and identify himself before saying, "I'm ten-fifty-three H. Hit and run. Just got T-boned by a white box truck that is now headed west on Surf Avenue."

"Copy," the dispatcher radioed back. "License?"

"Didn't get it," Reed replied with disgust. "I had a face full of airbag."

"Copy that. Injuries?"

"Negative, as far as I know, but I'm not the only one hit. It's going to take half the cops in Brighton Beach to sort out this mess."

"Affirmative. Units on the way."

He unfastened his seat belt and swiveled to face Abigail. "You're sure you aren't hurt?"

She was brushing off crystal-shaped bits of tempered glass. "My shoulder is kind of sore, that's all."

"Probably from the belt or the airbag," he explained. "Anything else? Did you hit your head?"

"No. How about you?"

"I'm fine."

Her voice rose. "Oh, no! What about the dogs?"

"I'll go check them. You stay put while I try to convince all these motorists that the police are on their way and there's no need to fight over who's to blame."

"I'll tell them it wasn't your fault," she vowed. Her fingertips brushed Reed's forearm as he left the damaged vehicle, sending a spark of awareness racing along his nerves.

How like Abigail to think of others first. Most of the women he knew, and half the guys, would be complaining their heads off. She, however, was concerned about him and the dogs.

Circling, Reed opened the hatchback and began to examine both dogs. Neither seemed injured but the pup was trembling in fright. He leashed Jessie first, then Midnight, and brought them around to Abigail while bystanders jostled and pushed past each other to capture everything on their cell phone cameras. It would be too much to hope that one of the onlookers had taken pictures of the truck that hit him, but he'd have incoming officers check anyway. Judging by the lights and sirens pulling up to the snarl, he'd have plenty of help.

The passenger door was caved in, its mechanism jammed, so Reed spoke to Abigail through the shattered side window. "See if you can slide out the other door without getting cut on this broken glass. If you can't get over the console, I'll have the fire department pry this side open."

"I think I can do it." She managed a lopsided smile. "If I can stop shaking long enough."

She wasn't the only one, he admitted to himself. It might not show on the outside but his guts were churning. Was it possible that the truck had hit them on purpose? The more he thought about it, the more he wondered.

A bigger question was, who was the target? His K-9 unit had suffered its share of attacks lately, beginning with the unsolved murder of Chief Jameson. It was possible the truck driver had seen the logo and had smashed into the blue-and-white SUV because he hated cops, especially K-9 ones.

On the other hand, Reed speculated, the passenger side had taken the hardest hit. Abigail's side. Anybody who had watched them walk back to the parking lot would have known who was on board with him and which seat she was occupying. Plus, this was her home turf. Perhaps her sense of ongoing menace wasn't all in her imagination.

He hurried back to the driver's door to help her climb out, then shepherded her onto the sidewalk before handing her both dogs' leashes. "Stay right here. You'll be safe. I need to go speak with the arriving officers."

The pleading look in those blue eyes nearly undid him. When she asked, "Do you have to?" Reed knew instantly that he wasn't going anywhere. Not until he'd arranged for a policewoman to stay with her.

"No," he said tenderly, "we can let them come to us."

When she sighed softly and sagged back against the side of the brick building where they stood, it was all he could do to keep from taking her in his arms and offering comfort.

Instead, he displayed his badge for the patrolman who was working his way through the crowd, clearly searching for the wreck's driver.

As the throng parted, Reed noticed two people in particular who weren't acting interested in the wreck, the dogs or the police presence. One was heavy and wearing a baseball cap while the other was thinner and peering between taller spectators. Clenching his jaw, he stared at them, then took out his cell phone, intending to photograph their faces.

By the time he held it up and zeroed in on the place where they had been, they had melted into the crowd. He lowered the phone and searched for them, deciding that they must have separated.

Abigail touched his shoulder, distracting him for the millisecond it took to lose track of the bigger guy in the baseball cap. Since he had nothing to show her, he chose to keep the incident to himself. But he wouldn't forget those men. They'd been standing stock-still, glaring directly at Abigail.

If Abigail had not had two loving, attentive canines at her feet and a policewoman close by, watching, she figured she'd have lapsed into hysterics long before she and Reed were allowed to leave the site of the wreck.

So weary she was almost tempted to sit on the dirty sidewalk, she perked up when she saw him approaching. The smile on his face was a plus. "Can we leave?"

"Yes, as soon as I transfer my gear to the replacement vehicle my unit is sending." He inclined his head toward the smashed SUV. "I broke that one."

"Not by yourself. You had help."

"No kidding. That's why they want to tow it even if it's drivable. Crime scene techs need to go over it before it's repaired and put back in service."

Many locals had lost interest in the scene and drifted off, leaving the sidewalk fairly clear. Firefighters were rolling up hoses they'd positioned as standby. Someone with an impressive-looking camera and an NYPD jacket was circling the scene and snapping photo after photo. A tow truck driver was hooking his implements to the rear bumper of the wreck.

Abigail did feel a little calmer by then, but she wasn't through being edgy. The hair on her arms and the back of her neck was prickling as if she were sunburned despite standing in the shade of the brick building.

Surprisingly, Reed scowled. "What's wrong? Are you hurt after all?"

She shook her head. "No. Why? Do I look that bad?"

"I can have an EMT from the fire department look

you over. It's no big deal." The frown deepened. "Tell me the truth."

"I am telling you the truth. I wasn't hurt. It's just…"

Reed stepped closer, scanning their surroundings and finding nothing amiss. "Just what?"

"Nerves." Her voice wasn't as self-assured as she would have liked, but there was nothing she could do about it.

"Understood. I should have had one of the other officers take you home earlier. Sorry."

"I probably would have argued with you then, but it has been a long day." She was scanning the street. "Look. Is that the car we're waiting for?"

"Yes. About time, too." Stepping off the curb, he flagged down an SUV identical to his. It pulled over and he leaned in the passenger side window. Abigail trailed after him, surprised to see a grinning uniformed woman behind the wheel. A closer look told her the pretty brunette was also a K-9 cop. And she was taunting Reed.

"That's some fender bender, Branson. You plan to polish out the dings on your lunch hour?"

Reed huffed. "It's gonna take a lot more than elbow grease to fix that mess." He noted Abigail's arrival over his shoulder and made introductions. "Brianne, this is Ms. Jones. Abigail. She was the victim of an incident that Jessie and I worked at Coney Island a few nights ago."

"And…?"

"And, she'll be fostering one of Stella's pups for us. The sweet one that was returned after failing the initial assessment for police work."

"Let's hope she can still become a service dog."

Looking past Reed, she said, "Nice to meet you, Abigail. I take it you have the necessary experience?"

"Well, I…" Lying was wrong, yet she loved the puppy already and did want to keep her.

"I'm going to be assisting until Ms. Jones is well prepared," Reed said. "So, how is Stella coming along?"

"Fine. Don't change the subject. Has this placement been approved by Noah?"

"He approved a trial placement," Reed informed Brianne. "Now, if you're ready I'll load the dogs and we'll drop you at headquarters."

"Won't be necessary," the other K-9 officer said, leaving the SUV. "I'll catch a ride in one of the patrol cars." She cast a sidelong glance at Abigail and raised her eyebrows. "Wouldn't want to cramp your style, Branson."

"It's not like that," Reed insisted. "This is community service. And I'm on my own time."

"If you say so." By the time Brianne started to turn away, she was grinning.

Concerned, Abigail followed Reed around to the rear in case he needed her to help. "I don't want to get you in trouble."

"Don't mind her. All cops tend to be cynical. If it looks suspicious, it probably is. That doesn't mean she's right. My boss understands why I brought Midnight to you."

"Something tells me it wasn't only for the dog's sake."

"What difference does it make? We need good foster homes and you can provide one. If you happen to get personal benefit from the placement, it's win-win."

"I don't want to do anything wrong."

"Let me worry about that, okay? Now climb in. I was starving before we were attacked and—"

"We were what? I thought this was an accident." She could tell by his expression that he hadn't meant to reveal so much.

Once she got that notion in her head, it was impossible to erase it. If the truck slamming into them was trying to hurt them, then the whole incident began to make sense. It had zoomed out of that alley so fast she'd barely had time to gasp, let alone shout a warning to Reed. Yes, New Yorkers had a reputation for aggressive driving, but entering traffic so carelessly wasn't something a delivery driver would do if he wanted to keep his job.

"I never looked at the faces of the people in the truck," she said ruefully. "Maybe if I had, I'd have gotten over my temporary amnesia and recognized them."

"Or maybe they had a beef with all cops and wanted to take one out," Reed countered. "You can't be sure they intended to hurt you."

"Hurt me?" Abigail gave an ironic-sounding chuckle. "If it was connected to the attack in Luna Park, I suspect somebody wanted to do more than just hurt me. Those people don't know my memory is gone so they probably believe I can ID them for whatever they've done." She swallowed hard. "I think they hoped to permanently eliminate the threat. Namely, me."

Reed didn't say much during the drive back to Abigail's apartment, but his brain provided plenty of opinions regarding the accident.

Getting a large truck into position to smack into the passing police vehicle would have been iffy at best, yet the notion that the seeming attack had been a real accident was hard to swallow. Taking the incident at face value was foolish. It might give him ulcers to keep assuming the worst, but that was the only way to stay on guard against a surprise attack. This afternoon was proof of that.

He'd been having a nice time playing escort for Abigail Jones. Too nice. And he had overlooked impending danger. Whether their attackers had meant bodily harm or not, it was unsettling to be the bull's-eye of anyone's target. He sure didn't want to have a working police K-9 named after *him* posthumously like his partner, who represented fallen officer Jessie Ramirez.

Deep in thought, Reed was jarred when Abigail reached across and touched his arm. "I'm sorry."

"For what?"

"For dragging you over to Brighton Beach and getting your car wrecked."

Reed was shaking his head as he glanced at her. "Don't be ridiculous. You didn't force me to go anywhere. That was my idea. And you weren't driving, I was, so the responsibility for the accident rests on me. Period."

"You said it wasn't an accident."

"It will be looked into. Nobody is sure the truck was after us."

"But they drove away."

"Maybe they had criminal records. Or maybe their cargo wasn't legit, and they didn't want it checked. There are plenty of reasons why people dodge the law."

Tears glistened in her eyes. "That's true, I suppose."

"Of course it is. This job, this life, is not for everyone. It can alienate you from friends and family, for one thing." Pondering his own past, he began to smile. "When my dad was trying to talk me out of going to the police academy, he used to say I'd be making myself the skunk at the Sunday school picnic."

"That's terrible."

"But it can be valid," Reed said pensively. "Dad was being realistic. Civilian attitudes toward cops aren't always complimentary." A red light stopped them, giving him time to study her expression in more depth. She looked slightly distressed, but unless he missed his guess, there was a lot more emotion boiling beneath her surface of pseudo-calm.

When she said, "You don't have to be a cop to get ostracized—it can happen to anybody whose ideas conflict with the latest public whims," her expression gave him confirmation.

"What somebody else decides is their right even if it's against the law," he added.

Abigail was slowly nodding. She'd averted her face, but he could see her reflection in the side window's glass. It looked as if her cheeks were wet with tears.

"That's the hardest part," she said quietly. "Sticking to your principles when you know other people are doing wrong. It's especially hard for kids like the ones I help."

"You must be good at your job for a tough teen like Kiera to want to confide in you," Reed told her. "I can tell you have empathy. That's a special gift."

Her head snapped around and she stared at him. "A gift?" She huffed. "It's more like the scar from a horrible wound, one I will never forget."

EIGHT

There was no parking available in front of her apartment building. Abigail said, "Stop and let me out here."

"You want me to walk you in, don't you?"

Yes, she did. And *no*, she was not going to admit it. Not after letting down her guard and revealing too much personal information. After unsnapping the seat belt, she used her shoulder to nudge open the door, then slid out. The polite thing to do would be to invite Reed in, but at that moment she was so disgusted with herself she simply wanted to be alone. No people. No dogs. If she let their camaraderie resume he was bound to start asking personal questions. Questions she did not want to answer.

"I can manage fine by myself." The keys to the foyer door and her apartment were on a ring tucked into the pocket of her jeans opposite her cell phone. Fishing out the keys, she left the street and hurried up the stone steps.

A sidelong peek showed that Reed was getting out of the car. "Hey! Wait for me."

Abigail's fingers were trembling as she tried to hold the first key steady. Noise in the street was making her head swim. What was wrong with that key? It had always fit easily into the lock before.

A car backfired. She jumped as if it were a gunshot. *Key, key. Come on.* Grabbing her right hand with her left, she managed to control the action enough to unlock the street door and step through. The automatic locking mechanism clicked into place behind her.

Fisting the key ring, she started up the stairs. By the time she reached the first landing she was running. Panting. Gasping. Hoping and praying to reach her apartment before her burst of nervous energy gave out. The sense that someone was pursuing her was strong and growing. That was ridiculous in the secure building, of course, but it didn't keep her imagination from insisting otherwise.

"Why didn't I let Reed come up with me?" she kept asking herself. "Why?" Was it false pride? Fear that he would look down on her if he knew the whole truth? Or had she somehow reverted to the frightened, lost teen she'd been when she'd fled her home and sought solace on the streets with others of her kind, throwaway kids nobody cared about or missed enough to look for?

Reaching the third floor, Abigail hurried to 312, managed to use the key and darted inside, slamming the door behind her and turning the dead bolt for extra security. Home. Sanctuary. Peace and quiet.

She leaned against the inside of the door, catching her breath and struggling against the panic, before she actually looked at her living room. There was a beige sofa and coordinating frieze on an occasional chair. Silk flowers waited in a milk glass vase atop a small dining table at the end of the kitchen, and the portion of the counter that was visible was tidy.

So why was she still sensing a threat? She folded her arms across her chest and studied the apartment as if she were a CSI looking over a crime scene.

Throw pillows? Check. Curtains pulled to dim the light from outside? Check. Library book on the end table by the chair? Check. Daily mail? Uh-oh. She began to scowl. "I'm sure Olga put it on the table when she brought it up for me." Was it possible she had merely imagined the daily routine happening again? And where was her purse?

Abigail's chest tightened with a band of tension that again restricted her breathing. She'd taken her purse to work with her. It was either still at the office or in the K-9 cop's wrecked vehicle! If that SUV ended up in a repair garage, there was no telling what would become of her personal property.

Her cell phone was cradled in her hand before she realized she hadn't saved Reed's number. Dialing 911 as if her problem was an emergency was wrong, so what other options did she have? She wasn't even sure he was connected to the precinct that patrolled her neighborhood.

Feeling guilty for calling out to God only when she was in dire straits, Abigail nonetheless prayed, "Lord, what now?"

Instead of receiving a sense of calm, she thought she heard an unfamiliar noise. She held her breath. Listened for it to repeat. Had it come from her bedroom? Walls between apartments weren't soundproof, so it could have come from next door. But what if it hadn't? Instinct insisted she should turn around and leave.

"And go where?" she said, barely speaking and relying on the sound of her own voice for slight solace. The deserted hallway could be just as menacing as what she thought she'd just heard. Suppose her imagination was on overload again?

Abigail pressed her back against the inside of her entry door. Reed had told her he'd seen at least two men leaving the scene of her assault, so what if one was in there with her and the other waited in the hall?

The phone in her hand vibrated! She fumbled with it, trying to answer. Instead of hello, she whispered, "Help," then hoped the call wasn't from a telemarketing computer.

"Abby? Abigail? Are you all right?"

It was Reed. *Praise the Lord*, it was Reed.

"Why did you run off? What's going on?"

Her mouth was so dry she could hardly speak. Cradling the phone, she cupped her other hand around her mouth and said, "I think there's somebody in the apartment with me."

"I'm already on my way. Hide!" he shouted in her ear.

Abigail would gladly have followed his orders if she could have. Unfortunately, her body was refusing to listen to her mind. Her sandals might as well have been nailed to the living room floor.

An interior door shut with a *snick*.

Abigail willed herself to flee. Nothing happened.

Footsteps made a slow, unmistakable cadence.

She inhaled. Swallowed a gasp. Watched for signs of the prowler she was now certain of. Her head was swimming. Her stomach lurched. Tight fists made her nails cut into her palms.

That pain was enough to jar her loose. She dropped to the floor and crawled behind the sofa. Heartbeats in her ears mimicked a bass drum. Intakes of breath were like a hurricane. Evil filled the atmosphere.

She held her breath as best she could and waited. There were no words for another divine supplication. All she could do was picture Reed Branson and pray in her heart that he reached her in time.

If Reed had taken the time to park before phoning Abigail's cell, it might have taken him longer to respond. As it was, he'd made up his mind to join her whether she liked it or not. That decision had supposedly been based on delivering Midnight, but he wasn't fooling himself. He wanted, he needed, to see with his own eyes that she was all right.

And now he knew otherwise. No wonder something inside him had kept insisting he must not leave her. She was in trouble. And it was her own fault. If she hadn't jumped out of the car and taken off he'd have been there to help her.

The staircase to the third floor was deserted this time. Breathing hard, he tried the knob on her door. It didn't turn. Should he knock and tip off a possible prowler or smash in the door and take a chance on traumatizing Abigail?

He knocked. "Ms. Jones?"

Nothing.

He rapped louder. "Abigail?"

TV and movie cops broke down doors with their shoulders. Real ones knew better. Lacking a battering ram and sufficient manpower to swing it, he readied himself for a kick.

The knob moved. Reed put a hand on the butt of his concealed .38, ready to draw if necessary.

Then he heard her whisper his name. "Reed?"

The door swung open. Abigail was standing there, tears streaming down her face, cheeks pale, hair mussed, looking more like one of the street kids she helped than she did a social worker.

Every muscle in his body was taut, his nerves primed. "You okay?"

She nodded, then stepped back and pointed to the hallway he hadn't explored when he'd visited before.

"The prowler?"

"Yes. I heard him back there."

This time, Reed did draw his weapon. Thumb resting on the safety, he gestured to Abigail with his free hand. "You stay here." Her lack of positive response made him hesitate. "I mean it. Don't move till I get back."

"O-okay."

There were only two doors off the short hallway and both of them were open. A tiny bathroom had no outlet. Her bedroom, however, had a window that provided access to a fire escape. Sea breezes were lifting the leading edges of the curtain.

Reed paused only long enough to make sure the prowler hadn't set a trap by hiding in the closet, then hurried to the open window and looked down the fire escape. A large person wearing a dark hoodie dropped down from the extension ladder and hit the sidewalk running.

"Police! Freeze!" Reed shouted, figuring his chances of compliance were zero to none. He was right. The fleeing man had a nondescript car waiting and disappeared into it.

Holstering the .38, he returned to Abigail. She had

obviously recovered some but was still far from sedate. "Sorry," Reed told her, "he got away."

"Did you see him?"

"Not enough to identify. He ran down the fire escape. I'll have the window frame dusted for prints but I doubt we'll find any."

"I always keep that window closed and locked."

He nodded and began investigating the rest of the apartment. "I'm glad I got here before he had a chance to harm you. Can you tell if he stole anything?"

"There's hardly anything in here worth stealing," she replied. "I live simply. My computer is at work and I keep a tablet in my purse. Which reminds me. I think I left the purse in your wrecked car. I really need it."

"Understood." Search completed, he studied her. Whether she realized it or not, she couldn't stay here. Not until she remembered enough for the police to recognize and capture her enemies. The question was, how was he going to convince her to find a more secure place to live when he knew she considered her current apartment a sanctuary?

Perhaps being blunt would save them all time and argument. "You need to find some other place to stay for a little while," Reed said flatly. "Call a friend."

All Abigail did was shake her head.

"I'm serious. You can't stay here now that we know how vulnerable you are."

"New York is full of burglars. I'll keep the window locked."

"I thought you said you already did."

"Well, he must have jimmied it." Beginning to pace, she waved her hands in the air as proof of her frustration. "I don't know."

Reed leaned back against the kitchen counter, folded his arms and gave her a steady look. "Think for a minute. The locks on the window are fine. I just checked. It seems more likely that he got in through the door and used the window for a quick exit when he heard me coming."

Rosy color drained from her face. Her lips parted. Her eyes widened, glistening. "How?"

"Our crime scene techs may have some idea after they've examined this place, but don't count on it. Old buildings are covered with scars." Waiting for her to come to a suitable conclusion was driving him crazy, so he stepped closer and clasped her upper arms gently. "Look, I know none of this is your fault, but that doesn't make it any less real. The more disturbing events pile up on you, the less likely you are to be able to recover your memory. That alone should be enough to convince you to move."

"I don't have any place to go."

"Friends?"

"Not any with extra room."

"How about the lady downstairs. Olga? She'd probably take you in."

"No way. I'd be putting her in jeopardy. The same goes for my boss, Wanda."

A solution to the problem had occurred to him already and he had discarded it for several reasons, not the least being his inconvenient attraction to this young woman. If—and that was a big if—he ever did decide to marry and settle down, his wife would need to be strong-willed and stable emotionally in order to cope with the trials and rigors of a cop's job. Abigail Jones was far too sensitive and empathetic for a life like that.

The arrival of patrol officers distracted Reed for the next ten minutes. By the time those men had spoken with Abigail he'd made up his mind. With nothing stolen and no harm to the occupant of the apartment, nothing would be done about this invasion of her privacy. That left only one alternative as far as he was concerned. He'd have to take her home to Rego Park, Queens, with him.

Reed grimaced. His sister, Lani, was not going to be happy about sharing her half of their place. Not happy at all. The only element of his idea that might appeal to her was taking in Midnight as well as Abigail Jones. Lani was a sucker for dogs. After all, she was also becoming a part of their K-9 unit and had never met a dog she didn't love.

That way the pup could learn manners from watching an older dog. He smiled to himself. Talk about coming up with the perfect excuse to include the young Lab. He was a genius! There was no way Lani could refuse to go along with his idea when there was a needy puppy involved.

NINE

All Abigail wanted after the stressful morning she'd had was to kick off her shoes and stretch out on the sofa. Instead, she had company that kept needling her. "I still don't see how sharing a place with you and your sister is better than staying here. Don't you both work?"

"Yes, but not necessarily the same shifts. Besides, nobody will know where you've gone."

"It's not practical. Queens is too far from my kids."

"I get it. I do," Reed said, "but I can arrange to drive you back to this neighborhood. It's not as if Rego Park is out of state."

Her glance drifted over the inanimate objects in her living room. Nothing she owned held particular importance for her. Resale shops had provided the furniture, tag sales the kitchenware and bargain stores the incidentals. It was all generic and nothing had been a gift.

The only photos she had displayed on the bookcase were of a few of the kids she had pulled in off the streets and rehabilitated. Many others had refused to let her take their pictures. She understood why. Life had damaged their capacity to trust, especially with regard to adults, and they didn't want to leave behind any clue to themselves, no matter where they went after leaving Brighton Beach.

She could identify with them. When she had run away and stayed on the streets during her sixteenth summer, she had acclimated far more than she had expected. If it hadn't been for a mentor, a woman like she had become, there was no telling how far she might have sunk and whether she would have even lived this long. Given that she was essentially paying back a debt to the loving group that had saved her from destruction, she couldn't knowingly throw it all away through false pride or stubbornness. She had to yield to Reed.

"All right," Abigail said, turning to him. "Call your sister and make sure she doesn't mind if I camp there for a little while. If it's okay with her, I'll go."

"She's fine with it."

Studying his ruggedly handsome face she half smiled. "You haven't asked her, have you?"

"Well, no, but I know Lani. She won't mind. And having a yard for the pup is a big plus. Otherwise you'd have to take her out and walk her on the street half a dozen times a day. You don't want to do that, do you?"

Abigail huffed. "I already agreed to go. You can save the big sell."

"Yes, ma'am." Reed was grinning at her.

"I do appreciate all you've done for me. I don't know anyone else who would have used so much of his free time for the benefit of a stranger."

"You're not a stranger," he countered. "Not anymore. Grab whatever you think you'll need and let's go. The dogs are waiting."

"I can't believe you left them both in the car," she said, intending to sound critical.

"I told you the AC was on. They were secure and fine. Did you expect me to take the time to get them out and lug that moose up the stairs when I knew you were in trouble?"

"No." She made a face. "You're right."

"Well, that's an improvement."

One eyebrow arched higher than the other and she tilted her head to the side. "What is?"

"You just said I was right about something. I may keel over from shock any minute."

"Hey, if I have an opinion, you're going to hear it, regardless."

Reed had to chuckle. "No kidding."

Hands fisted on her hips, Abigail took a stand in more ways than one. "Look. I know I've been traumatized. I'm not my usual self, nor am I the person you met at Luna Park. I'm no helpless weakling. I've had to fight to be taken seriously all my life and I'm not backing down. I will do whatever it takes or say whatever I need to in order to recover my memory and continue my career. It's my true calling, whether you realize it or not."

She had watched his expression fluctuate as she spoke. He was definitely listening.

"My apologies, Ms. Jones," Reed said soberly. "You're right. I was assuming too much." He noted the time. "The dogs have been alone for almost half an hour. I need to go check on them. How long will it take you to pack?"

"Not long." She wanted to keep him in sight, to lean on his strength despite her speech to the contrary. "Why don't you go get them and bring them up here for a few minutes while I grab an overnight bag and fill it?"

"I can do that," Reed replied.

She could tell he was as hesitant to leave as she was to have him go. When he suggested she walk down with him to get the dogs, she was more than happy to oblige. Noting how cautiously he entered the hallway before permitting her to join him helped reinforce her decision to move. Staying on edge day and night was not conducive to her mental healing.

To Abigail's consternation, she was literally yearning to remain near Reed. He'd become her anchor in the maelstrom whirling around her, the only steadying influence in her life.

Everyone else needed *her* to help *them*. Only Reed Branson stood ready to give support instead of taking it.

With Abigail to coax Midnight to try, the gangly pup made it up the stairs. By the third floor the younger dog was gamboling and panting and wagging her tail as if she'd just climbed Mt. Everest.

"She did it!" Abigail acted almost as excited as the ebony pup.

It pleased Reed to see how delighted the two of them were by their shared accomplishment. Let them celebrate while they could. He was still on protection duty. All he had to do was keep Abby from noticing his diligence.

Using the shortened version of her name in his thoughts made him ask aloud, "Does anybody ever call you Abby?"

Her smile disappeared. "My mother used to. I don't care for it, if you don't mind."

"Sorry."

"Don't be. It would have been better for me if Mom had hit the road with Dad when he left."

"Did your mother divorce him? Remarry?" He held the apartment door for her and they entered with the dogs.

"Nope. But she had plenty of boyfriends."

"Is that why you left?" He could tell she was debating whether or not to explain and he knew he shouldn't have pressed her, so he added, "Never mind. It's none of my business."

"I wasn't going to put it like that. I'd just rather not discuss it." Pink color rose in her cheeks. "Those are memories I wish I could forget the way I've blacked out getting attacked."

"Have you recalled anything about that night?" he asked, glad for a change of subject.

Thoughtful, she passed him Midnight's leash and stepped back. "Just little glimmers. A thought will start to form, then disappear. Like the foggy shadows."

"What shadows?"

"It's hard to explain. I can be thinking of something else and a picture of shadowy figures will flash into my mind. The harder I try to focus on it, the quicker the scene is gone."

"What did it remind you of? People?"

"I think so. More than one. And when we went to my office to meet with Kiera, I got a flash of something that made the hair on my arms stand on end." She shivered. "It was as though I was seeing her as part of the attack."

"Do you think she was?"

Abigail was shaking her head vigorously. "No. I do wonder if one of my other cases might have been involved, though. Those kids stick together. It's possible that Kiera knows more than she's willing to admit."

Reed nodded. "Okay. One thing at a time. I'll wait

with the dogs while you go pack. Make it fast. We want to get out of here ASAP."

"Do you think the prowler will come back?"

What should he do? Reed asked himself. Tell her the truth and make her fearful or reassure her when he could be wrong?

"I don't have a clue," he said honestly. "The only thing I am sure of is that you'll be safer someplace else."

Mirroring his nod, she squared her shoulders and stood tall. "Thank you," she said flatly. "I appreciate your candor."

The sight of this slightly built, lovely young woman displaying so much inner strength despite the circumstances took him by surprise. When she'd told him she possessed hidden fortitude, he'd doubted her. Now he was seeing it for himself.

Nothing changed about her either, as she left him and went to pack. Was she really as strong as she acted or was she putting on a front to keep from showing her true feelings?

Her bravery had to be genuine, he reasoned. When he'd first met her, she had been a basket case, so traumatized she could barely speak let alone function normally. There was no way she could be faking this much recovery. The real Abigail Jones was emerging and it gave him pause. While she'd seemed so broken, he could justify spending an inordinate amount of time looking after her. Now that she was regaining fortitude, she needed him far less.

Reed knew he should be glad she wasn't quite so needy anymore. Part of him was thrilled.

The disquieting element of the change in Abigail was his realization that he was also disappointed.

* * *

A last look at her apartment as she locked the door behind her made Abigail feel strangely sad. It wasn't much but it was home. No other place had ever seemed so dear, so safe, so comforting. And now that sense of peace had been stolen from her just as surely as if a thief had stripped the rooms bare.

Reed was waiting in the hall with the dogs. "I see you travel light."

"I don't need much besides my phone and a couple changes of clothes. Once you bring me my purse I'll have everything." She purposely neglected to mention that a large chunk of her salary was spent on others, especially the kids she was trying to coax off the streets. A Fresh Start had a budget for essentials but it barely covered the most basic necessities, and it gave her pleasure to add whatever she could. Although her boss was aware of some of her largesse the directors of the program had no clue about its scope, which was exactly how she wanted it.

"We'll go first," Reed said, gesturing at the stairwell. "Stick close."

"Hey, if you were wearing a backpack I'd climb into it," Abigail told him with a nervous chuckle.

"If we didn't have the puppy with us I could put Jessie at heel and carry you the way I did at Luna Park."

Hearing that caused her pulse to jump. "You what?"

"Carried you." He glanced over his shoulder. "Sorry. I shouldn't talk about that night because I don't want to influence your memories. The mind is a funny thing. People tend to fill in details they don't know, without realizing it, because their brain isn't satisfied with loose ends."

"Really?"

"Yes. Really."

Sticking close to his back, she almost ran into him when he stopped at the outer door to check the busy sidewalk and street beyond.

Abigail had to smile. "My neighbors will be glad to see me go. Anything to keep you from blocking traffic so often."

"It was necessary."

"I know. And I thank you. Again. I just hate to see so many drivers upset with the police."

"Yeah. Until they need us themselves. Then it's different." Reed shrugged. "Come on. Let's get your stuff and these dogs stowed and get out of here."

She followed closely, trying to help yet also stay out of his way. In seconds they were back on the road.

"Tell me about your sister," Abigail said.

That brought a smile. "Lani's amazing. She's been a dancer and an actress and also taught self-defense."

"I thought she was a cop, like you?"

"She is." Reed's smile spread. "The last time she re-invented herself, she decided she wanted to follow in my footsteps and work with K-9s. I didn't try to talk her out of it because I never dreamed she'd get this far. She surprised me and by not only getting into K-9 training but managing to transfer to my unit when she graduated."

"I'd have thought siblings wouldn't be allowed."

He laughed. "Normally, they aren't. My unit is unique, and Lani made the most of it."

"I hope she likes me."

"Lani likes everybody. She can be a bit overwhelming if you're not used to her personality. Just go with the flow."

With a silent sigh Abigail leaned back in the seat and folded her hands in her lap. Isolation and quiet was what she loved about the apartment she'd just left. Chaos often haunted her at work and she looked forward to calm, solitary evenings reading a good book or maybe watching an old movie on TV. Moving in with Reed and his sister, plus the dogs was likely to make going to her job seem like a sanctuary instead of the other way around.

Well, it couldn't be helped. She'd cope. Somehow. After all, the change was only temporary. Her apartment would be there when she was ready to go home.

A catch in her throat brought unshed tears to her eyes and she coughed to cover the reaction. When she had thought of home just now, she had realized that her feelings had been altered by the presence of the prowler. He might not have taken concrete objects from her, but he had stolen just the same. He had robbed her of what little peace she'd had left and there wasn't a thing she could do about it.

Casting a sidelong glance at Reed, she wondered how long his altruism was going to last. What if his sister pitched a fit at him for bringing home a houseguest and she had to find other accommodations? Where would she go? She could barely afford one place to live. Paying for a second one while trying to break her lease in Brighton Beach was out of the question.

Abigail turned to stare out the side window, barely heeding the passing cityscape. Her heart and mind turned to the only true anchor she had, her wavering yet tenacious faith. Sensible prayer was difficult when she was so confused, so adrift.

Out of her scarred memory came a Bible truth. *God*

*takes care of the flowers of the fields and the birds of
the air, so consider how much better He will provide
for his children.*

It didn't spell out the path she must follow, but it did
speak of trusting the Lord. Given her current circumstances, Abigail figured that was the best advice around.

All she had to do was make it happen.

Easier said than done.

Faith was not a tangible thing that could be grabbed
and stuffed into a box for safekeeping. It was a state
of mind, an acceptance of God's invisible power and
unqualified acceptance, no matter what a person had
or hadn't done. That was why turning your life over to
Christ was sometimes so difficult.

And yet, over time, Abigail had experienced the
Lord's kindness, His leading, His unending presence
in the midst of her worst trials. Looking back, it was
easy to see how He had protected her in the past and had
guided her steps into the present. Setting aside her mis-
givings, she knew without a doubt that she was blessed.

Her gaze drifted to the driver on her left. A week ago
they didn't even know each other, and today she was
on her way to live in his house. Either that was divine
guidance or she was about to dive into worse trouble
than she'd ever imagined.

Hopefully it was the former and would turn out to be
another blessing. That was certainly her unspoken prayer.

TEN

Reed's residential street in Queens was different from hers in Brighton Beach. For one thing, it was quieter. He slowed, waved at a group of neighbor kids shooting hoops in a driveway, then pulled to the curb across the street. "This is it."

"Wow. Parking practically in front of the house!"

He laughed. "Living out here has its perks. I would have stopped in the driveway if I thought our upstairs tenant was home. He gets the garage. I park outside. Having a police car out front is a great crime deterrent."

"I would think so."

Glad to see her spirits rising, Reed wisely avoided mentioning the mood change. Instead, he climbed out, leashed the dogs and released them. The pup was so excited she was running circles around Jessie and twisting together their light leashes.

Abigail retrieved her overnight bag and joined him. "Looks like they're glad to be here."

"Yeah. Me, too." He gestured at the white, two-story dwelling on its narrow lot. Houses on either side were clearly the same floor plan but had been modified over time by their various owners. The Branson place had a stone facade with short pillars next to the sidewalk to denote the beginning of the entry path. What lawn there was had been mowed recently, and flower beds graced a narrow strip fronting the porch.

"It's pretty," Abigail said. "Very welcoming."

"You can thank Lani," he replied. "She's the one who plants the flowers. I will admit I did some of the painting but only because she made me."

"*Made* you? I doubt that."

"Okay, she guilted me into helping her." He knew there was a goofy grin on his face but for some reason it felt right.

"That, I can believe."

As Reed shepherded his little group up the steps and onto the porch, he experienced an unanticipated surge of emotion. Lacking a different definition, he named it *joy*. Really? In the midst of all the conflicts in his work and home life, he was actually joyful? That seemed wrong, particularly in view of the mourning his unit was doing over their late chief, Jordan Jameson. Plus, they were all worried about Katie, Jordy's widow. Katie had been newly pregnant when Jordan was murdered six months ago and not only was she going to have to raise the child alone, she was still in limbo about the identity of her husband's murderer. They all were. So what right did anyone have to be this happy?

Reed had to smile at his twisted thoughts. Jordan Jameson had been a Christian. He'd see his family again someday. It was finding clues to his killer or killers that should be foremost on everybody's mind. Just when they thought they were getting closer to resolving the puzzle, something happened to pull them back. Crime never took a vacation. Drugs, gangs, muggings, drive-by shootings and myriad other events kept the entire police force engaged 24/7.

Opening the door for Abigail, he held back the dogs and paused to give his and Jessie's jobs serious thought. He couldn't help but be thankful that they were tasked with tracking instead of, say, bomb detection. Reed wasn't keen on working with a K-9 whose nose was trained to seek out destruction. His Jessie found lost people and that was fine with him.

Case in point. His gaze fastened on Abigail as she perused the small living room. If he hadn't been assigned to look for Snapper on the boardwalk at exactly the right time, not only might he have failed to meet her, she might have received more serious injuries. That thought deposited a boulder in the pit of his stomach. Thank God that he was around when she'd needed him.

"This is lovely," Abigail said. "You and your sister share the downstairs?"

"Yes. And the kitchen. Lani keeps telling me that cooking isn't necessarily a woman's job so we take turns."

"In other words, you order out?" Abigail was smiling at him and his cheeks warmed.

"Sometimes. I make a mean hamburger when I can grill in the backyard."

"How often have you done it with snow on the ground?" she asked.

Reed had to laugh. "A few. How did you know?"

"I'm a good guesser."

Reed passed her, leading both dogs. "I'll go let these girls out the back door and then show you your room. When I phoned Lani she said she'd move and give you her room but I figured you'd turn it down. The same goes for mine."

"You know me pretty well."

"I like to think so."

Just then the front door burst open, startling everyone. A young blonde woman wearing workout clothes that accented her athleticism was making her usual theatrical entrance. "Hi! You must be Abigail." She dropped overfull totes on the floor and stuck out her right hand. "I'm Lani, Reed's sister. Welcome to Queens. I picked up a few groceries. We'll order a pizza for supper. You like pizza, don't you? Of course you do. Everybody loves a good New York pizza."

Abigail briefly shook hands. "Hello."

"Has Reed shown you your room? I told him you could have my bed but he was sure you wouldn't accept it so I made up a cot in the spare room. It's usually an office. I hope you don't mind. I know it's not much but it's all we have."

Watching Abigail's reaction to Lani's monologue brought a grin and almost made Reed laugh out loud. His sister was a whirlwind of enthusiasm no matter what she was doing. Today was no exception. If Abigail ever managed to get a word in edgewise he was certain they would find common ground and get along well.

He held up a hand. "Whoa. Calm down, sis. We just got here a minute ago. I haven't even had time to put the dogs out."

Lani returned his smile and shrugged. "Sorry. I just want our guest to feel at home."

"I'm sure I will," Abigail said. "Right now, everything is kind of overwhelming." She met Lani's gaze. "Did Reed tell you about my loss of memory?"

"He mentioned it, yes." Lani took Abigail's hand and patted it. "We'll get you back to normal soon, I promise. He said you were attacked. I used to teach self-defense, you know. While you're here I can give you lessons."

The black puppy was tugging at the leash and trying to chew it. Reed ignored her long enough to counter his sister's suggestion. "I don't think that's such a great idea, Lani. Abigail will be plenty safe staying with us. She doesn't need instructions in hand-to-hand fighting. She's far better off relying on the police."

By the time he finished making his point, both women were staring at him. Lani was making a silly face and Abigail looked irate. That was not good. He figured he was about to learn plenty about her opinion. When she fisted her hands on her hips he was positive.

"You're joking, right?"

What could he tell her except the truth? "Um, no."

She rolled her eyes at him, then at Lani. "Do you believe this guy?"

"Sure," Lani said with a chuckle. "He's my brother. He's always underestimating me."

"Me, too." Abigail began to smile. "I'll be ready for my first self-defense lesson when you are. In the meantime I'll help you carry the groceries to the kitchen."

"My kind of houseguest," Lani said with enthusiasm. "C'mon, Abby. Grab a bag."

"She doesn't like that nickname," Reed called after them. A lot of good it did him. They disappeared into the kitchen together as if they had rehearsed a stage exit from one of Lani's little theater productions.

"Humph." Reed looked down at the dogs. Jessie was waiting for a command while Midnight nibbled on the bloodhound's ear. "I'm surrounded," he quipped. "Outnumbered by females." Starting for the back door he said, "All right, girls. Let's go outside and get some air. I need a break as much as you do."

Boy, was that the truth! When he'd suggested that Abigail meet and share a home with him and Lani, he hadn't imagined a joining of forces. It wouldn't hurt Lani to absorb a little of Abigail's sweet nature, but he sure hoped the influence didn't flow both ways. If it did, he was going to have more trouble than ever convincing Abigail to take his advice.

It struck Abigail funny that she had taken to both Branson siblings so easily. They were not terribly alike, yet each had a way of making her feel welcome. While Lani called to order a pizza, she busied herself pulling fresh vegetables out of the totes and lining them up on the counter.

"This romaine looks fantastic," Abigail remarked. "There's a greengrocer's close to my place in Brighton Beach. I shop there often." *When I'm not hiding from my own shadow.*

"Fresh is always the best. I have to walk a couple blocks farther but it's worth it." Lani paused. "Reed tells me you've had it pretty rough lately. I hope staying with us gives you a break. I can't imagine being by myself all the time."

Puzzled, Abigail tilted her head to one side. "Really? Why should you be worried when you're a cop and you know self-defense?"

Lani smiled sweetly. "I'm not afraid. I just know I'd be lonesome, even once I get my K-9 assignment. I like people around me." She giggled. "Even my stuffy brother."

"Stuffy? I never noticed that about Reed. He's always seemed very helpful and upbeat."

"Yeah? Pass me the salad makings," Lani said, opening a crisper drawer in the refrigerator. While she was bent over, putting the produce away, she said, "Personally, I think Reed is a great guy, too. Trouble is, he eats, sleeps and breathes the K-9 unit. That doesn't leave time for a social life."

Abigail was fairly certain Lani was issuing an unnecessary warning, so she countered with her own explanation. "I'm sure there is nothing *social* about your brother's concern for my welfare. He was the officer who first found me after I was attacked and has kindly shepherded me through the beginning of my healing process. It's not personal."

"If you say so. He seems to like you a lot, though. I'd hate to see him hurt."

The notion of her self-appointed protector being hurt, physically or emotionally, slammed into Abigail like a rogue Atlantic wave. All this time, while Reed had been looking after her welfare, she hadn't properly considered his. Well, she would now. The immensity of his sacrifice was just beginning to register. Before, she had let herself fall into the trap of feeling helpless and hopeless because of her lapse of memory. From now on she intended to be proactive.

How she was going to accomplish that remained as unknown as her insight into the attack at the park or the traffic accident or the break-in at her apartment. Although she already had all the human assistance she needed, she realized she had failed to pray for continuing guidance and wisdom. Doing so properly, however, was best accomplished in private, so she asked, "Would you mind if I went to my room to freshen up a bit before supper?"

"Not at all. Where are my manners? Hang on a sec and I'll show you to your room."

"I can take her," Reed offered, stepping in the back door without the dogs. "The furry contingent is playing on the grass."

"Okay, if you don't mind." For some reason Abigail found herself feeling shy.

"Not a bit." He picked up her suitcase and gestured with his free arm like a courtier in a medieval drama. "After you."

Abigail had not forgotten why she sought solitude, although if anything could have distracted her it was the handsome K-9 cop. They proceeded down a short hallway, stopping at the end. One look confirmed that the room Lani had prepared for her had been a home office. That didn't matter. It had a door and blinds on the windows. That was all the privacy she needed.

She paused in the doorway, blocking it and facing Reed. "Thank you. For everything."

He handed her the suitcase. "If you need anything, just ask. Lani says supper will be in about an hour, but if you want to rest longer, that's no problem."

"An hour will be fine," Abigail said. The small room behind her beckoned as if it wanted her to feel at home. She started to close the door.

Reed backed up. "Okay, then."

Truth to tell, Abigail didn't want to close him out, but she needed privacy in order to bare her soul to her heavenly Father. There was so much that she didn't understand, so many loose ends to the events of recent

days, she felt as if she were far beyond her depth and
being pulled under by an unseen riptide.

The latch clicked into place. Abigail pressed her
back to the closed door and sighed noisily. Her thoughts
reached out to God while her body was hit with intense
fatigue. She was spent in more ways than mere physical
exertion. Her heart was bruised by the way Kiera had
treated her, her thoughts were murky and disconnected,
and she was almost as bereft as she had been the day
she'd decided to run away to escape the unhealthy life
her mother had chosen.

After making her way to the narrow bed, she perched
on the edge, bowed her head, closed her eyes, folded her
hands and whispered, "Oh, Father, I'm so lost. I don't
know how I got here or what's next. Please, please show
me. Help me?"

In her mind she could almost hear, *Peace, be still.*
Wishful thinking sometimes manifested that way when
she was overwrought. And yet, there was a certain almost tangible peace flowing over and around her as if
she were being wrapped in a cloud of warmth and security.

Abigail resisted the sensation. She didn't want to be
cosseted, she wanted to be useful, in charge, making
a difference the way she did in the lives of the teenage runaways who came into her office. She wanted
to know what had happened to her and take an active
role in bringing her attackers to justice. She wanted…

Truth struck her hard. She wanted to tell the Lord
how to run her little universe. Of all the errors she'd
made lately, that was undoubtedly the worst, the most
foolish.

Turning her thoughts, her deepest heart, back to

prayer, she began with an apology. "Forgive me, Jesus. Forgive me. Please. I know you only want what's best for me." Abigail inhaled a shuddery breath and let it out slowly. As long as she relied upon her faith, she didn't need to know the details of God's ultimate plan.

Trusting Him was the key. It always had been, even when she'd been adrift and living on the streets like the kids she helped. That was when she had come to a spiritual awakening, thanks to several mentors. It had been as if the Lord had lined those believers up in His divine order and introduced them into her life at the exact moment when she was ready to accept the teaching each offered.

Grateful beyond words, Abigail realized that she still could have rejected the faith that now buoyed her up through this tempest. "Thank you, Father," she said, barely whispering as tears of thankfulness trickled down her cheeks.

Eyes closed, she continued in wordless gratitude, heart and mind. Each day demanded renewed commitment to her heavenly Father, just as each night required that she put her trust in His perfect wisdom and mercy.

Night Shadows. A memory wafted through her mind like windblown smoke.

Abigail tensed. Almost lost touch with the vision. There were three figures, two tall and one much shorter. The little one stood between the other two and was struggling.

Her eyes popped open. Reality immediately intruded, yet she managed to retain the elusive insight.

Jumping to her feet, she swiped away her tears, hurried to the door and jerked it open to yell, "Reed!"

ELEVEN

Hearing Abigail shout his name sent Reed's heart into orbit. They nearly knocked each other down when they collided in the hallway.

He grasped her shoulders and set her away so he could look into her face. "What's wrong?"

"Nothing." She was beaming through a mist of tears. "I remembered something. It was as clear as if I were looking right at it."

Struggling to control his pounding pulse, he slipped an arm around her shoulders and guided her toward the living room sofa. "Okay. Have a seat and tell me."

She twisted away, clearly elated. "No! I can't sit still. Listen. There were two guys at Luna Park that night. And a smaller person, probably a girl or young man. One guy was hanging onto the littler person and she— or he—was struggling to escape. I saw it all. I remember now."

He wasn't about to spoil her moment of triumph by mentioning that he'd likely observed the same two adults. Hearing that there had been a younger person involved was a definite breakthrough.

"Go on," Reed urged, working to keep his voice even and his tone casual. "What did you do then?"

Abigail deflated like a Mylar balloon on its third day. "I don't know. I didn't remember that far."

"It's okay," he was quick to tell her. "These things take time. You've made excellent progress. I have no doubt the rest of your memories will return soon."

"I should have tried to hold on to the vision."

"Not necessarily. You said you'd done that before with poor results. What you got, you got clearly. That's a big plus. We didn't know about the younger person before just now."

Abigail perked up a little and grasped his forearm. "Do you think it could have been Kiera they were holding? Is that why she was so evasive?"

"That's one possibility. Another is that she's the reason you were out there that night. Maybe you were going to meet her, she saw what was happening and split instead of trying to help. You told me she was obviously lying about why she wanted to talk to you at the center. She may have been embarrassed to admit deserting you the other night and wanted to know if you were aware she'd been nearby."

"You could be right." Sighing, Abigail looked to Lani, who had frozen in place to listen while holding a bowl of tossed salad. "What do you think?"

"Me? I'm just a rookie, but if this girl Kiera was acting funny after that night, I'd be inclined to peg her as a witness. Most victims put off different vibes. Did she seem afraid?"

"Not as afraid as I still felt," Abigail replied. "Just leaving my apartment was a major challenge." She shivered.

Reed slipped his arm around her shoulders without

stopping to think first. His instinct for protection insisted, overruling any sense of propriety. Although his sister arched an eyebrow quizzically, he didn't back down. The flashes of normalcy they were seeing from Abigail were promising, yes, but that didn't mean she was cured. Until she could willingly recall the entire incident at the carousel, she wasn't out of the woods. Figuratively or literally.

He guided her to the kitchen table, essentially turning her over to his sister. "I'm going to make a quick call to headquarters and notify the 60th Precinct, too. They need to be aware that there was a teenage victim involved in the first assault on Ms. Jones."

Lani was quick to reply. "Gotcha. If you're going outside to call it in, watch for the pizza man."

Nodding, Reed pulled out his cell and headed for the front door. Once he was outside he contacted his dispatcher and relayed Abigail's information, completing the call just as a pickup stopped at the curb. A man balancing a full pizza warmer jumped out and started up the walk.

Reed waved. "What do I owe you?"

He paid, took the hot pie and turned toward the open door, calling, "Thanks!" over his shoulder.

"No problem, man," the harried driver shouted back.

Reed had time to take only one step before he heard Abigail shriek.

She clapped both hands over her mouth. That voice. Did it belong to one of her attackers? At first hearing she'd thought so, but now that several seconds had passed she was growing less and less certain. Had the recent glimpse of lost memory triggered an aberration in her reasoning processes? Rather than remembering his voice, had she merely imagined a similarity?

Reed thrust the box at his sister and cupped Abigail's shoulders. "What happened? You're shaking."

"I thought... I thought..."

"You thought what?"

"That man's voice. It reminded me of someone. He couldn't have been the guy from the boardwalk, could he?"

"Of course he could."

"Did you know him? I mean, is he your regular delivery guy?"

"One of them," Reed told her. "Look, just because he sounded like the man who accosted you doesn't mean he's the same one, but there's nothing to prove he isn't until we check his alibi for the night you were chased." He guided her to the sofa. "Sit here while I make a couple more calls."

Abigail hated to keep following his orders but at the moment, sitting down seemed quite sensible. So did listening to his phone conversation. There was no doubt he was talking to the police, either his own unit or the one responsible for that Queens neighborhood.

"That's right," Reed said. "The pizza delivery was just made to my house. I want a check on the driver and his alibi for every night last week. If he was working, I want to know where his route took him." He listened for a brief minute, then added, "There's a chance he may tie to the Luna Park incident I worked when we were down there looking for Jordan Jameson's dog, Snapper."

Watching his expression, Abigail saw him listen and begin to frown.

"When? Where? Okay, stand by." Reed cupped a

palm over the receiver and spoke aside to her. "What do you know about a kid named Dominic Walenski?"

Her breath caught and she swallowed a gasp. "Why?"

"So, you do know him?"

"Yes. What's going on?"

"An anonymous caller reported that he's been kidnapped. When I mentioned Luna Park they told me that's where he was last seen."

"Oh, no!" Abigail managed to pull herself together enough to provide background. "Dom looks a lot younger than Kiera but he's almost her age. They're both part of a group that hangs out on the boardwalk most of the time."

"Okay." Listening to the phone, Reed held up his index finger to signal silence, so she waited. It wasn't easy. Dom was as much one of her kids as Kiera, maybe more so, considering the off-putting way that girl had been behaving lately. Abigail spread trembling hands wide, palms up, and mouthed, *Well?*

"All right," Reed said into the phone. "Jessie and I will stand by." He ended the call.

"What else did they say?"

"Not much. Apparently the tip came from an anonymous source. Female. Refused to give her name."

"We need to go. *I* need to go," Abigail insisted.

"In due time. Let the beat cops sort it out before we blunder in and cause more confusion. They're on scene. If they decide there's anything to the report, Jessie and I will be dispatched."

Lani interrupted, a pizza-laden plate in each hand. "You'd better eat, then. No telling how long you'll be gone if you get the call."

"Not both of us," Reed insisted, accepting the generous slices. "Abigail is staying here with you."

"Oh yeah?" Abigail was adamant. "Even if Jessie manages to track some of the kids down they'll take one look at you and scatter. You may not like it, but you need me."

"Aren't you scared?"

She huffed. "Of course I am! I'm terrified. Who wouldn't be? But that's no excuse for abandoning one of my kids when he's in danger."

"*If* he is."

Expecting further argument, she was stunned when Reed thrust the second plate toward her and said, "Then eat. And use a fork so you don't get Italian spices on your hands and confuse my dog."

She was going? Reed was including her? Just like that?

Averting her face to hide a flash of victory, she took a place at the kitchen table. Lani provided cutlery and a cold soda over ice.

Well, well, well, Abigail thought. *Just when I think I have him figured out, he goes and surprises me. What's up with that?*

A bigger question involved motive. Was Reed taking her along because he thought he would need her, as she'd claimed, or was he simply hoping that a return to the Coney Island boardwalk would further jog her memory? Either was possible. It didn't matter. As long as she continued to put others first and strive to do the job she was positive had been divinely ordained, she'd be fine.

Peeking over at him through lowered lashes, she realized she was ready and willing to follow him just about anywhere on earth. That admission was terribly unsettling. And patently true.

* * *

The dispatch for Jessie and Reed came a half hour after the initial report. He was in uniform by then. Jessie took one look at her official K-9 vest and harness and began quivering with excitement.

Reed eyed Abigail. She, too, was trembling, though not from eagerness, he concluded. *I have to hand it to her. That woman's got courage.*

"Ready?" He was strapping on his gear and checking the extra search and rescue equipment clipped to his vest and tucked into a go-bag.

Abigail's fingers were laced together at her waist and the knuckles had begun whitening. "I'm ready when you are."

"Okay. Come on. We'll go over procedure in the car."

He felt her following closely as he strode to the blue-and-white SUV. While he loaded Jessie, Abigail climbed into the passenger seat and was fumbling with her safety belt as he slid behind the wheel, grabbed the radio and reported his status.

"Branson leaving Queens. Do you want a code three response?"

"Negative," the dispatcher broadcast. "Units on scene report that the claims are so far unsubstantiated. Just keep your eyes open."

"What about a scent package?"

"Reporting party is supposed to meet you at the corner of West Fifteenth and Surf Avenue. She says she will have an article of clothing."

"Copy." Reed cleared his throat. "I have an outreach worker ride-along. She knows the Walenski boy personally."

"You cleared that with Noah?" was loud and clear.

Reed clenched his jaw. "Chief Jameson is aware I've been assisting this person in my off-duty time." He wanted to add that Abigail was up to her pretty blue eyeballs in this hot mess, but refrained. The less said, the better. He'd ask for forgiveness later rather than delay long enough to obtain official permission to include her.

"Copy," the dispatcher said.

He glanced across the front seat at his scowling passenger. "You knew I wasn't keeping track of you on the department's dime, didn't you?"

"I'd guessed as much." Her slim fingers had returned to their interwoven position.

"Just remember that this time is going to be different," Reed warned. "When Jessie and I are working you have to stay well behind us so you don't disturb any scent she picks up. Even a slight breeze can be too much. Got that?"

"Yes, sir. So how am I supposed to help you find Dominic if I'm trailing behind you?"

"Hopefully, whoever gives us the scented article of clothing will be connected to the group he normally runs with. You'll introduce me and vouch for me then."

"But…"

The quaver in her voice told him more than words would have. She was every bit as scared as he'd assumed she'd be even though she was putting on a brave front. How long she could maintain that facade was what concerned him.

"I won't be walking slowly after Jessie strikes a trail. Keep up with us as best you can. Run if you have to. Once my K-9 is committed I won't stop and wait for you. Understood?"

Abigail was nodding, her gaze wide. "Got it. What if I lose sight of you?"

"Then find the nearest patrol officer and stick to him or her. We'll return eventually, with or without the Walenski kid."

He had anticipated an argument he didn't get. The rest of the drive to Coney Island was uneventful until they approached the rendezvous point and noted the crowd.

Abigail leaned forward and pointed at a gaggle of teens amassed on the street corner. "That's them! Kiera's posse. There she is. Standing by the front patrol car. See?"

Reed saw all right. And what he saw was disquieting. If the entire group was worried enough to willingly meet and mingle with the police, chances were good that Dominic actually had been abducted as the caller had insisted.

He could tell these kids sure thought Dominic Walenski was in trouble. And since *they* did, that was good enough for him.

TWELVE

Abigail clicked off her seat belt and yanked the handle of the door before Reed had come to a complete stop. He checked in with the officers on scene while Abigail scanned the milling throng. Rides and concession stands were still open and the place was packed with New Yorkers and tourists eager to get in a last hurrah before the season ended.

Kiera ran forward waving a blue satin windbreaker. "I have Dom's jacket," the teen told Abigail. "He never leaves it. Never. His mom gave it to him right before… before she left."

"All right. That's good." Abigail gestured toward the approaching K-9 officer. "Kiera, this is Officer Branson and his bloodhound, Jessie. She's a tracker. Give the jacket to him and let him get to work."

The girl complied, eyeing Reed and Abigail suspiciously. "If you say so but I'm going too. We all are."

Hearing her own demand echoing back at her and realizing how off base she, too, had been, Abigail stopped. "We will. But in order for Jessie to work we all have to hang behind. Otherwise we can confuse her. Okay?" She slipped an arm around Kiera's shoulders to lightly restrain her. "The best way to find Dom is to follow the rules, even if we don't like them." A sidelong glance at Reed showed her his raised eyebrows. If the situation had not been so serious she might have smiled at the irony.

"I'll stay behind with these guys," Abigail told him, seeing his satisfaction with her choice.

He stepped forward, jacket in hand, and addressed the crowd. "Who was the last one to see Dominic?"

A dozen hands shot up.

Reed rephrased, eyeing a nearby patrolman. "You talked to that officer, right? Did he work out a timeline?"

Kiera pressed forward. "Yeah. It was me. Dom was supposed to meet us at our special place." She blushed. "We like to sit on a fave bench, eat hot dogs and watch the sunset."

"It's not dark yet. What makes you so sure something bad has happened to him?" Reed asked.

Abigail noted the way he was scanning the youthful faces and did the same. A couple of the boys were looking away as if they were hiding something, so she left Kiera and worked her way to them.

Keeping her body language relaxed, she slipped an arm around the slim shoulders of each boy and leaned in closer. "Okay, guys. Give. What do you know about all this?"

The taller of the two twisted away and ducked into the crowd of curious onlookers. The younger child was trapped, quivering. She kept a tight hold. "This police officer is my friend," she said. "He just wants to help us. Tell me whatever you know about Dom."

"He—he said he was gonna score. Be rich."

Abigail's thoughts immediately went to crime. "Drugs?"

"No! He'd never do that."

"Then what? What was he up to?"

"I don't know. Honest."

"Did you actually see him taken?" Reed asked.

The teen shook his head.

"Okay," Abigail announced. "Everybody listen up. Kiera is going to show Officer Branson where she saw Dominic last and then we'll back off so his dog can sniff and follow the scent. All of us. Got that?"

There were enough muttered assents to allay her fears that the kids would stampede through Jessie's scent trail. Grasping Kiera's shoulders, she turned her toward Reed and gestured to him. "Lead on."

Accompanying the teen, Reed guided Jessie toward the boardwalk. They weren't far from where he'd come upon Abigail that first time and he wondered what was going through her mind. Hopefully, having all those familiar young people clustering around her would be good for her taut nerves. And her lost memory. This was not the method he would have chosen to minister to her, but who was he to argue with God? After all, if he believed divine providence had led him to Abigail before, he almost had to credit the same source this time.

That was the trouble with faith, Reed mused. Sometimes it was easy to imagine the Lord's beneficial influence in a person's life while other times the choices seemed so impossible. It often boiled down to total acceptance or none. Too bad that degree of commitment wasn't as simple as it sounded.

Walking ahead, Kiera stopped just short of the boardwalk and waited for him. Yellow crime scene tape was draped across one side of the path while several patrol officers directed regular beachgoers out and around the cordoned-off area.

"Like I told the other cops, we were right here," she said. "Dominic promised to be back in ten minutes. It's been almost a whole day." Her voice broke.

Reed stopped short. "You reported that he was kidnapped so that we'd respond right away," he said. "Why? What's the rest of the story?"

She dropped her gaze to her sandals, suddenly fascinated with her toes. "I didn't say…" Her words faded.

"Speak up."

"I didn't say he was kidnapped," she admitted, making a face. "Not exactly."

"But you did mention it?"

The girl shook her head, pink-streaked hair fluttering. "Maybe. I just wanted you guys to find him, okay?"

"Making a false police report is a crime," Reed said gruffly. "We can't afford to run all over the city for no reason."

"I had a reason."

"So, nobody saw him actually being abducted?"

"Uh-uh. I just had a really bad feeling when he didn't come back. He always comes back when he says he will. Always." Kiera brightened and met his gaze. "Maybe he left to look for the dog again."

Reed tensed. "Dog? What dog?"

"The one he got when he was in foster care. Those parents said he couldn't keep it so he ran away and ended up here, with us. Dom said a man gave him that dog and told him it was okay, but the dog won't stay. He runs away a lot."

"Why would he worry about one stray dog? New York is full of them."

"Not like this one." Kiera began to sound enthusiastic. "He was like a super dog, you know? Big and smart and all. Dom said we should keep him for protection but he wouldn't eat good. I mean, we got hot dogs and nachos and stuff out of the trash, like always. He'd just look at the food like there was something wrong with it unless he dug it out himself—or Dom put it in a real dish for him."

Reed's pulse leaped into overdrive. His voice rose. "Was the dog a German shepherd? Was he wearing a collar?"

"Yeah. He had a metal name tag thingy fastened to it, too."

"Snapper," Reed breathed.

Kiera startled. "How did you know?"

"Because he's one of our specially trained K-9s. He's been missing since spring." He presented the jacket to Jessie and encouraged her to sniff it thoroughly as he spoke to the girl. "You go back and find Ms. Jones."

"Why?"

"Because I said so." Reed was nearly shouting. "Tell her what you just told me about Dom, then stay with the others. Those officers will be the first to know when my K-9 tracks down your friend."

And, God willing, Jordan Jameson's canine partner, Reed added to himself. He was beginning to see where this was going and the possibility of solving Jordy's murder loomed large. Finding Snapper, locating the missing boy and getting a lead on a ruthless killer all at once might seem impossible to most people, but it didn't to Reed. Not now.

* * *

Kiera dashed at the tears streaking her cheeks as she rejoined Abigail. "I'm sorry. Okay? I didn't mean to make the cops mad."

"Mad? What makes you think anyone's mad at you?"

"Your cop buddy was yelling."

Abigail folded her arms across her chest and stood firm. "Then you must have said something to set him off. I've seen Officer Branson in action and he's not short-tempered. He's always acted polite and professional, even when he's not on duty."

The fact that the teen had averted her gaze and was fidgeting told Abigail she was on the right track. "Tell me exactly what he said to you."

"I don't remember."

"Yes, you do. Give."

"He was mad 'cause I lied so they'd come look for Dom, okay?" Her voice was shrill, reedy. "I knew they wouldn't care if one of us kids was lost or in trouble. Not unless I told them a good story. So I said he was kidnapped." She sniffled. "I don't know why your cop friend had to make a federal case out of it. I mean, it was just a little fib."

Sighing and shaking her head, Abigail got the picture. Many teens didn't consider the consequences of an act before carrying it out. Their brains weren't fully developed yet and although they might look mature and try to behave like adults, their inherent immaturity regularly shot them down.

"Suppose someone else needed Officer Branson and his K-9 while he was here at the beach? What if a little kid got lost or something? Or suppose a murderer escaped because that tracking dog was too busy to chase him?"

"They've got a million dogs. I see 'em all the time."

"Not quite that many. That's not the point. Not all police dogs do the same jobs."

"How do you know?"

"I looked it up." Abigail gently touched the girl's thin shoulder. "Look, honey. I know your heart was in the right place. You guys feel responsible for each other. I think of all of you as family, too. But I'd never make a false police report. That sets a terrible precedent. What do you suppose will happen if you need to call for help again? Will they believe you? Huh?"

"I dunno."

"Well, I do. Come on. We'll start with the officers that came in patrol cars and then ask permission for you to speak to dispatch."

"What for?" The teen hesitated.

Losing patience, Abigail grasped her wrist. "So you can apologize."

"No way. Uh-uh. Not happening. Kids get snatched all the time down here and nobody cares. Nobody reports them missing. What's to say that Dom didn't really get kidnapped?"

Abigail froze. Kidnapped. At the beach by *the boardwalk. The smaller figure struggling between the two shadowy thugs. Was that what I saw?*

Wide-eyed, she stared at the girl beside her. Could Kiera have witnessed that same event? Was that why she'd sought Abigail out, had been so interested in what she might be able to recall?

Kiera cringed under the scrutiny. "Hey, why are you looking at me like that? It's creepy."

"You were there," Abigail said, hoping a forceful tone would carry her through. "You saw me get attacked."

Crimson infused Kiera's pale cheeks and clashed with the pink in her hair. "No way."

"Yes way," Abigail insisted. "That's why you insisted on meeting with me face-to-face. Somebody must have told you my memory was bad. You wanted to see if I remembered why I'd gone out that night and what I'd seen before I was attacked. Why, Kiera? Who are you protecting?"

"No-nobody." Twisting, she tried to free her wrist. "Let me go. That hurts!"

Realizing she had inadvertently restrained the teen, Abigail backed off, hands open and raised. "Sorry. Sorry, I wasn't thinking." Unshed tears of frustration filled her eyes. "Please. If you know anything about what happened to me, or to anyone else, you need to tell the police. At least give them a chance. Give me a chance."

"Snitch?" Rubbing her wrist, the wary teen gave a snort of derision. "No way, lady. You can keep your sodas and your food vouchers and your stupid clothes. We'll do okay without any help."

There was nothing more Abigail could say. One moment's lapse in judgment had probably undone most of the good she'd managed to accomplish all summer. Honesty had cost her the trust of this teen and probably would affect many more by the time Kiera finished re-telling the tale and giving it her own slant.

At that moment, Abigail yearned to rejoin Reed, to tell him her suspicions and ask his advice on what to do next. Looking past Kiera, she scanned the nearly deserted beach. The tide was coming in. A cadre of police officers were sweeping the shoreline with flashlights, following the path Jessie had taken before the waves rose and washed away all traces.

Abigail shivered. Folded her arms across her chest and hugged herself. One mistake. One little mistake. What had gotten into her? She wasn't a violent person, yet the grip of her fingers on the teen's thin wrist had left a temporary red mark.

She began to mindlessly chafe her own wrist. Sense the unwelcome touch of rough, masculine fingers. She closed her eyes and let the vision develop. Her pulse began to pound in her temples, her breathing the exhausted rasp of weakening prey.

Abigail could smell the sea and the concessions as usual, but beyond that was an odor of filth and sweat and unnamed revulsion. Her gorge rose. The remembered shadows took tenuous shape with noses and squinty eyes and ugly, ugly grins.

She gasped. Her eyes snapped open. The image vanished. But she had seen more this time. Much more. Those men had grabbed her, held her arms, kept her prisoner. Her fractured memory was healing. Returning. Piece by piece.

Inside the fences of Luna Park stood the antique carousel where Reed had found her cowering. She stared at it, hoping for more details. Trepidation now mingled with elation. Unnamed fear was being displaced by the joy of anticipated relief.

That segment of her escape might still be a mystery, but she was positive it wouldn't remain one for much longer.

THIRTEEN

Jessie led Reed down the shore toward Brighton Beach, then doubled back until they were nearly to the spot where he'd left Abigail and the others. To his right, a line of uniformed officers, augmented by official cleanup crew members in their neon vests, held on-lookers at bay.

To his surprise, Jessie paused, sniffed the air, then plowed straight into the gaggle of teens.

Reed noted Abigail standing prominently at the edge of the group. Where was Kiera? Had his impromptu lecture helped the teenager understand the seriousness of falsifying her crime report? He sincerely hoped so.

Instead of stopping to greet Abigail or anybody else, the trusty bloodhound kept her nose to the ground and shouldered through the human barricade at knee level. Jessie was clearly tracking. As long as she was on the trail he wasn't about to pull her back.

The clever K-9 circled a hotdog cart, ducked behind the vendor's portable sign and stopped at the bare feet of a crouching boy, her tongue lolling.

The youngster cringed but didn't try to flee. Reed

praised his dog, then met the gaze of the small, dark-haired teen. "Hello, Dominic. Where have you been?"

"I ain't…"

The purposeful scowl on Reed's face was enough to make the boy pause. "Yes, you are. Don't even try to lie to a police dog like my Jessie. She's never wrong." He held out the satiny jacket Kiera had given him earlier. "Lose this?"

"Maybe."

"Where's your girlfriend?"

"I got no girlfriend."

"Okay. Then where is Kiera Underhill? The three of us need to have a little chat."

Reed paused to radio news of Jessie's success and saw other officers begin to relax and return to their vehicles.

"Don't even think about running," he warned the fidgeting boy.

"Okay, okay. But it wasn't my fault."

"What wasn't? What happened here?"

"I-I heard somebody was down here asking about Snapper. I figured I'd get blamed for losing him so I split." He raised a hand as if taking an oath. "I didn't steal him. And I don't know where he is. The only reason I came back here is because I saw you and your dog going the other way."

Unconvinced, Reed pressed the question. "Suppose I believe you? How can you prove you're telling the truth?"

"Um, I don't know." The timbre of the boy's voice wavered from alto to soprano and back down again.

"Well, you'd better think of something, and quick," Reed said flatly. "If it was Snapper, there's no earthly reason for him to have wandered all the way down here by himself."

Dominic's dark eyes sparked. "Hey, I never said I found him here. Some guy gave him to me, back when I was still living in a foster home."

So, at least the kids had their story straight, not that he bought it. "Oh, yeah?" Reed said. "And where were you when this happened?"

He was fairly certain the boy was lying until he said, "Over by Vanderbilt Parkway. Queens."

Heart in his throat, Reed bent to stare into the teen's face, looking for clues that he'd made up his excuse. Deception might be this kid's modus operandi, but truth lay in his current expression.

"I can check your former foster placements, you know."

"Go ahead, man. Check. That's where I was when I got Snapper."

"So how did you wind up here?" Reed was hesitant to accept anything at face value. The department and his unit had chased down too many false reports and erroneous sightings for him to be easily satisfied.

"I ran away, all right? And I'll do it again if you try to send me back there. Those people hated Snapper. I promised I'd get a job to pay for his food but they wouldn't listen."

Softening his tone, Reed asked, "Did you have trouble getting him to eat?"

"How did you know?"

"Your friend Kiera mentioned it. There's a good reason. Snapper and all our dogs are taught to turn down food that isn't offered by their handlers or trainers. I'm surprised you got him to eat anything."

"Is that why he got so skinny? Man, that's twisted. He could've starved to death."

"I assume his survival instincts have kicked in by now. That's probably why he was okay finding his own dinner but balked when you kids tried to feed him. He still remembered his poison-proofing training."

"Hey! I didn't poison him. He was fine the last time I saw him. He just keeps running off, that's all."

Reed straightened, noting that Kiera and Abigail were lingering nearby. "So, where is he now?"

The skinny shoulders shrugged, then slumped. "Beats me. One day he's with me and the next he's gone. Nobody saw him go so I didn't know where to look besides around here." He sniffled. "Some stupid tourist probably took him."

"Tell me more about the guy you got him from in the first place? Can you remember what he looked like?" It was hard to keep from sounding too excited, given that there was a chance the boy had seen Jordan's killer.

"Sort of, I guess." Dominic's head bobbed up and down, his forehead knitting. "He was just a regular guy. Old, like you."

Reed snorted. "Got it. Do you think you could help a sketch artist draw his picture?"

"I might. What's in it for me?"

Fine, Reed thought, more than ready to barter. "Food. As much as you want for as long as these concessions stay open tonight. My treat."

"Seriously?"

"Seriously. I'm going to radio my headquarters with a report and ask an artist to meet us down here. That way you won't have to ride in a police car." *And I won't*

have to jump through so many technical, legal hoops,
he added to himself.

Abigail would probably volunteer to help, too, Reed
reasoned, making the boardwalk a perfect place to de-
brief the boy. If Dom kept playing it straight with the
adults, Reed intended to feed him until he couldn't hold
another bite.

Vanderbilt Parkway. Reed figured he'd never hear
that name without remembering the shock they'd all
felt when Jordy's body had been found. Images of that
body were branded in Reed's brain as if made by a hot
iron of sorrow.

God willing, the face of Jordy's possible killer held
as firm a grip on the mind of the wiry teen. Dominic
Walenski might be the only witness who could provide
clues to the elusive murderer. No way was Reed letting
him out of his sight until he had more answers.

Abigail spotted Dom when she caught sight of Reed.
Jessie had done it! It took a monumental effort to stay
where she was and make Kiera wait for Reed to finish
talking to the boy.

A wave of Reed's arm and the helpful actions of
other officers dispersed the crowd. Jessie was practically dancing, her tail up, her ears flapping and a knotted section of damp rope clamped between her teeth as
her reward for a job well done. Reed, on the other hand,
seemed almost morose. If the two teens hadn't been so
close by, she would have immediately asked him why
he wasn't as happy as everybody else, including his K-9.

Nevertheless, Abigail flashed a grin. Kiera might not
have forgiven her for the chastisement over making a

false police report, but she cared enough about Dominic to stick around. Good. One step at a time.

Despite the sour look Kiera got from the boy, Abigail continued to smile. "Good job, Jessie." She patted the broad, tan head, dodging the frayed end of the dog's reward toy before her gaze rose to meet Reed's and she added, "You, too, Officer Branson."

"Thanks." Although his expression remained sober, he did nod politely. "Dominic and I are going to go grab a late supper before the concessions close. You're invited."

"Thanks." Including Kiera seemed logical and smart, so Abigail looped an arm around each teen's shoulders and guided them toward the boardwalk. She didn't have to look back to know Reed and Jessie were following closely, because every second or third stride, the soggy rope brushed against her calf.

The kids were casting surreptitious glances at each other, clearly wishing a counselor was not walking between them. Well, tough. The thought of combining her efforts and Reed's gave Abigail hope of soothing tempers and learning more. All they had to do was foster a relaxed atmosphere and let these young people be themselves. Given their tenuous position as runaways and the way they viewed authority figures as the enemy, she and Reed had their work cut out for them.

She positioned herself on the outside of a small picnic table fronting a food stand and gestured to the teens. "Grab a seat, guys."

The look she got from Reed as he and his K-9 joined them was one of approval. Thanks to her, they were positioned to head off a dash to escape as well as clearly see each of the kids' faces. She gave him a smile. "I'll have one of their famous special hot dogs and a small soda."

He handed her the looped end of Jessie's leash, his gaze shifting from the dog to the teens as if reminding them it would be useless to try to run away. "What about the two of you? The same? I can always go back for seconds."

"Yeah, okay," Dominic said. Kiera nodded.

Abigail suspected that Jessie wouldn't do a thing about chasing anybody unless Reed gave her that specific command, but she pretended otherwise, grasping the leash tightly and acting as if she were the only reason the sweet bloodhound wasn't snarling and behaving like an attack dog. The ruse worked well enough that the teens seated across the table hardly moved a muscle.

Reed was back with their meal in minutes. He doled it out, reclaimed his K-9, then slid onto the bench closest to Dominic. "Okay. Eat. Then we'll talk."

Less hungry than she was curious, Abigail concentrated mostly on her companions. Reed remained tense. Kiera seemed relieved. The boy, though clearly starved and willing to eat, maintained a wary demeanor that she found strange. Of course, none of the kids was particularly fond of law enforcement because they were often apprehended and forced back into a system that, although designed to keep them safe and well, could easily fail. She knew that and clearly so did Reed, or he would have placed Dominic in official custody.

"I told you all I know," the boy muttered with his mouth half full.

"So, you said." Reed looked at Kiera. "What about you? Any chance you saw the guy who gave him Snapper?"

"Not me. I've been here all summer. Dom's kinda new."

"Is that why you lied to get us to come look for him?"

"Yeah, I guess."

Abigail saw the boy shoot Kiera a troubled glance. "*You* did this?" He muttered under his breath.

"Well, somebody had to," the girl replied. "We were worried about you."

"So you called the *cops*?" He was clearly annoyed. "Did you want 'em to arrest me for stealing the dog?"

"No, no!" Kiera insisted. Her meal was forgotten as she reached for his thin arm. "I didn't tell anybody about Snapper until they figured it out themselves." She began to smile as if enjoying a private joke. "I told 'em *you'd* been kidnapped."

Dom jumped back so forcefully he almost toppled off the bench. "You *what*?"

"It's okay. They know it was a fib. I just wanted to make them take me seriously and come look for you."

Expecting an explosion of angry words, Abigail was astounded to see the wiry teen overcome with what looked like fear. His hands gripped the edge of the table. His complexion blanched. His dark eyes widened and glistened as if he might be about to cry. His jaw dropped but no sound came out.

The instant she turned and looked at Reed's face, she knew that something crucial was happening. She just didn't know what it was. Or how to help.

Reed waited as he watched the boy's emotional upheaval. It was clear Dominic was hiding something, and although it probably didn't have anything to do with Jordy's murder, it was evidently frightening. Kiera had inadvertently scared the socks off her younger friend and it was Reed's duty to get past his facade of street courage and pull the details out of him.

And protect him, Reed added to himself. That kid was scared speechless. Biding his time, he took a bite of the hot dog he'd bought for himself, noting that he was the only one still eating. The girl looked confused, Abigail was obviously puzzled, and Dominic acted as if he was about to be sentenced to death row. Anything that serious called for finesse.

"You do know you're safe sitting here with me, right?" Reed said casually.

Dom was staring into the distance, his eyes shining, reflecting the overhead lights. When he shook his head, the spots of color glimmered.

"That's why I'm sticking with Officer Branson," Abigail explained.

When Kiera gave a derisive snort, Dominic's head snapped around. His expression was so poignant the girl shrugged and asked, "What?"

"Nothing." He was staring at his food but had stopped eating.

"Hmm." Reed took another bite, then washed it down with his own soda before concentrating on Kiera. "That was pretty smart of you to mention kidnapping. What gave you the idea?"

"Like I said, I wanted you cops to pay attention."

"Well, it worked." He paused. "So, why is your friend so mad at you? You must have some idea."

"Naw." She folded her arms in an expression of defense. "I don't have a clue. Maybe he's just a big baby."

"I am not!" marked the boy's return to the conversation.

Kiera shrugged. "Whatever."

Silence followed. Reed watched and waited. Both

young people were fidgeting, making him wonder if their angst was for the same reason or if each had a separate secret. Dominic seemed unduly upset about Kiera's subterfuge while the girl was acting clueless. Either she was a great actress or she truly didn't know why her friend was so angry.

Suddenly, Kiera gaped. She stared at the boy as if willing him to explain. But what? What had passed between the two runaways that he had missed? A quick glance at Abigail's frown told him she was as confused as he was.

Dominic gave a barely perceptible nod. That led to Kiera's exclamation of, "No!" followed by a grab at his hand. The boy's brown eyes filled with tears. His nod continued, gaining strength until his mop of dark hair flopped forward, masking the upper half of his face.

Whisperings between the two young people were lost in the noise of the crowds near the concession tables. Reed though he'd managed to pick out a few key words but there was no way to grasp the full meaning of the exchange without more detail. He did know that Kiera was now apparently as frightened as Dom, which might help once there was an actual crime to investigate.

"You can't stay here anymore," Kiera said flatly before switching to address the adults, particularly Reed. "You have to put him in protective custody."

He couldn't help smiling. "I think you watch too much television. Protective custody is only for innocent victims who can prove they are really in danger."

Kiera was on her feet in a flash. She grabbed Dominic's arm, jerked him off the bench and started to drag him away.

The boy didn't protest verbally but he did make a grab for his soda cup.

"Leave it," Kiera shouted. "We're out of here!"

FOURTEEN

Abigail was so startled she almost tumbled backward off the bench. When she regained her balance and looked over at Reed, he and Jessie were already on the move.

They zigzagged between tables, cleared the edge of the red-and-yellow canvas awning and disappeared among the milling vacationers and locals. There was no way she'd be able to catch any of them at this point, so she cleared off the table, dumped their trash and paced, waiting for one or more of her former companions to return.

An overview of people nearby proved unproductive. Not only was there no sign of Kiera's close friends, Abigail didn't spot any of the kids who were regulars at AFS, either. A few young adult males did look slightly familiar, however. That was a bit of a surprise. Most of the kids who aged out of the state foster care program, as well as her privately funded one, could hardly wait to leave the area once they turned eighteen. It never ceased to amaze her that many of them who could have signed on to stay in the system longer failed to do so.

Not only would it have helped them find a good job, they would have had support.

"I should know about poor choices," she murmured to herself. In her day, she'd almost let her pride cause her to miss a chance to get a higher education. Thankfully, the part-time job she'd been directed toward in her mid-teens had led to meeting mentors who had helped her turn her life around. Now she was dedicated to doing the same for others, like Kiera and Dominic.

Speaking of which… Reed's height helped her spot him before she could see who was by his side. Sadly, Kiera wasn't with Dominic any more. Oh, well, of the two, the boy was undoubtedly more in need of aid than the more street savvy girl was.

The crowd didn't exactly part for the police officer the way the Red Sea had for Moses in biblical times, but Reed's strength of presence seemed to cause quite a few human obstacles to give ground.

Dominic came into full view. Abigail studied his face, his body language. At first, he seemed resigned, then tense, then quickly scared to death. As far as she could tell, nothing about their surroundings had changed, yet the boy was obviously affected negatively.

She stepped close to Reed as soon as he'd cleared the throng. "Something is very wrong."

"Yeah. I lost your girl."

"No, no. That's not what I mean." Abigail cupped a hand around her mouth and stood on tiptoe to explain as privately as possible. "It's not Kiera I'm worried about right now, it's this one. You couldn't see the funny look that just came over him but I could. He's terrified. We need to get him away from here."

"You're serious?"

"Yes. I'll take responsibility. We need to go someplace quiet and safe. ASAP."

"All right. If you say so."

She fell into step on the opposite side of the boy, consciously guarding him. Until this second, she'd been so worried about Dominic and Kiera, she'd forgotten the bit of lost memory she'd uncovered.

"By the way," Abigail said, "waiting for you I had a surprising flash of insight into the men who grabbed me. One was masked to begin with. He had a round face and big, rough hands. The other one wasn't quite as large, the way I first thought. He had a face like a weasel and I think he was younger. I know he was skinnier."

To her delight, Reed looked pleased. "Wonderful. Let's go back to my car and wait for the sketch artist. You can make use of him after our friend here is done."

"I—I'm not sure I remember their faces that well," she hedged. "It's one thing to get an overall impression of them and altogether different to be able to pick out individual characteristics."

"At least you can give it a try. Right?"

She cast a sidelong glance at Dominic, ruing her thoughtless comments and hoping he wasn't going to adopt the same defeatist attitude regarding the man who had given him Snapper. It was too late to take back her candid remarks, but she might be able to counteract their deleterious effect.

"Of course I'll try. And once I've started to see the faces develop, I'll be able to make adjustments to get them just right."

"That's the spirit," Reed said. Although his voice sounded pleasant and enthusiastic, Abigail could tell his speech was as much for the boy's sake as hers had been. They both knew they were walking a tightrope here, balancing between what the law allowed and what her office could do. The main goal was, as always, the ultimate well-being of the street kids. She knew from experience that many of them were repeat runaways and would take off again the minute they felt threatened or abused or simply didn't like listening to parental-type authority figures.

She intended to treat Dominic equitably, yet she wasn't above giving him more leeway than usual if doing so led to the arrest of criminals and the solving of crimes.

One thing was certain. The German shepherd the youngster had been given was crucially important to Reed. If she was putting the pieces of this story together correctly, the person Dominic had met when he'd accepted Snapper could be connected to the untimely demise of Reed's boss, Snapper's former handler.

That wasn't simple dog-napping.

That was murder.

As soon as he had convinced Dominic that he wasn't under arrest and had talked him into climbing into the SUV, it was easy to load Abigail and his K-9. Reed radioed headquarters and explained his change of plans. He didn't want to panic the kid more than he already was, so he refrained from giving specific reasons for the relocation of the rendezvous with the police artist. Now that he'd had time to observe the Walenski boy more carefully, he agreed with Abigail. Something besides being with a cop had the kid spooked. Judging by the way he kept peering out of the windows and scanning the passing crowd, he was plenty scared of whoever he thought was out there.

It occurred to Reed to put Jessie in the back seat with Dom, and he would have if not for the artist's imminent arrival. With the AC running and everybody safe, he waited outside his vehicle, ready to flag down whichever artist showed up.

As he saw an approaching patrol unit slowing, he raised his hand to wave. The car pulled up beside his, hazard lights blinking. Reed reached to hold the passenger door as it opened and was pleasantly surprised to see the unit's ace tech guru, curly-haired, blonde Danielle Abbott, step out.

"Danielle! I assumed Joey Calderone would be assigned. Are you acting as my sketch artist tonight?" Danielle was not only a tech genius, she was also incredibly talented at digital art, particularly faces, and sometimes acted as a backup for Calderone.

She pushed her large, round-framed glasses up the bridge of her nose with one finger. "Sure am." Handing him her laptop and a red tote filled to bursting with who knew what, she flashed a wide grin. "Calderone was out of town so I volunteered. I've been dying to try my new face-building program in the field."

"This may work out for the best. My reporting party is a scared kid." Reed grinned. "If anybody can put him at ease and coax out the information we need, it's you."

She gathered a handful of curls at her nape before pulling an alligator clip out of the pocket of her flowery sundress. "Hang on a sec while I pin up my hair. I thought it'd be cooler at the beach but it's still too hot for me."

"September has its moments," Reed replied. He eyed

his parked car. "I'll introduce you and leave you with the boy. His name is Dominic Walenski. He's been in foster care and has a record of running away, so don't let him trick you. The most important thing is finding out what the perp looked like who gave him Snapper."

Her wide eyes looked enormous behind the large lenses. "Snapper? You found him?"

"Not yet, but I'm hoping we'll soon have an idea what Jordy's killer looks like."

Danielle pressed a hand to her clavicle and gasped. "Whoa! Okay, sure. Let me at him."

"Easy," Reed warned. "We think something else is bothering Dominic right now and I don't want you to spook him, okay?"

"Yeah, yeah. I'll be cool." She seemed to be struggling to control her excitement. "Are you sure the person who had Snapper was the murderer?"

"No." Reed shook his head. "But it's the strongest lead we've had since the guy who planted Chief Jameson's fake suicide note was killed. We have to start somewhere."

"Gotcha. Who's in there besides your witness?" She was peering through the windows of Reed's SUV.

"That's Abigail Jones." He decided to withhold details that were not pertinent to the case. "She works in Brighton Beach and along this part of the shore with kids like Dom. I thought her presence might settle him down if she kept us company."

One of the tech wizard's perfectly limned eyebrows arched and she gave Reed a mischievous glance. "Whatever you say, Branson. Just remember what's happened to some of the other K-9 cops recently. Zack Jameson,

Luke Hathaway and Finn Gallagher, for instance. Love is in the air, my friend."

He huffed. "The only thing in this air is the smell of popcorn, hot dogs and suntan lotion, so don't go imagining things, Abbott."

"Hey, can I help it if I'm a hopeless romantic?" She sobered again. "You interrupted my date tonight, you know."

"Sorry. You look nice in that dress," Reed told her, meaning it.

He saw the woman's sharp mind zero in on reality and heard her sigh. "It's okay. I know what's most important, same as you. We'll get justice for Jordan—and for poor Katie." A deeper sigh. "I can't imagine losing a husband, especially while being pregnant. She has to be going crazy with worry."

"You know the Jamesons are looking after her," he countered. "It's really a good thing they shared that multifamily Rego Park house to begin with."

"Still sad." The loose curls framing Danielle's face followed the shaking of her head. "It's hard to imagine how the whole family feels. Those brothers were close."

"Well, at least they didn't lose Carter, too," Reed said, recalling the officer's recent leg wound. "He's on the mend."

"From your lips to God's ears," she said, brightening and stepping past him. "Let's go meet this whiz kid so I can get started."

To Abigail's surprise and chagrin, she felt a twinge of jealousy when a pretty blonde got out of the other police car and stood speaking with Reed so intently.

What is wrong with me? He can talk to anybody he pleases. It's no business of mine. And yet, in some unfathomable way, her life had become intrinsically connected to Reed's. She could already sense his emotions, predict his responses. That wasn't natural. Not at all. At least not in respect to the handsome police officer. Most kids she could read like a book, even when they were mixed up with drugs or petty crimes or lying to her face. In Reed's case, however, the connection went deeper. Empathy explained some of it, of course. She accepted that. She shared his disappointment when plans didn't come together perfectly, such as when their vehicle had been wrecked.

Mulling over her situation as he and the other woman approached the SUV, Abigail felt a tug on her heart that was so poignant it almost made her gasp. Only the presence of the impressionable boy kept her from fully acknowledging her feelings. She cared about this man so deeply, so totally, she could hardly breathe.

The conclusion that shot into her mind as if fired from a gun was undeniable. *Impossible.* Yet true. Like it or not, she had fallen in love with K-9 officer Reed Branson almost overnight. That was crazy. He hadn't even kissed her. How could she possibly have fallen for him?

Making the best use of the moments before he reached her door, Abigail covered her face with both hands and prayed silently, asking God for insight into her own mind, her obvious confusion.

The door lock clicked. Reed was standing there. Abigail met his quizzical expression. "You okay?" he asked casually.

"Fine, fine. Just tired." She swung her feet out and stood.

"This is our tech wizard, Danielle Abbott," Reed said. "Danielle, meet Abigail Jones."

"A real pleasure." The amply endowed blonde extended a bejeweled hand.

Abigail accepted the gesture and shook hands. "Thank you for coming on such short notice." A slight eye movement indicated the boy in the back seat. "Dominic is ready to help us. As soon as you're through and satisfied with the face he chooses, I've promised him ice cream. Two scoops." She looked to Reed. "I hope you don't mind."

He smiled. "Not at all. You can sit with Danielle and do your faces while Dom and I go get his treat."

"Her, too?" the tech expert asked.

Abigail answered for Reed. "Yes. Me, too. I've been having some trouble recalling an incident in my past and had a flash of insight tonight. I suppose I'd better try to make something concrete out of it before it slips away again."

All business, Danielle gave Abigail the once-over. "So, you're the one."

"I beg your pardon?"

Danielle's smile returned. "We've heard plenty about a pretty assault victim our confirmed bachelor here has been keeping company with. Now I'm even more pleased to meet you."

It was all Abigail could do to keep from scowling at both of them. So she was the subject of gossip around their police station. "Terrific. It's good to hear that I've given you all something to talk about. Now, if you don't mind, Dominic needs to get started."

"Oops, sorry." Danielle shot a brief glance at Reed. "I didn't mean to make trouble, buddy."

"Not a problem," he said flatly. "I'm a big boy. I can

take a little ribbing. Just be sure you explain that this is work, not play, when you go back to headquarters."

"Work. Got it." The wink the blonde gave Reed was so blatant it made Abigail's blood boil. Talk about getting an immediate answer to a prayer for clearer thinking. Reed not only still classified her as a job and nothing more, he was openly flirting with a woman he obviously admired.

Sending thanks heavenward for such clear enlightenment was called for, Abigail knew. But right then and there, watching the way Reed and Danielle looked at each other, she was incapable of genuine gratitude.

"Ask and you shall receive," Abigail quoted to herself, wondering why she felt even worse after getting a definite response to her prayerful appeal.

As she watched Danielle join Dom in the back seat, Abigail found a trace of humor in the irony of her situation and whispered one more short prayer.

"Um, Father, do you suppose I could have do-overs and take back that last prayer?"

FIFTEEN

"I think we should take him home with us," Reed told Abigail. "I've talked to my chief and he's left it up to me for the present."

"Take Dominic home? Why?"

"Because it makes sense. There's no way to keep him safe when he's wandering all over the beach." He tried to subdue a smile and ended up with a quirky grin. "Look at it as informal protective custody."

"Kiera got to you, didn't she?"

"Maybe a little."

"If you keep taking lost souls home with you, you'll run out of house space."

Noting the rosy glow of her cheeks beneath the cute freckles, he reassured her. "They're not all lost. You're not. You just need a little TLC until you regain your memory." Reed's smile widened. "And it's working. You've already had two incidents that show recovery."

"Identifying that pizza man's voice was a mistake."

"I wasn't counting him. Give yourself credit, Abigail. You're a smart, intelligent, capable woman. You'll pull it together. I know you will."

"Yeah, right," she mumbled. Then louder, "I wish I'd known somebody like you when I was Dom's age."

Assuming a relaxed pose, Reed tried to draw her out. "Oh? Was it really that bad?"

For an instant he was afraid he'd angered her, because she seemed to be struggling emotionally. When she shook her head and said, "No, it was worse," his heart clenched. How could anybody hurt a kid, particularly a sweet one like Abigail had surely been?

Although she folded her arms across her chest and lifted her chin with evident pride, he could tell she was feeling vulnerable, so he stopped asking questions in the hopes she'd voluntarily reveal more about herself. He didn't realize he'd been holding his breath until she began to speak.

"I don't remember my father," she said. "That wouldn't have been so bad if Mom hadn't brought home so many new daddies for me to learn to love. When I was little it was easy to get used to them but as I got older and began to look…" She blushed. "You know. Pretty soon I was staying out late or not going home at all just to keep from having to dodge unwelcome advances from strange men."

"Your mother permitted this?"

"My mother was rarely sober. I doubt she noticed much. When I finally hit the streets for keeps at sixteen, I'm not even sure she reported me missing."

Reed gently touched her shoulder. "I'm so sorry."

"Hey, I lived through it. And it led to the start of my career in public service. If I could get squared away and turn out okay, it's proof some of these other runaways can do the same. That's what I tell them if I think they need that kind of encouragement."

"Good for you."

"Good for the people and organizations that were there for me, you mean. I didn't do it alone." She began to smile slightly, a dreamy look in her eyes that made them glisten in the neon flashes from nearby businesses and concessions. "I was really struggling, despite everything, until a mentor dragged me to a church youth meeting. It wasn't at all like I'd thought church would be. The music was upbeat, the snacks were great and nobody looked down on me."

"I know what you mean. I used to belong to a group like that. Mine even passed out free Bibles."

"Then you do understand. I'd never heard Jesus presented the way those kids did it. They talked about Him as if they actually knew Him personally, and I wanted the same relationship. It was after I committed my life to Him that things began to make sense." She huffed. "I don't mean all my troubles vanished. Getting it together took time and a lot of work. But I think I've managed to forgive my mother. She was a victim, too."

"I agree." Reed set aside the last vestiges of concern about his professional image and reached out to her. It was as natural an act as breathing, although once Abigail was in his arms, he did have a little trouble catching his breath.

At first she seemed reluctant, but in seconds she had relaxed into a shared embrace. Others on the sidewalk passed them by as if they were invisible. Coney Island was that kind of place, a place where romantic couples met and mingled with crowds of like-minded revelers, all intent on making the most of the last warm days of autumn.

Tucking Abigail against him, he rested his chin on

the top of her head, feeling the tickle of her hair, the whisper of her warm breath. He knew he should have been shocked when his mind had so easily provided the word "romantic" in connection to what was happening between them. Somehow, he wasn't even remotely surprised.

He drew a shaky, deep breath and released it slowly, admitting how much he cared for her and wondering what in the world he was going to do about it. This situation was akin to a hapless swimmer being caught in a riptide and pulled out over his depth. Way over.

That wouldn't have been so bad if he hadn't viewed himself as the lifeguard on duty.

Standing there, encircled by Reed's arms, Abigail closed her eyes and let herself absorb his strength, his support. Clearly her story had touched him, and of that she was glad. What remained puzzling was why, once he had offered solace, he continued to hold her. Not that she was complaining. No, sir. Given a choice she'd be glad to stand right there with her arms around him for as long as possible.

There was a very slight loosening of Reed's arms, a subtle easing away. Feeling that change, Abigail had no choice but to let go and step back. She forced a smile and gazed up, hoping she didn't look as if she were mooning over him.

"Thanks," she said. "I don't talk about my past often. Every time I do, it takes a lot out of me."

"I understand. Better now?"

The rumble of his voice seemed to convey more than concern. If she hadn't heard the sketch artist mention his confirmed bachelorhood, she might have imagined that they shared the same tender emotions she'd recently been battling against.

"Yes, thanks." Abigail let her gaze drift over the passing pedestrians without conscious thought. How long had she been denying her burgeoning affection for this special man? It was impossible to tell, probably because her psyche had been so frail to begin with. And now that she was healing? She huffed. Now that her normal sensibilities were returning, she supposed she should concentrate on self-determination and the pride of being her own person. It had taken years to mature to that point. She didn't want to abandon the courageous self she'd discovered and nurtured. It was what kept her together and gave her the strength to help others.

That was the trouble with falling in love, she mused. A person had to relinquish too much. Look at what had happened to her poor mother when she'd tried to rely on a man to complete her and had failed over and over.

Well, that pattern wasn't going to repeat itself in Abigail Jones. No way. As soon as she'd recovered enough to more fully describe the men who had attacked her, she and Reed would probably never see each other again.

Given the unwelcome reaction of her heart to that fact, she figured the sooner they parted the better. Yes, she was going to miss seeing him, being near him. But that didn't mean there was anything personal going on. He'd put it best when he'd instructed Danielle. They all needed to remember that he was merely doing his job.

Standing straight, shoulders back, Abigail left him and started toward the parked SUV. As soon as Dominic was finished she was going to take his place and describe the faces from her hazy memory. This was not the time to give up or give in. She was going to succeed or else.

Failure was not an option.

Reed hung back and let her go, knowing that nobody in his right mind would threaten her while she was standing next to a police car.

He'd been a fool to touch Abigail again, let alone embrace her, yet he'd been unable to stop himself. Every fiber of his being had cried out, insisting he offer comfort, and he had yielded. He must never step out of line like that again. It didn't matter how he felt personally, it was wrong of him to take advantage of her vulnerabilities. Later, when she was fully recovered and back to living a normal life, maybe he'd change his mind and ask her for a date, but right here, right now, he needed to keep his distance.

"As if that's going to be easy," Reed muttered. "I am in so deep already I can't believe it."

He saw her looking back. Watching him. Good thing she wasn't a lip reader.

Seeking something to do besides stand there and waste time, he decided to let Jessic out for a little exercise. To his chagrin, Abigail stepped back and seemed to tense up more when he approached.

He flashed his best fake grin. "Just checking on my four-footed partner. We won't go far. I'm keeping an eye on you."

She returned an equally forced smile. "Okay. I'm sure it will be my turn with the sketch artist soon."

"There's nothing to worry about," Reed told her, opening the rear hatch and liberating his leashed K-9. "Danielle will walk you through it. You'll do fine."

"Right." Sobering, Abigail made a face. "It seems like the harder I try to bring those faces back, the less I actually remember about them."

"Then think about something else until it's time to work for real. It'll come to you more easily if you don't force it."

Before Abigail had time to reply, there was a tapping on the window behind her. Reed hit the release on his key fob to unlock the door, and Dominic bounded out. "Ice cream!"

"Gotcha." Reed held up his keys for Abigail. "Climb in. The door will lock by itself. If you need to get out before I get back, use my keys." He tossed part of the ring to her. "Don't lose that or we'll have to walk home."

He waited until she was safely locked in the SUV before he turned to his young companion and pointed toward the boardwalk. "Let's go. We don't want the ice cream stand to close before we get there."

"Yay! Two scoops. Chocolate."

"Coming right up."

Reed followed the boy's zigzag path between groups of people, staying close and keeping Jessie on a short lead. Later, he'd ask how the session with Danielle had gone. While Dominic was acting carefree and happy, he was going to let him enjoy himself as much as possible.

Reed chuckled. Too bad ice cream wasn't enough to lift Abigail's spirits or he'd buy out the whole stand for her.

Danielle was easier to work with than Abigail had expected. She started with basic head shapes and added facial details with simple keystrokes until there was no more adjusting to do.

Danielle held up her laptop. "Well? What do you think?"

"The skinny one is pretty close. I'm sorry I couldn't be more helpful with the bigger man. He had a mask on when I first saw him, and I was pretty traumatized later."

"Not to worry. These guys run in packs like wolves. Locate one and chances are his buddies won't be hard to find." She reached out and patted Abigail's arm. "You doing okay?"

A shrug. "I guess so. Just disappointed."

"Don't be. You did great. I'll send this image to headquarters and make sure all the patrol units get emailed copies. It's a big city but we have eyes everywhere. We'll turn him up."

"I hope so. I've been too nervous to leave my apartment. If Reed—Officer Branson—hadn't encouraged me, I'd still be stuck there, staring at the walls and jumping every time somebody knocked on my door."

"He's a good cop. A good man. Our unit has had enough grief to last us all a lifetime and we'd hate to see another member hurt, if you get my meaning."

Abigail blinked rapidly. Had this stranger somehow glimpsed the truth and become concerned she'd break Reed's heart?

"I'd never lead any man on if I wasn't going to follow through," Abigail promised. "There really isn't anything between Reed and me. Honest. He's just helping out."

"Okay. If you say so." She smiled, and her eyes twinkled behind the large lenses of her designer frames. "Let me give you one of my cards. That way, if you do recall more and Reed isn't around, you can reach me directly."

If Reed isn't around? Was it possible? Of course it

was. There wasn't even a slim possibility that he was going to keep shepherding her up and down the boardwalk, let alone allow her to live with him and his sister for much longer. It would behoove her to keep that in mind above all else.

She glanced at the loathsome face staring back at her from the laptop screen. "Will you email a copy of that to me, too, please? I want to be able to show it to my boss in case he comes around my office. We both need to be prepared."

"Will do. You ready for your ice cream treat?"

That brought a real smile. "You think I need bribing?"

"Nope," Danielle replied, hitting the button on the key to unlock the doors. "But I do. I was supposed to be eating lobster and steak with a good-looking hunk about now. The least Branson can do is buy me a cone."

Stepping out first, Abigail felt as if a heavy load had lifted, physically and emotionally. Directing the formation of that little weasel's nasty face had helped release part of the burden she'd been carrying. Being out from under that weight was a big relief.

Providing I'm right, she told herself, sensing the mantle of peace slipping slightly. Had she seen that face somewhere else and imagined it belonging to her attacker? She'd been so positive while in the car, yet doubt was creeping in as the seconds passed.

She hesitated, frowning. "What if I'm wrong? What if the person I described is innocent? I don't want to blame someone who doesn't deserve it."

"Let us sort that out," Danielle said. "It's your job to do as well as possible and our job to take it from there."

"Right. Thanks." With a sideways nod she indicated

which direction they should go. "I know where the guys probably went. Come on. Let's surprise them."

As Abigail's gaze passed over the crowd, her subconscious gave her a start. *Whoa! Was that...? No way.* She had to be hallucinating after the recent sketch session. There was no other explanation why someone would look so familiar. Unless...

She turned and grabbed her companion's arm. "Look. Over my shoulder. Do you see him?"

"Who?"

"The guy in my sketch. He's standing by the ticket booth." The look on Danielle's face wasn't comforting. "You see him, don't you?"

Golden curls bobbed and earrings swung as the other woman said, "Sorry."

Abigail whirled. There was nobody around who even remotely resembled the person she'd described. So why was her pulse running wild and her mouth as dry as beach sand in July?

Chin up, she stood tall and reclaimed the shred of peace remaining, figuratively wrapping herself in hopes of anonymity. Maybe she had made a mistake. It was certainly possible. But that didn't mean she wasn't going to become complacent.

He was out there somewhere.

She could feel the menace.

And someday soon she was going to spot him for real.

SIXTEEN

The drive back to Queens seemed to fly by for Reed, undoubtedly because his brain was occupied by more than safe driving.

A glance in the mirror told him that the boy and dog had fallen asleep sharing the rear seat. Dom had one arm over Jessie's shoulders, his head pillowed on the K-9's soft fur.

Just to be certain, Reed cleared his throat before speaking. Nobody except Abigail paid the slightest attention. If he told her what he suspected, would it make matters worse or better? There was no way to tell. As he saw it, knowing to be cautious was the lesser of two evils.

"I was studying that face you and Danielle came up with," he began. "Something about him looked familiar."

Reed saw her eyes widen, her lips part as if she might gasp.

Instead, she said, "I thought so, too. Do you think I subconsciously described somebody else we saw on the boardwalk?"

"Not necessarily. That was where you were when you were attacked. Maybe the original thugs were hanging around and decided to come closer to check you out. See what you remembered."

"That's not a very comforting idea."

"No, but it can be a useful warning."

"Surely they won't try anything again. Not while I'm with you and Jessie."

"You're right." He wanted to reassure her without making her worry. "But life has to go on, Abigail. I won't always be close by. That's why it's so important for you to keep remembering more about your ordeal."

"I know, I know. You don't have to beat me over the head with it. Don't you think I'm doing the best I can?" She looked contrite before adding, "Sorry. It's not your fault."

He paused to regroup. "I was trying to explain that this isn't my regular area of coverage. The K-9s in my unit move all over the city, go to wherever we're needed most. I could be called away at any time. I want you to promise you'll stay aware of your surroundings and be very cautious."

She humphed. "Hey, I was doing fine hiding out in my apartment until you made me leave."

"Circumstances made you leave, not me," Reed countered. "You know that as well as I do. And while we're on the subject, what do you make of Kiera's panic earlier? When she got scared, grabbed the boy and took off, she was white as a sheet."

Abigail eyed the sleeping duo in the rear seat. "He knows what's going on. He must. Do you think we can persuade him to tell us?"

"I'm not sure. Getting him to describe the guy who may have killed my chief was a big step."

Abigail gave a cynical chuckle. "Hey, convincing

him to step foot inside this vehicle in the first place was giant. I thought we were going to lose him right then."

"It's thanks to you and Danielle that we didn't," Reed reminded her. "If I had been the only adult around he might not have agreed to anything."

"You've read his file?"

Reed nodded solemnly. "Yeah. He's all alone in the world. Little wonder he won't settle down in foster care. He has nothing left to go home to so he probably doesn't see the advantage of good behavior."

"Exactly." She leaned a little closer, making Reed's pulse jump. "Can I see the picture he came up with?"

"Sure." Hitting a key on the system in the center console, he displayed the criminal's face on a screen.

"He looks enormous. Beefy. But I suppose any adult male would look gigantic to a boy Dom's size."

"Probably. Still, it's a start. The image has already gone out to all units and been posted at every precinct."

"I hope and pray you catch him."

Hearing pathos in her voice, Reed replied, "I wish we could jail them all and throw away the keys. Sometimes I wonder if we're even gaining ground. It's ridiculous to imagine getting every scrap of dirt swept up, so to speak, but I can dream."

To his surprise, she smiled. "You'd better not wipe out all the crime in New York. If you do, you'll be out of a job."

"I don't think there's much chance of that," Reed said. "So, how are you feeling after your session with Danielle? I didn't want to ask while she was around."

"The session wasn't nearly as satisfying as the ice cream afterward," Abigail said. "I just wish Kiera had been with us."

"She'll turn up soon," Reed promised. "As long as she's more worried about other kids than she is about herself, she'll come back." Once more he checked the rear seat. Thankfully, nothing had changed since the last time he'd looked.

"That speaks well of her," Abigail ventured. "If she were more self-centered, I'd see less chance of helping her learn to live a normal life."

"The way you do?"

That made her laugh again. "Um, yeah, well, let's reserve judgment on that subject until I remember the rest of the details of my attack, shall we? Right now, nothing feels normal to me."

Reed almost snorted in self-disgust. Instead, he said, "Yeah, well, there's a lot of that attitude going around."

Home, to Abigail, was still her empty apartment, and she desperately wanted to return to it for the solace found there. However, since Dominic was now a part of their little displaced group, she felt obligated to remain with Lani and Reed, at least for the time being.

What surprised her was Reed showing up at breakfast the next morning in his uniform.

"I've been called in to work," he told his sister, Abigail and Dominic. "They need Jessie, so we'll be gone today."

Lying under the table, the bloodhound thumped her tail on the floor while the black Lab pup chewed a squeaky toy.

Lani reached over and gave Reed a playful punch in the shoulder. "You're obviously irreplaceable. I'll be glad when I get a dog of my own to partner."

Grateful for a benign topic of conversation, Abigail asked, "How long have you been a police officer?"

"Not quite long enough to be assigned a dog," the slightly younger woman answered. "But it won't be long now. I can hardly wait."

"Too bad Midnight isn't qualified." Hearing her name called, the pup began to paw at Abigail's knee, then switched to pulling on her shoelaces until he had them untied.

"Yes, you," Abigail said, grinning. "Stop that. Bad."

"Clip her leash on her collar so you have control," Reed said. "Then you can give corrections properly. Timing is everything. She won't know what she's done wrong unless you correct immediately."

"Okay. Sorry. There's a lot to learn, isn't there?"

"You'll catch on," Lani assured her. "Just be consistent and if you're not sure, ask. I'll be glad to coach you while Reed's gone today."

"Will do. At least Midnight will keep me occupied until I go back to work full-time." Thoughts of resuming her job gave her the shivers. She'd have to accept Reed's offer of a ride. Being shut up in a train car with strangers pushing in on her from every side was the stuff of nightmares.

Reed rose and carried his plate and coffee mug to the sink. "Gotta go. See you all later."

Abigail knew she was going to miss him something awful despite not being totally alone, but there was no way she'd let on. Whether Reed sensed her angst or not was a mystery. Part of her hoped he did while another part wanted to keep those inappropriate sentiments private.

Catching his eye as he donned his gear, she smiled,

hoping he'd reciprocate. Instead, she got a look that bordered on an unspoken warning right before he said, "Stay here and stay inside unless Lani is with you and keep an eye on Dom."

That was so clearly an order, she bristled. Nevertheless, she said, "Okay, okay. I get it."

Did he really think her troubles would follow her all the way to his house? That seemed highly unlikely. Although there had been a prowler at her apartment, the police had never proved who he was or why he'd broken in. It could just as easily have been an isolated incident. After all, the prowler hadn't tried to harm her when he'd had the chance. He could have been a total stranger. As Reed had said, they were a long way from ending crime in the city.

And she'd been of little help, particularly if her facial reconstruction had been of someone other than her original attacker. She visualized the thin, menacing face. Those squinty eyes. The bad teeth and lips that seemed ready to snarl like a rabid dog. His was a hard face to forget.

While she helped Lani clear the table, Abigail tried to pull her mind away from negatives and enjoy watching Dominic wrestle on the living room floor with Midnight. A half-grown boy and a rambunctious puppy were meant for each other. It was hard to imagine either of them becoming mature, productive members of society, yet that was her aim. It had to be. If her hard road in life had shown her anything, it was that redemption was not only possible, it was a worthwhile goal.

Left alone, without proper intervention, anybody could become a criminal, even the most tenderhearted people. Kiera was a prime example. At this stage of life she could go either way. She still cared about others. But she also looked out for number one. When a crisis came, would she choose the right fork in the road or barrel down the wrong one into the oblivion of drugs or other unspeakable acts?

Picturing the girl and recalling her attitude toward authority, Abigail felt her own stomach clench. She looked around the Branson kitchen and living room. Framed family pictures on the walls and a homey feeling weren't enough to take the place of Reed's actual presence.

His leaving had left a void despite it being temporary. For no logical reason she was scared. Again. Abigail shivered, glancing at Lani and hoping to draw comfort.

Instead, the other woman was drying her hands and peering out the window over the sink.

Abigail was hardly able to ask, "What is it? What do you see?"

"Not sure." Lani laid aside the damp towel and opened a nearby drawer. Her hand closed around the grip of a handgun. She pulled a clip from a higher cupboard and loaded, chambering a round while aiming at the ceiling and continuing to monitor the small fenced yard.

No one had to tell Abigail to step back and keep her head down. She was getting all too used to strategic avoidance.

Hunched over, she hurried toward the boy and puppy, wondering how in the world she was going to protect them when the only weapon *she* possessed was her wits.

If Lani hadn't been home with Abigail and Dominic, Reed didn't know how he'd have coped. Yes, the chances of trouble at his house were slim. He knew that. He also knew that Abigail's nemesis had struck unexpectedly before. Right now, however, he had other concerns.

A bank in Brooklyn had been robbed and witnesses reported one of the thieves had escaped on foot. Jessie followed his trail as far as an alley, then lost the scent.

"Looks like he caught a ride," Reed reported via radio. "We'll be ten-ninety-nine, available in a couple of minutes."

He allowed his dog to carry her reward toy as they backtracked. That was the trouble with this job. Not every task ended in definitive success. It was his duty to not only direct his K-9 partner but to also keep up her spirits. She had to be made to feel some accomplishment or she might become depressed over her failure.

"Kind of like I feel about Abigail's stalker," he muttered in disgust. Jessie looked up at him, her eyes questioning, her tail still. "Yes, you're a good girl," Reed assured her. "A good, good dog."

That obviously pleased her because the spring in her step returned and she paced happily at his side, wagging vigorously enough to cause bystanders to step back and give them extra room.

Normally, Reed was as eager as his K-9 partner to respond to an incident. This was who he was, what he did. His identity. And yet today, all he wanted was to be released and make his way back to Queens. To his home. To Abigail.

Like it or not, he kept having disturbing thoughts about her safety. Lani was home and would watch over her and the boy, he knew, so he should have been satisfied. Well, he wasn't. Not even close. The same instinct that often kept him alive in dark alleys and dangerous neighborhoods was currently prickling the short hair on the nape of his neck and sending shivers along his spine.

Pausing just short of the patrol cars grouped in front of the bank, he pulled out his cell phone. A quick call to his sister would put his mind at ease.

Although he wanted to phone Abigail instead, he figured Lani would be more inclined to deliver the kind of clear status report he craved.

The phone rang. And rang. And rang.

Reed stared at his phone, wondering if he'd pressed the wrong button. He hadn't. Maybe his sister was outside with Abigail and Midnight and didn't have her cell with her. As unlikely as that was, it soothed him to think it.

Ending that effort when voice mail answered, he tried Abigail's number. Surely one of them would have a phone on her.

Two rings. A shrill voice said, "Hello?"

It took Reed a moment to realize he was talking to Dominic. What was that kid doing with Abigail's phone? Had he stolen it and taken off?

"Let me talk to Ms. Jones," Reed demanded.

"She's…" The boy fell silent, but the connection didn't. In the background Reed heard the sound of splintering wood. Someone screamed.

Lani yelled, "Stop. Police."

"Dominic!" Reed shouted into his phone.

"He broke the door!" the boy yelled.

Multiple voices rose in fright. Anger. Confusion. A puppy yipped.

And then there was the unmistakable sound of gunfire!

SEVENTEEN

Abigail dragged Dominic behind the sofa with her and kept him there as long as she could. It was a monumental struggle to hang on to the wiry teen.

Lani's voice came across strong. "He's down. Call 911!"

"I'll do it," the boy answered. With a twist and scramble he was out from behind the couch and had hold of Abigail's cell phone.

"It's not working," he reported. "Hello? Hello?"

Abigail took it from him and managed to calm herself enough to disconnect from the previous connection and report the break-in. She relayed the street address Lani called out to her and was assured that patrol units were on their way.

"Tell them it's an officer-involved shooting and we need an ambulance," Lani insisted. "I don't want them busting in here and taking me down by accident."

"Is he… Is he dead?" Abigail asked.

"Not yet. But he's not doing well," Lani replied.

No matter how nonchalant she sounded, Abigail could tell how deeply affected the other woman was because of the quaver in her voice and the fact that she'd backed up to a chair and sat while keeping her gun pointed at the wounded attacker.

"Who is he?" Lani asked.

Abigail shook her head. "I don't know. I've never seen him before. At least, I don't think I have." She glanced over at the teen. "Do you know him?"

The boy shook his head vigorously. "Uh-uh. No way."

By this time the injured man was moaning and holding his thigh. "I could have hit the femoral artery," Lani said. "We need to try to stop that bleeding or we could lose him."

"I'll do it," Abigail said. "Have you got a scarf or something like that handy?"

"Use a towel from the kitchen and his belt," Lani told her. "And be careful."

"Okay." As she cautiously approached the man she sensed Dominic at her elbow and told him to stay back.

"I can help. I can. Honest."

Rather than waste precious time arguing, Abigail opted to let him stay close. Truth to tell, she wasn't keen on nursing this person's leg, and the teen's presence was soothing her jangled nerves.

"Okay. You take his belt off while I apply pressure to the wound with the towel," she told him.

The job was done in a jiffy. Abigail sat back on her haunches. If her hands had been clean she would have high-fived the boy. Instead, she started to stand.

At that moment, the victim lunged. His shoulder rammed into her and sent her reeling. Dominic fell back, too, landing on his hands and feet like a crab.

Lani shouted, "Get out of the way!"

One thing was crystal clear to Abigail. Their so-called incapacitated victim was back on the move and dangerous. She threw herself to one side, hoping to get out of Lani's line of fire. Dominic, however, sprang up and made a grab for the man, spoiling the officer's aim.

"Dominic!" Abigail's heart was in her throat. If the rookie fired again she was sure to hit the boy by accident. "Stop! Stop!"

The limping, bleeding interloper used the door frame to scrape off the slightly built teen and leave him behind in a heap before making it all the way outside and disappearing.

Acting stunned, Dominic began to sob. Abigail fell to her knees beside him and gathered him up in her arms, mindless of the bloodstains.

She saw Lani run past, swing around the splintered door jamb and assume a shooter's stance.

Abigail was holding her breath, too shocked to move. As Lani's body relaxed and the firearm was lowered, she knew it was all over. They had probably just lost their best chance to identify one of her former attackers and she was thankful he had been the only one injured in the melee.

Yes, she was supposed to forgive her enemies, but she'd reserve that noble attempt for *after* he had been captured and jailed.

Lani tucked her gun into a holster, clipped it to her waist and went out onto the front porch to wait for the first responders.

"Don't let Midnight out," Abigail called after her.

Frowning, Lani stuck her head back inside. "Where is she, anyway?"

"The last time I saw her she was hiding behind the drapes," Abigail said. "I hope she's still there."

"She is," Lani answered. "Poor baby is terrified." She fastened a leash to the puppy's collar and gently coaxed her to come out. Even then, Midnight continued to tremble from nose to tail.

Busy comforting the boy, Abigail cast only a cursory glance at her pup. Lani was patiently consoling her. That would have to do until she and Dom could get cleaned up and take over. It was sad to see how frightened Midnight was.

Until she noticed Lani's frown, she didn't realize that the negative experience might have done damage to her impressionable Lab baby. Obviously Midnight was going to need a whole lot of cuddling and reassurance in the days and weeks to come.

Abigail was more than all right with that notion. She, herself, needed the same kind of TLC that the pup did. It was going to be good for both of them. After all, she had only her street kids and a few coworkers to count as family. There was nothing wrong with adding a furry member, as well.

Part of her mind wanted to include the Bransons, both of them. Lani had saved her life this time and Reed had rescued her in the past. But that was from her point of view. Theirs was the key. Reed had often insisted she was part of his job. And Lani? Well, the rookie cop couldn't be thrilled with them since she and Dominic had inadvertently let the attacker escape.

Abigail sighed and soaped her hands. It seemed as though trouble followed her wherever she went. And now, despite monumental efforts to help, she had involved both police officers as well as at least one of her homeless kids. That was unacceptable.

Then again, she thought, using a brush on her already clean fingernails, so was getting killed when she hadn't purposely done one thing wrong. Or had she? Could there be facts obscured by her lost memory that would paint a different picture?

Reed skidded his SUV to the curb between two patrol cars and ran into the house. If he'd seen the blood on the floor before spotting his loved ones he'd have shouted in anguish. Knowing it could have been theirs had things gone awry, he gathered up his sister and Abigail in a group hug.

"You, too, kid," he said, gesturing to Dominic. "I was listening to my radio on the way back and they said you tried to tackle the guy. Come here."

Hesitant to approach, Dom inched closer to the adults. "He got away."

"Thankfully," Reed said. "Look, I know you were doing what you thought was right, but it wasn't. Promise me you won't try anything like that again."

"Yeah, okay."

That simple agreement should have sufficed, but Reed didn't like the intonation. Unless he was so overwrought he was imagining things, the teenager had his own agenda. That figured. After all, Dom was used to running wild and making his own decisions, the same as Kiera was.

Satisfied to hold Abigail and his sister however long they needed comforting, Reed found himself disappointed when they both eased away. In the background, one of the patrol officers was photographing the splintered door off the kitchen while a second inspected the backyard.

"I'll go get Jessie as soon as these officers are through," he said. "Where's the pup?"

"I put her in her crate in the bathroom to calm her down. She was a basket case after all this," Abigail said. "I didn't know what else to do and Lani said it would be best to give her some quiet time."

Reed nodded sagely. "That's fine. Where was she when the shooting started?"

"Hiding behind the sofa with me and Dominic," Abigail answered. "Lani was the only one who wasn't scared silly."

"Yeah, well," the other woman drawled. "I'm thankful I'd had the training to fall back on, but that doesn't mean I wasn't shaking."

"I'll talk to Noah Jameson and explain what happened here. How you had no choice," Reed said. "I don't think it will hurt your chances for being assigned a working dog. Might slow things down a little, that's all."

Lani gestured to the uniformed officer who was inspecting the broken door. "He took my gun and bagged it."

"Standard operating procedure," Reed assured her.

She pulled a face. "I know, I know."

Reed turned to Abigail. "Could this guy have been the bigger one with the round cheeks? The one you couldn't really describe?"

"I don't think so, but it is possible. If I had heard him speak I might have a better idea. Everything happened so fast this time I can't be positive, but I don't remember anything he may have said."

"Okay. I'm sure our lab can get DNA from the blood he lost. It may take a while, though. They're always behind."

"How about fingerprints?"

"He was wearing gloves," the teen volunteered. "Didn't you see?"

"I guess I was too busy worrying he'd die before we got the bleeding stopped," Abigail answered. "I've had a first aid course for my job, but it didn't cover serious stuff like gunshots."

Reed looked askance. "Really? I'd think that would be part of the normal curriculum. That and learning how to help victims of knife fights."

"Very funny," she said cynically. Reed could tell Abigail's nervousness was lessening. That was how this odd attitude worked for cops, firefighters and other first responders. They joked about the deathly serious aspects of their jobs as a tension reliever. The ones who never lightened up were bound to burn out a lot faster than their opposites did. Like what had happened to Abigail. The mind could take only so much trauma before it shut down.

Reed palmed his phone and thumbed through the photo albums before holding it up for her to see. "Take another look at the guy you were able to describe and try to picture him with the shooting victim."

Sighing, she seemed reluctant. Nevertheless, she stepped up and studied the face before closing her eyes. "Sorry. I'm not getting any flashes of insight. I really doubt they're connected, but if they aren't, then why come here and break down your door?"

"Good question." Reed was lowering his arm as the teenager inched closer. He raise the picture again. "What about you? Have you seen him down by the boardwalk or on the streets at Coney?"

Instead of offering a nonchalant no, Dominic began

waving his hands and backing away. His dark eyes were wide and glistening. "No. No way. Never saw him before. Uh-uh."

Well, that was overkill. Reed stood still, observing the boy's reactions. He was lying. Big time. Not only had he seen the thin face Abigail had come up with, he knew who the man was and probably had a good idea where to find him. That was newsworthy. And troubling.

"Okay," Reed finally said, pocketing his phone when the boy hurried out of the room. "I'm going to find out how much longer these cops will be working our crime scene, then go get Jessie and put her in with Midnight to help calm her down. Later, I'll grab a hammer and repair the door frame. We can't leave it like that overnight."

"I'm really sorry," Abigail told him.

Reed checked to make certain Dominic was long gone before he leaned closer and said, "Don't always blame yourself, Abigail. What happened here today may have had little or nothing to do with you."

She began to frown and make a face. "Are you serious?"

"Serious as a gunshot to a leg," he said, deadpanning the quip. "There's something else going on and I plan to figure out what. Just go along with whatever I say or do, okay?"

"Sure." She shrugged. "Are you going to let your sister in on it, too?"

Casting a glance across the room at Lani and reading unspoken understanding in her expression, he said, "I doubt that will be necessary. She has the mind of a cop, same as I do. We're naturally suspicious of every-body and everything."

"I'm not sure I like that," Abigail admitted.

"Yeah, well, it beats looking at the world through rose-colored glasses and making yourself so vulner-able."

"Meaning me?"

"If the glasses fit." Reed could tell Abigail was upset. That was fine with him. If he could do or say anything that opened her eyes to the evil in their world and made her safer as a result, he would. It was a personal sacri-fice to admit he didn't have a trusting nature because it showed him in a negative light. That could easily stop her from caring for him the way he cared for her. He could deal with that idea. He'd have to. But he didn't have to like it.

EIGHTEEN

Abigail spent the night tossing and turning, imagining all sorts of boogeymen hiding in the house or sneaking in and out through the windows the way the prowler had at her apartment. The old brick building in Brighton Beach had been noisier, but she'd been used to the ambient din of the busy city streets and her fellow tenants. Here, in Rego Park, it was so much quieter that every little noise stood out.

By morning she felt more weary than she had the evening before. Yawning, she joined Lani in the kitchen, drawn by the aroma of freshly brewed coffee. "Oh, that smells good."

The other woman filled a mug. "Here you go. Compliments of the cook."

Abigail chuckled, blew on the steaming liquid and took a cautious sip. "Mmmm. As good as it gets." She eyed Lani's jogging outfit. "Are you going running?"

"Been and back," Lani told her with a grin. "You have to get up pretty early if you want to run with me. I walked your puppy, too. She's out in the yard now."

"Wow. I guess I need to set an alarm. I don't hit my

stride until eight or so." She saluted with her mug. "And that's only after a couple shots of strong bean juice."

"Orange juice is better for you," Lani offered. "Want some?"

"No thanks." Abigail looked over her shoulder. "What about the guys? Any sign of Reed or Dom yet?"

"Nope. It's been nice and peaceful."

Laughing softly, Abigail nodded. "Believe me, I get it. I'm used to living alone."

"You don't get lonesome?"

"Sometimes." Another sip, another smile. "I am looking forward to having Midnight underfoot. She's a sweetheart. How was she acting this morning? Better?"

"Yes. I think she'll get over her fright from yesterday. If she'd been used to us and had developed more trust she'd have coped better. You have to remember, she hasn't been with you for very long. Socialization and bonding take time. You do realize you're only caretaking her, don't you?"

Sobering, Abigail nodded. "Yes, I know. How long can I expect her to stay with me?"

"As long as you participate in any formal training she may need, providing she improves enough to be considered for classes, you may be allowed to keep her at home for a year or two."

"That doesn't seem like very long at all." Abigail pictured those big brown eyes, velvety ears and feet almost the size of Jessie's, plopping against the floor like clown shoes. Midnight had just come into her life and she loved her already.

Reed's deep voice echoed down the hallway. "Dominic?"

Abigail swiveled to greet him as he entered. "Good morning."

"Where's Dominic?"

She and Lani shrugged. "We thought you were both sleeping in."

Instead of explaining, Reed stomped to the front door and jerked it open, then slammed it and circled through the kitchen to the rear. The patched door stuck slightly, but he strong-armed it open long enough to call, "Dominic!" without letting the eager dogs in.

"I didn't see him when I put the puppy out with Jessie," Lani said. "Wasn't he on the cot we fixed for him?"

"No. I thought maybe he'd moved in here to the sofa, but I can see he didn't." Raking his fingers through his short, dark hair, Reed began to pace. "We had a good man-to-man talk last night, and I assumed he understood that I wanted to be his friend and help him. Considering the rough life he's had, I should have guessed he'd take off instead of trusting me."

That conclusion settled in Abigail's stomach like a rock. "You think he's left?"

"Absolutely."

"Why? He knows he's safer here with us."

"Is he?" Reed strapped on his utility belt and opened the combination lock on the gun safe where he stored his duty weapon. "Tell me," he said, directing the query to Abigail, "when you said he was trying to stop the guy Lani shot, is it possible he was trying to leave with him instead?"

"No, I…" She reran the chaotic scene in her mind. Reed had a point. "I suppose he could have been. I just assumed, since he'd been helping me with first aid, that he was on my side. Our side. What makes you think he was trying to escape?"

"The way he reacted to the reconstruction of the face of your assailant. My mistake was thinking he was more afraid of that man than he was of staying here with us."

Reed's sister asked, "Do you want me to call it in as a missing person?"

"Not yet. I need to report to Noah Jameson before I do anything else. He left the decision up to me, and I'm the one who made the mistake of bringing Dom home. If Abigail hadn't been with us I probably wouldn't have. Let's assume the boy headed back to the beach and go there first."

"Are you going to put Jessie on his trail?" Lani asked.

It was clear to Abigail that her presence was posing a problem when both Bransons turned to stare at her. "I can stay here with Midnight if you need to go," she said.

"No good. Lani's trained in self-defense, but you aren't. The police still have her gun, and that puppy won't be any help. We'll all have to go."

"Even Midnight?"

"No. Lani can crate her for the short time we'll be away so she won't slow us down. I'll let Jessie track Dom as far as she can, then turn her over to you two and you can bring her back here—hopefully with a police escort—and wait for me. He's a savvy kid. He'll probably hop on the subway. Once he boards a train, Jessie's bound to lose his trail."

As far as Abigail was concerned, his plan was awful. However, this was not the time to argue. The sooner they put the bloodhound on the teen's trail, the better. When it came time to leave Reed and come back to the house with Lani, she'd speak her piece. No way was she letting that stubborn cop track down one of her special kids without her. Period.

Besides, she reasoned, she'd feel a lot safer with Reed by her side than she would if they parted. She might not be used to his house yet, but she was more than used to being with him. He was the glue that held her psyche together and the strength that gave her enough courage to keep trying.

That, and my faith in God, Abigail added. Lately it seemed she only remembered to pray earnestly when she was scared to death, so her next prayer was an apology to her heavenly Father and the promise to do better at trusting Him in all things, even the smallest detail.

Starting now, she told herself, giving thanks for Reed even if he was an opinionated, stubborn man who drove her crazy.

Reed felt overwhelmed and he was not happy about it. He couldn't report the boy when all he had was a suspicion. It was going to be hard enough getting somebody to look after Abigail when Lani had to go back to work and he sure couldn't divert the talents of his extraordinary K-9, he added. Jessie had found a trail the instant she'd hit the back door. Nose down, she was coursing back and forth, rarely lifting her head to sniff the air.

Reed glanced over his shoulder at the women. Lani was dressed for running but Abigail was going to get overheated in those jeans and that long-sleeve T-shirt. She was already wiping her brow.

"I can't stop now," he called back. "If you can't keep up, head back to the house."

A breathless, "No way," drifted back to him. He should have guessed Abigail would stick it out until he ended the search or she dropped from exhaustion. She was the most stubborn—and loyal—woman he'd ever encountered, with the possible exception of his over-achieving sister. Lani had always insisted she was as capable as he was, and now she'd met her doppelganger in Abigail Jones.

Streets grew busier and traffic thick. Trucks honked. Taxis squeezed in and out between other vehicles as if able to flex as they passed, much the way a terrier pursued a rabbit through brambles or down its burrow.

Jessie halted, circled once, then started down the stairway into the first subway entrance they came to.

"This is it," Reed announced. "As I suspected, he hopped a train."

Lani accepted Jessie's leash from him. "You really want us to go back home? Why don't you come along and get your car?"

"It'll take too long," he countered. "I'll contact Transit and make arrangements for them to keep an eye out, particularly near the Coney and Brighton stops."

"Okay," his sister said.

Pulling out his phone Reed covered the opposite ear with his hand to mute the street noise and turned away.

It took several minutes to complete his explanation and give the dispatcher a detailed description of Dominic. Since the boy owned so few clothes it was easy to tell what he had to be wearing. When Reed looked behind him, expecting to see Lani, Jessie and Abigail on their way back to his house, he was stunned. His sister and his dog were gone, all right. But Abigail Jones was still standing there, grinning up at him as if she had just won a prize.

"What are you doing here? And where's Lani? You're supposed to stay with her."

"I decided to stick with you, instead. Your sister didn't seem to mind." Abigail pointed back the way they had come. "She said she was taking Jessie home."

"Well, *I* do." He shaded his eyes to scan the busy sidewalk. There was no sign of Lani's blond hair, and Jessie was too close to the ground to spot at a distance, given the throng of pedestrians.

"Sorry," Abigail said, continuing to smile. "Too late. I'm going to be there for that kid, even if he is trouble with a capital *T.* You're stuck with me until we catch up to Dom."

Gritting his teeth and clamping his jaw, he stared at her. So pretty. So witty. And so, so…

She gestured at the descending staircase and the crush of passengers zigzagging past each other. "Are we going to stand here arguing or get a move on? I'm sure Dominic didn't waste any time."

Reed did the only logical thing. He clasped her hand tightly and started down the stairs, half dragging her behind him. There were no words adequate for this situation. None. Not even the unacceptable ones she had hinted at.

Right here, right now, all he could do was make sure she didn't lag behind or pull some other inane trick that made matters even worse. If that was possible.

He felt her resist. Heard her say, "There. That one. It's the most direct route."

She was breathless and softly laughing. He was not amused.

"You don't have to worry about me trying to ditch

you," she said, raising her voice to carry above the rhythmic clacking of the wheels on the tracks. "I told you. I intend to be there for Dom. The way I see it, you're my best chance of catching up to him."

Leaning closer, he spoke into her ear, his warm breath tickling her cheek and sending a shiver from there to the ends of every nerve.

"I'd be more inclined to trust you," Reed said, "if you kept your word."

She whipped around as best she could without staggering. "Hey, when have I lied to you?" Abigail wasn't sorry she'd used a harsh tone, but she sure wished she hadn't placed her face so close to his while doing it. Their lips were mere inches apart, and unless Reed straightened there was no chance she was going to be able to back away. The accidental closeness was overwhelming. Awesome. It was as if they were the only two people on that train, enclosed in a cocoon of intense awareness and emotional pull. Connected as never before.

To her delight, Reed seemed as stunned as she felt. Frozen in time, he stared into her eyes, studying, probing their depths, asking unspoken questions she didn't dare answer.

A little notion formed and grew beyond her wildest imagining. If the train jerked just a tiny bit and she let herself go with it, there was a chance Reed would feel the same urge she did and kiss her. They'd had their differences, sure, but the attraction felt mutual. It simply had to be. There was no way she'd have become so enamored of him if she hadn't sensed reciprocation.

When had it started? she wondered. How had she managed to meet and fall for this man in such a short

time? Was she deluded? Unbalanced because of the amnesia?

Amnesia. Abigail closed her eyes and stood stock-
still, her face still raised to his. She was seeing the carousel, the night, the men who had been nothing but
shimmering shadows until she'd worked through the
problem with Danielle and come up with a face.

She was in Luna Park. Alone. Frightened. And she
was watching two adults manhandle a smaller person,
probably a teen or preteen. Then they were after her.
Someone grabbed her. Threatened her. Hurt her wrists
and made her believe she was about to be murdered!

Abigail's lips parted. Her breathing grew ragged.
She remembered!

Her eyes flew open just as Reed was lowering his
mouth to join it with hers and her noisy gasp ended everything.

She had no time to lament the show of affection she'd
missed by moments. This was too exciting. She grabbed
his arm. "I know what I saw! It's all clear now."

"You remembered the whole event? Really?"

"Yes! It was—it was by the carousel. Two men, one
heavy and one thinner, just like I told you before. Only
now I know why they chased and grabbed me. I saw
them restraining a third person. I think it was one of my
kids. It had to be. Who else would be hanging around
down there at that hour? Besides…"

More details swam to the surface, giving Abigail a
jolt. "Hey! I know why I was there. It was because of
Kiera. She'd asked me to meet her."

"No wonder she was so nervous about your memories. She was involved. Do you think she set you up?"

Abigail's spirits plummeted from the mountaintop

of success to the valley of despair. "I don't know. I'd like to think she wouldn't do that to me but I can't be positive, especially after the way she made Dominic run away from us."

To her relief, Reed slipped an arm around her and held her close to his side while they swayed with the movement of the train. "One answer at a time," he said. "First we'll find him, then we'll look for her. If we have to round up every kid on the boardwalk, we will."

"Can you do that?"

He huffed. "Not out of uniform like this. But I do think I can get the acting chief of my unit to pull a few strings. We've had reports of a couple of newly missing teens anyway, so it's not a stretch to do a sweep."

"*My* kids? Why didn't you tell me?"

"Simmer down. These kids were visiting from out of town and disappeared during a day at the beach with friends."

"That is so sad." She leaned against Reed for support and to draw on his inner strength. "Sometimes I feel as though my best efforts are worthless. I can't rescue all the lost kids no matter how hard I try."

"Then you understand how I feel," he said with a sigh. "Only in your case, some of them actually come to you. I have to chase them down or try to outsmart them. A lot of times, my collars will make bail or alibi out and hit the streets again before I have time to grab lunch."

"I sometimes wish I could lock these kids up and force them to listen to good advice," Abigail said.

He gave her a tender squeeze. "And I wish my contacts liked me half as much as yours like you."

"*I* like you," she told him.

"Yeah," Reed said. She felt his voice rumbling in his chest where her cheek rested. "Don't tell anybody, but I kinda like you, too, Ms. Jones."

NINETEEN

"We could cover more ground if we split up," Abigail said.

Reed scowled at her. "You have to be kidding." It was a relief to see her blush behind those freckles.

"I thought I should at least suggest it."

"No. Period. You and I are doing this together or not at all. Got that?"

She squeezed his hand. "Yup. Got it."

"You're agreeing with me? What's wrong? Are you sick? Running a fever?"

"Ha ha." She held up one hand and placed the tips of her index finger and thumb less than an inch apart. "I don't want to get even this far away from you, okay?"

"That works for me." Reed couldn't help smiling. When he saw her sky blue eyes sparkling he almost embraced her again. If he could have come up with a good reason to, he would have.

"Since you're down here all the time and I'm not, why don't you choose where we look first?"

"Now you're the one who's acting strange," Abigail said with a wry smile. "But I get it. I do know where the kids like to hang out, although this is pretty early to catch any of them awake. They stay up late and sleep late."

"Where? Where do they sleep?"

She shrugged. "A lot of them stay on the beach in warm weather. That'll be ending soon, and it worries me. Come on."

Reed followed her down a ramp that led to the sand. It was too loose for comfortable walking, but he persevered. Sky that had been clear blue with a few puffy clouds was now darkening noticeably. "We should have brought jackets."

"Yes. I never dreamed it would turn so chilly in September."

"It's hard to imagine anybody spending the winter here, let alone a bunch of kids. That's a recipe for trouble."

"Don't I know it." Abigail shivered. "Most of them go into the city center when it gets too bad down here. A few come to us for aid and shelter. Those are the ones I look forward to seeing because it means they're ready to listen to reason. The state, as well as my organization, AFS, have plenty of programs to get them jobs or schooling or whatever they need. But they have to be willing to follow a few simple rules and that's where we sometimes run into conflict."

"I'm sure you do."

Just ahead, near the water's edge, a flock of gulls took flight and scattered, screeching in protest. Reed thought he'd seen something hit the beach near them so he wasn't too surprised they'd panicked. He did, however, inspect the wet sand where he'd seen the disturbance and he didn't like the narrow groove he spotted.

"What's that from?"

"My guess? A bullet trajectory." He began to scoop with his hands until he turned up a piece of lead-colored metal.

"That's impossible. I didn't hear any big bang."

"You wouldn't be likely to recognize the sound from this small a caliber. It would be like listening to plinking at a shooting gallery." Placing himself as a human shield between the boardwalk and the young woman, Reed scanned inland. All looked peaceful. A few folks were sweeping spots in front of food stands, and carts were delivering supplies for the upcoming day, but other than normal activity, there was nothing going on. If there had been a shooter he was either hiding or had left after firing the warning shot.

"Okay," Reed said, "we're getting off this sand and back to where we can take up defensive positions if we have to."

"But the kids…"

"Come on. We'll find a seat close to Kiera's favorite hot dog stand, watch and wait. If Dominic is around he may go there looking for her. Being in a crowd is smarter than wandering around like a row of lone ducks in a shooting gallery."

"So much for letting me take the lead," she muttered as they crossed the sand again.

"It's not your fault." He held up the tiny bullet. "I just have an aversion to ending up with one of these in me."

"I'd hate it, too."

"That's comforting." Reed told her.

Staying alert, he continued to scan the quiet stretches of boardwalk on either side of them while choosing chairs that backed up to an enormous menu sign. If the shooter was hiding, he or she would have to step into view to get a bead on them, giving Reed a chance to mount an effective defense.

The sigh Abigail loosed was almost as noisy as the wind off the Atlantic. Reed saw her shiver. "Cold?"

"A little. We left in too big a hurry to plan well."

"I know." He made a face of disgust. "My fault. Waking up and not finding Dominic rattled me. That's unacceptable for a cop. I know better."

"Yeah, well, when you care about somebody your emotions can take charge of your brain." She chuckled wryly. "I should know. I'm down here with you, just as unprepared."

He patted the concealed holster at his waist. "I'm not exactly unprepared. Underprepared is more like it." He glanced at the gray sky. "Once the sun comes out it'll warm up so much we'll be complaining of the heat."

"I suppose." Abigail had been fidgeting. She stood. "I can't just sit here, okay?"

Reaching out, Reed stopped her by touching her arm. "Wait. Look." He pointed as surreptitiously as he could. "Isn't that the girl?"

Abigail twisted around, squinted. "Yes!"

"Easy. It looks like she's coming to us. Let her."

"You're right."

As Reed watched, the teenager spotted them and broke into a run. She was approaching so fast he expected to see a pursuer. There was none. The boardwalk behind her was empty.

Abigail opened her arms and the girl collapsed into the embrace. She was weeping. Gasping. Trying to speak.

"He got me out…" Sobs interrupted.

"Who did?" Reed asked.

"D-Dominic. He was supposed to be right behind me, but he didn't make it!"

"Okay, slow down and explain," Reed said. All the response he got was more weeping, so he turned the job over to Abigail. "Get her calmed down. We need details."

"Right." Abigail shepherded the teen to the chairs she and Reed had been sharing. "Here. Sit with me and take some deep breaths. We need to know what happened. Where's Dominic?"

"*They* have him," Kiera blurted. "And they're going to put him on a ship." A gasp. "Today!"

"A ship? Why?" Abigail asked.

Speaking louder to be heard above the gut-wrenching sobs, Reed was hoping against hope that he was wrong. "How many kids do they have?"

"L-lots," Kiera blubbered.

"All young and mostly girls?"

The frantic teen nodded.

"Can you lead us back there?"

"I—I can't go back. If they catch me they'll kill me."

The puzzled expression on Abigail's face told Reed she was not yet seeing the whole picture, so he explained. "Human trafficking. We've suspected as much for months but haven't been able to gather enough evidence to make arrests. This could be the breakthrough we've all been praying for."

He pulled out his cell phone to report to his boss and saw light dawning in Abigail's eyes. Awareness was rapidly replaced by anger and determination.

She grasped Kiera's shoulders and forced a face-to-face confrontation. "Listen to me. This is what's going to happen. You are going to tell the police what you know and where the prisoners are being held. And then, if they have trouble finding the hiding place, you and I are going to lead them there. Understood?"

"Noooo!"

"Oh, yes. Somebody has to stand up for these other kids. Dominic risked his life to free you. Can you do less for him?"

Reed stayed out of it. He watched the girl sink to her knees, then saw Abigail lift her back up. They both had to be scared to death, particularly since both had been victims of similar attacks. It was only by the grace of God that Abigail had managed to outwit her pursuers and develop into a valuable ally.

He could not have been prouder of her if she had been his sister or a fellow police officer. All he had to worry about now was keeping her in the background while the NYPD handled the assault on the kidnappers' stronghold and freed their prisoners.

He huffed. That should be about as easy as turning the tide at will.

The best he could do was shoot a prayer toward Heaven and leave it to God, because no way was Abigail Jones going to listen to any other warning.

One element of the morning's operation was driving Abigail crazy. She hated waiting. However, she was also smart enough to realize that a Lone Ranger approach was foolhardy.

As patrol car after patrol car rolled up to the staging area along Surf Avenue and angled into the curb, she was astounded at the number of regular officers, SWAT team members and K-9s with their partners.

The only person she recognized for sure was Brianne, the one who had delivered the replacement SUV to Reed after his was wrecked. All business, the K-9 officer was accompanied by a golden Lab who looked more mature than the second dog of the same color who trotted along beside a male officer.

After shaking hands with many of the assembled police, Reed stepped back to listen to their incident commander issue instructions. As soon as assignments had been parceled out, Reed returned to Abigail, accompanied by the others with K-9s.

"Brianne Hayes you know," he said. "This is Stella, Midnight's mother. She's a former patrol K-9 being cross-trained at present."

Abigail nodded. Her arm remained firmly around Kiera's waist so the teen couldn't flee. "Yes. Hello again."

"And this is Finn Gallagher with K-9 Abernathy. His specialty is search and rescue. I hope we won't need either dog today."

"So do I." Abigail managed a slight smile for the others and their amazing canines. "I'm Abigail Jones and this is Kiera Underhill. She managed to escape from kidnappers this morning and is going to lead us to their hideout, if necessary." She gave the teen a squeeze. "Aren't you?"

"I guess." The face Kiera made to accompany her response was anything but amiable. Abigail didn't care. She couldn't let anything stop the rescue. There were some things that took precedence over the sentiments of a pouting, sniffling, uncooperative adolescent, and this was one of them.

"We saw your sister arrive in your car," Brianne

said to Reed. "She's got your dog and your uniform with her."

"Great!" Reed looked directly at Abigail. "Stay put. I'll go get Jessie and my gear and be right back."

Left with the other K-9 officers and their dogs, Abigail felt out of place. Nevertheless, she held her ground.

"I really admire what you all do," she told them. "I had no idea how complicated your job is or how hard you train to keep your dogs working well."

Brianne smiled down at the yellow Lab at her side. "Stella got off to a kind of slow start when she arrived from the Czech Republic. She was the gift that kept giving."

"You mean her puppies?"

Brianne's smile grew to a grin. "Yes. They're adorable, of course, but she couldn't work when we first got her and I don't speak her language so she had to relearn everything in English. If it had been German, one of our bilingual trainers could have taken over, but there's too much difference in the commands in Czech."

"It's probably harder for her than it is for us," Abigail guessed.

"I'm not sure of that. She's really smart." Fondness in the female officer's expression made it clear that she truly admired and loved Stella despite the obstacles they'd had to overcome.

"I hope Midnight takes after her," Abigail said. "She's so adorable. I'd love to see her succeed at something, even if she doesn't have what it takes to be a police dog."

"Don't feel bad. They don't all make the cut," Brianne said. "At least one pup from her litter has already washed out."

"How disappointing. Maybe they can become service or therapy dogs."

The officer was nodding. "Maybe. We only accept the best of the best in the NYPD."

"Dogs, you mean?" Abigail felt her cheeks warming.

"And men and women," Brianne replied, obviously enjoying the brief moment of shared amusement. "Reed Branson is one of the best." She paused before adding, "In and out of uniform."

"Are you and he…? I mean is he…? Oh, never mind."

Brianne laughed. "Relax, I do have someone special who used to be in the K-9 unit. Gavin Sutherland and I are engaged."

"I'm happy for you."

"I imagine there are personal reasons you're glad it's not Branson," Brianne teased. "Head's up. Here he comes. He's all yours."

In the background, Finn gave a cynical chuckle. "Better not let him hear you giving him away like a lost pup."

Abigail had been so enthralled by her conversation with the other K-9 officer, she'd forgotten that they weren't alone. The blush she'd sensed before probably developed into a crimson that washed out her freckles and clashed with her red hair.

To distract herself, she scanned the distant beach in the direction opposite of where the cops were gathering. All breath left her. She froze, barely able to speak. Finally, she managed to point with her free hand and say, "Look! Way over there by the steps. Are those the guys you're looking for? One is limping. Maybe he's the guy that was shot."

Everyone within hearing distance swiveled and

stared, including Reed. "I can't tell exactly what you're seeing but I'm going to find out." He grabbed his radio and broadcast the possible sighting. The pair had already reached and were crossing the boardwalk.

Shouting, "Stay here," Reed took off at a run rather than wait for backup and lose sight of his quarry.

Worried, excited and acting on impulse, Abigail thrust Kiera at Brianne and yelled, "Watch her," as a surge of adrenaline overpowered her usual common sense and convinced her to follow.

Struggling across the soft beach, she made a dash for the closest stairway leading up from the sand. This was her territory, the place where she'd felt most at home until she'd been attacked.

Once on solid footing, she didn't join the rush of police officers heading for Reed's last known position. Instead, she managed to stay parallel with him and Jessie, arriving at the junction of a street and an alley behind some concessions just as the other pursuers appeared down the block to her right.

Abigail felt like cheering until she noticed she was about to come face to face with the thugs they'd been after. "Oh, no!"

The two miscreants skidded to a stop and one pointed a gun at her. The thin-faced weasel was supporting his limping companion. That man fit the build of her second attacker. When he stared at her and said, "I should have killed you when I had the chance," she was positive it was him. The hair on her arms prickled. Her mouth was suddenly so dry she couldn't swallow, couldn't speak, couldn't move a muscle.

The larger man shook off his partner and faced her. She saw his eyes begin to squint. He pointed the muzzle of his gun at her, ignoring an ever growing cadre of armed police officers approaching with caution.

Abigail didn't know what to do so she simply stood there. Men were shouting over each other in the background, their individual commands lost in the din.

She saw her nemesis start to sneer, acting as if he didn't realize or didn't care that he was so greatly outnumbered. Then, something moved directly behind him. It was Reed!

Reed made a grab for the man's gun and missed. It fired, sending a bullet whizzing past Abigail's ear. She screamed.

An instinct for survival propelled her backward. She staggered. The gun came to bear on her once more. Was this the end? The part of her that knew she loved Reed kept insisting that her life could not end until she had told him how she felt.

She squeezed her eyes closed and covered her face with her hands, waiting for a second shot. Unidentified hands grabbed her roughly and lifted while fingers pressed tightly at her throat, choking the breath out of her. She was helpless. Finished.

Beautiful, colorful lights flashed behind her eyelids. Overwhelmed and overburdened she accepted the version of reality that was commanding her imagination and sank into oblivion.

TWENTY

Reed saw what was happening and roared with primal rage. He launched himself, landing on the back of the thug who was choking Abigail. One arm tightened around the front of the man's neck, elbow bent, and he completed the choke hold by grasping his own wrist for leverage.

Released, Abigail dropped limply into the arms of other officers who lowered her gently to the ground. Reed's anger consumed him, and he tightened his hold despite orders to let go. If not for Abigail's soft moan breaking through the haze of roiling emotion he might have continued indefinitely.

Reed picked out her moan above the sounds of traffic, the grunts and curses of his adversary and a multitude of police officers all shouting at the same time.

Abigail! She was still alive.

Reed pushed the burly kidnapper toward a nearby group of patrolmen. Abigail's eyelids were fluttering. He gathered her in his arms and began to rock back and forth.

"Wake up. Please, wake up." Gently kissing her hand,

he prayed with an intensity of pure faith that surprised him. "Please, Jesus. Please send her back to me."

Blue eyes opened and looked up. Thankful beyond words, Reed forgot his macho image. It was just them. Him and his Abigail. Together. "Thank You, Jesus."

Unashamed, he let the tears roll down his cheeks to mingle with hers in the instant before he pulled her to him and repeated his heavenly thanks over and over.

Abigail clung to him. Her breathing was raspy, her slim body shuddering as she struggled to take in enough air.

Finally, she whispered a weak, "Amen."

That was good enough for Reed. More of his tears dampened her silky red hair and his shoulders shook.

As others began to arrive and he was forced to pull himself together, Jessie pushed through and began to lick the salty drops off his cheeks.

It would have suited Abigail better if neither she nor Reed had been required to submit to a medical checkup. She kept repeating, "I'm fine. See? Standing up and breathing," which was punctuated part of the time by a croupy cough that negated what she was saying.

With her at the rear of the waiting ambulance, Reed was watching closely. Abigail was thankful he hadn't been hurt and felt terrible that she'd put everyone in more jeopardy because she'd gotten involved when she should have stayed back. She would have apologized ad infinitum if Reed's scowl hadn't stopped her.

Brianne had already reported that one of the two men they'd grappled with was in custody. The other had slipped away and escaped while everyone's attention was focused on Reed and the man trying to strangle Abigail.

Finn and Brianne showed up at the ambulance to deliver news of the latest developments. Wisely, Abigail kept silent as they briefed Reed.

"Danielle is putting a trace on the calls made from the big guy's cell," Brianne said. "As soon as we get solid info we'll mount a strike against the rest of the gang. In the meantime, precinct cops raided the place where the girl said she'd been held."

"Let me guess," Reed said, wincing when he moved. "It was empty."

"Unfortunately," Finn answered. "We're checking street view cameras to see if we can get a lead. If that teenager is right and they plan to ship out a load of trafficked kids tonight, it will probably be at high tide, meaning we have until 10:00 p.m. to locate them."

Although Abigail was listening, her mind was also spinning. If she were the kidnappers, where would she hide prisoners? They'd probably want to stick close to the shore or a harbor even though patrols would be thick now that the authorities knew what was going down. Those poor, poor kids must be so scared. And unless Kiera had lied, Dominic Walenski was still among them. So where could they be?

There were a couple of abandoned warehouses in Brighton Beach that came to mind. Abigail knew that kind of place was a favorite of homeless kids, especially once the weather worsened. Those buildings also would provide a fertile hunting ground if the kidnap ring was short of victims.

She cast a surreptitious glance at Reed. He was straightening his uniform, clearly intending to continue to assist with the ongoing search. If she was going to divert him, now was the perfect time.

Waiting until he looked ready, Abigail gently touched his shoulder. "Please, don't go."

"I have to."

"But…" She looped her hand through his arm and urged him to step aside. "I have an idea."

"Uh-oh. The last time you had an idea we got shot at."

Not about to be deterred, she tried another approach. "I think I may know where the kidnap ring stashed those kids."

"What took you so long to say so?"

"I didn't say I was positive. I just have an idea. What will it hurt to go with me and see? You'll hear about any new leads over the radio in your car wherever you are."

"I gather you want me to drive you somewhere?"

"Not just anywhere. To a couple of places where homeless kids tend to gather in the winter. What can it hurt?"

"My job," Reed quipped. "I'd like to keep it."

Abigail ignored his cynicism. "We won't be going far. You'll be close by if and when these other officers nail down a location." She pulled a face and directed it at the bevy of squad cars along the street. "Personally, I think it would be a lot smarter to try to sneak up on these traffickers. Look at all those cops. You'd think they were going after the mafia."

"This is organized crime, whether it's a worldwide organization or a hometown operation," Reed said. "Chances are, unless these kids get sick and die on the voyage, they'll be sold to the highest bidder. Think about it. They leave home looking for freedom and end up a prisoner in the worst kind of jail."

The weight of his words settled in her heart and left a bleeding wound that might never heal unless they rescued the helpless young teens. Then she spied something in his expression that she could only hope she understood.

"You're going to take me, aren't you?"

Reed gave her a cynical look and shook his head as if disgusted with himself, not her. When he said, "Yes, God help me," Abigail couldn't hold back a grin. Okay, they might not be successful. Other searchers might have better results. But that wasn't the takeaway here. Reed was *trusting* her. *Completely.* She felt like cheering, and would have, if she wasn't afraid of triggering another coughing fit.

Jessie trotted along beside Reed, tail waving like a flag, nose up, testing the air. On his opposite side, Abigail felt as much elation as the K-9 was demonstrating. Only Reed, bracketed between them, seemed morose.

It wasn't until they were back in his car and halfway to Brighton Beach that his mood lifted. A radio call was asking their location in relation to the block of empty warehouses she had already pinpointed.

Abigail was ecstatic. "That's it!" she shouted across the car. "That's where we're headed. And we'll get there a good ten minutes faster because we have a head start."

Reed radioed their position, then glanced over at her, his eyebrows raised. "How did you figure that out?"

"Logic," she said, pointing to her temple, "and brains."

"Ha!" For the first time since that morning, she heard

him start to laugh. Really laugh. From her crate in the rear, Jessie joined in with a howl.

Abigail would have enjoyed the moment a lot more if Reed's laugh hadn't sounded so sarcastic.

Pulling up a block short of the designated warehouse, Reed parked in an alley and got out.

As he released his K-9, he gave Abigail a stern glare. "You are not going."

"Yes, I am. I've been inside before. You need me."

"Only if I want to complicate everything," he countered. "This time somebody might aim at me instead of you."

"Have I mentioned lately how sorry I am for getting in your way?"

"Yes, you have. That doesn't mean I'm ready to make you my partner. Jessie is all I need." With that, he started off, assuming she'd stay behind.

When she hustled to keep up with him, instead, he halted. "Go. Back. To. The. Car."

"I don't think so."

"Aargh!" Pausing for a deep, calming breath, he regained his composure. Faced her. Said, "Ms. Jones, you are the most obstinate person, man or woman, I have ever met. However, if you're half as intelligent as you claim to be, you'll realize that you're putting everyone in more danger by insisting on sticking with me. Stop and think for a second. Please."

That did it. Reed saw the fire leave her blue eyes and watched her shoulders sag. She finally got the picture. With a barely discernible nod, Abigail returned to the SUV, fished around in the passenger seat and emerged holding Dominic's satin jacket.

"You may need this," she said calmly. "I noticed he'd left it in the car after he worked with your tech person."

"Perfect. Thanks." A tense moment came and went. "Well?"

She pulled out her cell and waved it. "If you need me, call. I'll be right here."

"Good." Wondering how long her promise was going to last, Reed silenced his radio and left her. Circling the old brick warehouse, he turned the corner to the loading dock in the rear and glanced back. No Abigail. What a relief.

He understood why she was so bent on being in on the capture. She loved those mixed-up kids. Identified with them, according to what she'd told him about her past. But that didn't mean it was smart for her to get underfoot when a police operation was in play.

Once the other units arrived and they had the building surrounded, he'd be ready to show Jessie the jacket and give her the command to seek. Entry was bound to be chaotic. When he located Dom, however, chances were good that the other kidnapped kids would be close by.

Jessie heard the noise first and froze, fully alert. Reed stiffened. Followed the dog's cues and stared at the roll-up door above the concrete loading platform. Chains rattled. Muted voices drifted out through the corrugated metal portal.

The door began to rise.

Reed fell back, taking Jessie with him and giving her the signal for silence. The only close hiding place was behind a large trash bin, so he hunkered down there to watch.

A box truck like the one that had smashed into his

first SUV was rattling up the street behind the warehouse and turning in to the drive. One headlight was shattered, its chrome frame flapping. The front bumper was canted, too. He didn't need forensics to decide this had to be the same vehicle that had been aimed at Abigail.

Anger rose. He tamped it down. Emotional responses were self-defeating. What he needed was to radio his position and report on the developments before the kidnap ring loaded the truck and it sped off crammed with victims.

He keyed his mic. Static echoed in his earpiece. "On scene, ten-ten. This is a ten-thirteen. Repeat, officer needs assistance."

A garbled reply told him little. Either the Dumpster was heavy enough to interfere with radio transmissions or dispatch had more than one incident working at once. The latter was most likely. After all, this was New York City, even if this particular raid was taking place on the fringes.

The truck made a three-point turn and stopped, its rear to the dock. The driver was new to him, but he recognized Abigail's remaining original assailant as the passenger. This was the right place for sure. So where was his backup?

Reed looked down at Jessie with affection. She hadn't been trained for anything but tracking, so he wasn't going to put her life in danger by taking her with him if he was forced to act alone. That would not have been his choice. Not in the slightest. But he couldn't just stand by and watch a bunch of kids loaded into a truck that would take them somewhere so terrible it was almost beyond imagining.

I still have a little time, Reed told himself. *It's only a matter of minutes until backup arrives.*

Did he have minutes? He thought so, hoped so.

Someone inside the dark warehouse started to wail. The sound of a slap echoed out the open bay door and the noise ceased immediately.

Shadows began to fill the portal. Myriad feet shuffled forward. The victims were chained together at the ankles. They could walk but there was no chance any of them could run, even if Reed somehow managed to distract their captors.

He heard sirens in the distance. So did the kidnappers. One of the guards prodded the group of abused teens forward with a rifle. "Faster or I'll shoot you where you stand."

Reed was about to show himself in a last-ditch effort to prevent the thugs from loading their prisoners when he heard a familiar voice coming from across the dock.

"You won't shoot anybody," Abigail shouted. "If you do, nobody will be able to move a step because they'll be dragging dead weight."

Where was she? Reed couldn't tell. Thankfully, her common sense warning seemed to have gotten through to the armed men. One called to the other. "See, dummy? I told you it was stupid to tie 'em all together like that."

"Well how was I to know? I didn't wanna lose any more."

Multiple sirens overlapped each other. The cacophony grew. A patrol car skidded across the driveway to Reed's left, blocking the truck's escape. Officers piled out, crouching down and running for cover.

The man with the rifle turned and fired at the car.

Reed shouted, "Everybody down!" at the frightened teens.

To his horror he saw that Abigail had joined the group of victims and was trying to drag them, en masse, back into the warehouse. Her task was a jumble of legs and arms and toppling bodies.

Gunfire continued from the thugs while cops circled the building, taking care to not aim at the teens.

One of the criminals chose a human shield and appeared at the door, illuminated by police floodlights.

Reed was both shocked and terrified.

The man had grabbed the only civilian who wasn't chained. Abigail Jones.

Abigail was not about to become a victim again. She hadn't had time to learn much about self-defense from Lani but she had seen one move that might work. Cupping her fist in her opposite hand she drove her elbow into the man's stomach as hard as she could. He gasped, released her and folded like a limp rag. She threw herself to the side.

Recovering quickly, the rifleman straightened and pointed his weapon at the prisoners. Abigail cringed next to Dominic and held him close. There was no way for her to shield all the captive teens. If this was the end, then so be it. She'd done all she possibly could.

A volley of shots echoed.

A kidnapper threatening them collapsed. The weasel-looking guy from the truck and its driver immediately raised their hands. Weasel screeched, "Don't shoot! I give up."

In seconds the officers closed in and it was over.

Abigail hugged the teen she'd grown so fond of. "Dom. Are you okay?"

The only reply she got was a tightening of his hug and shaking of his shoulders. She stroked his dark hair.

Reed soon joined them. Abigail was delighted that he included them both in his embrace and she clung to him, unashamed, unafraid. It might take weeks to sort out all the crimes this gang had committed but that was inconsequential measured against the astounding rescue. She didn't even care if she got a royal chewing out from every cop in New York. Saving those kids had been worth the risk. If she hadn't physically forced them to move, to try to get themselves out of the line of fire, there was no telling how many would have, could have, been wounded. Or worse. That horrible thought made her weak in the knees.

Reed's breath was ragged against her hair. When he kissed the top of her head she thought she heard him swallow a sob. Tears filled her eyes. Relief filled her heart and mind. The nightmare was over. Her memory was restored. The threat had been eliminated and lives had been saved. It was possible her joy-filled dreams could now unfold.

So what should she do? Apologize again for interfering? Give Reed time to set aside possible anger and decide they belonged together despite everything?

The idea of waiting was unacceptable. Ludicrous. She wasn't going to stand by wasting time. Not when she could act. If facing her enemies had taught her anything, it was that life was short and should be lived to the fullest.

Overflowing with love for this man, Abigail leaned away slightly and gazed up at Reed while the traumatized boy celebrated by giving high fives to some of his fellow captives as they were unshackled.

Reed's cheeks were visibly streaked, as were hers, and she rejoiced. If he had not cared, deeply, he wouldn't be showing emotion so openly. Now was the time.

She started to say, "I…" and was silenced immediately by the most amazing kiss she'd ever experienced. Myriad thoughts swirled through her consciousness. She slipped both arms around his neck. Not only was Reed not angry, he seemed more than ready to hear what she intended to say.

As soon as he broke contact she tried again. "Reed, I…"

Another kiss. Another thought ended in the beauty and assurance of his affection. Dare she try again? Was it even necessary?

With her eyes closed and her heart wide open, Abigail let her thoughts thank her heavenly Father for leading her to this man and keeping them together long enough to fall in love. Then she tried to concentrate on how to tell Reed.

That would be easier to figure out if he wasn't kissing me senseless, she thought. This time, when he let her come up for air, she merely smiled.

That was apparently enough, because he mirrored her joy. "I hope you were trying to say you love me, because I'm head over heels in love with you, Ms. Jones."

"I was." The smile spread. Relief triggered humor. "Does this mean I get to keep training the puppy?"

"Only if I come along with her. We're a package deal."

"You are, huh? Are you well trained, Officer Branson?"

"Perfectly. I have the commendations to prove it."

He was grinning broadly, his dark eyes sparkling. "I don't mean to rush you, I mean, you can take all the time you need. I'd just like your promise you'll marry me someday."

"Someday? Then we have a problem. Midnight needs specialized training ASAP whether she goes on to become a working K-9 for the police or serves some other purpose. I'm afraid we'll have to sacrifice for the sake of the dog and get married pretty soon."

His hearty laugh made her spirits soar. "I guess we will," he said. Then he kissed her. Again and again.

In the background, Abigail saw Dominic slowly walking away from them and her heart leaped. Was it feasible to become his guardian or even adopt him? she wondered. Was that asking too much?

Still in Reed's arms, she raised on tiptoe to whisper the question in his ear. His answer wasn't immediate, but he did seem willing to consider a family of three. That was good enough for Abigail. A husband, a son, a K-9 tracker and the perfect cuddly puppy. It was more than she had ever wished for. What more could she ever want?

EPILOGUE

It was Reed's idea to treat Abigail––and Dominic––to lunch at Griffin's. He wanted to show her the special areas designated for K-9 officers and their dogs as well as discuss their shared future in a homey, relaxing atmosphere. They had both decided it was time to tell the boy what they hoped to do and see if he was on board with adoption.

"You're sure we can take the dogs inside?" Abigail asked.

Reed smiled. "Sure can. The owner, Lou Griffin, designated a special section for K-9 officers and their dogs. He even added a sign that says The Dog House."

"Wow. Awesome."

Chuckling, Reed glanced at Dom, who had walked on ahead. "You're starting to sound like somebody else I know."

"Well, we have spent a lot of time together lately." She sobered. "I wish I knew why he sometimes seems so unhappy."

"I think what we have to ask him will fix most of that," Reed said. He'd passed the wide front window and was reaching for the handle of the door before he noticed the hand-lettered note taped to the inside. It read, "Closed due to family emergency."

Cupping his hands around his eyes to cut the glare, he tried to see inside. The place looked deserted. Reed sighed in frustration. "Not good. I thought they were going strong when they reopened after the explosion."

"Explosion?"

"Don't worry. It won't happen again. Like our kidnappers, the bomber is done causing trouble, although there are still developers who would love to get hold of this chunk of land and build something new here."

"I love the old neighborhoods and shops. It gives New York character."

"I know." Reed thought he saw something move inside so he decided to knock. "Hey, Lou! What's up? We're starving here."

A grumpy-looking gray-haired old man with his arm in a cast opened the door and peered out. "We're closed. Barb has the flu and as you can see, I won't be able to get orders up fast enough by myself. Sorry."

"Aw, c'mon, Lou. At least a cup of coffee. There's no other place around here that allows dogs."

The door swung back. "Okay, okay. Coffee. I'm always open for my buddies in uniform and their K-9s. I've got some Danish left. Or pie." He eyed the wiry, dark-haired teen with them and arched a bushy brow. "Who's your friend?"

Reed placed a proprietary hand on Dominic's thin shoulder and looked to Abigail for unspoken permission. When she nodded, he said, "I'd like you to meet Ms. Abigail Jones, who has agreed to marry me. And this is Dominic. He'll soon be our son if he agrees to being adopted."

The old man gaped, then recovered and stuck out his good hand to shake Reed's. "Well, I'll be. When you do it, son, you go all the way. Instant family. Congratulations."

Abigail lightly patted the boy's opposite shoulder. "What about it, honey? We talked about this a few days ago and you seemed open to the idea so we've looked into it. What would you say to having a couple of new parents?"

"You guys were serious? Yes!" His shout startled both Jessie and Midnight into a chorus of barking while the adults laughed.

"Let's go sit in there," Reed said, gesturing at the French doors leading to the separate section Lou kept for officers and their dogs.

By the time they'd settled down around a table, they were joined by Reed's commander, Noah Jameson.

Reed stood to shake his hand, then made introductions, inviting Noah to join them.

"I can't stay. I just stopped because I saw you come in," Noah said. He pulled out his cell phone as he glanced at Dominic. "Is this the teenager who had Snapper?"

Defensive, Reed was quick to say, "Only for a little while."

"Fine," Noah said, displaying the composite Dominic had done with Danielle and holding it out for him to look at. "Is this pretty close to the way you remember the man?"

Dominic nodded.

With a telling sigh, the interim chief put the phone back in his pocket. "I'd like to believe that's the face of my brother's killer." He focused on Reed. "What do you think?"

Although he trusted his son-to-be, Reed realized it had been a long time since Snapper had been handed over. Memories were funny things, as he and Abigail well knew. Still, he wanted to be encouraging as well as support the teen.

"I think that's the best, most logical assumption to make," Reed said. "We'll get the guy. None of us will give up or rest until he's behind bars."

The strong emotions he read in Noah's expression hinted at a desire for revenge. If Reed hadn't known what dedicated cops the remaining Jameson brothers were, he might have worried about a vendetta. He wouldn't have blamed them.

Gazing at his loved ones, Reed silently thanked God that they had made it through their personal crises. Abigail was going to be his wife, Dominic was eager to become their son and even Kiera had mellowed enough to return to the foster parents who had been so worried about her welfare.

Now it was time for him and his unit to go back to rallying around the Jameson family and work on solving their mystery. Justice was waiting.

* * * * *

"Mom!"

That had been a child's cry. State police officer Patrick Sanders glanced across the open desert at the base of a mountain.

Had he found what he was looking for?

Tucker sniffed, nose turned to the breeze.

Patrick's K-9 partner, an Airedale terrier he'd gotten from a shelter as a puppy and trained, scented the wind. His body stiffened and he leaned forward. As an air-scent dog, Tucker didn't need a trail to follow. He could catch the scent he was looking for on the wind or, in this case, the winter breeze rolling over the mountain.

Patrick's mountains, the place he'd grown up. Until right before his high school graduation when his mom had packed them up and fled town. They'd lost their home and everything they'd had there.

Including the girl Patrick had loved.

He heard another cry. Stifled by something—it was hard to hear as it drifted across so much open terrain.

He and his K-9 had been dispatched to find Jennie and her son, Nathan. A friend had reported them missing yesterday, and the sheriff wasted no time at all calling for a search and rescue team from state police.

The dog had caught a scent and was closing in.

As a terrier, it was about the challenge. Tucker had proved to be both prey-driven, like fetching a ball, and food-driven, like a nice piece of chicken, when he felt like it.

Right now the dog had to find Jennie and the boy so Patrick could transport them to safety. Then he intended to get out of town again. Back to his life in Albuquerque and studying for the sergeant's exam.

Tucker tugged harder on the leash; a signal the scent was stronger. He was closing in. Patrick's night of searching for the missing woman and her child would soon be over.

Tucker rounded a sagebrush and sat.

"Good boy. Yes, you are." Patrick let the leash slacken a little. He circled his dog and found Jennie lying on the ground.

"Jennie."

She stirred. Her eyes flashed open and she cried out. *"We need to find Nate."*

Don't miss
Desert Rescue *by Lisa Phillips,*
available wherever Love Inspired Suspense books and ebooks are sold.

LoveInspired.com

LISEXP1220

LOVE INSPIRED

INSPIRATIONAL ROMANCE

UPLIFTING STORIES OF FAITH, FORGIVENESS AND HOPE.

Join our social communities to connect with other readers who share your love!

Sign up for the Love Inspired newsletter at **LoveInspired.com** to be the first to find out about upcoming titles, special promotions and exclusive content.

CONNECT WITH US AT:

Facebook.com/LoveInspiredBooks

Twitter.com/LoveInspiredBks

Facebook.com/groups/HarlequinConnection

LISOCIAL2020